THE EQUUS, BOOK 1

DAWN IN ETRASCO

by

J. R. Rada

AIM

PUBLISHING

DAWN IN ETRASCO (THE EQUUS, BOOK 1)

Published by AIM Publishing, a division of AIM Publishing Group.
Gettysburg, Pennsylvania.

Printed in the United States of America.

ISBN: 979-8-9903256-3-0

PROLOGUE

This was the last day of paradise, and Equ cried because he was the one who had to end it.

Before the sun had even cleared the tops of the snow-topped mountains that ringed Etrasco, the colts and fillies were awake and playing in the green valley. The horses raced each other across the valley floor, their hooves pounding against the soft grass and soil. It yielded beneath them without being torn up and thrown behind the young Equus. The unicorns playfully jousted with each other, thrusting and parrying with their gleaming white horns. The pegasuses tested the strength of their downy wings in short, hopping flights, occasionally trying more-complicated loops and drops. When their stunts succeeded, the other Equus cheered them on with loud whinnies. Many of the zebras, ponies, and donkeys danced around each other with their forehooves kicking out in their rough-and-tumble play.

The sight of his beautiful children and the innocent pleasure they took from life reminded Equ to reinforce his form. Today, he chose to be a white unicorn with a golden horn. Yesterday, he had been a golden pegasus, and the day before, a black-and-white striped zebra with a yellow mane and tail. The golden-horn unicorn was his favorite form, though. Perhaps, in the future, he would choose a different favorite, but he knew that it would be an Equus. In all his millennia of life, he had created no other creature.

As the antics of the young brought them more enjoyment, the air filled with the sound of their joyful and loud whinnies. The noise and the warmth of the sun were a wake-up call to the adults, and they stirred from their sleep. Some stood and kicked out their legs —

first back and then front until they created a rocking motion — to stretch their stiff muscles. Other Equus rolled in the grass for their morning grooming.

"Good morning, Father Equ," they called out as they noticed him. It didn't matter how far away they were from him. He heard their thoughts in his head through the mind-link as clearly as if the Equus circled around him.

"Good morning, my children. Enjoy the day," he replied.

The adult Equus walked around the lush valley, drinking water from the wide stream that ran through Etrasco from the east before they grazed on the sweet grasses and wild grains and berries that were so plentiful in the valley. The grass on the valley floor was thick, but not high, while low trees and bushes covered the mountain foothills.

It was another morning in paradise, which is just as Equ would have it. Always, if he could. He had created and maintained Etrasco with his life-giving power, giving the earth life in such a way that it remained earth and did not become a new creature.

Perhaps Etrasco could be considered his second creation apart from the Equus. If so, Equ was just as proud of this beautiful valley as he was of the Equus. Etrasco was his refuge from his brothers and sisters in this world of pain and sorrow. Life in Etrasco was how life should be lived, and Equ had shared this valley with his children. The Equus numbered just over 100 creatures. Compared to the numbers and variety of creatures that Equ's brothers and sisters had created, it was not a significant amount, but they were enough to bring Equ joy, which was all he sought for both himself and the Equus.

Etrasco was a world without pain and without predators. It was a symbiotic creation; the Equus drew nourishment from it and the Equus, in turn, fertilized the earth with their bodies in death when they grew old and spread seeds through their wastes during their long lives. Equ made sure that all injuries to the Equus were healed as soon as they occurred. The grass here was succulent, as he could attest to, and the water tasted sweet. Both were plentiful.

Yet, today would be the last day in paradise for the Equus.

Equ turned away to hide his tears because he did not want to alarm his children. He wanted today of all days to be the best, to be perfect, for it would be the one he remembered when his children were gone. He watched the Equus play. He raised his muzzle in the air as a warm breeze blew and smelled lilacs and honeysuckles. He listened to the delightful melee of sounds, both auditory and psychic.

While the sounds he heard with his ears conveyed emotion, it was the psychic sounds that revealed thought between the Equus. Conversations nearer him were easier to understand because the mind-link bond was stronger. All the conversations he listened to told him that his children were happy.

As Equ stood in the valley, apart from the herd but still close enough to watch and enjoy them, he saw a woman walking across the open field. He knew at a glance that she must be his mother, for she had not been there a moment ago. Today, his mother was blonde-haired and young, perhaps twenty but no more than twenty-five years old. His mother could make any form look beautiful, but this human form was a recent one and her own creation.

The younger Equus and even some adults began to romp around the woman as she neared the herd. They feared no animal within the valley, but they always displayed a great curiosity about the different creatures that visited. Even now, the Equus recognized Equ's mother; not by her form, which changed often, but by her love for them, which she exuded in every glance, thought, and motion.

"Good morning, Mother," they called to her as they tried to push their muzzles into her hands so she would pet them.

She laughed out loud, a high-pitched twitter, as her thoughts said, *"Good morning, children. May the day bring you great joy."*

Her mind-voice that she used to communicate with the Equus was richer and lower-pitched than her human voice.

During some visits, Equ's mother tried to fool the Equus and hide herself from them until a clever Equus discovered her in one form or another. She would reward that Equus by assuming whatever form he or she chose for her, whether it be a simple bee or some unknown creation invented by the lucky Equus. Today was not one of those days.

Equ watched her, giving her time with the Equus. She loved them almost as much as he did, so it was not surprising that she would want to spend this day with them. His mother reached out her hands to stroke their necks. As she did, she assumed their form, whether it was horse or unicorn or zebra. She stood neck to neck with them and groomed their manes and withers with her teeth, giving them affection in the manner they understood. Some Equus neighed while others returned the grooming. Eventually, all the Equus had greeted her, and she re-assumed human form and walked to where Equ stood watching.

The woman smiled, showing her white teeth. It was an action that meant danger or anger to the Equus, but Equ was familiar with the human form, so he knew the expressions and how to interpret them. Besides, he had never seen his mother angry in any form.

"I see you have taken the form of your children once again," she said, her voice as soothing as the sound of the river that watered Etrasco as it rolled over the rocks in the foothills. They did not need the mind-link to communicate in their language. "I always thought it was the children who took the form of the parents."

Equ nuzzled his broad, white muzzle against his mother's neck. He stood nearly a meter taller than his mother's form, so he had to lower his head to reach her.

"In my children, I have created the perfect creation; why would I not want to assume it for myself?" he asked her. The Equus could not speak, but Equ was not truly one of them. He was a creator, and he could speak when he chose to do so.

His mother stroked his muzzle. "I've given this form my great love for your children. There may come a day that they will create a symbiosis with each other like the Equus have created with Etrasco."

Equ knew that given the opportunity, it would happen. The Equus were herd animals, but they would let any willing species be a part of their herd.

"May it one day be so," Equ said.

"Don't be so formal."

"I'm sad."

His mother stroked his neck and turned to look over the herd. The Equus had gone back to grazing and playing. "You are right in one thing, Equ. You created the perfect form, or as near to it as possible."

Equ drew back from his mother and looked towards the tops of the mountains. "Then how can you expect me to let them go, knowing what is out there?"

Not only was his despair apparent in his voice, but his unicorn form started to destabilize. His hide changed to skin, causing his color to darken. Then it pebbled into scales. Equ realized what was happening and brought his emotions and his form under control. How could he tell his mother just how much he did not want to do this? He would do it because he loved his mother and respected and trusted in her wisdom, but he was afraid of what would happen to the Equus because of his actions today.

"I know you love the Equus, my son, just as I love you. It is the love of a parent for a child." She waved her arm toward the mountains. "What is out there is also my creation, just as much as you are. I love the land, and I think the Equus will, too."

"But the land can be harsh."

In deciding about the future of the Equus, he had gone out into the world in the form of an Equus, trying to feel what it would be like for them to live beyond the mountains of Etrasco. He knew of the icy winters and the deadly predators and the dry deserts. He knew what these things would do to his children. He realized that Etrasco was an oasis in this world, and that made him treasure the valley even more.

"I created this world as a testing ground, but it is also wonderful to behold and experience. It is not without its beauties." She paused and stroked his neck. "I have not asked you to do anything that I haven't asked of your brothers and sisters," his mother said.

Etrasco was not home to any other animal life, other than the Equus. Other animals visited Etrasco, but only with Equ's permission and only those that meant no harm to the Equus. Etrasco was Equ's world within this world, and it housed his only creation. His mother's world was created to fill the habitat needs of a variety of animals, such as sharks, polar bears, sidewinders, and mice.

Equ nodded his head and said, "That is what I fear the most. Not all of my brothers' and sisters' children are as peaceful as the Equus or humans."

His mother smiled. "I think you would be surprised at the levels of violence both the Equus and humans can do if presented with the right circumstances."

Equ shook his head. "I made the Equus peaceful."

His mother tilted her head forward and gave him a stern look that made her look years older. "Equ, the Equus are not toys. You have created living creatures that must be allowed to live. It is part of the responsibility that you must accept as a creator."

Equ nodded. "The Equus live here. Etrasco is their home. I created it for us. Here, the Equus can live in peace without need."

He controlled the conditions in the valley and what happened within its boundaries. Not even his brothers and sisters could enter here without his permission. Only his mother had that right.

His mother dug her bare toe into the rich soil. "*Here*, the Equus exist. I would not say they live. Etrasco is an artificially maintained reality. It could not survive without your intervention. Is that what you fear of the Equus, that they could not survive without you?"

Equ shook his head vigorously. "No, they are strong."

These were his children, his creations. He had lived as one of them for many decades now. Equ knew their limitations and strengths. He had not created weak children, but that did not mean he wanted to push them to their limits only to have them fail.

"How do you know they are strong if they cannot discover their individual characters on their own? In Etrasco, there is no growth or progress unless you introduce it."

"What would I do if they were killed, though? Other creations have vanished from the world because they were ill-equipped to handle its chaos."

"Randomness is not chaos, Equ. Besides, you said yourself that the Equus are strong. If any species of Equus should not be able to live up to your praise, they can be returned here, where they can once again be safe from the world."

Equ nodded. "Yes, I suppose so, but the pain it would bring…"

His mother leaned toward him and touched her forehead to his. Equ's eyes could not see her when she was directly in front of him because of the blind spot in his field of vision, but he could feel the warmth emanating from her… and her love. It was just as real to him as her body heat. "It is not much more than death, my son. It happens to all of us eventually, even you and I, though our deaths will be in our time, not this time."

"It is not the death of my children I fear, Mother. They age and die here. I just don't want them to die in pain or fear."

His mother shrugged. "I can't promise you it won't happen, Equ." She paused. "It may be hard, but you must do it. I know how you feel. I felt the same way when I allowed you and your siblings to leave my presence. Until I gave you this world, you all also existed in a state of innocence, much like the Equus. You are a creator, Equ. Creators create. I have given you leeway here because your one creation was so beautiful that your changes only give it a variety of appearances and skills. However, a species created must be tested. That is the purpose of this world: to test viable life so it may be seeded elsewhere."

Equ pranced a bit, alternating his hooves in quick steps. "Don't you see that we—your own children—are an example of what can go wrong, Mother? Your children are no longer innocent. Look at what has happened to us without your constant presence."

Equ remembered the days in his mother's presence as some of the happiest in his life. It was a time of peace, and it was that world… that feeling… that he had tried to recreate in Etrasco. He felt that he had done a good job of doing so.

His mother nodded. "That is true, but it is not this world that changed you children. It was the fact that this world allowed your true natures to be revealed that changed you. I created you all as individuals, and at least in your innocent states, I loved you all equally."

Equ was suddenly afraid that his mother was about to say how disappointed she was in him and his resistance to her plan.

"But no longer?" Equ asked.

His mother shook her head. "I did not say that. You have all changed. You are all different from you were before you set out on your own. Some of you have done things that have greatly displeased me, but all life is not beauty and plenty." Her expression took on a distant look as she remembered some of those displeasing moments. "Some of the most viable life forms that have been proven worthy to be seeded on other worlds are those that I detest. However, they were not created to please me but to survive."

Equ lowered his nose to the ground and imitated a grazing unicorn. It was an act of submission for an Equus. Though his mother was not angry, she was speaking in the stern, lecturing tone that she had used when she had taught Equ about his powers.

"Do you still love me?" he asked, his voice faint.

His mother bent down and gently lifted his head with her hand so he could look her in the eye. She scratched behind one of his ears with her free hand. It helped ease the tension in his neck.

"Of course, I still love you. You are one of my children. I do not think I could ever not love you or any of your brothers and sisters," she told him.

Equ glanced at her sideways. "Even Carn?"

His mother flipped her blonde hair over her shoulder and nodded. "Yes, even Carn."

Carn was one of Equ's older brothers. Carn was destruction. Carn was death. He chose no one form to exist in like most of Equ's other brothers and sisters. From the moment Carn had learned of his ability to change shape at will, his will had changed. He had embraced his mother's vision to be free and to grow in the world beyond theirs. In fact, he had been pressing for it before their mother had even made her final decision about sending her children out on their own. Perhaps the insistence of Carn, even while in the protective shielding of their mother, had led her to decide that creating life in an experimental world might be a good experience for Carn. Equ could not say that it had been.

Life had only allowed Carn more freedom than he had had with his mother and more avenues to vent his savagery. No one was spared Carn's destruction, even his own children. One day, he might run with a pack of wolves to bring down one of his sister Perl's buffalo. Those magnificent creatures were quite capable of defending themselves against wolves… unless they met up with Carn as a predator, and then the herd would be lucky to survive. The next day, Carn might take the form of a lamb and wait until the wolves he had run with the day before circled to attack him. He would then take the form of some monstrous creature resembling a lamb and destroy the wolf pack.

Carn made no sense to Equ. If what Carn had become indicated what happened when one lived in the world, then Equ wanted nothing of it or of him or his children.

"How can you love him?" Equ asked his mother.

She thought for a moment and smiled. "He is strong willed and very imaginative. His creations vary greatly in habitat, size, and abilities. He uses this world to its fullest capabilities and seeks to stretch his creative abilities."

Equ shook his head. "But he kills wantonly."

The corners of her mouth turned up slightly in a smile. "You asked what I loved, not what I hated. Yes, your brother has decided that predators are the most viable species he can create."

It took Equ a moment to understand his mother's point. Creatures either had his full love or none. "You can separate what you love and hate from an individual?"

His mother nodded. "I must. I've had to find things in you and your siblings to love rather than focusing on the negative aspects."

"And me?"

She turned and waved her hand over the herd. "You, I love because you can create a thing of such beauty and grace as the Equus. Others have chosen many unique forms to bless with life. You found the one form you preferred and gave it not only life but love."

Equ nodded his elongated head and then asked, "And the negative?"

His mother sighed. "We are experiencing the negative now. You are the last of your siblings to release your children into this world. This is as much a growing experience for you as it will be for them. I will cry for you as you cry for them."

Equ looked over the herd with sadness in his eyes. "How will it be?"

His mother pursed her lips as she thought. "Challenging. They will have their triumphs and tragedies, but they will live. They will learn how to survive in a world with predators. They will survive as the Equus, although individuals will suffer."

Equ had nothing more to ask her after that, and his mother had nothing more to say. Both of them had made the decision. They stood on a slight swell in the valley floor and watched the Equus enjoy their last perfect day in Etrasco. The young frolicked and tested each other but without animosity towards one another. The adults groomed and foraged, and some gamed with the colts and fillies.

Sometime during the day, Equ's mother vanished, leaving Equ to watch his children alone. He did not feel her leave or notice her going. He wanted to record this day in his memory, for this memory would have to last him a long time.

Night in Etrasco fell, and the young, the first to rise, were the first to sleep. They bent their legs and lay in the soft grass, nestling near their dams.

That will change in the world, Equ thought. *They will have to learn to sleep standing up and for shorter stretches of time or risk being taken by surprise by predators.*

He watched and waited. When all the Equus were asleep, he walked among them, touching his nose to the nose of each of the Equus.

"Goodbye, Fale. One day, we shall meet again," he said to a zebra.

"Goodbye, Gryen. I love you," he said to a donkey.

"Goodbye, Calvn. Live well."

On and on, it continued as he moved through the herd, bidding farewell to each of his children and calling them by name.

When he had bid goodbye to each Equus, he stepped away from

the herd and said, "Goodbye, my children. Always remember me."

Then Equ closed his eyes, and the Equus were gone.

Calvn, the oldest of the unicorns, awoke with the terrified cries of the young shrieking through his mind and frightened squeals ringing in his ears. He had never known the young Equus to be afraid. Didn't Father Equ protect them and care for them in Etrasco?

He shook off the effects of sleep and stood up. Not only were the young ones running around in panicked circles, but many of the adults were, too.

"Where are we?"

"This is not Etrasco!"

"Where are we?"

"Father Equ!"

Calvn looked around and saw what had frightened the Equus. They were no longer in Etrasco. The mountains that had always surrounded their home as a barrier to the world were missing. The Equus stood instead on a great plain that stretched as far as their eyes could see. The grass here was also a paler shade of green and tougher on their hooves. Much of it stood knee high.

He felt a chill run through him. They were no longer within the shelter of Etrasco. How had they gotten here and where was Father Equ?

Others had the same thought. *"Father Equ!"* they called through the mind-link. *"Help us! Where are we?"*

Father Equ never appeared to them, no matter how impassioned their pleas were, no matter how long they implored him to help them. Where had their creator, their father, and their protector gone? He had abandoned the Equus. They were alone, wherever they were.

Calvn walked around the herd, listening to their pleas and trying to keep the Equus together because some of them tried to run away, hoping to find Etrasco. Somehow, he realized that if they were to separate, they would die. Their strength lay in the size of their herd and their ability to act together; the only thing they had that was still familiar to them.

But the Equus were scared now, even Calvn was scared now, and not thinking clearly. They had to first be calmed, and their attention needed to be directed to solving their problem.

Calvn reared onto his hind legs and kicked out his forehooves. He sent out his mind-voice as forcefully as he could to all the Equus. *"Brothers and sisters, calm yourselves."*

"But we are alone!" came the reply from many.

"We are not alone," Calvn said. Their panic had caused them to miss the obvious.

"Where is Father Equ? Where is Etrasco?"

"We are not alone because we have each other," Calvn clarified.

"But where is Father Equ?"

"If you calm yourselves, I think I can answer you," Calvn told them. He wasn't sure that he could answer them, at least to their satisfaction. He had been thinking about the problem as he struggled to hold the herd together. It wasn't hard to do on the open plain. When one of the Equus began to drift away, Calvn would gallop over to him to turn him back. Yes, it wasn't hard to do, but it required a lot of running back and forth, and Calvn was no longer a colt.

Calvn knew that panic would do them no good. Some Equus might hurt themselves by rushing around looking for a land that was no longer nearby. To discover what had happened to the Equus, they first had to calm themselves down so they could search for the answer and not ignore the obvious, like they had about being alone.

At Calvn's urging, the Equus quieted and slowed down. The adults nipped at the flanks of the young to urge them to be still. Gradually, they turned to the side to expose their flanks to Calvn, showing him they were ready to listen. They were eager for answers and guidance.

When Calvn had their attention, he said, *"It is true we are without Father Equ. If he has not come in answer to your sincere pleas yet, I would not expect him to do so. The question to be answered is: Why would he banish us from the land of our birth and abandon us?"*

The words *banish* and *abandon* sent a ripple of unease through the herd. Some pranced around. Again, some Equus denied the obvious; perhaps it was a character flaw among the Equus. This group called out, *"We are not banished. Father Equ would never leave us."*

However, others recognized the reality and wanted answers. *"We don't know why we are here. You said you could tell us why."*

Calvn tossed his head back and stomped on the ground to draw the attention of the Equus. *"And I shall. Do we not know that Father Equ loves us?"*

"Yes, and we love him. Why has he left us?"

"We must have displeased him," Calvn told his brothers and sisters. The answer seemed simple to him.

"But we did nothing wrong!" was the dominant response from the herd.

"We must have, or he would not have banished us."

Again, they ignored the obvious and logical. If the Equus had been sent from Etrasco, then it was a punishment, for nothing could be better for the Equus than Etrasco, which had been created for them. And because Father Equ loved them, if he had sent the Equus from this perfect place, it must be because they had displeased him.

"Then how do we return to Etrasco?" the Equus asked.

Calvn shook his head. *"We don't. We wait for Equ to return for us, but first, we must prove to him we are worthy of his love."*

"How?"

"We must live the way he taught us until we once again please him."

The skies seemed to open then and soft rain poured down upon the Equus, even though the sun continued to shine in the cloudless sky. The raindrops tasted of the sweetness of the waters of Etrasco. The Equus turned their faces to the sky, allowing the taste of the rain on their tongues to remind them of their lost home.

In doing so, they tasted the tears of Equ as he grieved at the misery of his children.

1

As the morning sun crept over the tops of the white mountains to the north, the purity of the mountains' color spread the light across the plains of Hemlaza and amplified it. With the morning light brighter, the morning seemed as if it was later in the day than it actually was. One had to look at the height of the sun in the sky to realize it was just barely dawn.

Varon, a five-year-old chestnut stallion, was one of those who awoke with the warmth of the sun shining in his face. He opened his eyes and immediately closed them again rather than stare into the sunlight.

It shouldn't be so bright! How could he have slept so long that it was now late morning? He rarely slept this long and then only when he was exhausted after galloping or wrestling with some younger colts to show off for the mares. Movement from others in the herd or the general melee of thoughts in his head should have awakened him by now.

Certainly Pautin would have been calling for him louder than any other Equus in the mind-link. It was pleasant not to have her complaining about something, though.

He peered out through slitted eyelids and gradually opened his eyes as they adjusted to the brightness. He stared at the sun above the horizon a moment, wondering at the time of day. He moved his elongated head up and down on his thick neck so that his stare could focus on the mountains.

Mountains! He could see mountains in the north. Mountains had never been in the north. The only mountains on Hemlaza were the eastern Meshack Mountains, and they were not white.

But unless the sun had changed its waking spot, there were now mountains to the north of Hemlaza. They were not tall, jagged peaks like the Meshacks, but a smooth, semi-regular line across the horizon. However, they were so far away that they might be taller than the Meshacks, which were much closer to the herd's current grazing area. Where were the vast fields of alfalfa to the north, reaching all the way to the Horizon Sea?

This was not a typical morning.

Seeing the mountains reminded Varon of the old stories that the zebras and ponies told, about how the Equus had been abandoned in Hemlaza because they had shown themselves unworthy to live in the presence of Equ 193 generations ago. The Equus had been a single, great herd then, not the many herds that roamed the Hemlaza plains today. They had dwelt in the beautiful valley of Etrasco under Equ's protection. Then one morning, all the Equus had awakened in Hemlaza. Where Etrasco had been wooded mountains surrounding the lush valley within, Hemlaza, while lush, was an island surrounded by forests and beaches.

And now white mountains. Varon thought for a moment that perhaps Equ had taken them back to Etrasco. Perhaps the Equus had learned what they needed to know to return to their creator and father.

It was the material of dreams.

He shook his head to wake himself and then looked around for Pautin, his season mate. She had been standing beside him when he fell asleep. Pautin was a lovely palomino and had caught his attention last year with the shapely flow of her leg muscles as she ran with the herd. He had mated with her and impregnated her last year during the Season of Life, and so they were season mates until after the foal was born. Varon had mated for the first time last year, and he was not sure he had made a good decision by impregnating Pautin.

Now, she was heavy with what Varon hoped would be a fine filly and nearing her due date. She was big and wide and waddled when she walked. The sleekness of her muscles was gone, and the bitterness of her personality remained.

With Pautin near her birthing time, the Season of Life should be coming, but he had yet to see the new grasses that usually marked the beginning of the season. The long Seeking Season for grasses and fruits to eat was over, and yet, there was still a chill in the air, as if the Seeking Season did not want to leave Hemlaza. This was unusual, but it had its advantages, for the chill kept the annoying insects still. Pautin was moody enough with the birth coming soon. Varon was glad for one less thing to aggravate her. He tired of having her nip at his neck when he tried to groom her. Worse, he hated when she overwhelmed others' mind-voices by keeping herself close to him so that hers was the dominant voice in his head.

Varon lowered his head and grazed until he had his fill, which hadn't happened often lately. With his hunger satisfied, he walked over to see Pautin. She turned to stare at him with her round, brown eyes. Her eyes still enchanted him with their size, even if her personality left him cold. Varon backed away and kept his distance from her.

"What is wrong?" he asked her.

"You did not let me graze first," came the tart response in his mind.

Varon snorted. *"First? Yesterday, you told me that this grass was too bitter for your taste and that you would eat your feces before you ate this grass."*

Yesterday had definitely not been one of Pautin's better days. She had tried to bite him six times. Varon judged how good his season mate was feeling by how many times she tried to bite him. Once or twice was a good day. Three or four times a day was average. Anything over four meant it was a terrible day.

"That was yesterday." Her tone was haughty now, nearly echoing in his head because she stood so close to him. He thought she would try to bite him again.

Varon would not be choosing her as a season mate again. Pregnancy did not become her as it did with some mares. He was glad he hadn't chosen her as a life mate as some older Equus did when they continued to choose the same season mate year after year.

"Today, this grass tastes sweet," Pautin said as she lowered her head to graze.

"It's the same grass," Varon insisted.

She snorted. *"It is not. The grass yesterday was bitter. How could they be the same if one is bitter and one is sweet?"*

Varon just shook his head. It was no use. Pautin would never admit that it was her taste that had changed, not the taste of the grass.

He turned his gaze outward in search of predators. His function now was to serve as his season mate's protector. It was largely symbolic since they were nowhere near the edge of Scola's Herd and the herd scouts would warn them long before Pautin was in danger.

He allowed his attention to drift somewhat as he touched the mind-link and heard the non-directed thoughts of others in the herd. He hadn't been the only one who was surprised to see mountains on the northern horizon this morning, and the other Equus seemed just as confused as him over their appearance and meaning. Some still thought, as he had for a short time, the Equus had returned to Etrasco. Others thought the sun had shifted its waking spot. The change terrified more than a few.

What it came down to was that no one knew what the mountains were; only what they weren't... and they weren't there yesterday.

"What do you think of the mountains?" Varon asked Pautin.

"They are mountains." Pautin wasn't known for her in-depth analysis of situations.

"But they weren't there yesterday."

"So? They are mountains, not predators. Mountains can't kill you."

She might be right, but did that fact apply to mountains that appeared within the span of a morning? If mountains could appear where there had been no mountains, what was to say they didn't pose a danger to the Equus? Could they wake up tomorrow high on a mountain top? Knowing the Ravagers existed in this world had taught Varon that one could not always trust appearances.

Perhaps Calvn Scola would have more information about the white mountains and where they had come from. Varon doubted it, but some other Calvns might have passed on the information through pegasus messengers. Some herds had to be closer to the white mountains than Scola's Herd.

Pautin finally raised her head from the rye grass, signaling that she was finished grazing for the moment. Varon raised his head high and searched for Calvn Scola. He wasn't surprised to find the unicorn at the center of a gathering crowd.

Varon walked over to the edge of the crowd of Equus. The zebras, ponies, donkeys, and horses parted to make way for him as he moved through the herd. He saw his sire, Tola, staring at the white mountains and walked over next to him. Tola was a ten-year-old gray stallion, and Varon had been his first colt. Tola was also the horse leader of Scola's Herd.

"The morning has brought change to Hemlaza," Tola said.

"Do you know what they are?"

Tola whinnied in good humor. *"I raised you better than that, Varon. They are mountains."*

"Are they?"

Tola cocked his head to the side. *"You think not?"*

"Mountains don't suddenly appear and they usually aren't all white."

Tola nodded. *"Ah, you have been thinking. Excellent."*

Varon arched his neck at the praise. He enjoyed it when his sire honored him with kind words. *"So if they probably aren't mountains, what are they?"*

"I have no idea."

"Unfortunately, neither do I," Varon said. *"Does Calvn Scola know why the mountains have appeared or from where they came?"*

"Of course not. No one does," Tola responded sharply.

What was wrong with Tola? His sire was very good-natured. Why this sudden change in attitude? Was Tola worried about his increasing age? Varon had heard no rumors about a horse seeking to challenge Tola's leadership of the horses. It was Tola's job to ease the tensions between the horses and any of the other species in the herd. He also spoke for the horses to the Calvn. Perhaps he was more upset about the white mountains than he appeared.

"I thought for a moment when I awoke that we were back in Etrasco," Varon said.

"It would never happen." The mind-voice was not Tola's. Varon turned and saw that it was Sartino, the zebra leader in Scola's Herd. *"When the Equus are taken back to Etrasco, Equ will announce it through the zebras. It will be a joyous occasion for celebration as we say goodbye to the homeland and return to the birth land."*

Varon could have argued the point. There were as many theories on how the Equus would return to Etrasco as there were Equus on the Hemlaza Plains. No one knew for sure how the Equus would return; they only hoped that it would be soon.

"Father, if you hear anything about the mountains, will you please tell me?" Varon asked.

"You and all the horses. A horse leader cannot show favorites. As horse leader, I speak for all the horses in Scola's Herd, and I must care for all of them as well as I can," Tola told him.

Tola seemed to have calmed down now. Varon was glad. He didn't want to argue with his sire.

A pregnant pony approached Varon and said, *"Varon, my foal is being especially active; so much so it hurts me. Do you think my birth time is near?"*

The pony was young, and this was her first pregnancy. Not that Varon had much experience with birthing, but he was a horse, and as such, had been trained in the healing arts.

"Not for another few weeks, Tangie. You probably ate something that the foal didn't like," he told her.

"It's not as if I have much choice."

Varon nodded sympathetically. *"Pautin had the same problem. Doverweed worked for her then. I'll find some and bring it to you."*

"Thank you, Varon."

"You're welcome, sister."

Tangie wasn't his sister, but he called all Equus brothers and sisters to remind him they were all children of Equ. Even Pautin.

As Varon walked back to where Pautin was grazing with two

other mares, he was not satisfied with what his sire had told him. Mainly, because he hadn't been told anything. Neither the Calvn nor Tola knew what had happened or why the white mountains had appeared.

Hemlaza now had boundaries. It always had, but they had never been so apparent before today. He knew the Equus lived on a large island. In his life, he had been from one end of Hemlaza to the other. He had been in the mountains to the east, to the high cliffs overlooking the sea to the south, and the sandy beaches to the west coast. Did the fields of alfalfa still reach the north coast?

Varon tried to go about his normal routine of speaking with his friends, who were generally the other Equus his own age in the herd. Today, though, all the Equus wanted to speak of were the white mountains.

"The unicorns are so self-absorbed that it's amazing they see anything beyond themselves," Marsallin, a roan mare the same age as Varon, told him. Marsallin hated the unicorns. Varon could have told her of Pautin's own self-absorption and that horses were not immune from that fault. One did not speak ill of one's season mate while they were mated, though. Anyway, most of the herd already knew about Pautin, particularly stallions who had been her former season mates. Pautin was seven years old and had mated many times already and been a season mate twice.

"This is an evil sign, Varon," Stoni, a heavily muscled horse, told him. *"The land is changing and who is to say it will not happen here tomorrow or next week?"*

"We can't worry over something we have no control over," Varon said.

"How do we know that we don't have any control over it?"

That was a good question to which Varon had no answer, but he knew where he might find one. If Tola did not have the answer, Calvn Scola would, or eventually someone would tell him what the white mountains were.

"What do you think of the white mountains?" Varon asked Jalon, a four-year-old chestnut pegasus mare, who was Varon's closest

friend. The pegasus' ability to fly had always fascinated Varon, and Jalon counted him a friend since he had healed her broken wing two years ago.

"I think everyone's imagining them. If we all close our eyes, they will disappear," she said.

"Everything will disappear if we close our eyes."

Jalon nodded. *"That's my point."*

"Haven't you thought about what they might be?"

"I'll consider them mountains until I know differently, but guessing what they are accomplishes nothing," Jalon told him.

Varon shook his head. *"What do you dream about, sister?"*

"Etrasco."

"Don't we all?"

"Yes, but I dream not just about what it's like, but how I can get there."

"If anyone can get there, you will, Jalon."

Once time allowed him, Varon searched out Calvn Scola. The black unicorn with the white horn was standing so he faced away from the white mountains. Like so many others in Scola's Herd, he did not want to face the unknown. His season mate, a roan mare, was grooming his mane while the Calvn grazed on a pile of grass the donkeys had brought him.

The unicorns, at least the unicorns in Scola's Herd, regularly flaunted their ruling status and exercised it. They did not move around to graze. They had the donkeys forage for them. Many ponies were used as personal groomers for the unicorns. The unicorns' actions within Scola's Herd did nothing for their image among the other Equus when the stories of their behavior spread, but as long as the unicorns were the ruling class, stories did not matter to most of them.

"My Calvn, I seek to speak with you," Varon said.

Calvn Scola raised his head slightly. *"Then speak, Varon. I will listen to any of my herd who seek my wisdom."*

Varon sincerely doubted Scola's wisdom, but he was the herd leader, the Calvn. He was the one who was supposed to have answers to questions.

"The mountains are troubling the Equus, Calvn," Varon said.

"They are mountains. We have seen mountains before."

Varon had to force himself not to snort at the Calvn's purposeful blindness. He didn't want Calvn Scola to refuse to listen to any ideas concerning the mountains, which he would do if his ignorance was pointed out to him.

"We have not seen white mountains before, Calvn, and especially not white mountains that apparently appear on their own," Varon pointed out.

With his head turned to side, Calvn Scola eyed him from the side. *"You're not superstitious, are you, Varon?"*

Varon shook his head. *"I've never considered myself so, Calvn."*

"Good, then you are not one of the fools who will tell me that Equ is bringing Etrasco to us," Calvn Scola said.

Varon shook his head. *"I had not heard that, but many other rumors about the white mountains are running through the herd. No one knows the truth."*

Calvn Scola nodded, his horn dropping so it pointed almost threateningly at Varon. *"Agreed."*

"Could we not send a group to investigate and find out the truth? If we could know something about the mountains, it could eliminate many of these rumors. It would calm the herd if they knew that you knew what these mountains are."

The Calvn's ears perked up. *"I could send a group of pegasuses. They could travel the quickest to and from the mountains, and therefore, return things back to normal in the shortest time. I dislike this unnatural change I see."*

Unnatural. Varon thought that was an appropriate word to describe the mountains.

Scola was supposedly sired by a descendent of the original Calvn, the first of the Equus to unite all the Equus after their arrival in Hemlaza. That is why the herd leaders used Calvn's name as a title, to pay homage to his exceptional skill as a leader. It was also a constant reminder to others that the Calvns were direct descendents of Calvn and supposedly shared in their sire's leadership skill.

Privately, Varon thought the original Calvn's leadership skill was being diluted with each succeeding generation of unicorns. Tola had been the first that Varon knew of to give voice to doubts of the leadership ability of Calvn Scola. Since then, Varon had studied Calvn Scola enough to develop his own opinion of the black unicorn, which agreed his sire's view. All Varon had seen of Calvn Scola's leadership was his ability to steal the ideas of others and claim them as his own; unless, of course, the idea proved a failure. Then Calvn Scola readily gave credit for the idea to someone else, even if it was his idea. Varon had no doubt the herd would be told that the expedition was the Calvn's inspiration. Varon didn't mind as long as the expedition found the answers to his questions.

"That would probably be best, Calvn," Varon told his herd leader.

"Father Equ, hear us. Father Equ, hear our pleas," came the undirected pleas of the zebras. It was the daily call for Return.

"I will announce the expedition after Return," Calvn Scola said.

Varon nodded and turned to leave. He would have to find Pautin first before he gathered with the others for Return. His season mate was grazing when he found her. She didn't even look up when he approached.

"Did you hear the call to Return?" he asked her.

"I was waiting for you."

"I have been with the Calvn."

Pautin ignored him and continued grazing. Though he did not raise his head, his tail flicked in irritation with her attitude towards him.

"And what about the needs of this horse, your season mate who carries your foal?" she asked.

"You were not left wanting," Varon told her.

"How would you know?"

Varon did not reply because he knew it would do no good. Pautin was not making sense again. He turned to move off to Return. Pautin did not follow.

"It is time to go," he told her.

"I will come when I am ready," she snapped.

"If you offend the zebras by arriving late to Return, it will be a matter for the Calvn to reconcile between you and the zebras, not me," he said.

Return was a daily ceremony that the zebras performed. It reminded the herd of where they came from and what they needed to accomplish before they could return to Etrasco.

He moved off again, not bothering to look back. He hadn't gone far when something bit him on the flanks. He jumped, but luckily he didn't kick out. If he had, he would have injured Pautin and perhaps their foal. She had bitten him because he had forced her to trot, and quick movements – especially the bouncing motion of a trot – at this stage of her pregnancy were very uncomfortable.

"Wait for me, my season mate," she told him with false sweetness.

Varon stopped walking until Pautin caught up with him. Together, they walked slowly to the gathering herd. Varon found a place near the front of the gathering. Calvn Scola stood just in front of him.

"Father Equ, hear our plea. Father Equ, come for us. Return us to the birth land. Father Equ, help us. We want to be with you," the zebras chanted to begin Return. Their mind-voices were now the only voices on the mind-link.

The herd pressed tightly together. The zebras approached the Calvn with Sartino, the leader of the zebras in the lead. Before Sartino reached the Calvn, he turned to the side and kept walking. The zebra walking behind him was holding Sartino's tail in his mouth. He also turned and followed Sartino. One by one, the forty-eight zebras, each holding the zebra's tail who walked in front of him, formed a walking chain that encircled Scola's Herd of 249 unicorns, horses, pegasus, donkeys, and ponies.

"In the dawn of time, the Equus were one with Father Equ," Sartino said. *"We lived in peace but fell short of Father Equ's desires for us. So we were banished from the birth land of Etrasco."* The zebra ring stopped moving. The opening between Sartino's nose and the last zebra was in front of Calvn Scola. Calvn Scola walked through the opening, followed by the unicorns, pegasus, horses, po-

nies, and donkeys. *"In our struggle to find a way back to Equ, there arose a great unicorn who spoke for Father Equ. Calvn, the Voice of Equ, told the Equus what was needed to return to Father Equ and Etrasco."* The Equus formed a circle around Calvn Scola with their noses toward him. Sartino stood outside the circle. *"In Calvn's lifetime, Return did not happen because the Equus continued to fall short of the perfection needed to prove ourselves. Father Equ still watches us, though. He sent the Ranglan Stone, the stone of leadership, to the Calvn to end the herd wars and remind us of our single purpose."* Sartino galloped into the center of the circle and stood next to the Calvn. *"And so we have been given a piece of Equ in the form of the Ranglan Stone. As Father Equ guides the Calvn, so the Calvn guides the Equus."* The Equus all turned away from Calvn Scola and Sartino as if to form rays of a sun. *"We seek for Etrasco. When we are perfect, the Voice of Equ will lead the Equus back to Etrasco."*

"Father Equ, hear our plea. Father Equ, come for us. Return us to the birth land. Father Equ, help us. We want to be with you." This time it was the other Equus in the herd who said the chant.

When Return was finished, the Equus went back to their daily activities, which consisted mostly of trying to find enough to eat and watching out for predators. However, before they could move far away, Calvn Scola reared up on his hind legs and called, *"Wait, my children. I have come to a decision about what to do about the white mountains."*

"Yes!" some Equus shouted.

"This afternoon, I am sending three pegasuses to fly to the white mountains and discover what they are." There was an angry rumble from the pegasuses, but no distinct thoughts that could be understood. *"They will return to us and report on their discoveries. This should put many of the rumors I have heard to rest. So try to restrain your speculations until the pegasuses return."*

Varon looked at Jalon and wondered if the pegasus had been speaking to the Calvn. Their comments about the mountains sounded too much alike. Varon doubted it. Most of the pegasuses avoided talking to the Calvn if they could, since Scola was jealous of their ability to fly.

"*Thank you, Calvn,*" the Equus said.

"*Chinarvo,*" Scola called to his pegasus herd leader. "*Select three of your fastest pegasuses who can make the journey quickly and bring us word of the white mountains.*"

"*It will be done, Calvn,*" Chinarvo replied. He bowed his head to the ground and spread his great, black wings forward in a wide, sweeping motion so that the tips pointed toward the herd leader.

Chinarvo made his selection of pegasuses that would fly to the white mountains that evening, and Varon watched them fly off to the north into the coming darkness. Not surprisingly, Jalon was among them. The small pegasus was eager to be away on the journey. She was always eager to explore.

He wondered what his friend would find to the north.

Varon raised his head to the sky and offered a plea to Equ.

"*Father Equ, hear my plea. Guard my brothers and sister on their journey. They are alone and without a herd. Protect them from the Ravagers. Allow them to accomplish their mission and return them to their mates.*"

"*Thank you, Varon.*" Varon heard the voice faintly. It came from Jalon. She had heard Varon's plea on her behalf.

Varon stood back up and searched the skyline again. The pegasuses were out of sight.

"*Good luck, sister,*" he called.

He heard no reply. The pegasuses were out of range of the herd's mind-link. They were alone now and would form their own mind-link.

Varon turned and walked away, looking for Pautin. She would need to complain about something to him before she went to sleep.

For the first two days after the band of pegasuses flew off to explore the white mountains, speculation about what they would find continued to run rampant among all the species in Scola's Herd except the donkeys. Perhaps they didn't propose theories because their chief duty was to concentrate on the plains around the herd to warn the herd if predators came too close. Or, it might have been that their lowly position in the herd hierarchy had taught them to be very flexible to whatever situation they faced.

Once the speculations had ended over what the white mountains were and weren't, the Equus began to wonder when the pegasuses would return to put their questions to rest. This was what interested Tola, for what could take the pegasus so long to make the journey to the white mountains and back? Had they met with predators or were the white mountains further away than they appeared?

The world was changing, but was it changing for the better or worse? Tola wished he had the answer or knew who did.

He tried not to look at the white mountains, but knowing that they were there, just at the edge of his vision, drew his eyes to them. And when he saw the thick line of white along the horizon, his body trembled against his will as if he were cold. What he felt was not a drop in temperature but fear of change.

Concentrate, he told himself. *Duty to life mate. Duty to horses. Duty to herd.*

He took deep, sucking breaths, pulling the cool air in over his teeth and blowing it out through his flaring nostrils. His sides heaved as he concentrated on his mantra. To others, it would look as if he was running while standing still. Slowly, his thoughts refocused themselves.

When he was calm, Poins, his life mate, said, *"It is taking longer for you to regain control."*

Poins was Tola's life mate of three years. She had been his first season mate in his fourth year and the season mate of his seventh year. In Tola's eighth year, they had become life mates. Neither of them would ever take another season mate again. Becoming life mates was a serious commitment between two Equus. It meant the two Equus committed to mate with no other.

Poins was a ten-year-old mare whose coat had brown and white patches of color. Her legs were long and her body thick.

"I know, but I can still regain control," Tola replied.

"What will we do?"

We? How he loved Poins! To her, it was not even a question of whether they would face this problem together. The sickness was his alone. Poins could have left him, and no one would have faulted her, but she remained with him, honoring their commitment to each other.

"We must continue. The familiarity of life helps me maintain my control."

Poins said, *"Then you will have to communicate to the horses. They have questions, and they need their herd leader's counsel."*

"White mountains!" Tola snorted. *"It is because of them I am lost."*

"You are not lost."

Eventually, Poins would have to admit the truth to herself and do what she could to protect herself from him.

"I am. I can only postpone the inevitable," he told her.

When he heard no reply from Poins, he looked up. His life mate looked terrified. She stared at him with her ears pointing in different directions to mark her indecision. The muscles in her neck quivered with tension. She lifted and dropped her tail continually.

He walked over to her and massaged the base of Poins' neck at the withers with his lips. He rubbed the trembling muscles in her neck until they stilled.

"We should just leave the herd," Poins said.

He shook his head. *"We can't."*

"Why not? If the herd even suspects you have mind-sickness, the Calvn will declare you a renegade," she said as softly as she could to him.

Mind-sickness was the most feared disease among the Equus. Not only was its cause unknown, but it was highly contagious. An Equus with mind-sickness acted erratically and sometimes heard and saw things that weren't there. From the initial Equus who carried the disease, it spread to the other Equus in the herd through the mind-link. An entire herd with mind-sickness had once galloped off the southern cliffs and plunged to their deaths in the Shadow Ocean.

Tola said, *"I know, but my first duty is to my life mate... you. We can't survive as exiles, so I need to do what I can to keep you alive. My second duty is to the horses. I can't relinquish my position as horse leader. No one else is ready to lead yet. Stoni and Varon show promise, but they aren't ready now. Dissa is ready, but he's a Scola sycophant. He would not be a talented horse leader. My third duty is to the herd, and while I am endangering them, it is not a fatal disease to them. If I must balance my failure to the herd against you and the horses, I select you and the horses."*

Poins groomed Tola's withers. It sent a pleasant tingling sensation through his body that relaxed him as it spread.

"Tola," Calvn Scola called.

Tola blew air through his mouth to flap his lips. *"Yes, my Calvn?"*

"Join me and the other herd leaders. We need to have a council."

Calvn Scola rarely held council with his herd leaders. He much preferred taking advice from other unicorns. Tola walked to the center of the herd where Calvn Scola, Sartino, Chinarvo, Benju, and Drusinos were already waiting for him. Poins accompanied him, but stayed far enough away from the council meeting that she wouldn't be thought to be intruding on the conversation of the herd leaders.

"The white mountains are a problem," Calvn Scola said.

Tola noticed the Calvn had his back to the white mountains. Tola wondered if the sight of the mountains disturbed Scola's own control. Could the mind-sickness be affecting Calvn Scola? Had it spread despite Tola's efforts?

"Have the pegasuses reported?" Drusinos asked.

"No." Calvn Scola paused. *"The white mountains are so… unnatural."*

"How so, Calvn?" Chinarvo asked.

"Mountains just don't appear!" Calvn Scola snapped.

"We should wait until the pegasuses return. Then…"

"And then what? What can we do against mountains?" Scola asked.

"Calvn," Tola asked, *"are you feeling fine?"*

Calvn Scola's head swung around to stare at Tola. *"Of course I'm fine."*

Tola felt his own control wavering on the brink of dissolving. His anger and panic boiled and rumbled just below the surface of his control.

"You seem upset," Scola countered.

"Aren't you? Aren't all the Equus? Mountains are moving on the Hemlaza Plains!" Tola snapped.

Tola realized that Scola didn't have his back to the mountains because it shook his resolve; Scola was afraid of the mountains because he knew he couldn't control them like he could an Equus in his herd. Tola felt a deep shame that his Calvn, the Equus that was supposed to lead this herd, should show such fear. Tola could remember when Calvn Alle had led this herd before he had died. Alle had *led.* He had been Calvn. Scola was only a poor imitation. Why Equ would have chosen him was beyond Tola's understanding. Scola was another reason Tola couldn't leave the herd. Tola needed to lead the horses because Scola wasn't, wouldn't, and couldn't.

Tola's control wavered again, and he felt anger. He wanted to strike out at Calvn Scola. He felt his control slowly return and then fade just as quickly. His emotions were raw now. He was about to lose control. What could he do to protect himself?

Poins snorted and began stomping her hooves. The unicorns near her moved away.

Tola and the other herd leaders turned to stare at her.

"What is wrong?" Tola asked her.

"Your anger. It's overwhelming me," Poins said so that the others couldn't hear her thoughts.

"My anger?" Then the realization hit him. He had suppressed his anger too easily, but it hadn't been because of any skill of his. Poins had used their special bonds as life mates to aid his self-control. *"Poins, don't take on my madness."*

Poins shook her head. *"I will."*

"No!"

Realizing he was losing control, and doing so would only hurt Poins more, Tola started concentrating on the mantra he had developed. *Duty to life mate. Duty to horses. Duty to herd. Duty to life mate. Duty to horses. Duty to herd.*

"I don't want to cause you pain, my mate," Tola said.

"Tola, either I accept your pain now and help you, or I will have it forced on me later by your mind-sickness," Poins explained.

To the others, Tola said, *"She is not feeling well. If there is nothing more to speak of, I would like to find some calming herb for her."*

"But we have not finished discussing what can be done about the white mountains," Calvn Scola said.

"You said yourself we can do nothing. We don't even know what they are. We should wait until the pegasuses return. Who knows? They might even bring us good news."

Tola turned and walked away, nudging Poins along with his nose. Poins still hadn't calmed herself from the rage and confusion flowing through Tola. He tried to relax himself even more as he groomed Poins, hoping it would bring her back to her senses.

"We should leave," she said, *"before they drive us away."*

Tola shook his head. *"No, I should leave."*

"If you left the herd without me, I would die."

Tola shook his head. *"No, you wouldn't. Life mates live on after one dies."*

"But I don't want to."

What could he say to that? He and Poins were life mates because they loved and honored each other. Would he feel the same if his and Poins' roles were reversed? Yes, and he wouldn't let her talk him out of remaining with her either.

Being a life mate meant making a great commitment, which was why so few Equus went to the effort to forge the bond. Once forged, the bond only grew stronger with time until life mates shared their own mind-link within a herd.

Duty to life mate. Duty to horses. Duty to herd.

He had to hold on to his sanity for Poins' sake.

Tola knew that he should leave, but he also knew that he wouldn't. If he left the herd, Poins would follow and they would both die. He would fight the mind-sickness until he could fight it no longer. Only in that way would Poins have a chance to live.

Duty to life mate. Duty to horses. Duty to herd.

The path he had chosen was a betrayal of his duty to herd and horse, but it was the only way that Poins would have a chance at life. When Tola was dead, there would be another horse leader, but not another life mate for Poins.

3

Jalon flapped her wings harder, taking longer strokes in the hopes of catching more air under her. She wanted to fly higher, always higher. She had always wanted to climb high enough into the sky to soar within the fluffy, white clouds and to feel their feather-light softness against her hide. She wondered if they felt as she imagined and was eager to know. Were they as light as they looked? Were they warm or cold? Were they dense like she heard smoke from a wildfire could be, or lighter like the morning fog that was sometimes in the valleys of the Meshack Mountains and the rolling foothills?

Jalon's wings tired with the intense effort to lift her higher, and she knew she could rise no further unless her wings had lengthened lately. She stretched her legs out in front and behind her and leaned her neck forward to minimize her wind resistance. Then she stopped flapping her wings. Gravity took hold and sent her into a dive.

Jalon whinnied with glee.

She pulled out of the dive well above the ground and zoomed over a herd of moose, sending them scattering in all directions.

Jalon whinnied and kicked her legs with delight.

"Jalon, this is an expedition, not a competition," Trenea scolded her.

Jalon swerved and flew around until she was paralleling the course of the older pegasus. Trenea was a gray stallion who was a full head taller than she was. He had tried to be her season mate this year, but he was too serious for Jalon.

"I am just happy to be away from the herd for a while, Trenea.

The pegasuses in other herds get respect. Why don't we?" Jalon asked.

She hated how the pegasuses in Scola's Herd were kept near the edge of the herd; the few that he had left with his herd. Most of the time, Scola had Chinarvo sending the pegasuses on one useless mission after another, and the pegasus leader did not have the courage to stand up to Calvn Scola. The pegasuses needed a new herd leader, and the herd deserved a new Calvn.

"Respect depends on the Calvn and ours is jealous of our wings," Trenea said.

"Why? I am not jealous of his horn. I am not jealous of any stallion's horn," she said.

"Who can say? It does not even matter. If the Calvn is jealous of the pegasus, it is up to the pegasus to change his feelings."

That made little sense to Jalon. If Calvn Scola's jealousy was causing a problem between two species, then Calvn Scola should be the one to fix the problem. Besides being too serious, Trenea was too willing to accept whatever life handed to him without trying to change the bad to the good.

"Still, you must enjoy being away from the herd," Jalon said.

"I miss my season mate," Trenea said. After Jalon had turned him down, Trenea had mated with Fofit, an attractive five-year-old mare.

"As do I," Pars, the third pegasus in the expedition, added.

Jalon hadn't taken a season mate this year. She had been in heat and felt the urge to mate, but she had also seen how poorly Varon and Pautin got along. While Jalon had wanted to mate with some stallions, she hadn't wanted to make a mistake like Varon had. So she hadn't encouraged the stallions by winking her vulva at them, although they still had realized that she was in heat from the scent of her urine. There was no getting around that unless she would have flown far away from the herd every time that she needed to urinate.

Jalon was a methodical Equus. She wouldn't rush into things. If there were a stallion for her, he would have to fly faster than her because Jalon would not wait for him to catch her and court her.

Jalon looked at the white mountains, which seemed just as far away as they had been when the pegasus had started their journey.

"By the Creator, those must be gigantic mountains!" Jalon exclaimed.

"Tell me something I don't know, Little One," Pars said. Since he was the largest pegasus in their band, Pars tended to lord it over the others, particularly Jalon.

Jalon looped under Pars' hooves and flapped her wings hard to swing up above the large pegasus in a graceful arc. Then she gently landed on top of Pars and stopped flapping her wings. Pars immediately sank under the extra weight. He flapped his wings harder, but they weren't strong enough to hold two pegasuses aloft.

Pars squealed.

"Get off my back, you fool!" Pars shouted. *"You'll make me crash!"*

Pars twisted, trying to knock Jalon off his back. Jalon stretched out her wings to steady herself and maintain her position on Pars' back.

"The problem with being big, Pars, is that you have too much weight," Jalon taunted him.

She lifted off with a single flap of her wings. Pars tried to bite Jalon's haunches, but the young pegasus easily evaded him. Jalon might be small, but she was agile.

"And you have no grace!" Jalon added.

"Enough of your foolishness, Jalon," Trenea scolded. *"Since you have so much energy, fly ahead and see if you can find us a place to set down and graze. I, for one, am hungry."*

"I am, too," Pars added.

"That's another problem with being so much larger than other pegasuses; you eat too much," Jalon said.

Pars snorted and shook his head.

"Don't taunt him, Jalon," Trenea warned.

"Fine. I'll fly to the east. Why don't you stay to the north? I'll parallel your course to the limits of the mind-link. Why don't you send Pars to the west? That way, we'll cover more territory."

"Good thinking, Jalon," Trenea said.

Jalon veered away, gliding off toward the east. It was past mid-day now. The sun was behind her to the south, so she didn't have to squint as she flew north. The air was cooler, not only because of her altitude, but there was a winter chill in the air.

It amazed Jalon how large the land of Hemlaza was. Millions of animals, including the thousands of Equus, lived on the island, and yet, looking across the land now, Jalon could only see a couple rabbits, one rattlesnake, and a small herd of deer. All the rest of the animals were too far away or hidden from view. Jalon couldn't even sense their mind-links. That is, if they even had one. She wasn't sure.

The land was that immense, and still the white mountains seemed to dominate it.

Jalon noticed six black dots in the air off to the north. At first, she thought they were birds. They weren't. She realized that they weren't small; they were just far away like the mountains. To be that large and flying meant that they were pegasuses, but they were too far away to join her in a mind-link. That was odd. If she could see them, she should be able to link with them. She watched them as they drew closer. Their bodies were oddly proportioned for pegasuses, and their hooves were much too thick.

Then Jalon recognized what she was seeing.

"Trenea! Pars!" she called.

"What?" Trenea answered.

"I see six griffins coming from the north."

"The griffins are dead. Chicac killed the last three generations ago."

Jalon veered to the west. *"Tell that to these six if they catch up with us!"*

The griffins had all supposedly been killed during the Griffin Wars. The griffins had been the one major predatory threat to the pegasuses. Their raking claws and sharp teeth had been deadly weapons in air battles. Not only were the griffins usually victors against the pegasuses, they were just as deadly to any of the Equus locked to the ground. The pegasuses from all the Equus herds had banded together in one great, single-species herd and sought out the griffins at their aviaries, killing them by overwhelming them with much greater numbers. The griffins had killed nearly half of the pegasuses in the wars and one in ten had been wounded so badly that he never flew again. The few griffins who had escaped had been hunted relentlessly over the next few years, but it was thought that all the griffins had eventually been killed. The Equus had been relatively safe since then.

Jalon flew as fast as she could, searching for her two companions. She watched behind her as she flew. The griffins were closing the gap. She could make out their general shape now. They were definitely griffins, despite what Trenea had said.

"Fly east, you two! Don't wait for me! If you do, you might not get away!" Jalon called out her warning to them.

"Are you going to get away?" Pars asked.

"I don't plan on missing the look on Scola's face when I tell him that the griffins still live. It will make his horn go limp!" She wished she were as confident of her success as she sounded.

"But where have they been since the Griffin Wars?" Trenea asked.

"It doesn't matter where they have been. They are here now."

The griffins drew closer, and Jalon couldn't seem to fly any faster. She cursed her small wings, wishing, not for the first time, that she had the wings of a larger Equus. Not because she wanted to fly higher. Her life now depended on her speed. Even fear wasn't adding to her speed. Unless something changed, the griffins would catch up with her in soon. She had heard the tales that griffins could fly faster than pegasus because they had the lighter bone structure of an eagle. The pegasus, on the other hand, was a horse with wings.

So Jalon needed to use her size and weight difference to her advantage. One griffin screeched like an eagle and dove at Jalon from above. It extended the claws on its four legs to rip at Jalon's back, where her wings joined her body. If they could cripple her, it would be easier to kill her.

Jalon leaned her head forward and dove toward the barren plain 300 feet below her. As her haunches tilted up, she kicked out behind her. Her kick missed the griffin, but it startled the creature and gave Jalon some extra thrust downward. She angled down so sharply she might as well have been falling. At the last moment, she pulled up. The griffin couldn't pull up fast enough and smashed into the ground behind Jalon. Jalon could tell by the odd angles that the griffin had broken, her right wing and three legs.

Jalon eased off her ascent and landed gently. She didn't waste time checking to see if the griffin was dead. She broke into a gallop.

Behind her, she heard a second griffin land with a loud screech. Jalon was not the fastest Equus she knew, but she was faster on the ground than a light-boned lion.

The other griffins landed and surrounded their fallen comrade. Jalon expected to see them carry the wounded griffin between two unwounded ones back to where her wounds could be treated. It was what one pegasus would have done for a wounded companion. Instead, the five griffins snarled and lunged at the wounded griffin. Despite herself, Jalon whinnied in fear as the five griffins killed and ate their companion.

Jalon galloped even harder; fear fueling her speed. The gap between her and the griffins widened now that they were on the ground and momentarily distracted. Two griffins that apparently weren't satisfied with cannibalizing their companion took to the air to pursue Jalon.

Her muscles strained as she ran since she wasn't used to galloping for long stretches, but she knew that if she let up for a moment, the griffins would be on her.

And she really did want to see the expression on Scola's face when he found out about the griffins.

She galloped, and the gap held. Her stamina held, and the gap widened again. It wasn't because Jalon was galloping faster. She wasn't. She couldn't have. The griffins were tiring of the chase. Soon, they slowed to a walk one by one.

Jalon kept galloping in case the griffins took to the air again. She got her second wind, and it became easier to gallop. She began wondering where Trenea and Pars were. She hoped that they were safe.

"Trenea!" she called.

There was no answer. She assumed that the other two pegasuses were out of range of her thoughts and couldn't establish a mind-link. She slowed to a walk only when she saw a stream and realized how thirsty she was. She drank her fill of the cold water and began walking again.

She turned to the north. It wasn't because she felt a need to complete the mission that Scola had set her upon. She was curious as to what the white mountains were for herself. In fact, she reasoned that she was probably closer to the white mountains than she was to the herd, so she might as well continue to satisfy her curiosity.

Jalon glanced behind herself frequently, half expecting to see the griffins approaching. She was tempted to take to the air again. That was where she felt the most comfortable, but she was safer on the ground for now. She didn't enjoy making herself a target for any other griffins that might be in the area.

Of all things! Griffins!

Where had they come from? Were these six—these five—the only ones that were still alive or were there more?

One thing for sure was that the pegasuses were no longer the masters of the air.

When night came, Jalon was still walking to the north. She found some sweet wheatgrass and ate until she was full. It was the first satisfying meal that she had had all day. The blueberries were green and weren't very juicy, but they were filling and had a fresh taste. She judged that the white mountains were at least three more days away. That is, if she flew and didn't walk the entire way there. She hoped that reaching them would be worth the journey.

"Jalon!" the mind-voice was faint.

"Pars?" Jalon replied.

"Yes. You're alive!"

"Alive, scared, and tired."

"Were they griffins?" the older pegasus asked.

"I've never seen one, but what I saw matches what the ponies described as a griffin; an eagle's head on a lion's body," Jalon explained.

Pars' mind-voice was getting louder as Pars moved closer to her.

"This is not good news," Pars said. *"I think the ages are changing."*

What was he worried about? He hadn't been chased by griffins. *"Six griffins do not mark the changing of an age."*

"No, but six griffins, the white mountains appearing, and the extra-long Seeking Season might mark a change," Pars said, and Jalon had to agree with him. Taken together, it all might mark a change.

Jalon began searching the sky for a dark, moving shadow. Pars should have been close enough for Jalon to see him.

"Where are you, Pars?"

"Close, judging by the sound of your mind-voice."

Pars dropped to the ground next to Jalon. Startled, Jalon began jumping and kicking and screaming in terror.

"Griffins! Griffins!" she screamed.

Pars whinnied with amusement.

Jalon turned and galloped away into the night as fast as she could. Pars stopped whinnying and called, *"Jalon! Jalon! Wait! It's me, Pars."*

Jalon stopped, her sides heaving. She stared at the form just to make sure it was Pars. He approached her slowly this time, and the young pegasus kicked out. Pars jumped away in just barely enough time to avoid being hit by her hooves.

"Careful, Jalon! I told you it was me, Pars!"

She kicked at him again, and he dodged. *"I know! I'm trying to kick you because you scared me!"* she screamed.

"It serves you right for all the times you've scared me."

"But I thought you were one of the griffins!"

Pars stared at her. *"They must have been frightening. I've never seen you so jittery."*

Jalon calmed down, but she still glared at Pars. *"I told you I was scared, didn't I?"*

"I didn't believe you."

Jalon shook her head. *"Let's go find Trenea. Do you know where he is?"*

Pars nodded. *"We set up a meeting place and time. He is searching for you further to the east."*

"Then let's find him. We shouldn't be separated with five griffins in the area."

"I thought you said that there were six griffins."

"I tricked one into crashing and her companions killed her and ate her."

Pars whinnied. *"Ate her? No wonder you are nervous."*

The two of them took to the air. Jalon followed the older pegasus and stayed close by him. At times, they were so close that their wings almost touched. Having Pars with her meant an increased degree of protection to Jalon, and she didn't want to lose that right now. The two of them would still be no match for five griffins, but just having Pars nearby was a reassurance.

They joined up with Trenea near dawn, and Jalon explained everything that had happened to her since they had separated the day before. They decided to continue on to the white mountains since they were so close to them. They reached the mountains three days later and landed atop a flat surface thousands of feet above the plains.

They were white mountains and cold under Jalon's hooves. No vegetation could be seen anywhere within sight.

"These are like no mountains I've ever seen," Pars said.

Jalon kicked at the surface of the mountains and it flaked away. She lowered her head and sniffed at the surface.

"This is ice," she said.

"You sound surprised. The Meshacks have ice on them during the Seeking Season," Trenea said as he licked at the ice.

"Yes, but you can scrape away that ice and find the earth beneath. This is such a hard pack that I doubt we could scrape away more than a few inches of it."

"Look at how steep this mountain face is," Pars said, peering over the edge. *"It's as if the ground just broke apart and shoved these mountains into the air."* He shook his head. *"It's not natural."*

"It may not be natural, but is it dangerous to the Equus?"
Jalon stared out over the vast plain of ice. It was just as flat as the Hemlaza Plains. Because of the glare off the ice, it was hard to stare at the surface. Jalon squinted and shook her head. She couldn't see the opposite edge of the mountains.

"It looks more like the Hemlaza Plains than the Meshack Mountains from up here," she noted.

Pars nodded. *"But do we fly further inland?"*

Trenea said, *"We've barely looked at these mountains. If they are so different from what we expected from only a casual glance, how many more differences will we find further inland?"*

"None!" Pars shouted. *"Look for yourself. These mountains go on and on without end."*

"If what you say is true, then we have discovered a way off of Hemlaza to other lands," Jalon suggested, staring off to the north.

Pars' jaw snapped shut; not in anger, but in confusion. *"A way off Hemlaza? To where?"*

"Who knows? Etrasco, perhaps," Trenea said.

"Etrasco?"

"This plain reaches into the Horizon Sea, but how far? This might be the path the griffins used to return to Hemlaza. We need to know." Just speaking of the griffins made Jalon shudder.

They agreed to fly inland to find where the white mountains began. They flew north for a full day and night and saw nothing but a white field of ice below them. It was as unending as Pars had suggested and barren of life.

When they stopped to rest, they could scrape at the ice and suck on the shards to quench their thirst, but there were no plants to eat. It was hard to imagine anything being sparser than the Hemlaza Plains, but the white mountains were. The pegasuses grew hungry. Jalon was relieved she had a smaller stomach to fill than Pars. She was famished. He must be starving.

"This is a wasteland," Pars said.

Trenea agreed. *"This might very well go to Etrasco, but there is no way that the Equus could follow it. We would die before we reached the end."*

Jalon looked around, seeing nothing but ice. Could the Equus cross this expanse, and if they could, what would they find? More ocean?

There were ways Jalon could envision this expanse being crossed, but not with the small band they had now. It would require a large, coordinated effort by many Equus to cross these mountains, but it could be done. The question was: would it?

"We can't accomplish anything more without risking that we won't have enough strength to fly back to the plains," Jalon said.

Trenea and Pars agreed. They slept for a brief time, sucked on some ice, and then flew back toward Hemlaza. Jalon was exhausted from the lack of food, as were the others, but they pushed themselves onward, knowing that the sooner they were off the white mountains, the sooner they could graze.

To Jalon, the white mountains were the greatest change that she had ever known. The griffins were terrifying, but they could be conquered. They had been in the past, but how could the Equus conquer a mountain range?

4

The continued absence of the pegasuses, particularly Jalon, disturbed Varon. He missed his friend, but more so, he wondered if something had happened to the small band of Equus.

The sight of the white mountains on the horizon each morning also upset him. He kept telling himself they were simply mountains, but he must not have believed himself. The white mountains were threatening in a way the Meshack Mountains weren't. During his longer periods of sleep, Varon dreamed of waking up with the white mountains right next to him.

It was the change in the pattern of life that disturbed Varon. After five years of life that followed a general pattern, he expected the rest of his life to be like that. The herd would graze for a week in one area and then move onto an unfamiliar area. The Season of Life followed the Seeking Season. Beaches lined the north coast of Hemlaza. But now grazing was so scarce that the Equus moved daily, the Seeking Season still held the land, and there were white mountains to the north.

Calvn Scola wouldn't have the answer unless someone told it to him, but Tola or one of the other species leaders might. Tola kept close counsel with the other species leaders, even when the Calvn didn't.

The horse leader was grazing near his life mate, Poins, when Varon approached him.

"Father?"

Tola jumped back onto his rear legs. His front legs flailed out, striking Varon in the muzzle. Varon squealed and hopped backwards. Varon tensed, wondering if he would have to fight his sire. He hadn't expected this reaction from Tola.

"Do you seek to challenge me?" Tola shouted with his mind-voice.

Others in the herd stopped grazing and looked up at the sound of Tola's mind-voice and the challenge he'd issued. Varon lowered his head to the ground, imitating grazing as he submitting to his sire's authority as horse leader. Tola was only ten years old, and he could still best younger stallions in the herd, which was why no one sought to challenge him. Varon's throbbing muzzle told him he was not ready to challenge his sire.

"Father, I don't want to challenge you. I came to speak with my horse leader," Varon said, hoping his sire heard no challenge in his tone.

Tola dropped down so that all four hooves were on the ground, but he still continued to paw at the ground to show his agitation. Varon kept his gaze directed down so his species leader would not think Varon was issuing a challenge.

"You want to be horse leader of this herd. You think because I am your sire that the position is yours for the taking. Do you think yourself a unicorn?" Tola demanded.

Varon knew his sire was suspicious of challengers to his position in the herd, but he had never been so openly hostile about it, especially towards Varon. Tola knew Varon was just beyond being called a colt and not wise enough or strong enough to best his sire.

"I want only to know if you have heard anything about the pegasus band or know what has happened to them," Varon said.

"What? Do I look like Chinarvo? Do I have wings sprouting out of my sides? I am horse leader, and I will tolerate no challenger. Do not let the gray in my coat fool you. I am still young and able to face down any challengers." Tola snorted. He held his tail high, swishing it back and forth.

This wasn't getting any better. Varon wasn't sure what he could say to ease his sire's worries, but he knew that everything he had said so far only seemed to upset Tola more. It would be better to submit to the horse leader and leave. He and Tola could speak at another time.

Hopefully, it would be a time when Tola was more at ease.

"I am sorry to have disturbed you, horse leader," Varon said.

Tola calmed. He stopped moving around and looked at Varon

with compassion in his large brown eyes. Even if Tola's actions were not normal, these were the eyes of the Tola that Varon loved.

"Do not be sorry, Varon. I always have time for a fellow Equus, especially one who is of my blood," Tola said.

The non-threatening thoughts scared Varon because he knew the sudden change in mood wasn't right. He backed away from the tall stallion.

"Thank you, father."

Tola nodded and went back to grazing. Varon saw his dam nearby and trotted over to her. Poins saw him coming and observed his approach. She seemed tense, but not in a way that would explode in aggression. Her tension was more worried.

"Say nothing, Varon," she said when he was close. The pressure from her mind-voice was soft enough not to attract attention from other nearby Equus.

"But…"

"Let's walk."

Varon nodded, and his dam began walking beside him. He felt his dam continually brushing the mind-link, but not joining in the flow of thoughts. She remained silent and tense. When they were yards away from any other Equus, she looked at Varon.

"Now we can talk," she said.

"You are afraid of being overheard," Varon said. It was a statement, not a question. That they had walked away from the herd showed Poins wanted a private conversation between the two of them. Her testing of the mind-link showed her fear.

"Because I know what you will say."

"So you know my thoughts before I form them?" That had always irritated Varon about the mind-link. It was an intimate form of communication, and it made some Equus feel they knew everything about you. No one knew Varon's innermost thoughts, those he did not give voice to. The need to link with the herd did not drive him. He used the link to communicate, not to live.

"Calm yourself, Varon. I know what you are thinking because I saw your reaction to Tola. You think Tola has mind-sickness."

Varon snorted, and then he calmed himself. That was the reaction most Equus had at hearing the words mind-sickness. *"Does he?"*

Poins' ears pointed in different directions, showing her indecision. *"Who knows, but an accusation, right or wrong, will make him an exile."*

"But if he has mind-sickness, you endanger the entire herd by hiding the fact," Varon said, beginning to prance besides Poins.

Poins lowered her head below Varon's. *"He is my life mate, Varon."*

Varon shook his head. Mind-sickness was not something he wanted to contract. His world was changing enough without distorting it through mind-sickness.

"It isn't right, mother."

"What is? Should I kill Tola by making an untrue accusation? I would be killing myself," she told Varon.

"You exaggerate."

Poins shook her head. *"Do I? He is my life mate. One life mate without the other is incomplete. My life is joined to his life. We are as one. That is what the term means."*

Varon blew air past his lips and let them flap. He wanted to show loyalty to his dam, but his first loyalty was to the safety of the herd. Above all, the herd must survive. Individual Equus died every day, but as long as the herd survived, new individuals were born to replace the dead.

"How long have you known?" he asked.

Poins stopped walking and turned to face Varon. *"I don't know."*

"Then how long have you suspected?" Varon pressed.

Silence fell between them, and Varon wondered if Poins would answer him.

"Three days," she said.

"Three?"

If Tola had mind-sickness, then the entire herd was already infected now. It took less than a day for mind-sickness to spread through an entire herd. How long would it be before the herd started showing signs of paranoia? But if Tola had infected them, why hadn't any of the other Equus shown signs of having mind-sickness already? In three days, the signs should have manifested themselves. The odd behaviors. The unexplained actions.

They weren't apparent.

Maybe his sire didn't have mind-sickness. Maybe Tola was only preoccupied with other things going on in the herd. Hadn't Tola always said that Varon had a curious nature, much like his own? Perhaps Tola was curious or worried about the white mountains appearing. Perhaps it was his single-minded concentration on unraveling their mystery that caused him to act as he had?

What should Varon do? Did it matter at this point?

"Mother, I can do nothing now. After three days, you have either proven yourself right or endangered us all," Varon said.

"Varon, don't sound cross," Poins said.

"Why shouldn't I? What if Pautin gets infected and harms herself or the foal? I am her season mate, but how can I protect her from mind-sickness?"

"I didn't choose this path because of my fears. For if it was mind-sickness Tola has, I would have endangered myself as well as the herd. I had to make a choice. Do you understand?"

"Yes, you chose possible madness over exile," Varon replied.

Poins snorted and stamped her front hooves. *"I chose life over death, my colt."*

Varon noted that she had called him a colt, though he was older than four years. She was reminding him that though he was mature, his life experiences and wisdom to this point were still lacking. Poins was telling Varon not to be an upstart.

"What a herd does or doesn't do is not always the best for the individual Equus," Poins explained. *"Individuals can think and decide. A herd can only react. When the individual acts like a herd, the herd suffers. You see what you believe to be a sign of mind-sickness. Did you think through the consequences? No, you reacted on an emotional level."*

"Mind-sickness is dangerous."

"You are reacting to the words, my colt. Mind-sickness equals

danger to you. It is instilled in the herd, but who is in danger?" She paused. Varon said nothing. *"Only the carrier of the disease is in danger when the zebras are available. It's death to the carriers and an inconvenience to everyone else. Given that choice, which would you choose for your mate?"* Poins asked him.

Varon nodded his head. *"I understand."*

Poins groomed Varon's withers. *"Tola always said you truly understood what it is to be an Equus. Don't disprove him now."*

"All equal under Equ."

"That is the literal meaning," Poins said. *"And the other?"*

"Equ's children," Varon said with a moment's pause.

Poins nodded. *"Yes. You understand the caring love of a sire for a foal without yet being a sire. You will make a good sire when your foal is born."*

Varon understood why Tola had taken Poins as a life mate. Varon had always known his sire was wise as horse leader, but now he could also see that same wisdom in his father's choice for a life mate. Poins was just as wise as Tola.

"It is because I had a fine sire and dam," Varon said.

"I can only imagine how great your compassion and love for the Equus will be when you are Tola's age," Poins told him.

When they rejoined the main body of the herd, Varon stood and watched Tola while Poins walked over to stand beside him and groom him. He had to admit that his sire seemed normal now. Tola was calm and seemed at ease with his surroundings.

Maybe Tola was alright.

By the evening of the fifth day after the pegasuses had left, the herd opinion was that the band was not returning. Varon wondered at that and questioned those who mentioned their belief. When pressed for a reason they would believe the pegasuses would not return, they could give no facts but only suggest that it was something the herd knew.

The herd.

No individual seemed to be at the origin of the rumors, only the herd. It was as if the herd was an individual among the Equus who was greater in authority than even Calvn Scola and worse than him in its ability to make a correct decision.

But the Equus cannot survive individually, Varon thought. *If the herd thought is so wrong, how do we survive as herds, but perish as individuals? And if a Calvn were to work to make herd thought correct, would the herds then perish?*

Varon would have to speak with Tola and Poins and see what their opinions were. They could make sense of the confusion.

A surge of anger flooded the mind-link, and Varon felt like lashing out at the nearest Equus. He reared up before he could bring his violent emotions in check by focusing on his own thoughts instead of the herd's.

"I am not angry. I am not angry," he repeated to himself.

Others, however, gave into the raw power of the emotion. Fights broke out among the herd and not just between stallions, either. Mates fought, biting at each other's necks and haunches. Individuals between species fought, kicking and gouging. Hooves tore at hide and teeth bit deep.

What caused this? It was more than herd thought. He had felt the surge of emotion within the mind-link, but the mind-link wasn't for conveying emotion. Something had contaminated it.

Varon looked around the herd and spotted Tola. His sire was on his knees. His body shook as he fought to remain calm amid the confusion.

Tola did have mind-sickness! There was no hiding it!

"Varon, open your thoughts to me," Sartino, the zebra leader, said as he trotted up next to Varon.

"No, then the madness will overwhelm me," Varon said more harshly than he had intended. The zebras were only trying to identify the carrier of the mind-sickness, but Varon was afraid to open himself to the mind-link's contamination. If he did, the raw emotion would overwhelm him.

Sartino walked over next to Varon. *"Now, Varon, open your thoughts to me. The power of Equ will shield you for now."*

Varon allowed his thoughts to touch the mind-link. He could feel anger from the herd surging through the mind-link. It burned like fire and ran like a wildfire, but when it neared Varon and threatened to engulf him, it instead slid around him. Within the link between Varon and Sartino, there was only peace and calm.

"You are not the carrier," Sartino said.

"No, I am not," Varon replied with relief.

"Sartino... it... is... me," Tola said, barely controlling his emotions. *"I... am... the... carrier."*

Sartino turned around and saw Tola on his knees. The zebra called to the other zebras in the herd and they galloped from wherever they were and surrounded the horse leader. Zebras were immune to mind-sickness, so they did not have to worry about being overwhelmed by Tola's nearness.

"Tola, by your own admission, you are the carrier of mind-sickness. For the safety of the herd, you are now exiled from this herd and declared a renegade to the Equus. No other herd may accept you as a member. Leave now," Sartino ordered him.

"I cannot... My strength... has... left... me. I... am... losing... control. The Equus... must... run," Tola said. He threw back his head and screamed in pain. Deep pain saturated the mind-link and many of the Equus joined in Tola's scream.

"Equus, to the north. Now," Sartino ordered. Usually, the Calvn would command the herd, but when confronting mind-sickness, it became the zebra leader's duty to lead because he remained unaffected by the mind-sickness. Calvn Scola was just as debilitated by Tola's mind-sickness as the other Equus. He had been fighting with a donkey that had been grooming him. Now he was staggering around as if he were in pain and kicking at phantoms.

At first, only the individual Equus who had remained in control of themselves against the surge of violent emotions heeded Sartino's order. Then the others galloped to the north as herd reaction took over individual thought and the entire herd stampeded. When the mind-link with Tola broke, the herd slowed to a trot. Before they had even caught their breaths, fights broke out again as individual Equus gave into the mind-sickness that contaminated the mind-link.

The forty-eight zebras in the herd each paired with one of the other Equus. The closeness of a zebra protected each Equus as it had Varon. Once all the zebras had paired off with others, the ninety-six Equus galloped away until they could break from the herd mind-link and form a new link between themselves. With a new mind-link formed free of the mind-sickness carrier, the zebras used their shielded links with the other Equus to link to each other. Unable to find a mind to infect, the mind-sickness gradually faded away like frost melting in the sun's heat.

No one, even the horses, knew the cause of mind-sickness. Thankfully, it was a rare disease, and only one member of a herd was a carrier at any one time. Because of this, the horses had discovered that the cause didn't come from drinking contaminated water or food or else more Equus would have been carriers. The zebras were immune from mind-sickness, which only further compounded the problem of understanding what the mind-sickness was and how to treat it. However, the zebras' immunity provided a cure for all but the carrier. The theory that the horses had come up with was that some Equus' minds rebelled against the mind-link and sought, unknowingly, to destroy it.

When the last vestiges of the mind-sickness faded from the new mind-link, the zebras backed away from their partners. The mind-sickness failed to reappear, and the zebras left the cured Equus to return to the herd and pick another set of Equus to cleanse from the mind-sickness.

The zebras had left with their second group of forty-eight from the herd when Tola came charging into the remaining herd; mane flying, eyes wide, and neighing with terror.

"They come! They come!" he shouted.

Varon felt a fresh wave of panic run through the mind-link. Some Equus bolted in fear, but enough of the herd kept their senses to keep the herd together. They circled the herd, turning the most-susceptible Equus back while Tola leaped around yelling, *"They come! They come!"*

A young unicorn named Llall turned and faced Tola.

"You're an exile! A renegade! Leave now before we kill you," Llall yelled.

"They come! They come!"

Tola reared up, flailing out with his forehooves. Llall held back, staying out of range of Tola hooves. He lowered his horn, preparing for a fight with the gray stallion.

Varon could see that his sire was out of control now. By his actions, Tola showed not even a hint of restraint. All of his control had fallen away. Whatever the mind-sickness was, it was in complete control of Tola now.

"My mate."

Varon saw Poins approaching Tola and Llall. She seemed calm, as if the mind-sickness hadn't affected her. Then Varon noticed the tremors in her legs as she placed her hooves down. She walked as if she had to force her body to obey her command.

"Stay back," Llall said. He turned on her. In his state of mind, he was ready to fight. It didn't matter who he fought.

Ignoring Llall, Poins said, *"My life mate, my life is yours."*

Tola stopped kicking and lowered his hooves to the ground. He still snorted and pawed at the ground, but he wasn't an immediate danger to the Equus. However, when Llall approached him, Tola snapped at him, nearly locking onto the unicorn's neck and drawing blood. Llall jumped back.

Poins came closer. *"Life mate, do you not recognize me?"*

"They come! They come!" Tola shouted.

Unperturbed, Poins said, *"Then we will face them together."*

Tola paused. *"Together? Yes. Together."*

Poins stood next to him and began grooming him. Tola stopped pawing at the ground, but he kept throwing his head back and snorting. Yet, he allowed Poins to stand near him. She was a calming influence on him.

"You tried your best, my life mate. You held the mind-sickness in check for longer than any other Equus has ever done, but now you must admit defeat. You can do more," Poins told him.

"I am horse leader of Scola's Herd. Duty to life mate. Duty to horses. Duty to herd. I am horse leader," Tola chanted.

"No longer, my life mate. You must protect the herd and obey the

exile order. Duty to herd must come first this time."

Tola tensed, and for a moment, Varon thought he might rampage again. Poins kept grooming him, though, and he stayed calm.

"Exiled? But what have I done wrong?" Tola asked.

"Nothing. You have done nothing wrong, but you have mind-sickness."

"I am horse leader of Scola's Herd," Tola repeated.

"It is time to leave, life mate."

Tola turned his head so he could see his life mate. There was sadness in his eyes as he stared at her. He blinked once and then looked over the herd as the Equus stared at him. Even at such a great distance, he could see faces filled with violent emotion staring back at him, emotion that he had given them.

"I thought I could stop the sickness. I could have shown the way to heal carriers," he said with clarity of thought.

"Yes, my life mate, but now you must prevent the sickness from spreading. Only your sacrifice can end it. That is what you can do as a healer now."

Tola lowered his head. *"I've caused harm to the herd."*

"Nothing that cannot be healed."

Tola walked away from Poins with his head drooping. When Tola had left the herd, Varon walked up beside his dam.

"How could he resist for so long?" Varon asked.

Her split ears showed her indecision. *"I don't know. Tola has always had a powerful sense of self. Perhaps that helped him, but it wasn't strong enough."*

"But it could lead the way to cure mind-sickness."

"Perhaps, but how many horse carriers will have to die before the Equus will find a cure?"

"Horses are healers. If Tola has opened a path toward a cure, we need to follow it."

"The cost is too great," Poins said, staring after Tola.

"If he had stayed, the herd could not have been healed," Varon told her, trying to ease the pain she felt at sending her life mate away.

"And now he will die."

"It might be a relief from the madness."

"For him, perhaps." She watched as Tola walked away with his head down.

The zebras made four more trips to take infected members of the herd away and cleanse them of the mind-sickness and rejoin them to the clean mind-link. When the zebras shielded Varon from the madness in the mind-link, Varon felt the tensions ease out of his body as he no longer had to fight against the raw emotions of the mind-sickness. Varon's muscles relaxed and the edge on his emotions dulled.

He looked over at his dam. Her head hung low, and she stared to the west; the direction Tola had galloped to begin his exile from the Equus. It was almost as if she could still sense him, though he was no longer part of Scola's Herd's mind-link. Was that part of being life mates, being joined by a bond tighter, more intimate, than the mind-link?

"Your sire was a menace," Pautin said from beside Varon.

"Why do you say that?" He didn't bother turning his head to look at her.

"Isn't it obvious? He tried to drive the entire herd mad."

Varon snorted. *"Pautin, no one knows the cause of mind-sickness, so how could Tola have meant to drive the entire herd mad? He would have had to get the disease intentionally, but how could he do that since no one knows how the Equus contract mind-sickness?"* She didn't answer him. *"Besides, you're fine now. Tola is the only one who will truly suffer from his mind-sickness,"* he told his season mate. *Tola and Poins,* he added for himself.

Calvn Scola called the herd together once the mind-link was cleansed. He took a count of the members of the herd and made sure that no one had run off during the cleansing. The horses inspected the wounds of those injured in the fighting and treated them with hooked thorns and herbs as best they could. Luckily, no one died during the fighting.

No one had died, but Scola's Herd had lost its horse leader, and Varon had lost his sire.

5

Tola wandered the plains in a daze as the sun rose over the white mountains. His emotions changed from one instant to the next. Anger. Despair. Confusion. Frustration. Contentment. Nothing stopping them or even controlling their intensity. He felt like a leaf being blown about in a storm. He gave up trying and tried to put distance between himself and the herd.

Duty to life mate. Duty to horses. Duty to herd.

But the herd and the horses had turned him out and declared him a renegade. What did he owe them? Why should he worry about their safety?

They will keep Poins safe, he told himself.

He galloped hard and fast. It was a way for him to tire himself and bleed off some of the energy his emotions carried. If he was tired, then hopefully, the emotions wouldn't be so intense.

What was he going to do now? How long would it be before the disease killed him?

Anger. Joy. Frustration. Confusion. They all pounded his head, making him dizzy and disoriented. They surged in his body, making his blood pound and his muscles tense. He galloped with no destination in mind, only knowing that he should run.

The rising sun brought no relief, for he felt that its light exposed his sickness for all to see. If he slept, he did not realize it.

I am alone, he thought.

"You are not alone," came an answering voice.

Tola looked around, but he didn't see another Equus nearby. His thoughts had touched a mind-link, though. How could he be part of a mind-link without seeing the Equus?

"Who are you?" Tola asked.

"We are the foals of the Ravagers."

"We? I don't even see you."

The Equus appeared as if from nowhere, charging toward him. Dozens of Equus of all species. They galloped hard, encircling Tola, and still they galloped in a circle around him.

Foals of the Ravagers?

"Whose herd is this?" Tola asked.

"We are no herd. We are a pack," answered a different Equus.

Which of the Equus was speaking to him? Tola couldn't tell. It only added to his confusion.

This was wrong. It made little sense. It had to be a part of the madness of the mind-link.

"But you are Equus," Tola said.

"No longer. Now we are hunters. We are the forsaken, the exiles, the renegades."

Tola felt a surge of fear that was not associated with his mind-sickness. Exiles? This was a band of exiles?

One unicorn of the herd—the pack—reared up as his mind-voice asked, *"Who claims this kill?"*

What kill?

A dun-colored unicorn reared up and answered, *"I do. I found him."*

"He is yours."

The unicorn dropped back to the ground and charged Tola. Tola wanted to gallop away, but the Equus who surrounded him kept him confined in one small area with their moving circle. He tried to push through them, but they held their line tight.

Tola turned in time to see the dun-colored unicorn's horn plunging toward him. It pierced him in the neck, sliding across his bones and tearing his muscles and blood vessels. He screamed into the mind-link as he died. He only hoped that his mind-sickness would infect this herd, but then, maybe they were infected already. They certainly were mad.

Tola collapsed to his knees. He could feel his blood pumping from the hole in his neck. The unicorn rose over him and smashed his forehooves down on Tola's back. Tola screamed, but it was cut off as he died.

Two days later, the herd scouts from Scola's Herd found Tola's body. They called to Scola and told him that the body was Tola's.

Varon was surprised. Given the immensity of Hemlaza, the bodies of exiles or renegades were rarely found. Scavengers carried off various parts of the dead to their dens and warrens so they could feast with their families, out of sight of other predators. The remaining bones would eventually be buried or covered over by grass. In the end, the Equus always returned to the land what they had taken.

Varon approached the body to make sure his sire was dead. He couldn't understand where the predators who had brought down Tola were. They had made the kill and left it alone. The only wounds were on Tola's throat and neck and the back of his hind legs.

Tola's body looked like a fresh kill. Predators had hamstrung him and then had ripped out his throat, killing the horse leader. Most of the Equus avoided the body once it was recognized. They didn't enjoy being reminded that predators could kill them, too.

Why hadn't the predators eaten Tola? Only Ravagers killed for the sake of killing, and Tola's wounds weren't savage enough to be from a Ravager.

Varon stared at the body with detachment. He wouldn't allow himself to feel grief over his sire's death. Tola had done what was needed to preserve the herd. He had performed his duty to the end, and that is how the horses would remember him in their memories.

Tola's leg wounds had bled a little, but if they had hamstrung Tola as the donkeys suggested, then there should have been a lot of blood around Tola's legs. The only reason for there not to have been a lot of blood was that the leg wounds must have come after Tola had died. Why? That made little sense. Hamstringing was a method to stop a fast Equus. This predator had been fast enough to catch Tola and kill him, but then why had the predator hamstrung a dead Equus?

Varon shook his head.

It didn't make a difference. Tola was dead either way, but Varon liked to understand things, and he did not understand how his sire had died.

"I hope you have now found Etrasco," Varon said softly.

As Varon walked back to the herd, he saw his dam staring out at the body. She did not try to approach it, but simply stood looking. Her expression betrayed nothing of what she was feeling.

"It is Tola," Varon told her.

"I know."

He stood next to her, wanting to talk about how she felt, but not wanting to intrude on her grief. Instead, he settled on grooming her as she stared at Tola's body. When she said nothing, he moved back into the herd to find Pautin.

When the herd moved onto other grazing, Poins stayed in the same position, just staring at the body of her life mate. The donkeys called to her to stay with the herd. They sought her mind to speak with her, but couldn't find it. Finally, one donkey approached her.

"She's dead," Jossnal called to the herd.

"Are you sure?" Varon asked.

He broke from the herd and galloped back to his dam's side.

"Her sides do not move with breath," Jossnal said.

"Mother!" he called.

When she didn't respond, he touched his muzzle to her neck and nudged her. Her body fell over, her legs sticking out.

"She is cold," he said flatly. Her body no longer held the warmth of life in it. How long had she been dead? Had she died while Varon groomed her? No. He would have sensed that... at least he felt that he would have sensed her death.

The herd returned to stand around Poins. Calvn Scola walked around her body, examining it, and then turned to Sartino.

"She has returned," Scola announced.

"Then let us send her away with our pleas," Sartino replied.

The Equus began to gather grass and drop it on Poins' body. The grass signified many things. Each blade and stalk held a plea of an Equus to Equ, which Poins would convey to their creator. The grass was also meant to provide her with nourishment on her journey to Etrasco. And, the grass showed that the earth had accepted her body back.

This close to Tola's body, the difference in how the herd treated the two bodies struck Varon. Tola's body lay wounded and uncovered while Poins' body was shown great care and attention. But Poins had been an Equus. As an exile and renegade, Tola was no longer considered an Equus. He was simply another dead animal.

Except to Poins. Varon was sure his dam had died because Tola had been killed. Hadn't she even predicted it? In this case, the mind-sickness had been fatal to someone other than the carrier.

When the Equus had covered Poins' body, the herd moved off to find new grazing and fill their stomachs.

6

Multiple times each day, Scola scanned the northern horizon, searching for the return of the three pegasuses whom he had sent to explore the white mountains. He would watch the plains for predators, but his gaze would move further out, and upwards, to stare at the white mountains and then to the sky, searching for pegasuses.

The sight of the faraway mountains that loomed so large chilled him. Where had they come from?

Scola hated change. He needed the stability of knowing which fields blossomed earliest in the Season of Life and which ones were late. He enjoyed knowing just where to find alfalfa, rye, and wheat. He enjoyed knowing where the different fruit trees and berry bushes could be found. He liked the comfort of knowing where the sweetest water ran across the plains.

But to see such a drastic change! How could it be?

Now that he was Calvn, he resisted change. Why should he want to see a change in the conditions that brought him to power? Change might weaken him and leave him open to a challenger to his authority. He wanted the white mountains to go away. They were too big a change.

When they wouldn't go away, Scola tried to ignore them.

But the white mountains were always there whenever he looked to the north; the pegasuses never were.

Where were those flying beasts?

After sixteen days, many of the Equus gave up believing that the pegasuses would ever return. This scared Scola more than he would admit. The pegasuses were strong; not that Scola would tell them that, but they were. If they had failed to reach the white mountains or the white mountains had conquered them, what did that mean for the future of the Equus?

"The white mountains have killed them," Scola heard Broshin, a twenty-year-old pegasus, say.

"How?" Scola asked him.

"How could mountains move, and yet they have? We live in an age where nothing can be depended upon to be the same tomorrow as it is today. It would not surprise me to see the sun rise in the east tomorrow instead of the west."

That was not what Scola wanted to hear. He wanted to hear that the mountains would be gone with the dawn.

Had the ages begun to shift? If so, would the white mountains bring a radical change to the Equus like when the Equus had awakened one morning in Hemlaza, or would it be a minor shift like when the Season of Plenty changed to the Preparation Season?

If Equ returned the herds to Etrasco, would there be no need for Calvns? What would happen to Scola? Who would groom him and forage for him if he were no longer the Calvn of his herd? He enjoyed the privileges of his position.

Scola tried to voice his concerns to Revan, his season mate. *"I wonder if the pegasuses will return. What are three pegasuses against the white mountains?"* he said to her as she grazed. It was the closest he had come to saying that he was afraid of the mountains.

"You speak as if the mountains are predators," Revan said.

Predators? Could mountains seek to kill like a lion? Scola didn't think so. Mountains just were part of the land like the plains, the rivers, and the oceans. *"I don't know if the mountains are, but I do know the white mountains are not normal mountains."*

Revan raised her head to stare at him. *"What is normal nowadays? Is the extra-long Seeking Season normal?"*

"No."

"That bothers me more than white mountains. The mountains are far away, but my belly tells me to eat now, and it is harder to find grass."

Toward evening, the herd scouts called out in loud brays, alerting the herd. Usually, their calls warned of night-stalking predators, but this time their thoughts carried with the brays.

"The pegasuses are returning. We saw them pass the smaller moon as it sat on the horizon. They will be here soon," Shev, a young donkey, called out.

The herd scouts were primarily donkeys with a few ponies and horses when needed. Their job was to watch for dangers and warn the herd if predators were nearby. They patrolled around the fringes of the herd. Since the donkeys were the lowest species in the Equus hierarchy, their placement on the outskirts of the herd also made them the most likely targets for predators. Their sacrifices gave the rest of the herd time to break into a gallop and run away to safety or form a defensive circle.

It was the way of nature, Scola thought. The unicorns lead and the donkeys give themselves so that others might live. Why should he want it to change when a change might endanger the Equus or him?

The mind-link suddenly filled with with dozens of mind-voices, calling out over each other. Were predators attacking? Scola looked around and saw the dark shapes of the pegasuses landing among the herd near him. Despite the lateness, the herd gathered around the pegasuses, eager to hear of what they had seen. Equus did not sleep at night any more than did during the day, and they slept in brief stretches as a defensive measure. The pegasuses they had thought were dead had returned, and no one wanted to miss the story of their adventures.

Scola snorted as he watched the pegasuses arch their necks and spread their wings. They were the center of attention, and they relished the fact. Scola was sure that the pegasuses would try to lead the herd, given a chance. Chinarvo and some older pegasuses were too ambitious.

"What happened to you?"

"Where have you been?"

"What did you find?"

The questions mixed and became jumbled as each Equus sought

to have their question heard above the others. They tried to move closer to the pegasus or to shout their questions in the mind-link.

Trenea tried to speak, but the sound of his mind-voice only brought a flood of more questions. So the pegasuses waited until the confusion calmed, and they had everyone's attention.

"The white mountains are not mountains at all, but a wall of ice," Jalon announced.

"No! They can't be! There could not be so much ice in all the world to make such mountains," Shuse, a young pony, called out.

"It is true," Jalon insisted. *"I doubt that even the warmth of the sun during the Season of Life and Season of Plenty could melt all of this ice."*

Calvn Scola stepped forward, his neck arched.

"Where does this ice come from?" Calvn Scola asked.

"It stretches as far as the eyes can see to the north, and it appears to be moving southward."

"How fast is it moving?" Scola asked, concerned. Perhaps Broshin had been right, and the ages were shifting. What change would an age introduced by ice bring to the Equus?

"Not very fast at all. The movement is not apparent in days, probably only in years, but there has been movement. Otherwise, how could the mountain have gotten to the north coast? They did not rise from the ground. Given time, the white mountains will cover all of Hemlaza."

"How much time?" Varon asked.

That young horse was another upstart. Scola was glad to be rid of Tola. The horse leader had been too well liked. Varon was proving to be just as bad. Everyone wanted to lead this herd. They all wanted Scola's power for themselves.

"I could not say, Varon," Jalon answered after a moment's thought.

"Guess, sister," Varon urged her.

Jalon nodded. *"If we assume the mountains were just beyond our sight on the Horizon Sea this time last year, then they have moved the distance we can travel in half a day."*

Varon's tail came up and his ears leaned forward. *"Half a day?"*

"That is the visibility out on the Horizon Sea. The pegasuses have measured it in the past."

Varon shook his head, his mane splaying across his neck. *"Then the mountains would cover Hemlaza in five or six generations,"* Scola said. *"Impossible."*

Jalon nodded. *"That is what Pars, Trenea, and I thought, too."*

"The land will be dead well before then, though," Pars said.

"Equ created this land. It will not die," Sartino proclaimed.

Jalon said, *"I'm not so sure, zebra leader. My companions and I spoke of this on our return flight to the herd. The land near the white mountains sleeps in the Seeking Season so the mountains' effect on the land is more than their physical presence. It is probably the cause of the long Seeking Season that we are feeling now. In addition, as the mountains move south, they push the Equus and all other creatures on Hemlaza into a smaller area. That will cause a problem for food, water, and living space."*

Scola turned to stare at the white mountains, staggered by what he had heard. He looked from edge to edge along the mountain line. It ran across the horizon as far as he could see. He did not doubt what he'd heard because his own eyes could verify it. There were mountains where there hadn't been last year. A morning's travel in a year!

How?

How could all the mountains be ice? How could they move so fast or even move at all? How would the Equus survive?

What could have brought on such a change? A major change of ages happened only when the Equus reached a turning point. Scola had always thought the turning point would be as obvious as the change, but if the white mountains appearing was a major change, then Scola hadn't noticed what the turning point for the Equus had been.

Had the Equus pleased or displeased Equ?

Were the white mountains a reward or a punishment?

"You lie, Jalon!" Trahnison, a zebra, accused the pegasus.

Jalon lifted her nose and stared at Trahnison. *"I do no such thing. The Calvn sent us to the white mountains to discover what we could and report on it to put some rumors to rest. Now you speak as if you prefer the rumors to the truth."*

Scola did. The truth was scarier than the rumors.

"What is truth to a pegasus?" Trahnison said.

"The same as truth should be to a zebra," Jalon said.

"Silence!"

The shout came from Calvn Scola's mind-voice, and it caused the entire herd to fall silent. Scola lowered his horn so it pointed at the herd to let them know he was angry enough to charge.

"I thank you for your report, Jalon," Calvn Scola said, his mind-voice heavy with formality. He tried hard not to let his fear show itself in what he said.

"There is something else you should know, Calvn," Jalon said.

Calvn snorted impatiently. *"What is that?"*

"My companions and I were attacked by griffins."

Calvn's eyes widened. After a moment, he calmed himself, and said, *"Thank you for this information."*

"As you command, Calvn," Jalon said formally. She lowered her head to the ground and swept her wings forward.

"But what you speak of is impossible."

Jalon stiffened. She raised her head and retracted her wings. *"No more impossible than some rumors we have heard circulating about the white mountains, Calvn."*

Calvn Scola looked around the herd. His large brown eyes looked confused.

"But I cannot accept the impossible without verification," Scola said.

He heard murmurs throughout the herd. Many of the zebras and unicorns nickered. The pegasuses flicked their tails in irritation. The general tone of the herd seemed to be agreement with Calvn Scola. He knew that he was on the right track. Deny the mountains. They did not exist. Things would return to normal.

"Then why were the pegasuses sent to explore the white moun-

tains? Are we not the verification of what your eyes can see already? The white mountains are made of ice!" Jalon's thoughts bordered on outright anger.

"Do not take that tone with me! I do not accept insubordination, even if you were a species leader!" Calvn Scola snapped.

"As you command, Calvn." Perhaps Chinarvo was not the one to fear. It might be Jalon. She was young enough to think she might lead. Maybe being a servant of the Calvn would not be enough for her. She bowed her head and swept her wings forward again, but it almost seemed a parody of her previous gesture to the Calvn.

"How far away are the white mountains?" Scola asked.

Jalon raised herself up and said, *"At a gallop, a fast stallion could make it in seven days out and seven days back."* Calvn Scola dipped his head as he contemplated the numbers. *"But you can't take the mares, not with so many ready to foal, and you can't travel in a straight line to the mountains either. Some rivers are too deep and fast moving to cross without finding a ford."*

Scola pawed at the ground. He looked up and scanned the herd, staring at him. No other Equus offered an opinion. What should he do?

"Your report is accepted. I will say more of this in the morning," Calvn Scola said.

The herd dispersed back to where they had been sleeping. A few of the pegasuses walked over to groom the returned trio and welcome them back to the herd.

Scola watched the pegasus' reunion in curiosity. He let his mind search out the various conversations in the mind-link; at least those that were loud enough to be heard.

What should he do about what the pegasuses reported? Could the white mountains be a wall of ice? He couldn't imagine it.

As if reading his deepest thoughts, Wevco, an older unicorn, said, *"Imagine! Thinking the white mountains are made of ice!"*

"That's what happens when you trust flyers with their heads in the clouds instead of your own species," replied Oyen, Wevco's life mate.

Scola was tempted to add his own comments to the conversation, but he didn't want the unicorns to know that he was listening in on their conversations. Still, he thought he might glean some useful information from listening. After all, Wevco and Oyen were both older than Scola. They had much more life experience than he had. Not that Scola would tell them that.

"Who can trust a pegasus?"

Oyen nodded her agreement. Scola almost did, too, until he remembered he was not supposed to be a part of the conversation.

"Still," Oyen asked. *"Where could those white mountains have come from?"*

"If the unicorns had been sent, then we would know by now."

"Yes, the white mountains concern all the Equus, not just the pegasuses."

"You can't trust their flights of fancy concerning important matters."

Scola nodded without realizing it. *This concerns all the Equus,* he thought. His solution would have to include all the Equus.

In the morning, Calvn Scola waited once again until after Return to speak with the gathered herd. With the Equus gathered so closely to him, his thoughts could more easily command their attention.

"I have decided what to do about the pegasus report, my children," he announced.

The herd stopped spreading out from the tight configuration of Return and conversation on the mind-link stopped. Scola enjoyed once again being the center of attention. Varon knew the Calvn must have hated giving some of that attention up to the pegasuses last night. The Calvn arched his neck to give himself a more authoritative appearance.

"We must know more about the white mountains, if they pose a danger to Equus as the pegasuses report. I will send a group of Equus—three unicorns, a horse, a pony, a zebra, two donkeys, and a pegasus—to make their own investigations of the white mountains. In that way, all the species will have representatives who have seen the white mountains for themselves. Jalon will accompany the group as the pegasus, and she will act as the scout to show the group the safest path to the mountains."

"As if they could miss them," an Equus near Varon said. He thought it was a pegasus, but the touch on the mind-link was so soft that he couldn't pinpoint who had said it.

That Calvn Scola was sending out three unicorns and three donkeys was not lost on Varon. The donkeys would be potential sacrifices to predators, and the unicorns would be the leaders of the band.

"Who will go?" someone asked.

"Fles, Chalo, Millotin, Varon, Vinel, Corriate, Shev, Fome, and

Traball," Scola said.

"What is our aim?" Fles, a golden colored unicorn, asked. He was already trying to exert his supposed leadership on the band. Ambition must come with the horn.

"Find out what is happening to the Hemlaza Plains. Will it continue? What is beyond the white mountains?" Calvn Scola told him.

Fles lowered his head. *"We will find out the answers."*

Somehow Varon doubted that. The Equus had experienced nothing like the white mountains before. What was there to compare it to, especially if Scola refused to accept the truth when it was presented to him? Did the unicorns somehow think they could change the truth?

Varon turned and walked away from the gathered herd. He had only gone a short distance when he saw Pautin hurrying toward him, her belly swaying heavily underneath her. She was upset enough to accept the pain of moving quickly. Her breath came in harsh snorts.

"So are you so eager to be away from me, my season mate?" she asked when she saw that he had noticed her.

"I must make some arrangements before I leave."

Pautin snorted. *"And what about me? Who will care for me while you are gone?"*

Varon stopped and turned to face her. *"Would you like to tell Calvn Scola that he can't send me away? I'd prefer to stay."* Varon wasn't sure that was the truth. He was curious about the white mountains. How better to learn about them than to visit them himself?

Pautin's pace stuttered. *"No, he is Calvn,"* she said.

He was glad she didn't press the issue. Calvn Scola might have changed his mind if she had asked, just to keep her from pestering him.

"Well, it is the Calvn who has commanded me to go with this group," Varon told her.

She snorted. *"But what about me?"*

"These arrangements I need to make are for you, and I must do them before I leave with the others."

Varon kept moving, even quickening his pace to a trot because he knew it made Pautin ache to move that way while she was pregnant. It was petty, but he wanted to be away from her.

"*Varon.*" It wasn't Pautin's mind-voice.

Varon stopped walking and turned back to see Jalon approaching him. He liked to look at who was speaking to him and to have whoever spoke to him look at him. It ensured that each had the other's attention, and it strengthened the sound of the mind-voice in their heads.

"*Do you believe me and what I said about the white mountains?*" Jalon asked.

Varon flicked his ears forward. "*I do. It is hard to believe, but the mountains are there, which is just as hard to believe.*"

Jalon nodded. "*I have seen them myself, and I still doubt they exist.*"

"*Then have patience with everyone else, sister. We'll do what the Calvn asked, which will only prove what you and the others said. You don't mind getting away from the herd for a couple of weeks, do you?*"

"*You have not seen mountains like these, Varon. They are as tall as the Meshacks, but much steeper. I dislike them.*" Jalon paused and said, "*We – Trenea, Pars, and I – thank you for your pleas to Equ. I am sure that your voice to Equ made the difference between life and death when six griffins pursued me.*"

Varon shook his head. Griffins. He had hoped he would grow to forget that word.

"*I thought they were all dead,*" he said.

Griffins were deadly predators. They seemed to be a conglomeration of other species. They had an oversized eagle head and wings, a lion body, and a lizard tail. It was a fearsome predator created by Sarton, a sister to Equ. It was also the only predator that could compete with and kill a pegasus in flight.

"*Apparently not,*" Jalon said.

Varon's ears pointed forward and back. "*I'm not sure what scares me more: the white mountains or the return of the griffins,*" Varon admitted.

"The griffins," Jalon said quickly. *"I can fly away from the mountains."*

Varon nodded his head. *"Let's hope we don't meet any griffins along the way then."*

The herd scouts were still moving along the outer boundary of the herd to protect it against any predators. Varon found Benju, the herd leader of the donkeys in Scola's Herd. He could have spoken to Benju from a distance like many of the species did when they wanted to speak with the donkeys. It was a means of keeping the donkeys in their subservient role.

"So you are going to the white mountains?" Benju asked when he saw Varon approaching.

"It appears so."

"Do you think they are dangerous?"

"Not in the same way as lions, but Jalon thinks they are dangerous. Until I am convinced differently, I will accept that."

Benju nodded his agreement. *"What brings you out here then? I thought you would have things to do before you leave other than talking with a* donkey.*"*

Varon noted the emphasis that Benju placed on "donkey." Someone must have put him in his place recently, probably a unicorn. He rarely seemed so sensitive about being a donkey.

"I need your help, my brother," Varon said.

Benju raised his head somewhat. Varon asked him for help; not ordered him to do it. It was nice to have a choice. *"How so?"*

"As you noted, I have to leave. I will be gone at least the large moon cycle, judging by how long the pegasuses were away."

Benju nodded. *"A long time. We will have moved far from here by then."* With the long Seeking Season, the herd needed to move almost daily to find enough to eat.

"It is a long time also when Pautin is near to the time that she will bring forth new life. She is worried about who will help her while I am gone. The other mares will do much, but I would feel more comfortable knowing brothers I trust were watching over her. She has little patience, and the horses may grow tired of her antics. I

was hoping the donkeys might monitor her because you have more... " He tried to choose an inoffensive word.

"Patience?" Benju suggested.

"Tolerance for others' shortcomings," Varon said, trying to sound more diplomatic. *"She can be trying, but the donkeys have shown themselves able to endure the worst of the Equus."*

"You need the donkeys then."

"Knowing how Pautin is, I would understand if you don't want to help. She is not known for her kindness to donkeys," Varon said.

Benju tossed his head up and down. *"Don't worry, Varon. Pautin is no worse than some unicorns, and at least we can decide this matter for ourselves. We are not being ordered to do this."*

Varon lowered his head to the donkey. *"Thank you, my brother. Would you like me to bring you back a piece of the white mountain?"*

Benju nickered. *"I would much rather prefer good news; say, that that mountains are melting."*

"I will do my best to find it then."

Varon galloped off to find Pautin and let her know of the arrangements. However, when he saw her, she fixed him with a direct stare that told him he needed to stay away from her.

"I thought you had left," she said.

"Not yet."

"You might as well have gone. You wish to leave me alone."

Varon sighed. *"You are not alone. You are part of Scola's Herd."*

"If I have no season mate at my side, I am alone."

Varon could see the Equus who were going on the journey beginning to gather around Calvn Scola. They had said their goodbyes to their mates if they had any, and now there was work to be done and a journey to be started.

"I will see you when I return, Pautin."

He turned and walked away. As he approached the expedition group, he felt old. None of these Equus was any older than four years old. Why had Calvn Scola chosen Varon to be among the group? He didn't mind going, but he wanted to know why.

"Calvn, I seek to speak with you."

"Speak, Varon," Calvn Scola said.

"Why was I chosen to be among this group?"

Calvn Scola tilted his nose up and turned his head to stare at Varon. *"Are you questioning my decision as Calvn of this herd?"*

Varon ignored the challenge in his mind-voice and said, *"No, I am trying to understand your decision. These other Equus are younger than me. The pegasus said that speed is essential on this journey. I assume that is why you chose colts. I am no longer a colt."*

"In any herd or band, there is always one who is the oldest and the slowest. In this small band, you are both. Besides, was it not your idea to send the pegasuses to the white mountains?"

His idea. So Calvn Scola had decided that the pegasus expedition had failed, and he was placing the blame on Varon. But it hadn't been Varon's idea; at least it hadn't been his idea to send only pegasuses to explore the white mountains.

"I only suggested you should investigate the white mountains, Calvn," Varon reminded Scola.

"But by pegasuses only! This concerns all the Equus, not just the pegasuses."

Varon tried to keep his anger from showing. No matter how this conversation went, Varon would be responsible for any failure, real or perceived. Who would failure fall upon when this band returned to verify the pegasus report?

Calvn turned to the rest of the group. *"It is time to depart, my children. Make haste. Go with the aid of Equ and bring us the blessings of Equ."*

The ten Equus rose on their hind legs and kicked their front legs. When all forty hooves touched the ground, the band galloped off toward the white mountains.

8

Galloping northward from Scola's Herd, the small band of young Equus made good time during their first two days of travel. They rested and ate when they came across good grazing. Given the scarcity of food that was occurring across the plains, they couldn't risk passing up any grazing, since they didn't know when they would eat again.

Vinel the zebra struggled the hardest to keep up with the band, but he didn't complain. Vinel's legs were shorter even than the ponies and donkeys, and he had a stockier build than the others in the band did. He also insisted on conducting a version of Return each morning just after sunrise. Vinel would walk narrow circles around the band as he spoke the story of Return while Fles filled the Calvn's place in Return.

Varon thought the sight of a single zebra trying to appear as forty-seven zebras looked ridiculous. The zebra would gallop around the other nine Equus and then try to look majestic as his sides heaved and sweat dampened his hide.

Given Fles' anxiousness to lead the band, he assumed that acting for the Calvn in Return meant that he was acting for the Calvn throughout the expedition. Varon didn't mind much. He was used to following a unicorn, but Chalo and Millotin, the other two unicorns in the band, disputed Fles' leadership. The three fought at every opportunity, trying to take control of the band's direction by galloping in the front of the group or calling breaks without consulting Fles. Yet, Vinel continued to choose Fles to serve in the Calvn's place. It gave him a certain amount of power in the group that did not go unnoticed.

Though the unicorns fought over the leadership position, it was actually Vinel who controlled the group, and hence, was the real leader. Fles tried to remain in the zebra's favor so Vinel would continue to choose Fles as the Calvn's representative during Return. That seemed to be the symbol of leadership between the three unicorns.

Fles called rests whenever Vinel appeared tired, and he made certain to point out to the zebra where to find the best grazing grass. The only thing Varon could have done without was the ever-constant arguing that he had to listen to as he galloped. Because he was forced to stay with the band, he had to stay in range of their sniping mind-voices, and he had to stay joined with the mind-link so he knew what was happening. Listening to them put Varon in a poor mood and gave him a headache.

That was why Varon was relieved to see Jalon drop down from the sky and land in front of them. Fles used the interruption as a reason to halt the group so that Vinel could rest.

"Why aren't you scouting, Jalon?" Fles asked, assuming command.

"Because I am reporting that you are being trailed."

"By what?" Fles asked, concerned.

Jalon cocked her head to the side. *"That is the odd part. It is wolves and lions, about sixty of them."*

Corriate interrupted. *"But they don't share the same lands. They don't mate. They have nothing in common. Why would they be trailing us together?"*

"They share one thing," Jalon said.

"What's that?"

"They're both predators."

"Are they Ravagers?" Chalo asked Jalon.

Just hearing the word made Varon nervous. Not all the creators were as loving as Equ. The fathers and mothers of the predator races often took the form of their children and hunted the creatures of the land. They were savage in their ferocity. What made this group seem like there might be Ravagers among them was that there were two different species of predators running together. The only time Varon had seen that happen was when a creator was with the pack; and when a creator, such as Carn, ran with a pack, they became Ravagers, which described what they did to any living creatures they encountered.

"I cannot tell if they are Ravagers or not until they ravage something. Let us hope it is not you," Jalon warned him.

"What should we do?" Varon asked the pegasus.

Fles glared at him. He thought Varon should have addressed him since he considered himself the leader.

"Gallop," Jalon said.

"Gallop?" Fles repeated.

"Run as far and as fast as you can."

"Why should we do that?" Fles said.

"You are all young. Use your speed to your favor more than you could if you were part of a herd filled with foals and the aged. Neither the wolves nor the lions can match your speed, especially over long distances. Use it. Put distance between you and them now so they won't even get close to you. That will give you time to think and plan what to do next if they continue to track your scent," Jalon explained.

"Do you think they will follow us?" Varon asked.

Jalon's ears took opposing positions, showing her indecision. *"I would not have thought wolves and lions would travel together, but they do. I guess it depends on how hungry they are and if they come across the scent of easier prey."*

"It's cowardly," Fles said.

"We're not talking about jousting between unicorns or wrestling between ponies. These are predators. Equus run from predators when they can. You've never had to face a pack like this. You send the donkeys out as herd scouts, hoping they will appease the predators, but have you ever seen what predators do when they catch a donkey you've sent out?" Jalon snapped.

Fles tossed his head back. *"I am a unicorn, I don't..."*

"That's right! You don't! Unicorns don't do a lot, and one thing they don't do is learn what's going on beyond the herd. Now the herd no longer surrounds you. You... not just the donkeys... you have to face the predators. If they catch up with you, three donkeys

will not appease the appetite of this pack."

Varon had never seen Jalon so upset. The sight of the two predators joining forces in such an unusual pairing must have upset her. It upset Varon, and he hadn't even seen them. Two different predators joining their numbers to form one enormous killing pack. If the predators could continue increasing their numbers through unusual alliances, they would create an overwhelming pack that could destroy all the Equus if they desired. One advantage the Equus had over predators was that their packs comprised a couple of dozen animals, much smaller than the average-size Equus herd. However, this predator pack was larger than usual and the Equus herd was only a small band of animals. The Equus did not have the advantage of numbers. Fles pawed angrily at the ground. *"You can't talk to me that way! I am Cal... leader of this group."* He neighed to cover his mistake.

He stopped and trotted off a short distance from the band, still prancing around as they tried to bring his anger under control.

Claiming to be a Calvn when the unicorn wasn't was an offense punishable by exile, which meant certain death under the teeth and claws of the predators on Hemlaza. Varon was certain that Chalo and Millotin had also noticed the near slip. They would watch Fles more carefully now.

"Lead the Equus away from here. Only a unicorn would consider honor when, without survival, there can be no honor," Jalon said in a tone that sounded like a command.

Millotin stepped forward; his head high and his neck arched. *"Enough of this arguing! We gallop, and we gallop now!"* he scolded.

The tone of his mind-voice brooked no opposition. He took off in the opposite direction from where Jalon had said the predators were coming. Jalon immediately took flight to follow the brown-mottled unicorn.

"I did not say we should gallop!" Fles insisted, trying to regain control of the band.

"No, you did not," Varon replied and galloped after the other two Equus. The donkeys followed, then Chalo, and finally even Vinel.

Fles stood alone. He realized he had allowed himself to be ostracized by the band. He galloped hard to catch up with the rest of the group.

"Upon considering, I realize that avoiding the predators is wise," he said.

No one commented, but everyone knew that Fles had forfeited his right to lead by silent decree. Now Millotin would lead the band. Varon wondered if this style of command could carry over into the herd. Doubtful, but one could hope.

They galloped hard until the gap between the donkeys and zebra and others grew too great. The rest of the Equus then slowed to a trot until the donkeys and Vinel caught up with them. Then they moved into a canter. The donkeys and Vinel could keep up with the group if they galloped while the rest of the Equus cantered.

The sun was dropping from its zenith when Varon felt something suddenly rear up in front of him, causing him to skid to a halt. His legs stiffened as his hooves dug into the ground. He threw his head back to avoid whatever was in front of him that he couldn't see. As he did, he noticed the donkeys and Corriate stopping. However, the unicorns, zebra, and Jalon continued forward without even noticing the problem. Varon saw nothing with his eyes, but his mind screamed at him to "stop" because there was something there in front of him.

The others noticed Varon, Corriate, and the donkeys had stopped and they turned back.

"What's wrong?" Millotin asked. *"Why did you stop?"*

"The land," was all that Varon could think of to reply.

"Something's wrong with the land," one donkey said.

"What?" Millotin asked.

Then Varon realized what he was sensing. *"We're crossing where the creators have crossed."*

"You could say that about most places," Millotin noted as he approached the invisible line. He sniffed at the ground. Then, finding nothing, walked back and forth across the invisible line.

"I think you just wanted to rest," Fles said. *"You are too old and the donkeys are too slow to keep up with us."*

"And what about me?" Corriate snapped. *"I am still a colt. I can run faster than you, and I cannot pass."*

Fles snorted. *"You are too lazy."*

Millotin turned to nip at Fles' muzzle. Fles lowered his horn in a defensive gesture and skittered backwards. Millotin ignored the challenge and turned back to Varon.

"Creators have crossed here recently," Varon told him.

"How recently?"

Varon nosed forward, sensing the firmness of his mind's resolve to not let him pass. The firmer his resolve, the more recent the passing.

"A day at most," Varon estimated.

"He wants to rest," Fles insisted.

Varon threw his head back angrily. If he could have crossed the path at that moment, he would have charged the arrogant unicorn and pummeled him with his hooves.

"Be quiet, Fles. Haven't you heard of or seen how the sixth sense manifests before?" Millotin ordered the other unicorn.

Fles shook his head. *"I don't believe it. It's just the lower species trying to claim to have something that the upper species don't have."* Unicorns, particularly those in Scola's Herd, called themselves the upper species.

"Are you claiming I'm a lower species?" Varon challenged. He fixed Fles with a direct glare that would have done Pautin proud.

"Enough," Millotin shouted. *"It does not matter if you believe what Varon says, Fles. I do. Varon, as long as we don't follow the path, you should be able to cross it, shouldn't you?"*

"Usually. Even if the path was fresh, we should have been able to cross it, but there is something wrong about this path that is holding us back. I sense death about it."

"Death on a creator path means a Ravager. That would mean that this is a path tread by Sarton, Puven, Clemintin, or Carn. They must have shifted shape, or else you would not sense it."

Varon nodded.

"Then it is certainly good that we are not following the path. I would not want to catch up with Ravager creators, even if they took

the form of a snail. We will wait until the power of the path fades enough so you and the others can cross."

"Can you tell what was killed?" Jalon asked Varon.

Varon looked at the donkeys. They only shook their heads. *"No, only that it was a massacre. The death scent almost matches the creator scent."*

Varon felt a sense of curiosity and fear about the Ravagers. They had massacred some herd or pack, but were all the members dead? The reason the Equus knew about the Ravagers was that they weren't thorough in their killing. They attacked suddenly, killed savagely, maimed what was easily reached, and then moved on. They did not eat their kills, but left them to rot and scare others.

"Millotin, I want to backtrack the trail," Varon said to the unicorn.

"Why?"

"They may have left wounded behind after the attack who I can help. I should check. I am a healer. I could help them if they are wounded."

"There might also be predators left behind who are feasting on the kills," Millotin pointed out. *"I don't think it's wise. I think we should move on."*

"We'll have to wait until the death scent fades enough that we can pass to continue on. Until then, we have to wait anyway. Allow me to go. If I see predators, I can return here. Otherwise, I might be able to give help."

Millotin didn't like the idea. He paced back and forth in front of Varon.

"It's foolish," he said.

"I'm a healer, by nature and by training," Varon said, reminding him of the duty of horses. Varon had been trained as a healer since he was old enough to understand what Tola and the other healers in the herd had explained to him. He took pride in his ability to help other animals heal their wounds and cure their sicknesses.

"But I don't feel good letting you leave the safety of the band. If you are killed, it would leave this band without a healer," Millotin said.

"If there are Ravagers along the way, the band wouldn't be able to protect me. The herd wouldn't be able to protect me," Varon pointed out.

"I could send Jalon to fly over the area to see if there are survivors," Millotin suggested.

Varon shook his head. *"No. Why risk your scout? She is more valuable to the expedition than me. I hope to investigate, and it should be my risk to take. I wouldn't risk anyone else's life."*

Millotin nodded. *"Fine, go if you must, but I still think you are being foolish."*

"If we knew Ravagers had attacked Scola's Herd, you would feel different about what I am doing," Varon said.

"Yes, that is because it would be my herd."

Varon nodded. *"Well, the horses look at all Equus as our brothers and sisters. Equ made all the Equus, and of all creatures, he gave the horses the knowledge and ability to help and heal. Should I forsake my creator-made nature now?"*

Millotin pointed his horn toward the east. *"I said go, Varon, but don't expect me to honor you for taking a fool's journey."*

"I thank you for your understanding, Millotin." He was only being half sarcastic, for Millotin had at least granted him permission to leave the band.

Millotin neighed and turned away from him. *"Start looking for food and water,"* he told the others. *"If we are going to be here for a while, we should rest."*

Varon broke into a canter, heading east. He realized that the death scent was getting stronger, not weaker.

Varon slowed to a walk to verify what he was feeling. The invisible barrier had seemed spongy back, where the other members of the band waited for him. Now it was much firmer.

He didn't understand how that could be, but he knew what it meant. He was moving closer to the Ravagers, not away from them.

Varon stopped. Should he turn back to avoid a chance of encountering the Ravagers and warn the band? But what he had told Millotin was true. Varon might find creatures who needed his healing skills. He might be able to save a life if he continued.

Varon walked forward, wondering how far away the Ravagers would be.

He got his answer when he heard a llama scream. The sound unexpectedly shattered the silence of the plains. The scream abruptly cut off, and Varon knew that the llama had been killed.

He hurried forward. As he topped a low rise and saw what was beyond, he backed off a couple of steps and lowered himself to the ground. He was in a dangerous position. If a predator saw him, he would be as vulnerable as the prey. However, he was in greater danger right now if he stood up.

Varon raised his head so he could stare over the top of the rise. About a half a mile beyond, he saw a large herd of llamas jumping and kicking. Occasionally, one would lean its head back and scream in a high-pitched squeal.

What was happening to them?

Then he noticed the small, gray foxes that were attacking the herd. One launched itself from the barren ground onto a llama's back, sinking its teeth into the llama's neck. Another fox hamstrung a llama. As the llama collapsed, the fox ripped the llama's throat out. There were about twice as many foxes as llamas, which should have been enough for the llamas to handle. If nothing more, they should have been able to outrun the foxes.

But there were too many foxes.

Varon picked out the Ravager in the fox pack easily. It moved faster than the other foxes. When it attacked a llama, the llama died quickly rather than screaming. Varon watched the Ravager's fox paws stretch out to four times their normal length, encircle a llama's neck and slice the throat open with a quick swipe of his claws.

The sight of the carnage roiled Varon's stomach. His head throbbed, and he had to look away.

He could do nothing to save these llamas; not as long as the Ravager foxes attacked them. He would have to wait and see if there were any survivors. He suspected he would wait in vain.

How could there be survivors when a creator fought as a Ravager?

Varon looked up. Only a few of the llamas still stood.

The Ravager increased in size until it was as large as a llama, but it still looked like a fox. It towered over the fox pack and roared like an angry lion.

Which of the creators was this?

The Ravager's gaze focused on Varon. The creature grinned, showing a mouth full of a double row of sharp teeth.

The sight startled Varon. He scrambled to his hooves, knowing he was about to die. By the time he stood up, the Ravager was only a few yards away from him.

Varon wondered if he should even try to run from the Ravager. He didn't want to point the killer toward his band of Equus. If Varon was going to die, let it be him alone. Besides, if the Ravager wanted to kill him, Varon could not outrun it. The Ravager could change into a cheetah or some other fast-moving creature and overtake Varon within a quarter mile.

Just as the Ravager was about to reach him, a large unicorn charged the fox-like beast from its side. His golden horn plunged into the Ravager's neck.

The Ravager reared up and roared. It pulled away from the unicorn and turned to face him. The unicorn danced around, keeping itself between Varon and the Ravager. Varon stood still, watching numbly.

Who was this brave unicorn? Varon wondered. He was a large white unicorn with a golden horn. The unicorn was even larger than Wisvel of Tika's Herd. Wisvel was a horse who stood half again as tall as many donkeys. This unicorn had to be at least another head taller than Wisvel. Varon had never seen such an enormous Equus. He had never seen a unicorn with a golden horn, either. Unicorn horns were made of bone, so they were always white, no matter what color the unicorn's coat might be.

"Go, Varon," the unicorn told him.

Varon felt guilty that he wanted to leave the unicorn to fight the Ravager on his own. No Equus could stand up to a Ravager. The Ravager would kill this brave unicorn because it chose to defend Varon.

"I can't leave you alone," Varon said.

"I can defend myself."

"This is a Ravager," Varon said, as if it wasn't already obvious.

"I know."

"I can help you."

"You will, but not here or now. Now, you must go." Varon still hesitated. *"Go, Varon. With you gone, the Ravager will lose interest in me and move on to easier prey."*

Varon turned and galloped away. He paused at the top of another rise and looked back. The golden-horned unicorn and the Ravager were still circling each other; sometimes darting forward in a quick attack. Varon was amazed that the unicorn was still alive, but the Ravager seemed afraid of him.

"May Equ protect you," Varon called in his mind-voice.

He heard the unicorn neigh loudly, as if what Varon had said was funny.

Varon galloped away. He found his band grazing in an area of too-sparse grass and waiting for him to return.

"Did you find anything?" Millotin asked.

"A Ravager disguised as a fox led a pack to destroy a herd of llamas," Varon told them.

Millotin pranced nervously. *"How do you know what the predators looked like?"*

"The Ravager doubled back on its trail, and I saw the pack he was with attacking the llamas," Varon explained.

That caught everyone's attention.

"And you escaped?" Millotin said, amazed.

"Just barely. The Ravager saw me and was coming after me, but a great, white unicorn with a golden horn rescued me."

Millotin looked skeptical. *"A golden horn? Are you sure?"*

Varon nodded. He looked around and saw the skepticism in the others' expressions. *"It's true. He was close to me and larger than any Equus I have ever seen. He had a golden horn, and he held off the Ravager and gave me time to escape."*

"Varon, only one unicorn was ever said to have a golden horn."

Varon was too upset to remember who that unicorn was, but he wanted to know. He wanted to thank him. *"Then they must be the same. Who is it?"*

"Equ. The ponies say that his favorite form in Etrasco was a white unicorn with a golden horn," Millotin said.

Varon was dumbfounded. *"Are you saying that I saw Equ?"*

Millotin shook his head. *"You're saying it."*

Equ? Why would Equ appear to him? Why would Equ save him? *"But it couldn't have been Equ."*

"Why not? Ravagers are creators in animal form. Why couldn't Equ appear to his children in their form?" Millotin asked.

Varon shook his head and flicked his tail. *"But he didn't appear to the Equus. He just appeared to help me."*

"He must have wanted you to live."

"Why me? Ravagers and predators have killed Equus before, and Equ never saved them. I'm not special. I'm only a horse and not even a horse leader," Varon said, surprised at how self-critical he was being with himself.

"I can't explain it, Varon." Millotin turned to the zebra. *"What about you, Vinel? Do you have an answer?"*

Vinel shook his head. *"I'm still not convinced that Varon saw Equ,"* the zebra said.

"What other unicorn would have a golden horn?" Millotin asked.

"Maybe it only appeared golden in the light."

"Varon?" Millotin said, turning to the horse.

Varon's eyes flicked back and forth between the two of them. His ears took opposing directions as he shook his head. *"I don't know. I don't think it was the light."*

Vinel said, *"Perhaps we will see this golden-horned unicorn at Champion Days and find the answers we need."*

Varon nodded. *"I would like to meet him and thank him for his timely help."*

Varon lowered his head to graze. He paused when he noticed the white vapors coming from his nose. It was colder here than where

Scola's Herd was grazing. Yet, it shouldn't be cold at all during the Season of Life. If the seasons could change their eternal pattern, why couldn't the ages change?

"Jalon," Varon called, *"are we close to the wall of ice?"*

"Not really. Why?"

"The air is colder here."

"That wall has a lot of ice, Varon. I suspect it will chill the air far away."

The donkeys and Corriate had crossed the invisible path while Varon had been gone. Once Varon had eaten what he could, they started toward the north again. They were wary of any creatures they saw, fearing that they could be Ravagers.

Three days later, Varon's band asked for shelter with Calvn Lacinus' Herd when they entered the herd's grazing territory. This herd lolled in their fields when Varon and the others approached at a cautious walk. They didn't want to alarm the herd with a sudden approach, but Varon doubted that anything could have alarmed this herd. Some Equus rolled on their backs in the grass. Others lay stretched out, languishing in the sun, trying to warm themselves. The few Equus who were standing seemed to do it on shaky legs.

As Varon's small band approached the herd, none of the herd scouts challenged them, which was foolish; deadly at worst.

"What is wrong with them?" Varon asked.

"They all seem sick," Vinel noted.

Millotin snorted. *"The herd is unprotected. They wouldn't need Ravagers to destroy them. Predators alone could do it... and not many at that."*

"We should find Calvn Lacinus. He may need our help," Vinel said.

"Calvn Lacinus," Millotin called with a loud projection of his mind-voice.

They heard no response.

"Together," Millotin told the band. *"Calvn Lacinus!"*

"Too loud," came a faint reply.

They concentrated on tracing the thought until they found Calvn

Lacinus lying on his back and kicking his legs in the air. He wasn't trying to scratch his back by rolling on the ground. He flailed his legs like an overturned turtle trying to right itself. Calvn Lacinus was a roan unicorn who was slightly overweight. Bits of grass and dirt knotted his mane and tail. He had none of Calvn Scola's majestic appearance.

"Calvn Lacinus?" Millotin asked.

The unicorn rolled onto his side and raised his head.

"What is it? Who are you?" Calvn Lacinus asked.

The unicorn had a cloudy look in his eyes, as if he had been asleep. His gaze didn't focus on any of the Equus in Varon's band.

"We are from Calvn Scola's Herd," Millotin said.

"Then what are you doing here? I'm not Scola."

The Calvn still hadn't bothered to roll over and stand upright, but at least he stopped kicking his legs. Varon wondered if the Calvn could right himself. The unicorn was just as impaired as the other Equus in his herd.

"We are investigating the white mountains to the north. Calvn Scola sent us to see them for ourselves and discover what we could about them," Millotin said.

"White mountains? There are no mountains to the north, especially white ones."

How could he not see them? His herd was even closer to them than Scola's Herd.

Millotin remained respectful and pointed his white horn to the north. *"Please look, Calvn. They are there."*

The Calvn's head rolled to the side to look to the south.

"I see no mountains," Calvn Lacinus said.

"You are looking to the south, Calvn," Millotin said, now having a hard time keeping the exasperation in his mind-voice.

"Oh." Lacinus rolled his head to the other side. Varon saw his expression change when he noticed the mountains. How could he not have noticed them before now?

"Look, mountains. How did they get there?" Lacinus asked.

"That is what we are looking into," Millotin explained.

Calvn Lacinus nodded. *"Good. When you find out all about them, let me know."*

Millotin looked around at the others in his small group. Vinel tossed his head. Varon was afraid that the zebra would say something offensive.

"Calvn, is there anything wrong?" Millotin asked.

"No, why should there be? Everything is wonderful. Cravist sees to that."

"Cravist?"

"Herd leader for the zebras in my herd."

Vinel snorted and stomped his front hooves. *"A zebra finds this behavior proper?"*

Calvn Lacinus' large brown eyes focused momentarily on Vinel. His lips drew back over his lips and seemed to ripple like a wave from side to side.

"We are honoring Equ, zebra," Lacinus said.

"Honoring him by leaving yourselves open to predators?" Varon snapped.

"Equ will protect us," Calvn Lacinus said. He sighed as he shut his eyes.

"How do you know this?"

"He told me."

"He... told... you!" Vinel's eyes flashed with anger, and he danced around in a circle. *"Impossible."*

"Calm yourself, Vinel. Remember, he is Calvn of this herd," Millotin warned him. Many zebras jealously guarded the fact that they believed that they were the only Equus who could speak to Equ.

"But a zebra would not do this," Vinel insisted.

"Calvn, where is Cravist? We would like to speak with him," Millotin asked.

"I don't know. Probably by the river gathering more of the Creator Moss." Lacinus smacked his lips. *"I hope so. Talking to all of you has distracted me from listening to Equ. I have to eat more Creator Moss to find him again."*

"What is Creator Moss?"

Calvn Lacinus nodded. *"If you are nice, maybe Cravist will let you have some moss for yourselves. Then you will learn the truth."*

Vinel started to say something, but Millotin silenced him with a glance. *"Equ's blessings, Calvn. We will find Cravist and speak with him,"* Millotin said.

The Equus from Scola's Herd walked away slowly, weaving to avoid staggering and prancing Equus. Vinel looked at them disdainfully.

"What's going on here?" Millotin asked to no one in particular.

"I have suspicions, but I don't know why it would be so," Varon said. *"It's the Creator Moss that causes this state, like when Soma ate too many fermented berries last season."*

It was all that Varon could think of to explain this. It fit what Calvn Lacinus had said and what Varon was seeing. The question was why would so many Equus act so recklessly? The Ravagers Varon had seen destroy the llamas weren't all that far to the south. This herd wouldn't even offer a Ravager any resistance.

"But why would everyone in this herd do something so foolish? Soma was an idiot. Are all the Equus in this herd fools?" Millotin asked.

"They do it because they believe it allows them to talk with Equ. You heard what Calvn Lacinus said. Who wouldn't take a risk to do that?"

"Are you speaking from experience, Varon?" Millotin asked.

"I didn't set out to search for Equ. I was looking for survivors of the Ravager slaughter."

"How could they be so stupid?" Vinel asked.

"Because Cravist told them that was what the Creator Moss could do," Varon said.

Vinel shook his head. *"No, a zebra would not do something so foolish to the Equus. Our purpose is to judge; not execute. If Cravist is doing what they say, then he would endanger himself and the members of the herd."*

They found the zebra Cravist standing in a small, shallow stream that ran northeast from the Meshack Mountains to the Shadow

Ocean. He did not seem to be in the same condition as the rest of the Equus in his herd. He was standing steady. The zebra snorted when he saw the band approaching him.

"Stop where you are," Cravist ordered with his mind-voice.

Vinel jumped forward to the front of the band. *"And if we don't?"* Vinel challenged. *"Will you call upon your herd to stop us?"*

"Who are you? I don't know you. You aren't from this herd."

"We are from Calvn Scola's Herd," Millotin told him.

"They were running far to the south the last I heard, though they are probably moving toward the Ranglan Depression now."

Millotin nodded. *"They probably are. We are a small band sent to explore the white mountains and try to find out what they are."*

Cravist snorted. *"The white mountains are Equ's retribution upon the Equus."*

Millotin shook his head. *"Retribution? Why would he do that? We are his children. He loves us."*

Cravist snorted again. *"Loves us? If he loved us, why would he send us away to Hemlaza? The creator's ways are his own. I believe he has watched how the Equus have dissolved into herds with interspecies squabbling, and he hates us for destroying the beautiful unity he created when we lived in Etrasco. Now he seeks to punish us. Mark my words: the Equus will perish."*

Vinel flicked his tail. *"For someone who doesn't presume to know the creator's ways, you have strong opinions."*

"I am the herd's Voice to Equ."

"That is not what Calvn Lacinus says. He believes the Creator Moss allows him to speak with Equ," Vinel said.

Cravist snorted again. *"Calvn Lacinus is a fool! Creator Moss opens their minds to see what the Equus could be if they could fulfill their potential. It does not allow him to communicate with the creator."*

"It opens this herd to predators," Millotin snapped.

Cravist nodded. His ears pointed forward in contrast to his apologetic tone. *"So be it. If the predators destroy us, it shall be the creator's will."* He whinnied at the comment as if he thought the destruction of the Equus was amusing.

He did not seem upset he was endangering his herd's lives or even his own life. Varon wondered if Cravist was under the influence of the Creator Moss. He seemed steady, but what he was saying made no sense. Something odd was going on.

"It will be the Ravagers' will, not Equ's will!" Vinel shouted at him.

"This is herd business. It does not concern you," Cravist said, dismissing Vinel.

Vinel hesitated and looked at the others in the band. When he turned back to Cravist, he said, *"We came seeking the herd's protection for the evening, but it appears we would have to protect the herd. Even the donkeys can barely stand."*

Cravist snorted. *"We need no protection. We are at peace and are happy. I am species leader of Lacinus' Herd, and I so judge the Equus of Lacinus' Herd."*

Millotin turned to his band. *"We will not stay here tonight. We are safer on our own. This herd invites death, and one day it will come. Let it not be while we are here."*

Their band turned and left Cravist standing in the river as they moved further north. He did not stop them or follow them. Varon turned and looked over his shoulder. Cravist still stood defiantly in the middle of the stream. Cravist snorted when he saw Varon staring at him.

The small band left Lacinus' Herd and traveled north for a long time until Vinel broke the silence.

"I don't understand why," Vinel said.

"Why what?" Varon replied.

Vinel stomped his front hooves in the dirt. *"Cravist is condemning his herd to death."*

"So it would appear."

Vinel shook his head; his stubby mane waved back and forth along his neck. *"But why?"*

"I don't know. He seemed intelligent enough, so he must have reasons he feels justify his actions. He seemed to have a lot of un-

pleasant feelings about his Calvn," Varon said.

Vinel shook his head. *"Nothing could justify what he has done, not even jealousy."*

"Just the same. It is a herd matter for the zebras in the herd. We cannot interfere this time. Champion Days will have to do," Millotin said.

"They may all be dead by then."

Millotin nodded. *"Then it would be the will of Equ. To try to impose our standards on Calvn Lacinus' Herd would tie our fate to theirs and open us up to exile from Scola's Herd. If they continue using Creator Moss, they could make us take the moss, however it is used, and we would die with them."*

As part of the agreements that ended the Herd Wars forty-three generations ago, each herd of Equus agreed that as long as issues remained within a herd, it was herd business and subject only to the decision of the Calvn who led the herd. Where herd business might eventually cause future problems for other Equus herds, species could try to cross herd lines to influence their own species within the problem herd to change their behavior. It was a lengthy process that was seldom used; though Varon thought it might be worth it in this instance, especially if the knowledge of Creator Moss reached beyond Calvn Lacinus' Herd, which it now did since Varon and the others knew about it.

Then again, it might be safer for the Equus if the secret of the Creator Moss died with Lacinus' Herd.

The band put as much distance between themselves and Calvn Lacinus' Herd as they could before nightfall. They did not want to be anywhere nearby should the predators attack the herd this evening.

9

At nightfall, Varon's band picked up the scent of another herd's territorial markers. The scent was still strong, so the herd, wherever it was, still claimed this territory for grazing.

"Do you recognize the scent?" Millotin asked the others.

"Friez's Herd," Jalon replied.

"You recognized the scent from the air?" Millotin sounded impressed. It wasn't often that a pegasus impressed a unicorn.

"No, I just returned from meeting one of the pegasuses in Friez's Herd while I was scouting. I can lead you to them. They aren't far away."

"Should we go?" Millotin asked. Friez was very territorial for an Equus. He claimed far too much land for his herd when they grazed. Many Equus preferred avoiding territory that still carried his scent, even if Friez's Herd was not grazing there.

"It's custom to ask another herd's permission to pass through their current territories. We wouldn't want to start a herd war between Scola's and Frieze's Herds." Jalon let it pass without comment that they would need to observe the utmost decorum to pass through Calvn Friez's lands.

"But we are not a full herd. Friez's Herd might think we're renegades and drive us out of the area," Millotin suggested.

"I spoke with the pegasus Li. He will let Friez know that we are not exiles, but an exploratory band from Scola's Herd. We should be fine as long as we don't give Friez any reason to be angry. Now that he knows we are nearby, we should present ourselves to him."

"Let's hope that his herd hasn't discovered Creator Moss."

Jalon shook her head. *"They haven't."*

"Besides," Varon added, *"we can rest easier tonight as part of a larger herd. Friez's Equus are excellent fighters, even if they are a bit paranoid. We increase the safety of Friez's Herd and our own band by joining them for a brief time."*

Corriate snorted. *"A bit paranoid?"*

Millotin agreed with Corriate's comment, but said, *"However, we would still be safer with Friez's Herd. Lead us to them, Jalon."*

As they approached the large herd, Varon was surprised to see it bustling with so much activity this close to nightfall. The herd numbered nearly 500 Equus. It was the largest of the individual Equus herds. It said a lot for Friez's leadership that he could hold such a large herd together. Yet the size of the herd deterred most predators, leaving the herd with no outlet for the aggressiveness Calvn Friez encouraged in the Equus in his herd.

The donkeys patrolling the outer edges of the herd as herd scouts challenged Varon's group when they came upon them.

"Hold, Equus, we do not know you." The donkeys had to be careful not to allow Ravagers disguised as Equus to enter the herd where they could decimate it. It seemed to happen to at least one herd a year. It hadn't yet happened this year, and hopefully, it wouldn't.

"We are from Scola's Herd to the south," Millotin said.

Other donkeys raced over and encircle the band. They did not know if they were throwing their lives away or not, but they did not hesitate to do their jobs of protecting the herd. It said a lot for the loyalty that Calvn Friez had among his herd members.

"We seek the safety of the herd for the night from Calvn Friez," Millotin said.

A long silence followed as the donkeys called to Calvn Friez through the mind-link and requested his permission to let Varon's group pass. The answer must have been affirmative because the encircling donkeys broke away and began to return to their patrols.

"Calvn Friez is in the center of the herd. He is expecting you," one donkey said.

The unicorns and zebras passed the donkeys, not saying anything or even looking at them. Varon stopped next to the lead donkey and said, *"Thank you, brother."* If Varon surprised the donkey, he didn't show it. He turned his attention back to the plains, watching for predators. These were not the downtrodden donkeys of Scola's Herd.

Further in, the rest of the herd seemed to be playing. The unicorns jousted, their horns clacking together loudly. The pegasuses attempted complicated flying maneuvers that made Varon dizzy just to watch, although he stopped to watch anyway until Millotin told him to keep up with the rest of the band. The horses raced back and forth as their hooves threw dirt clods into the air, and the ponies wrestled.

"They are practicing for Champion Days," Millotin noted.

"That's not for another moon," Varon said.

"Some herds prepare early."

"And some herds are more worried about finding good grazing rather than competing." Competition was fine, but survival was paramount.

As they penetrated further into the herd, more and more of the Equus stopped what they were doing to stare at Varon's band. No, not the band, he decided, but at Vinel. Varon looked around at the herd. There were no zebras in Friez's Herd.

"Why are there no zebras here?" Varon asked.

Vinel shook his head. *"The herd has forsaken Equ. They will perish."*

Millotin turned to glare at Vinel. *"I don't know why there are no zebras among the herd, but don't you dare say such things in front of the Calvn. We are seeking not only his protection this evening, but his permission to cross his current grazing lands. This herd could be just as dangerous to us as any predator if we should find disfavor with the Calvn,"* Millotin warned him.

Vinel snorted. *"I will not forsake the creator."*

"No one expects you to. I just want you to respect the Calvn of this herd."

Calvn Friez was a large, thick-muscled unicorn who stood three heads high at the shoulder. He was dark with three white socks. As

Varon's band was led before him, they lowered their heads to imitate grazing.

"*I have been told why you are here, and you are welcome to the safety of my herd tonight,*" the Calvn said.

"*Many thanks, Calvn. I am Millotin. I lead this band,*" Millotin said. Then he went on to introduce the others in the group.

"*Why is Calvn Scola so interested in the white mountains? I am surprised he had the initiative to send a band to explore them,*" Calvn Friez said, nodding toward the mountains.

"*We have been told that they are not mountains like the Meshack Mountains, but walls of ice. Our Calvn would have us see this for ourselves before we decide what to do.*"

"*Ice? In all of my herd's speculations of what they are or what their appearance means, ice did not come up,*" Calvn Friez said. His herd was known for their physical prowess, not their imaginations.

"*I saw the mountains myself, Calvn,*" Jalon said.

"*I do not doubt your word, pegasus. I was only observing that we hadn't considered the possibility,*" Calvn Friez said.

That was unusual. Calvn Scola always seemed to doubt the pegasuses in everything; loyalty, intelligence, ability and honesty. Pegasuses obviously had more respect among Friez's Herd than among Scola's Herd.

"*Calvn Friez,*" Vinel said as he stepped forward. "*I see that your herd is without zebras.*" Millotin glared at Vinel, but the zebra ignored him. "*Undoubtedly, that means it has been some time since your herd had Return to remind them of the purpose of our existence on Hemlaza. In appreciation for your hospitality, I would like to offer to perform Return tomorrow morning for your herd before we depart.*"

Calvn Friez's brown eyes focused on Vinel until the zebra turned away. "*No!*"

"*But...*"

"*No, this herd does not perform Return, and it will not have one performed as long as I remain Calvn. Pleas to Equ cannot save us from predators and Ravagers. Only preparedness and vigilance will.*"

There will be no Return here. I have offered you the safety of my herd for this evening. If you abuse this generosity, we will drive your entire party from our territory."

Millotin bowed his head. *"We intended no offense, Calvn. We appreciate your kindness and abide by your decisions as they regard your herd."*

"See that it is so."

As Varon's group moved away, Millotin said to Vinel, *"Don't even talk of Return or Equ while we're here, Vinel. We need to return to our herd through this land. If we're driven from this area, you will make our return much longer."*

"What do we do now?" Corriate asked.

"Mix with your species, if you wish. I will call all of you together tomorrow so we can take our leave of Calvn Friez," Millotin said.

Mixing meant finding the herd leaders of the various species and talking with them to spread the news of what was happening with other herds. News was always a common exchange when the herds met. Varon sought out the horse leader of Friez's Herd. Yulmis was a dun-colored stallion who seemed overly impressed with his limited prestige. Varon had never liked him when they had met at Champion Days, and he liked him even less seeing him within his own herd. Yulmis was obeisant with pegasuses and unicorns, those above him in the social structure of the Equus, but hard with everyone else. Upon meeting Varon, as a horse not of his herd, he seemed unsure of which approach to take.

"Well met, Varon of Scola's Herd."

"Well met, Yulmis of Friez's Herd."

"What has brought you here?"

"My brothers and I seek to explore the white mountains."

Yulmis looked over his shoulder toward the mountains, which now appeared to glow red in the light of the setting sun.

Yulmis snorted. *"Why? They are mountains. Other than being white, why should you care to explore them? They do not appear hospitable in the slightest."*

"Mainly because until twenty-eight days ago, we did not know

they were there. These mountains apparently move," Varon explained, growing impatient with the horse leader.

Yulmis turned away from the mountains, uninterested. *"It is your time lost in preparing for Champion Days."*

Varon looked around and saw Vinel walking through the herd alone. With no other zebras around, he was a single species with no zebra with whom to converse. He was a pariah in this herd. No one would risk associating with him for fear of angering Calvn Friez.

"You were foolish to bring a zebra to this herd," Yulmis said, seeing where Varon's attention had been directed.

"Why?"

"We are the only Equus herd with no zebras."

That was news. *"Why is that?"*

"Calvn Friez exiled them all three moons ago and declared them renegades. This herd will have no more of the foolishness of the zebras."

"Exiled?" This news hadn't reached Scola's Herd yet. To exile an entire species from a herd was unheard of. Typically, if a species was cut from a herd, they went to another herd and moved from herd to herd until a herd adopted them. There were herds without pegasuses, ponies, and even donkeys. Many times Varon wondered how long it would be until Scola sent the pegasuses of his herd away. It would be a foolish thing to do given the pegasuses' ability as scouts, but Scola was a foolish leader. He would blame his poor decision on some other Equus.

But to declare a species renegades was to sentence them to death. Even Scola wouldn't do something so stupid, and Calvn Friez didn't seem stupid.

"What could the zebras have done that would have so angered Calvn Friez that he exiled their species?" Varon asked.

"Four moons ago, a Ravager that looked like a sparrow killed Calvn Friez's life mate."

Varon remembered how the mind-sickness had taken his sire and how Tola's death had affected Poins. Varon couldn't imagine feeling that way about Pautin. She was only his season mate. However, he could understand Calvn Friez's grief at the loss of his mate.

Yulmis continued, *"The zebras had told Calvn Friez that Equ desired him to take a life mate. He did. When predators killed her, Calvn Friez could not accept that Equ would want him to take a life mate just to have her and the foal she carried ripped apart by a Ravager sparrow. That is all it took for him to lose his faith in Equ."*

"And with no faith in Equ, he had no use for zebras," Varon added.

Yulmis nodded. *"He hates them. He blames the zebras for his loss, and since he had proclaimed Maysene his life mate, he cannot mate again. No other Calvn blood will take over this herd when Friez dies. An outsider will have to become Calvn. Two actually, since no other Calvn can control a herd this size. It will have to be split between two Calvns. The zebras have destroyed this herd's future, and the Calvn felt it only just to destroy them."*

Varon nodded.

"Vinel," Varon called, in a way that Yulmis couldn't hear his thoughts.

"What is it?" came the reply.

"Where are you?"

"Grazing by the stream."

Varon looked around and saw him standing alone and far from any of the other Equus.

"I think it would be best if you stay with the donkeys this evening," Varon advised him.

"The donkeys? Never!"

"If you don't, you may be dead by morning. These Equus declared the zebras of this herd renegades," Varon warned him.

"Renegades? But that..."

"I know what it means. I also know the donkeys are the only species that won't challenge you." Varon paused and added, *"I think. Your appearance is an offense to this herd."*

"But we have the Calvn's protection while we are here."

"Do you think Calvn Friez will protest if another unicorn gores you in the night? Do you think the Calvn will mind if a zebra dies

among them when he is the one who exiled them?"

Varon heard no reply from Vinel. He was probably thinking over his options.

"It's your choice, Vinel. I've warned you. Don't be stupid."

Their small band left in the morning after thanking Calvn Friez for his shelter. Varon was relieved to see that Vinel was still alive. Varon didn't ask him if he'd spent the night with the donkeys, though. It didn't matter. He was alive.

In the afternoon, they stopped to graze and Jalon landed near them.

"Jalon," Millotin called to the scout. *"The mountains do not seem to be moving closer after five days of travel toward them."*

Jalon cocked her head to the side to stare at the mountains. Then she turned to look back at Millotin.

"They must be since we are moving toward them. Are you saying that the mountains are running from us?" Jalon seemed in a peculiar humor. *"Are they afraid of us?"*

"I am saying that by your reckoning, we should reach them to-morrow. I don't see that happening," Millotin told him.

"It won't. We still have far to travel."

"But you said six days!"

Jalon lowered her head. *"It seems I misjudged your abilities as gallopers."*

"Our abilities? It is you who told us the wrong time," Millotin said.

"Only because you all are not as agile and fast as I had been led to believe."

That stung the unicorns' pride, and they trotted off to sulk, though not too far. They didn't want to be beyond the help of the rest of the band should they need it. The rest of the group grazed quietly. No one else wanted to speak of the white mountains or how much further it would be before they reached them.

"That was a mean thing for you to say to three- and four-year-olds," Varon scolded his friend.

"They should have expected it. After all, I'm unreliable. Calvn

Scola always doubts my word," Jalon replied.

The pegasuses in Scola's Herd enjoyed few pleasures when dealing with the unicorns. This apparently was one of them. Varon would not cloud her joy.

The band stopped for the night near a shallow stream. The water was colder than in most streams. It hurt Varon's teeth to drink it, but it had a sweet taste. He did not stand in the water, though, because its biting cold hurt his legs to the bone.

Varon spent much of the evening grooming Jalon while Jalon groomed him. He liked the soft, but stiff, feel of the feathers in Jalon's wings against his chest. He was careful not to pull them out, though. Jalon had warned him long ago that losing feathers other than by molting could cause difficulties with her ability to fly.

"Jalon, what do you think the white mountains appearing means to the Equus?" Varon asked the pegasus.

"It means the world is changing. I think... I know that things are different now. You can see it just by looking around. I don't know if the white mountains caused it, but they are a part of it and not the part that I fear," she explained.

"You're worried about the griffins."

"Yes, I've never had to fight a predator that could match me in flight. The griffins not only matched me; they were overtaking me. I had to gallop along the ground to outrun them." Jalon shook her head. *"Pegasuses weren't meant to gallop."*

"I understand your fear, sister, but the griffins are not unknown creatures, just unexpected. The white mountains, mountains of ice, are new. Where are they from? The water in the stream does not move when it turns hard in the Seeking Season."

"Perhaps the answer lies at the other end of the white mountains. Maybe they don't move on their own, but are, instead, pushed," Jalon said.

"Remember what Cravist said to us? Would Equ do this to us? What's his purpose?"

"Equ sent us from Etrasco. If he did that, he could do something like this."

"But what would he mean for us to do? Equ had a purpose in sending us from Etrasco. We may not know it, but there is a purpose. So what is the purpose of what is happening now?" Varon asked. *"If the white mountains cover Hemlaza with ice, what could the Equus do but die?"*

"They could leave, I suppose," Jalon suggested.

Varon nodded his head. *"Perhaps, that is the purpose, but where would we go?"* Varon pawed a hoof at the dirt. *"It makes little sense. When he wanted us to leave Etrasco, he moved us himself. Why would he not do it now?"*

"Am I a creator? How would I know?" Jalon asked.

"Where would we go? Hemlaza is an island."

"I don't know. Pegasuses have tried to fly to other islands. None has ever returned. We're not even sure if another land other than Hemlaza exists," Jalon told him.

Varon slept easily, if a bit too heavily. Dreams he couldn't remember troubled his sleep. They weren't nightmares, but they weren't typical dreams either. All he could remember was that he did not like what the dreams were telling him.

He heard a loud, low-pitched snort from one donkey who was standing guard around the band.

"What's wrong, Fome?" Varon asked.

"Predators," the donkey announced.

"Ravagers?"

"I don't think so. Ravagers would have attacked by now. These are circling the herd."

"Is everyone awake?" Millotin asked, moving closer to Fome.

"Yes," came the replies from the band.

"Is there a route to run?"

"I'm not sure," Fome said. *"We are outnumbered, and they are tightening their circle around us. It will be hard to run now."*

The Equus turned their attention outward. Varon could see the movements of the predators among the shadows. He saw a lot of slinking shadows out there, but he couldn't tell what the predators were. Their smell was indistinct.

He heard growling from all sides and knew what they faced. Wolves had surrounded them and were trying to frighten the band into splitting into smaller groups.

"Jalon, to the skies," Millotin ordered.

From the air, Jalon could dive and attack the predators by kicking them from above. She would also be safe from attack there.

The pegasus did not argue the point. She knew her most useful position in a fight would be in the air. From the air, she could attack the predators at their blind spots.

"Unicorns, horns out." The unicorns turned to point their horns, their most-effective weapon, outward. They would gore predators with their horns. Since the unicorns would watch the predators, they would also direct the attacks of the others.

"Everyone else, hind quarters out. May Equ favor us." The rest of the Equus would kick with their powerful hind legs at the predators. It was a classic Equus defense and effective when performed by a large herd. Dozens of striking hooves had been known to decimate attacking packs as well as a Ravager could.

The wolves charged as a pack, still hoping to scatter the small band, but it was their pack that broke. Jalon swept down from the sky. Her flaring hooves struck the lead wolf's back, snapping his spine. The pack broke around him.

"Unicorns, charge and retreat," Millotin shouted through the mind-link.

The three unicorns charged the wolves at various points. They gored two wolves, and Millotin barely missed killing a third. The wolf flipped over on his back to avoid Millotin's horn, but the unicorn still kicked him in the side. The three unicorns retreated to the band just in front of the wolves.

"Vinel, kick!"

The zebra obeyed. His hooves connected with the head of a wolf. Blood flew from the wounded wolf's scalp as a flap of fur was scraped free of the wolf's skull.

The unicorn snapped orders at the Equus, who obeyed. The wolf bodies began to fall and not rise. The predators clawed some Equus, but Millotin kept the band together so none of them were separated enough that they could be surrounded and brought down.

It seemed to Varon as if they fought for most of a day, but the moon barely moved. He kept his head down so he wouldn't be a target for a leaping wolf. He kicked whenever Millotin ordered it. Varon was exhausted at the end of the brief battle. Fourteen wolves lay dead. All the Equus were injured, but none seriously. Vinel and the donkeys rolled in the stream to clean themselves off. The icy water stopped their bleeding wounds. Varon found some thorns on a low bush and used them to hold the flesh of deeper wounds on Corriate and Fles together until the flesh healed.

"We should leave here," Vinel said. *"The blood smell will bring others before too long."*

It was agreed, and the Equus band galloped to the north, away from the battle scene.

Three days later, the Equus reached the base of the white mountains. As the mountains became clearer, Varon had felt a sense of dread for days. However, it terrified him to finally reach them.

The mountains did not rise gradually from foothills to ever-steeper mountains. They were a sheer wall of ice that rose thousands of feet above the Equus.

The band was quiet as they crossed the final few feet to the ice wall. Varon smelled it and then licked at it. It was ice. He could feel the intense cold in the air this close to the mountains.

Corriate kicked at it with his forehooves. The ice flecked off in small chunks, showing nothing beneath it but more ice.

"It's ice," he said.

"So I said," Jalon said.

"It is not a mountain then."

"It is. It is a mountain of ice."

"Look there," Fome said, pointing with his muzzle.

They turned to look further down the mountain. The roots of a large tree stuck out of the sheer wall of ice.

Varon realized what the sight meant. It scared him.

"The mountains are moving. There are no trees in this area of

Hemlaza. It had to have been torn up somewhere other than here, and the mountains have held onto it long enough that some ice has formed around it," Varon said. What he also realized was that there was land elsewhere other than Hemlaza.

"But mountains can't move," Millotin insisted. He shook his head.

"These aren't mountains. It's an ice wall."

Varon arched his neck and looked up. He shuddered. The Equus were losing their land to these mountains. No longer were there fields of alfalfa along the northern shore of Hemlaza. How could they resist giving ground before its massiveness? Was it true that ice would cover Hemlaza in four generations?

"Are we close to the sea?" Varon asked.

"A few hundred yards away, perhaps," Vinel said.

"Can you see over the top?" Millotin asked Jalon.

"We landed on the top of the mountains when we made our original journey," Jalon answered.

"How far have you seen?"

"Much further than the ocean should be and the mountains keep going. The mountains reach beyond Hemlaza and stretch into the ocean and beyond."

Varon shuddered. He wasn't sure if it was the implications of what Jalon had said or the chill in the air. Was there enough ice beyond the ocean to cover all of Hemlaza?

"How much further?" Millotin asked.

"Further than my band could fly in a day when we were here earlier."

"Could you travel to the end of the ice in more than a day?"

Jalon flicked her tail in irritation. She knew if she answered wrong, she would be asked to take another journey.

"I suppose I could if there was food or fresh water along the way," Jalon said.

"There isn't?"

"None that we saw. We were very hungry by the time we reached Hemlaza again, having gone two days without food. We chipped the

ice and sucked on the chips for water."

"Where does all the water come from?"

"It must come from behind the mountains somewhere. Saltwater doesn't freeze, and the rivers on Hemlaza are still at normal levels, though I fear what will happen when these mountains touch our rivers."

Varon did, too. It meant that the rivers would ice over and add their volume to the white mountains. It would mean a drought to those areas of Hemlaza fed by the rivers. It meant an end to life on Hemlaza.

10

Carn let the stream wash around his legs. Ice was forming at the edge of the banks. The stream would freeze over in a day or two. He ignored the biting pain of the cold water. These Equus were so pampered; their tolerance to cold was too low. Carn took pride in his ability to withstand the pain of freezing cold, even in this imperfect form.

He listened to the night sounds and sounds of the herd of which he was currently a part. The mind-link was quiet, but he knew that most of the Equus were still awake, just lost in their own visions. Carn heard whinnies and snorts coming from the direction of the herd. He even heard an occasional Equus run across the land.

That would have to change. He couldn't risk one of these Equus escaping to warn the other herds of all that he had done to them. Worse, he couldn't risk Equ or his mother learning of this. They would stop his deception.

Carn should have destroyed the small band that had come through here earlier. He wasn't sure if they could do anything to change his plans. He hadn't thought so. He had just wanted them to leave so he could savor Lacinus' Herd's decay.

Decay!

How lovely. Carn was using their own pampering to destroy the Equus. Perhaps now the lesson would be learned. If not, he could teach the lesson to dozens of other herds.

Equ would realize Carn was attacking Equ's beloved children from within, and the Equus would die just as Carn had predicted to the small band yesterday.

Carn lowered his head into the icy water. The single-digit temperature shocked even him because his muzzle was much more sensitive to the cold than his legs. He suppressed a chill and used his teeth to work a sizeable piece of moss free from the rock to which it clung.

With the shortage of fresh grass and fruits, some Equus had developed a taste for river moss. When Carn had seen how this species of moss affected the Equus, he had also seen a way to exact his revenge without drawing his mother's punishment.

Carn lifted his head from the water and walked out of the stream, holding the moss in his mouth. The chemicals, proteins, and minerals that affected other Equus had no effect on him. He could counter their effects at once with only a thought. Oh, he had let the chemicals work their magic on him once. The effect had been interesting. Colors had seemed sharper while he had lost all sense of pain. It was as if one sense had drawn its enhancements by dulling another. The shift had been uncomfortable at first until the chemicals had stimulated the pleasure centers in his brain so strongly that the moss' effects had caught him up in its rapture.

He could give pain through pleasure. What an interesting concept!

Carn found Calvn Lacinus and stood before the rolling fool.

"My Calvn," Carn said.

Calvn Lacinus' legs pointed straight up in the air, but they moved as if he were trotting. The Calvn was still under the influence of the moss, but his eyes were less glazed over than they had been earlier in the day. The effects of the moss were diminishing. Carn couldn't risk that. It had taken weeks of living as Cravist to introduce the entire herd to the moss. Calvn Lacinus and the horses had resisted more than the rest, unsure of the safety of the moss, but even they had given themselves over to its power and pleasure.

"My Calvn," Carn repeated.

Calvn Lacinus stopped moving his legs and tried to focus his attention on the zebra. He failed and closed his eyes instead. Good, the effect still hadn't worn off.

"I brought you more Creator Moss, my Calvn," Carn said.

"Moss. More moss? Good. Good. I was having trouble hearing

Equ. I kept running toward his voice, but it kept getting fainter," Lacinus said without opening his eyes.

"Well, the moss will help. Just open your mouth, and I'll give it to you now."

Lacinus lifted his chin and opened his mouth. How easy it would be to rip out the unicorn's throat. He could kill them all so easily, but he had to restrain himself. He couldn't attack. All it would take was one Equuus to realize the weapons at their disposal and Carn would be in trouble. No, he had a plan, and he had to follow it through to its delightful conclusion.

He lowered the strip of moss in Lacinus' mouth so that the Calvn could chew it and swallow it. Cravist did so, knowing it was important, above all, that Lacinus remain incapacitated. He couldn't be allowed to rally his herd and command them.

As Calvn Lacinus finished eating his moss, Carn heard a wolf howl in the darkness. A few moments later, another howl answered the first.

Carn whinnied. Good. A wolf pack had found the herd. Before too long, they would attack. It would happen as soon as they realized there were no herd scouts at the edges of the herd to warn the Equus to prepare themselves.

Carn turned and walked back to the river. He might make sure the herd leaders were incapacitated before the wolves attacked. That would make devastating the herd even easier. As he walked, he noticed shadows moving out of the corner of his eyes. The large moon was full, and the small moon was waning. It was good hunting light.

The howls grew in number. Carn picked out at least fourteen separate howls, but more would answer. The wolves would wait until their numbers were larger before attacking even an incapacitated herd ripe for destruction.

Carn lowered his muzzle into the water to pull more moss free. When he raised his head, he saw the wolves moving in slowly, unsure of what to expect from the herd and wary of traps. He could count at least three dozen wolves within range of his vision.

***

This would be fun.

The first Equus that died was a prancing donkey who was probably imagining that he was a unicorn commanding a herd. A large, gray wolf charged him from the front and bit into the donkey's throat, ripping it open. Blood darkened the wolf's muzzle as the donkey dropped.

Carn laughed out loud, not worrying if an Equus or a wolf saw him and wondered how a zebra could laugh.

Carn saw other Equus fall; donkeys, unicorns, horses. It made no difference. Their blood was always red, and their lives were all short. They fell quickly because none of them offered any resistance to the pack. The wolves swarmed over them, feasting as if they hadn't eaten at all this season.

Most of the Equus died in silence like the donkey. A few squealed as they died.

At first, Carn worried that their cries might startle the herd into a stampede. Instead of scaring the herd, it only angered the few who gave voice to their feelings, telling the squealers to be quiet.

That was how a herd should die, quickly and quietly. How fun this all was, Carn thought.

If this did not show Equ that pampering the Equus was useless in their developing their ability to survive, nothing would.

A wolf charged out of the night toward Carn. The creator stared at the wolf without fright. The fearless stare gave the wolf pause.

Carn opened his mouth. He let his tongue reach out like a snake striking. He let his tongue change to a viper as it closed the gap between himself and the wolf.

The cottonmouth snake bit the wolf on the neck, injecting it with venom far deadlier than a cottonmouth's venom. The wolf yelped and backed away. As it turned to run from him, it fell to the ground. It lay twitching in the dirt until it died.

Carn retracted his tongue, changing it back as he did.

Yes, pampering was not a survival trait for a species. Not for Equus and not for wolves, either.

11

Miskala held back from galloping full out because he didn't want to outdistance Capsta and Qarel, the two horses running with him. Not that he was too sure he could outdistance them. His sides already heaved from his exertions, and the horses hadn't even begun to sweat.

Miskala knew he wasn't the fittest Equus in the herd. Unicorns, as the leaders of the Equus, lived a pampered life. Miskala's sides bulged with extra weight from Calvn Conllal's ability to know where the best grazing was and when it was in season. That ability had failed of late because there was no new grazing. Now Miskala was helping forage for others in the herd, particularly the pregnant mares, who couldn't move swiftly.

"Why are you running so slowly, Miskala?" Capsta asked.

His pace faltered, and for a moment, he was galloping until he fell back into the rhythm of the run.

"I thought you said you wanted to find a grazing area quickly, so why are you moving so slowly?" Qarel asked.

"Slowly?" was all Miskala could say. He was crestfallen. He knew he wasn't as fleet of hoof as some Equus, but if this pace was considered slow, then galloping fast would kill him!

Then he heard Capsta and Qarel whinnying, and he knew they had been joking with him.

"We wanted to see how fast your pride could make you run," Qarel said and whinnied again.

"I would like to finish quickly, but galloping is not my idea of fun," Miskala told them.

"Well, we're not finding anything in this direction. Should we turn?"

Miskala said, *"Maybe we should split up to cover more ground."*

Capsta reared up on his rear legs. Miskala and Qarel stopped to stare at him.

"Splitting up will accomplish nothing. With the land as bare as it is now, any grazing will stand out like a predator on the horizon," Capsta said.

Miskala nodded. When would the Season of Life come to the land? *"If the barrenness continues much longer, Equus will die."*

"Hemlaza is a land of plenty, Miskala. It won't happen," Qarel said.

"Look around you, Qarel. Where is the plenty? We are eating less and working harder to find what we do eat. If it continues much longer, I may actually become svelte," Miskala joked.

Qarel whinnied. *"If that were to happen, no one would recognize you."*

But what Miskala had said was true. Calvn Conllal was one of the oldest Equus on Hemlaza, and even he said he had not known a year this barren. It was as if the Seeking Season did not intend to end this year. Already they were a quarter day from the herd with no signs of food. A barren land could not support life. Hemlaza was not barren yet, but it soon would be, and when that happened, Equus and other animals would begin dying, with the predators being the last ones to die.

"Let's go out for a while longer. Then we'll head east before turning back," Miskala suggested.

"It's as good a guess as following the wind nowadays," Capsta commented. He was the horse leader of Conllal's Herd.

As they galloped again, Miskala said, *"Try not to make my heart give out this time. I'll try to gallop faster."*

They galloped north for a while and then turned east. Miskala saw something on the horizon. He might not have been fast, but he had sharp eyesight. Still, at this distance, he couldn't be sure what he was seeing.

"Stop. Look east. What is that?" Miskala said.

The horses stopped and stared. *"Is it a predator?"* Qarel asked.

"It looks too small, and it seems to keep... falling down."

The moving brown shape did seem to stand and then fall.

"Let's go see what it is," Miskala said.

"It could be a trap set by the predators. It could be a Ravager," Capsta said.

Miskala nodded. Capsta was right, but Miskala was curious to know what he was looking at. He was forever curious.

"You're right," Miskala said. *"You two stay here. I'll go by myself."*

He galloped toward the creature. He noticed his two friends were galloping on either side of him.

"If you galloped any slower, you'd be moving backwards," Qarel joked.

"I thought you two would stay behind," Miskala said.

"You need someone to keep you from slacking off," Capsta told him. *"If we didn't come along, you would probably be walking."*

"Thank you."

They had covered about half of the distance to the animal when Miskala realized what it was.

"It's a foal!"

"A foal!" Qarel said. *"What's a foal doing out here by itself?"*

"It's a trap," Capsta warned. *"No foal could survive out here. It's a Ravager trying to lure us in because we'll feel sympathetic to the foal."*

They continued galloping until they neared the creature. Then they slowed to a walk and approached it cautiously. It was a reddish-brown colt who couldn't have been more than a day old, so he was too young to become a part of the mind-link.

The colt cried out as the three Equus approached. It tried to move away but only succeeded in falling. Miskala studied it from a distance. It was hungry; that much was obvious. It needed its mother's milk.

"Qarel, hurry back to the herd. We need a lactating mare out

here to feed this little one until we can get him back to the herd," Miskala said.

"A lot of the mares are stingy with their milk nowadays because of the lack of food."

Miskala shook his head. *"I don't care whether it's a donkey or a horse or a unicorn mare. Just bring whoever you can find. We need to fill this little one's belly, or he won't make it through the day."*

"I'll be back as soon as I can," Qarel said as he turned and ran off.

"Why would a mare leave a foal here?" Capsta asked.

Miskala shook his head. *"I don't know, unless maybe the herd feared they couldn't support any more young. If so, they were cruel, and I can't imagine that."*

"This one doesn't seem hurt or deformed," Capsta observed as he walked around the colt. The colt watched him, occasionally crying for milk.

The foal had a good shape. He would grow to be a handsome stallion if he lived. He'd be a credit to any herd to which he belonged.

"What herd was last through here?" Miskala asked.

Capsta walked in slow circles, sniffing the air and the ground for the territory markers of the last herd, or if not finding that, a scent of a familiar Equus.

"I smell a horse named Buser. She's in heat, and she's with Gee's Herd," Capsta reported.

"Is she this foal's mother?"

Capsta shook his head.

"Why would a mare leave a healthy foal behind?" Miskala asked, more to himself than Capsta. He couldn't imagine any foal abandoning this little one, but an Equus had.

"Maybe we should go to Gee's Herd and ask them," Capsta suggested.

Miskala shook his head. *"They would just deny it because, in leaving this colt, they knew they weren't giving it a chance to live."*

"Then that raises the question of why again, especially since this

colt is healthy."

"We'll just have to find out the answer."

Miskala moved closer to the small colt and began grooming him around the withers. The colt moved closer to him for the warmth of his body. When he began searching Miskala for nipples, the unicorn nudged the colt away. When Qarel arrived with Jazi, a lactating mare horse, it was a relief to Miskala.

"Move aside, Miskala. This requires a mother's touch," Jazi said.

"His mother may have been the one who left him," Miskala snapped.

"She might have. Not me. I came as a favor to you."

Miskala lowered his head. *"I'm sorry. I'm just angry about what has happened to this little one."*

"What has happened?"

"This foal's mother abandoned him," Miskala said.

"Are you so sure?" she countered.

"What else could it have been?"

Jazi flicked her ears back and forth. *"A multitude of things. The truth doesn't always lie near the surface, Miskala. It sometimes takes a lot of digging to reach it."*

Jazi moved up next to the colt. He sniffed at her for a moment and then realizing her nipples offered him food, his lips grabbed at them. He began sucking.

"He has a strong survival instinct," Jazi commented. *"Why don't you go on back, Miskala? I'll head back with this one when he's full."*

"I'll stay. I'm not much, but I'll stay here in case we run into predators on the way back to the herd."

"What are you going to do about this colt, Miskala?" Qarel asked.

"I'll have Calvn Conllal adopt him into the herd, and I'll take care of him."

Capsta shook his head and stepped forward. *"No, Miskala."*

"Then what?"

"You're a unicorn, and this colt is a horse. It is the responsibility of the horses to care for him. I appreciate your concern for the horses, but you can't even feed him. My season mate is lactating. She should be able to feed both this colt and our filly," Capsta said.

"I got the impression you didn't like this colt."

Capsta shook his head. *"No. I didn't trust the situation. I thought it was a trap. I will accept responsibility for the colt as I do for my horses in Conllal's Herd."*

Miskala nodded. *"I don't think this colt will disappoint you."* He paused. *"I will concentrate on trying to find out why someone left this colt here."*

"I would be curious to learn that myself."

Miskala watched the young colt tug at Jazi's feat and he marveled at the young life's desire to live. Most newborns, left alone, would have been dead already. This young colt wanted to live, and Miskala intended to see that he did.

What disturbed him was to think an Equus wanted this colt dead. Why?

<h1 style="text-align:center">12</h1>

Scola's Herd was in full training for the upcoming Champion Days when Varon's band returned after their moon-cycle-long absence to investigate the white mountains. Unicorns jousted. Donkeys worked at kicking rocks out of the air. Zebras wrestled. Horses raced each other. Pegasuses flew their air antics. The intense competition reminded Varon of the scene that had confronted him with Friez's Herd.

Varon had developed a better understanding of his nine companions on the journey. They had faced predators, jealous Equus, and the unknown white mountains together. They had learned to do more work than usual, for in a small band such as theirs; everyone was required to work hard, even the unicorns.

Varon had even noticed the beginnings of a breakdown in species bias within their small band. Even Varon had seen beyond the species of an Equus to the strengths Fles and Vinel showed as well as the others. Vinel and Fles had surprised him though, because he had expected little from them at the beginning of the journey. However, Vinel had shown his indignation with his own kind at Lacinus' Herd, and Fles had proven himself a valiant fighter against the wolves.

As soon as the small band rejoined, they gathered around Calvn Scola who was watching the unicorns practice their jousting. The actual champions wouldn't be chosen until the day of the various contests at the Ranglan Depression.

"We worried about you," Calvn Scola said as they approached. He did not sound worried or overjoyed to see them. By the way his attention was focused on the jousting, Varon thought the Calvn would

much rather be watching that than listening to Millotin's report.

"We did not live up to Jalon's expectations of how fast we could travel," Millotin said as he bowed his head in front of the Calvn.

Scola stared at Jalon but said nothing to her. Jalon lowered her head and spread her wings. With false humility, Varon was sure.

"What did you see?" Calvn Scola asked.

"An ice wall, as the pegasus reported. We saw it from the base. The wall is quite tall. You can call them mountains, though they are made of ice."

"From where does it come?"

Millotin shook his head. *"We cannot venture to its end. There is no food along the tops of the mountains. The pegasuses already tried on their first exploration and failed."*

"Are the mountains moving?"

Millotin paused in his reply. *"We did not see them move, but they are where no mountains were before."*

A restless murmur ran through the mind-link. The news was not received happily. How could they stop a moving mountain range? They could not cross them to be safe behind the mountains because they were too steep and deep. They could only run in front of the white mountains, but the land would end at the southern cliffs. The mountains would pushed the Equus into the sea if they did not die from starvation first.

"You bring us very distressing news. I had hoped to hear better. It will have to be discussed among the Calvn Council at Champion Days. We should be able to decide what is best for the Equus," Calvn Scola said.

Maybe it would even be a good decision if some of the wiser Calvns carried the day, Varon thought. He did not count on it, though. If the Calvns wanted to do what was best for the Equus, they would disband the council and turn leadership of the herds over to the genuine leaders among the Equus, not just the unicorns.

"Perhaps the ponies should try to explore our history to see if something like this has ever happened before," Millotin suggested.

Corriate stepped forward. *"We would be eager to try, Calvn. Per-*

haps Equ will grant us instruction on how to deal with this problem."

"*You make this sound like a critical crisis,*" Scola said.

Millotin bobbed his head. "*You did not see the white mountains, Calvn. If you had, you would realize that nothing will stand in the way of those mountains as they move across Hemlaza. We must be prepared.*"

Scola nodded stiffly, as if hurt him to bend his head. "*We shall be, but our preparations can wait until after Champion Days.*"

They could say nothing more. Calvn Scola had decided, and he would only dig in his hooves if they challenged him.

"*Varon,*" Evin called with his mind-voice.

"*What do you want, brother?*"

"*The horses are gathering on the west side of the herd.*"

"*Why?*"

"*It's time to select a new horse leader. We've been too long without one, but we had to wait until all the horses in the herd were present. With your return, they now are.*"

Varon had known a new horse leader would have to be selected since Tola was dead, but he hadn't wanted to think about it.

Who in the herd would serve the horses as well as Tola had? Varon's sire had been known for his wisdom and leadership. Both were much-needed traits in a herd where Scola was Calvn.

All seventy-three of the horses of Scola's Herd gathered. When Evin saw that all were in attendance, he spoke since he was the eldest horse in the herd. He would serve as the default horse leader until a new one was chosen.

"*With Tola gone, we must now choose a new horse leader by mind-voice rather than challenge. I will hear the debate,*" Evin said.

Varon's head was filled with lots of conflicting thoughts as the Equus put forth the names of the various stallions for consideration. No sooner were many names suggested before they were shouted down. When Varon heard his own name called, the predominant reason against him he heard was his age. Most horses thought him either too young to lead or too young to hold leadership in the herd against challengers.

Varon wondered about the last one himself. If he won leadership by consent, could he hold his leadership position against horse challengers? It wasn't unheard of for an unliked stallion to champion a weaker, better-liked leader, only to challenge and defeat the leader once he was named horse leader. Was that what was happening here?

After the horses argued over the merits of each name, Evin called for silence. *"All the eligible horses have been spoken for. Those who still want to be considered for horse leader of Scola's Herd, step forward and present themselves."*

Varon was eligible, but did he want to be a leader? Could he live up to Tola's example? He watched as Stoni, Unta, Dalis, and Marveesi stepped forward. Unta was a devoted follower of Scola. Dalis was too aggressive, and Varon thought he lacked wisdom. Marveesi was aging, but he would make a competent leader. Stoni had a lot of wisdom, but Varon didn't consider him a talented leader.

Was this the best that the horses of Scola's Herd could offer to follow Tola as horse leader? None of them would even come close to being as good a leader as Tola. What would happen under their leadership? Did Varon want to find out?

What would Tola have told him to do in a situation like this? Easy. Never leave your future to others. Act if you can.

And Varon could act.

He stepped forward.

No one else followed him.

Evin arched his neck and said, *"Now is the time for the choosing. Choose well, for the horses of this herd need not only strength, but wisdom in their leader."*

"Who chooses Unta?" Twelve horses reared up.

"Who chooses Marveesi?" Seven horses reared up.

"Who chooses Dalis?" Twelve horses reared up, tying him with Unta.

"Who chooses Varon?" Nineteen horses reared up. Varon was surprised he got such substantial support from the herd, but he noticed that Pautin, his own season mate, had reared up for Dalis. She

was hoping to become his season mate once her and Varon's foal was born.

"Who chooses Stoni?" Evin called. Seventeen horses reared up.

Evin nodded. *"It is decided then. Varon is the new horse leader of Scola's Herd. May Equ guide you in wisdom as he did your sire."*

Varon looked over the horses, wondering if there had ever been a five-year-old horse leader before. He had no doubt someone would challenge him within a few days. He would have to be ready for that if he meant to continue ruling the horses.

No… leading. Scola ruled. Tola had led. Varon would follow his sire's example as much as he could and lead the horses.

"I thank you all for your faith in me, and I will do my best to lead with my sire's wisdom and my dam's love," Varon said as a way of accepting the responsibilities of a horse leader.

"What do you think of the white mountains?" Marsallin asked. She was not one for celebrating when there was work to be done.

"I believe that life on Hemlaza will change. It will have to change, or the land itself will die."

That brought silence to the horses.

"How will it change?" Evin asked. *"I am nineteen years old and have not seen life on Hemlaza change. Not ever."*

"I don't know all the ways change will occur, but we can see the first change already in the way the Seeking Season is refusing to give way to the Season of Life. What will happen if there is no Season of Life? I don't know if this will be, but it may happen. We must be ready for the worst even while we hope it doesn't happen."

Once the horses separated to go about looking for food or tending to their foals or mates, Varon walked over to Pautin. He said nothing to her. He was afraid that his anger at her betrayal would slip out, and he did not want to show his anger and get into another argument with her.

"So I am the season mate to a horse leader," she said.

"I know you did not wish it," he responded.

"Why do you say that?"

"You did not rise for me."

"I think Dalis would serve the herd better."

"Do you really? Why?" He took a deep breath to calm himself.

"His is older and stronger. You may have the wisdom to lead, Varon, but I doubt that you have the strength to lead. What good would it do to rise for you when another horse will take your place within a day or two?"

"Thank you for your faith in me," he said, unable to keep the sarcastic tone out of his mind-voice.

"Oh, is that the way it is with you now that you are a horse leader?"

"What way is that?" Varon snapped.

"You like to speak of wanting and giving honesty until it hurts your feelings."

"I did not stop you from voicing your opinion."

"But you didn't like hearing it."

"I didn't enjoy seeing the white mountains either, but I faced them. The truth may be unpleasant sometimes, but I don't deny it," Varon told her.

"Then do you think you can remain the horse leader of this herd?" Pautin asked.

"I don't know. It depends on who tries to challenge me," Varon answered.

"It will be Dalis. He wants to lead the horses. Can you defeat him?"

Varon's ears flicked back and forth as he thought about it. *"I don't know. He is stronger, but I am faster than he is."*

Pautin snorted.

Varon didn't feel enjoyment at arguing with her anymore. He veered away from her and walked toward the center of the herd where Calvn Scola would be. Varon needed to let the Calvn know he had been chosen the new horse leader. How long he would be horse leader was up to fate and his own strength.

Calvn Scola stood in the center of the herd, turned away from the white mountains. Four unicorns clustered closely around him, trying to curry his favor. From the way they stared at the Calvn and their closeness to him, Varon guessed that Scola must be speaking to them quietly through the mind-link. They all turned their attention to Varon as he approached.

"I seek to speak with you, my Calvn," Varon said. He lowered his head to the ground and imitated eating the non-existent grass.

"What is it, Varon?"

"I wanted to let you know I have been chosen as the new horse leader for this herd," he said as he raised his head.

Calvn Scola seemed surprised. *"I did not realize that the horses now chose their leader by bloodline."* Varon knew what surprised Scola was that the horses had chosen someone as young as Varon.

"They don't, Calvn. They chose me because they felt that I could lead them wisely," Varon told his Calvn.

"Let it be so then."

Then Calvn Scola turned his attention back to the other unicorns. Varon walked away to find something to eat. With grass and grains getting scarcer and fruit all but non-existent, the Equus were spending more time searching for food than eating it.

Jalon fell into step beside Varon. *"Congratulations, horse leader."*

"For today. Who knows about tomorrow?" Varon found he was willing to be more honest with Jalon than his own season mate.

"If the horses are wise, they will let you continue to lead."

"It is not wisdom that threatens my position. It is ambition. Some stallions in this herd are ambitious."

Jalon nodded. *"Even so, there will come a day when you are strong enough to hold dominance among the horses and you will."*

"Thank you, sister."

The first challenge to Varon's leadership didn't come from Dalis as Pautin had predicted. It came from Unta, a six-year-old palomino. He had been the next-youngest stallion to be considered as horse leader.

The other challengers had been making threatening gestures toward Varon since his selection, laying their ears back against their heads when they saw him approaching and blocking his path when he walked. Mostly, Varon ignored the challenging stances and concentrated on talking with the horses to learn their concerns and fears. Varon wanted to win his position through respect for his wisdom, not fear of his presence.

Unta broke the tense truce between Varon and the other challengers. Varon was walking through the herd when Unta not only blocked his path but also made a bite threat. He snapped his jaw open and closed while shaking his head up and down and back and forth.

Varon stopped and stared at the challenger. Unta's tail swished, and he stomped his front hooves. Varon held his ground.

"You seem upset, Unta," Varon said.

"I claim the right to be horse leader."

The Equus surrounded them anticipating a fight between Varon and Unta.

"The horses have already rejected you as their leader. How can you lead if the horses won't follow you?"

Unta stomped harder, but Varon didn't back away or lower his head to show his submission to a stronger challenger. He wanted to appear relaxed, but he didn't know how he could do that and still be prepared for the attack that was sure to come.

"I challenge your authority," Unta said.

He charged Varon with his head extended forward to snap at Varon's neck. Varon lowered his own head as if to meet the charge, but at the last moment, he jumped to the side. Unta's bite missed Varon while his momentum carried him past Varon. As Unta passed, Varon kicked out, striking Unta in the haunches and drawing blood. It wasn't a deep injury, but it was enough to cause Unta to limp.

Unta squealed and turned to face Varon. They came together and reared up on their hind legs. Their forelegs kicked out, trying to strike at one another. Their hooves clacked as they hit together. Varon kept his head back. If one of Unta's hooves struck his muzzle, it might cause a lot of damage.

Unta pressed the attack, forcing Varon back. Then one of Varon's rear hooves slipped in the soft earth, and he had to drop to all four hooves to keep from falling. He saw Unta's legs dropping toward him and he jumped forward.

He hit Unta in the stomach, throwing the bigger horse backwards. Unta squealed as he tumbled backwards onto his back. The horse rolled onto his side and lay still except for his heaving chest.

Varon snorted and charged Unta. He reared up in front of the palomino.

"Do you yield, or do I mark you?" Varon threatened. Marking an opponent was wounding him so he could never challenge another horse leader. Usually marking took the form of breaking a leg, in which case the would-be challenger would have a weak leg for the rest of his life that horse leaders would recognize for what it was. More violent markings by harsh horse leaders had been gouging an eye out or even death. Varon did not want to be forced into any of the choices. He was a healer, not a fighter. However, if Unta did not yield, he would have to mark him or continue fighting stronger opponents until one eventually defeated him.

"You are lucky," Unta said.

"I am horse leader," Varon said, though he suspected that Unta was right.

Unta lifted his head and nodded. *"You are horse leader. I yield... for now."*

His mind-voice held no threat, just the promise of a future challenge. Varon wondered how long it would be before he would have to face another challenger. Pautin thought Dalis would challenge him. Would Dalis be the next challenger?

It would be up to Varon to prove himself and win the respect of any potential challengers. Defeating Unta had won him a few days of peace. He would have to use them wisely.

He was horse leader of Scola's Herd. He had won the right by mind-voice and challenge. Now he would have to hold it.

13

Scola's Herd moved northward toward the Ranglan Depression for Champion Days. The speed they moved at depended on how well the grazing was along the way. Some areas had already been overgrazed and no fresh grasses had grown back because of the cold. The herd moved quickly through those areas to find better grazing further on. Where the grass was more plentiful, they took their time moving because the pregnant mares tired easily and needed more food than usual. Unfortunately, they didn't find much except for a few berries, fruits, or grains.

Varon and the other horses attended to the delivery of the foals along the way. Pautin's own time of delivery held off, though.

Calvn Scola still pushed the herd on, even when the grazing was good. They had to be at the Ranglan Depression by the end of the third moon cycle of the Season of Life.

Champion Days was more than an athletic competition that allowed the various herds of Equus to work off the tensions that arose between them in a non-destructive way. It was a memorial service. As the thousands of Equus gathered at the Ranglan Depression, ponies, who were responsible for remembering the history of the Equus, told the ancient stories of the Equus Herd Wars to the young over and over. The heroic epic of the original Calvn taming the new land of Hemlaza and uniting the Equus was a favorite among the colts. Other popular tales were the ill-fated pegasus flight to find Etrasco, the Griffin War, and Jos the pony who had created the peace the Equus now lived under and was himself mysteriously killed. And the story of the Ranglan Stone was told repeatedly as Champion Days grew closer.

It was at the Ranglan Depression that the Equus had nearly destroyed themselves. Forty-three generations ago, all the herds had come together for one massive battle of Equus against Equus. Alliances between herds shifted daily, and war fronts ranged in the double digits. Equus died in the hundreds, but the battles were so fierce that even the carrion couldn't reach them for fear of their own safety. The herds fought day and night, and entire herds vanished in death. The Equus were accomplishing for themselves what the predators had failed to accomplish. It had been the beginning of self-annihilation.

After twenty-two days of fighting, a large burning rock fell from the sky and smashed into the Hemlaza Plains. The ground shook, throwing many of the weaker Equus off their balance. Dirt and rocks filled the sky in a haze. When it settled, the Equus had stopped fighting.

"It is a sign from the creator."

"Equ has shown his displeasure with us."

"The creator has shown his might."

All of these things were said, and all were believed. So the Calvns, through the wisdom of Jos, created the pact that guided how the herds could co-exist on their island world. Two very important things came out of that pact. The first was that while individual herds ruled themselves, the species also ruled themselves, which allowed crossover in governance between the herds to hold the Equus together as one, even while living separately in herds. The second was the creation of Champion Days; a time for uniting, remembering, and deciding the future of the Equus.

To seal the pact, each Calvn left his mark and story scratched onto the walls of the Valley of the Equus. Since then, each new Calvn had also left his mark and story on the walls of the Valley of the Equus, though none but the Calvns could see the scratchings, let alone understand them. The Ranglan Stone, the remnant of the burning rock that had fallen from the sky and ended the Herd Wars, had been placed in the valley. New Calvns wore the Ranglan Stone on their horns on their day of their election as a Calvn. It allow them to commune with Equ and receive his guidance.

"What is the future of the Equus?" a small unicorn asked the pony, Corriate, who had been telling the young ones the history of the Equus this day.

"To return to Etrasco," Corriate answered.

"Will that be decided on these coming Champion Days?"

Corriate shook his head. *"We will make a step in that direction."*

"Only a step?"

Corriate nodded. *"The journey to Etrasco is not a flat path laid across the plains the Equus can run at a gallop. It is a vaguely seen path up the side of a steep mountain. We must make the journey one careful step at a time, lest we fall back and lose more ground than we have gained."*

"It must be hard being Calvn and having to make those decisions," the small unicorn said with great seriousness.

Corriate nodded. *"So they tell me, but I am only a pony."*

The gathering of the Equus at the Ranglan Depression was an awesome sight. This many Equus gathered only once a year. The size of such a great herd numbering in the thousands deterred predators, so that the Equus there were safer than usual.

It was good that Champion Days were only once a year because it took that long for the grasses in the area to grow back after such heavy grazing. Even as Scola's Herd approached the depression, Varon noticed that the grass was already growing sparse. The donkeys would forage long and hard to feed all the Equus before Champion Days were through.

The Ranglan Depression was the crater the Ranglan Stone had made when it hit the earth. However, although the Ranglan Stone was barely the size of a unicorn's hoof and could fit on the horn of a unicorn, the Ranglan Depression was at least fifty Equus wide and as deep as four Equus standing atop each other. It truly showed how angry Equ had been with the Equus and their senseless wars.

Varon liked to think he would not have taken part in the killing because he was a healer. Other horses had killed during the herd wars, though. Anger and jealousy had divided the Equus and nearly killed them all.

As was the custom for all the Equus approaching the depression, Scola's Herd filed into the crater, marking the descent of the Equus from their glories in Etrasco when they had dwelt with Equ. Then they walked out of the depression on the opposite side, marking what they hoped would be their return to Etrasco. The symbolic turning point was the point where the Ranglan had impacted the plains, which was now at the very bottom of the crater. The Equus also hoped that the impact of the Ranglan Stone was also a turning point in actuality for the Equus.

Varon was not convinced of the fact. The Equus had lived in peace since the Herd Wars, at least peace within their kind, since the Ranglan Stone had ended the wars, but were they any closer to returning to Etrasco? He wasn't sure.

What did Equ expect of them?

Once the Equus filed out of the depression, Scola led them to the outskirts of the gathering Equus and urinated at various spots in a large circle. It was a miniature version of their grazing area and honored as such by the other herds. This would be his herd's gathering place during Champion Days. Once the boundaries were marked, Scola gathered the herd around him.

"We will gather here each morning, and I will choose the champions for the day's events.

Until then, you are free to go about your species business. I will see you in the morning. Let us see that our champions excel during these days of competition. We need more mares to keep up with our stallions," Calvn Scola told them.

The Equus separated and searched out others of their species from other herds. Varon walked away with Pautin.

"Are you hungry?" he asked.

"Not at this time."

"Since I am now horse leader, I will have to be about horse business while we are here," Varon said. He expected Pautin to react angrily and decided he might as well get her arguments out of the way now. He was still in a precarious position as a new and untested

horse leader, and he wanted to make a good impression among the other horse leaders when he met with them. Having a sulky season mate would not make a good impression on the other horse leaders.

"I know," Pautin told him.

She was too calm. Varon wondered what was wrong with her.

"Are you all right?"

She nodded. *"I suppose. Last year, when Scola's Herd came to the Champion Days, I was not with a foal. I was the herd champion for the horse filly race."*

Varon could not remember much about last year's Champion Days. So much had happened between then and now. Much of it was more important to the survivability of the Equus than a few days of physical competition. Why couldn't Calvn Scola see that?

"How did you perform in your race?" Varon asked.

"I came in second. Many mares thought I would win the race this year, and yet, I can barely even move. I had hoped that the foal would have been born already." Her mind-voice held no accusation, but Varon knew he was the reason she was carrying a foal.

"I'm sure you would have won. Perhaps next year," Varon said, trying to console her.

Her head drooped. *"Perhaps."*

They found the vast herd of horses to the southwest of the Ranglan Depression. A group of mares surrounded Pautin and peppered her with questions about her pregnancy. They wanted to know the details and offer their advice to her.

"When are you due?"

"Is it a colt?"

"Who is your season mate?"

Varon left her. He doubted that she would miss him now that she was the center of attention among the mares. Varon began searching out the other horse leaders. He found twenty-five of them gathered in a cluster near the south end of the horse herd. From the harsh tones he was hearing in his head, the horse leaders did not sound happy.

"Brothers," Varon announced. *"Scola's Herd has arrived."*

"Where's Tola?" one of the horse leaders asked.

"He was killed two moons ago." Varon didn't elaborate on the circumstances. Saying that Tola had had mind-sickness would only stain his sire's reputation. All that the horse leaders needed to know was that Tola had died. *"I am horse leader now."*

"You are young," Gryn of Plu's Herd said.

"I have met my first challenge and won," Varon boasted.

"More will come."

Varon raised his head high. He didn't want to show weakness in front of his peers or they might not accept him. *"Then I will force them to yield."*

"Enough Gryn. Varon is the chosen horse leader of his herd. It was not your choice," Capsta of Conllal's Herd said.

"You all sound upset," Varon said.

"It's the unicorns again," Wasn of Ploithi's Herd told him.

Varon nodded. *"It usually is."*

"But this time they have violated the First Law of the Equus."

"A species cannot do that," Varon reminded him. As bad as unicorns could be, he did not believe that a species would risk violating the First Law. There was too much coordination, and too much danger involved. An individual might risk it, but not a species.

"But it was the unicorns' decision," Tamia insisted.

"What did they do?"

"A unicorn colt was born in my herd," Tamia of Gee's Herd said. *"It was a unicorn without a horn."*

Varon shook his head. *"How can it be a unicorn if it has no horn? It's a horse."*

"It was born of unicorn parents. That makes it a unicorn, despite what it looks like."

"If it was a unicorn, it would have a horn."

Capsta shook his head. *"This one does not."*

Varon nodded. *"Interesting."*

"Interesting? Is that all you can say?" Gryn snapped. *"Don't try to sound like Tola, Varon, you don't have the experience. This is disastrous."*

Varon fought to keep from feeling intimidated. *"Why is that?"*

"Because the unicorns feared this foal. Calvn Gee sired him, and it showed the unicorns they are not as far above a horse as they thought if a pure-bred unicorn and a descendant of Calvn could be born and appear only as a horse," Tamia explained to him.

"What did the Calvn and the unicorns do about the foal?" Varon asked.

"Calvn Gee ordered the colt to be exiled."

"Exiled? A foal! But it wouldn't last a day as an exile."

Capsta hopped back and forth between his forehooves and rear hooves. *"Exactly. They were trying to kill it, and in so doing so, the unicorns of Gee's Herd violated the First Law."* The First Law of the Equus was that Equus would not kill Equus.

"Was the colt exiled?" Varon asked.

Capsta nodded. *"Yes. A few of the horses from Gee's Herd went back after the unicorns had left the area, but I and others in my herd had already found the foal. We didn't know that he was a unicorn at the time, though. He was only an abandoned colt that needed food. Now I've adopted the colt as my own. My season mate and I will raise it."*

Varon shook his head. *"Horses raising a unicorn. The Calvn Council won't allow it."*

"They won't learn of it. If the council learned of this unicorn, they would only enforce Calvn Gee's exile and leave him to die. In my herd, only I know that the colt is truly a unicorn. Horses, at least, do not kill Equus. My season mate and I will raise the foal as our own and be happy doing it," Capsta said.

The idea chilled Varon, but what was the option? To allow the foal to be killed by predators? That was just as distasteful. Life was already dangerous enough without having Equus kill Equus. If there was one thing the Equus should have learned from the Herd Wars, it was that divided, the Equus are more dangerous to themselves than predators.

"But you still can't charge a species *with violation of the First Law. At best, you might disband the herd."*

"Then that is what we will do," Capsta said. He seemed angrier

than the other horses at the unicorns' actions.

"*But you will punish the innocent along with the guilty. Not only innocent unicorns, but the other species as well.*"

"*We will accept the punishment,*" Tamia said.

"*You speak for the horses of Gee's Herd, but what of the donkeys, zebras, ponies, and pegasuses? Do you speak for them as well?*" Varon asked.

Capsta flicked his tail in irritation as he shook his head. "*No, but something must be done. Calvn Gee cannot be allowed to believe that he is above the First Law.*"

"*Then bring the charge if you must, but you will need two-thirds of the Calvns to agree for the zebras to pass sentence. It won't happen. You will only make enemies of the council and not just Calvn Gee,*" Varon warned him.

"*But at least all the Equus will know what Gee has done. They will see the hypocrisy of the unicorns, and Gee will be that much more careful about abusing his charges again,*" Capsta said.

14

Carn walked through the thousands of Equus gathered around the Ranglan Depression. It was just a hole in the ground, but the Equus worshipped it like it was a creator. He didn't understand the Equus' fascination with this place. Why should they want to honor a meteorite? It just showed their foolishness. The Equus were an unfit species to live.

Even now, Carn could shift his shape and wreak carnage among them. He could kill hundreds of them before they would have even run off too far for him to follow.

But that wouldn't do.

No.

Not now. Even the slightest shift would allow some of these fools to detect his scent. He had to remain fully an Equus for now.

Carn had a mission… a purpose… now. He wanted to show his brothers and sisters, and even his mother, that the Equus, despite their supposed beauty, were a foolish species, even a useless one.

As he walked, Carn heard speculation through the mind-link about Lacinus' Herd. They were the only herd that hadn't arrived at the Ranglan Depression yet, and it was past the time for all the herds to be at the depression for Champion Days.

Lacinus' Herd would never appear.

One herd of forty was now destroyed because of their own foolishness. Who could be blamed for their destruction but themselves?

Oh, another alpha male would break off to form a new herd to replace Lacinus' soon enough. For every herd lost, two more sprung up to replace it, but would it be soon enough if predators killed all the herds, or would it be soon enough if new herd wars broke out among the Equus?

They are like weeds, Carn thought.

And the only way to destroy weeds was to destroy the roots. The Equus would be destroyed from within through their own faults. If Equus could be turned against Equus, they would do much more damage to each other in a quicker time than a dozen Ravagers could do. Not only would it destroy life, but it would also shake the unity of the Equus. Just look at how effective the Equus Herd Wars had been. They had nearly destroyed themselves entirely.

As he walked, Carn spoke with various Equus. It didn't matter whether they were zebras or unicorns or donkeys. He did not distinguish between castes, for outer appearances were something he could shed or change at will if the situation dictated it. What Carn sought was those Equus who were dissatisfied with the herd system.

He watched their body language, searching for aggressive stances where none was required. He listened to their conversations for anger and pettiness underlying their thoughts. These were the emotions that Carn could use to bring down the Equus.

He saw Oralum from a distance. The gray unicorn was speaking with a small group of younger unicorns. Carn studied the prideful arch in Oralum's neck, the nervous pawing of his front hooves, the almost-unnoticeable disturbance in the link of their mind-voices, and the fully erect ears.

Yes, Oralum was doing something he shouldn't be and was trying not to draw more attention to himself and his co-conspirators than was necessary.

"Are you a Calvn?" Carn asked, though he knew Oralum wasn't. A Calvn wouldn't have been so circumspect in what he was doing.

The question shocked Oralum, which is why Carn had asked it. The unicorn group immediately separated and walked away as if they were afraid of having been found out. Oralum lost the arch in his neck and turned to see who had spoken to him.

"I am Oralum of Conllal's Herd and I am of Calvn blood," the unicorn said.

Interesting. He hadn't denied that he was a Calvn, but he had tried to leave the impression that he was. Oralum was trying to place himself as high as he could in the Equus hierarchy, but he still wanted to be higher. He wanted to be a Calvn of his own herd. Ambition was an emotion that Carn could mold to his purposes.

"Well met, Oralum. I can see that you are of Calvn blood. I am surprised that you do not have your own herd," Carn said.

"In time, I will have it, zebra."

"I am Entro." Names did not matter to Carn, nor apparently to Oralum, because he chose not to use the name that Carn gave.

"When Calvn Conllal dies, I will be the unicorn that replaces him as Calvn of the herd," Oralum said.

"You sound so sure."

Oralum nodded. *"I am. I am the most able unicorn in the herd."*

"But when Calvn Conllal dies, the new Calvn can come from any herd," Carn pointed out. He had been in this form long enough to have learned the ways of the Equus.

Oralum arched his neck. *"I am still the most capable."*

"Then why not break away and form your own herd now? A powerful leader such as yourself should be able to attract enough followers to form a herd of your own."

This gave Oralum pause as he thought about it. Not that he hadn't considered the option before. A power-hungry Equus would have had to consider the advantages and disadvantages of trying to form a new herd. New herds were smaller and more open to predator attacks. No, Oralum paused because he needed to select a lie to tell Carn.

"My herd is my life. I was born into this herd, and this is the herd I want to lead when my time comes. There have been other herds that I could have become Calvn of, but I chose to wait until I could lead this herd," Oralum lied.

This was a fine opportunity for Carn. Oralum wanted to lead. He wanted to believe that he had ability, but he was afraid that he would fail. Equus were so easy to manipulate.

And if Calvn Conllal should die, what would happen then? The possibilities were intriguing. Would Oralum win the herd and become the new Calvn?

"You truly have vision and dedication, Calvn Oralum." Carn paused. *"I guess that I shouldn't call you that yet, should I?"*

The proud arch in his neck and flared nostrils had returned to Oralum when Carn had called him Calvn. Oralum might not be the leader he considered himself, but he would make an excellent follower as long as his ego was inflated. Carn could do that easily enough.

"Oralum, I want to be a part of your herd," Carn said, as if the idea had just occurred to him.

"But I don't have a herd yet."

"You will, though, and I want to be a part of that herd. If it means I must join Conllal's Herd until it becomes your herd, then so be it."

Oralum nodded. *"You are wise and farsighted, Entro. If it was in my power to choose my herd leaders, I would choose you as the zebra leader."*

Carn lowered his head and imitated grazing. *"I am honored that you think so highly of me."*

"I do. Hopefully, Bronelin, the current zebra leader will think so, too. Let us go find him, and I will speak for you and the honor you will bring to the herd."

Carn walked dutifully behind Oralum. As they walked, Carn was delighted that this would be so easy. All he had to do was create an itch and the Equus would scratch it. And if they scratched themselves hard enough and in enough places, they would tear themselves apart.

Instead of using Creator Moss, this time, Carn would work through another Equus to accomplish his goals. Besides, if he continued using the same technique of destruction, it would lead to suspicion. Weren't the Equus always on the alert for Ravagers because they attacked always in the same manner?

This way was better. Carn was a creator. What he was doing now was no different to him than creating life. He was destroying; finding the keystones that, when removed, would collapse everything. Here, the keystone was Oralum's ambition. Ambition was a good trait, but it needed to be tempered with wisdom.

And there wasn't enough of that among the Equus, as Equ would soon find out.

15

The thirty-nine Calvns present—one from each of the Equus herds—spent the first day of Champion Days greeting each other and examining the various Equus among the different herds. Based on how well their herd champions did in the competitions, they could attract mares to bring fresh blood into their own herds. New stallions weren't as desired because of the competition they could create for the leadership roles in the herd, including the Calvn.

Scola enjoyed these meetings with his peers. Though he wasn't senior Calvn, he still garnered respect from the lower species. He enjoyed speaking with the other Calvns and sharing his wisdom with them, for they among all the Equus understood him.

"I tell you, the white mountains are connected to this extended Seeking Season," Calvn Plu was telling Calvn Gee.

"How can that be? Since when do mountains affect the weather?" Gee replied.

"These aren't true mountains, though," Calvn Scola said.

"What?" Plu said.

"What are you talking about, Scola?" Gee asked.

Scola appreciated the advantage he had of knowing something that the others did not. He was the center of attention now. Even Calvn Mika has stopped talking and was watching to see what Scola had to say.

"The white mountains are an ice wall," Scola said.

"Ice wall?" Calvn Gee shook his head. *"You're crazy, Scola."*

Scola remained calm and shook his head. The insult didn't disturb him because he knew that he had the answers.

"I know what I'm saying. Have any of you sent a band to investi-

gate the white mountains? I did. I sent a band representing all the species, and what they returned to tell me was the white mountains are made of ice," Scola said.

"But that's impossible!" Calvn Plu said.

"And if there is that much ice to the north, it is no wonder that the cold still holds this land in its grip," Scola added.

Calvn Mika stepped forward. *"This is something we will have to discuss in council. Now, we have the competition to begin. You did well to investigate the white mountains, Scola. It is better for us to act on knowledge than ignorance."*

Scola bowed his head. *"I've always thought so."*

Near midday, all the Calvns ringed the edge of the Ranglan Depression. From there, they called their herds to gather. The heat of so many bodies close together took the chill from the air and caused many to forget about the ever-present white mountains.

"Thus, we begin Champion Days," Calvn Mika, the senior unicorn, said. *"Do well, and do your best. The first event will be jousting among the unicorns. All champions to their Calvns."*

Beside him, Scola nodded and tried to look as regal as he thought Mika did. He planned on living long enough to be the senior Calvn of all the Equus someday.

By tradition, the eldest Calvn was the speaker for all the Calvns at Champion Days, supposedly because he was the closest one by blood to the original Calvn.

The Calvns made their choices for their herd champions for the jousting, calling them forth from their herds to stand in front of their Calvns. Scola chose Lascinon, a three-year-old gray unicorn with a very long white horn. The extra-long horn would give him an advantage where his skill might fail. Scola made a grand gesture of touching the tip of his horn to the tip of Lascinon's horn, as if to grant him part of his power.

"Do not fail me, Lascinon," Scola said.

"Never, my Calvn."

The rules of the contest were simple. As this was a contest of speed and agility, the object of the contest was to draw blood along the necks of the other unicorns using only a unicorn's horn. Drawing blood anywhere other than the neck did not count. Kicking was not allowed, nor was gouging. When a unicorn had his blood let, he was disqualified and sent outside of the contest area.

Calvn Mika explained the rules to the thirty-nine unicorns competing as herd champions. The large herds of Equus circling the champions to watch the competition would serve as the boundaries of the competition.

The champions touched their horns to the ground to acknowledge they understood and accepted the rules of the competition.

Then Calvn Mika said, *"Then show us, herd champions, who the unicorn champion of the Equus is."*

There was an immediate flurry of activity as the unicorns flung their heads around to strike first at the nearest champion to them. First strikes eliminated about a third of the unicorns from the competition right off. Those defeated moved off to have their wounds treated by the horses, who stood ready with moss.

After this first initial rush, the unicorns spread out enough to watch each other. Some unicorns formed temporary alliances so they could team up to draw blood from another champion. Vole, a daring young unicorn, escaped one of these traps by vaulting over the back of one unicorn charging him. He looked almost like a pegasus. His actions brought neighs of approval from the herds.

When about half of the champions had been dispatched, a loud shriek brought all action to a halt. Ricie, a white unicorn, lay on the ground. His side heaved in ragged breaths as blood pumped from the round hole in his neck. Tayven, Calvn Hol's champion, stood nearby, his white horn glistening with blood on nearly all the shaft.

Horses rushed from the crowd and surrounded Ricie. One of them tried plugging the hole with moss, but the blood seeped out around it.

Another horse pulled the moss away and held the sides of the wound closed with his teeth.

"Thorns! We need thorns to seal the wound first!" the horse called through the mind-link.

Three horses ran off looking for thorns. The horses used the hooked thorns of the tackleburr bush to hold flesh together on deeper wounds until they healed on their own.

Scola stood quietly, mimicking Calvn Mika's stoic approach to the disruption of the unicorn competition.

Ricie squealed and kicked his hind legs. It was a weak kick, which was a grave sign. Even from his position to the side of the competition, Scola could see that the wound was mortal. It didn't take a horse to see that.

"*Calvn Sarov*," the horse working on the wound called through the mind-link.

"*Yes.*"

"*Ricie will die, I think. The wound is deep, and I can feel the pulse weakening.*"

The other horses brought back branches of thorns. As they prepared to seal the wound, Ricie gave a weak whinny and died.

Calvn Sarov walked from the Calvn ring to where the dead unicorn lay. He touched his nose to the dead unicorn's nose and then raised his head. The horses backed away and went into the Equus herd to wait and see what would happen.

Calvn Sarov stared at the unicorn for a few moments and then said, "*I charge Tayven of Hol's Herd with violating the First Law of the Equus!*"

Tayven reared up on his rear legs and kicked his hooves. "*It was not intentional. He turned into me. I did not mean to kill him!*"

Calvn Mika walked out to Tayven. "*You have no say, Tayven. The matter has been placed before the Calvn Council because a unicorn of a different herd committed the offense.*" Calvn Mika turned to Calvn Sarov and said, "*Choose the unicorns you wish to guard, Tayven, until we reach a decision of guilt or innocence.*"

Calvn Sarov called out three unicorns' names, who circled Tayven and led him away from the competition field. They would guard him until the Calvn Council decided what punishment Tayven would face.

Once Tayven left, Calvn Mika said, "*Resume the competition.*"

The champions did not question the command. To hesitate was to be eliminated. They charged. They parried. They drew blood. However, they were more careful about their thrusts now. None wanted to face what Tayven would face for violating the First Law.

Lascinon was one of the last seven unicorns in the competition. He was grazed on the neck as he tried to dodge around Ricie's body and was eliminated. The eventual winner of the competition was a white unicorn named Dig of Lapp's Herd.

He took his victory lap around the edge of the competition area, but Ricie's body laying on the field muted his victory. When Dig had finished, the champions galloped off to celebrate together as unicorns.

The zebras from all the Equus herds carried mouthfuls of grass and dropped them on Ricie's body. From nearby, the Calvns watched, as did some other Equus. The grass covering over the body showed that Ricie would return to the land and nourish it as it had nourished him. The grass would also feed him on his return to Etrasco.

Scola wondered how he should judge Tayven. Violating the First Law was a serious charge. He would have to follow Mika's lead. That brought Scola peace of mind.

16

When the sky turned a deep red with the coming night, Calvn Scola called his herd to gather near the Ranglan Depression along with all the other Equus herds. Many of the unicorns staggered to the meeting. The first day of Champion Days was their day, and many of them celebrated by chewing on fermented berries saved for this celebration. The berries caused any Equus eating them to feel a sense of euphoria, but in actuality, the unicorns staggered around and made fools of them. Usually showing such weakness was not allowed, but because the gathering of Equus was so large and the threat of predators minimal, the unicorns did not have to stay in a general state of readiness.

When most of the Equus had gathered, Calvn Mika stepped forward upon a pile of dirt that elevated him above the heads of even the tallest Equus so he could be seen by all.

"We use this time to celebrate our history and resolve our differences," Calvn Mika announced to the Equus. *"This has always been a time when all Equus have met together. This year, Calvn Lacinus' Herd has not shown up. We fear the worst for them because only the worst would keep them from breaking tradition. To know for sure, I will dispatch eight of my pegasuses to search for Calvn Lacinus' Herd."*

Scola knew Calvn Mika feared that Ravagers had destroyed Lacinus' Herd. No predators had ever destroyed a herd so that there were no survivors to tell the story of the destruction, but no herd had ever missed Champion Days before either.

"As for the more recent matter of Ricie, the Calvn Council has reached a decision about Tayven of Calvn Hol's Herd. He is to be

exiled and declared a renegade for violating the First Law," Calvn Mika said.

"No! It was an accident!" Tayven tried to shout over Calvn Mika's thoughts.

"The council and witnesses saw it otherwise. You were overly aggressive in the competition and deliberately killed Ricie. Feast well tonight, Tayven. In the morning, you will be sent from the Equus to endure life alone. May you return swiftly to Equ."

Scola was surprised at the decision, although he had risen to support the exile. The Calvn Council rarely took action against unicorns, especially such harsh action. However, Mika thought Tayven's exile was warranted and so Scola had supported the decision. It must have been because many at the competition saw Tayven's actions as forcing the council into action. Scola did not question the wisdom of Calvn Mika.

"Celebrate tonight, champions of the Equus. In the morning, the pegasus champions will compete," Calvn Mika said.

Capsta, horse leader of Gee's Herd, called out, *"I am glad to see that the Calvn Council does not fear punishing its own species."*

Calvn Mika arched his neck and flicked his tail back and forth. *"Was there a doubt?"*

Capsta arched his neck just as proudly. *"There was, but knowing justice is obtainable from the council, Capsta of Gee's Herd has charges for the council to consider."*

The Calvns stopped moving away from the edge of the depression. *"What charges?"*

Capsta reared up on his hind legs so that the Calvns could see him.

"I charge the unicorns of Gee's Herd with violating the First Law of the Equus."

"Absurd!" Calvn Gee called out from the group of Calvns.

"Two weeks ago, a pure-bred unicorn was born, sired by Gee. However, because the unicorn was born without a horn, it was exiled and left to die."

Angry murmurs sounded throughout the gathering as the different Equus jumped into the argument. Some wanted an immediate exile of Gee. Others denied a unicorn could be born without a horn.

"That is a lie! I sired no such creature! My foal was stillborn," Gee insisted.

Gee glared at Capsta, but the stallion didn't back away from his claim. Calvn Mika didn't look very happy, either. He lowered his head and shook it. Scola watched him, uncertain of how he should react to this disturbing news.

"Capsta, you have leveled an extreme charge against an entire species within a herd. By your charge, you claim that all unicorns of Gee's Herd took part in this… this exile of a foal," Mika said.

Capsta nodded. *"I know, Calvn, but justice must be served as it was served with Tayven. The unicorns, particularly Gee, ordered this exile for no other reason than the foal was an embarrassment to him and his species."*

"Justice will be served, but the Calvn Council must consider the charge and the evidence before we decide on how it will be served."

Capsta bowed his head. *"I understand."*

When the Equus had dispersed and separated into their species groups, the Calvns gathered in a tight circle at the bottom of the Ranglan Depression. They could counsel among themselves there with no other Equus being able to come close enough to hear their conversations through the mind-link without being seen.

"You can't exile all the unicorns in my herd," Gee said. *"It's absurd. The herd would be destroyed without leadership."*

Calvn Mika nodded. *"No, we can't. A Calvn must lead all the herds. If the unicorns were exiled from your herd, it would have to be dispersed. The question that interests me is: Are the charges true?"*

Gee hesitated, looking away from Calvn Mika and pawing at the ground. *"Yes. Kri delivered her foal. It wasn't stillborn, but it was not a unicorn colt."*

A soft murmur rippled among the Calvns, but not loud enough to be heard outside their immediate group.

"Are you sure it was your foal?" Mika continued.

"Yes, Kri chose me for a season mate," Gee replied.

"But she birthed a horse."

"Are you suggesting a horse sired the colt?"

Mika's ears twitched in opposite directions. *"It has happened before."*

"Kri hates horses. The colt was mine, unfortunately."

"It must have been defective."

"That's an understatement," Gee said.

Mika glared at him.

"Did it show other defective signs other than lacking a horn?" Mika asked.

Calvn Gee shook his head. *"No, it was healthy otherwise."*

"And you exiled it."

"What else could I do? Let the monster live and show to all that a unicorn could be born without a horn? He appeared to be a horse. A horse cannot be allowed to be a part of the Calvn line. What if he one day claimed the right to be a Calvn? Would the Equus allow a horse to lead a herd? A Calvn's foals are unicorns in blood and appearance."

Calvn Mika nodded. *"I agree, but if we do not take action, the other species will be angry. They will claim the council does not offer justice, and if that result became a widespread belief it could be almost as bad as a hornless unicorn."* Calvn Mika paused. *"Let me consider the problem tonight. We will talk about this again in the morning before we exile Tayven."* Calvn Mika paused. *"Is there anything else?"*

Scola took a deep breath, stepped forward, and said, *"The white mountains."*

Calvn Mika stared at him. He was not used to hearing Scola's mind-voice. *"What about them?"*

Mika blew out through his mouth so his lips flapped. It was a sign of exasperation.

"I sent a small band to investigate them. They said the mountains are moving."

Calvn Mika's eyes widened. *"Are you sure?"*

"I sent three unicorns with the band. They all said there were tree roots and other debris sticking out from the side of the mountains."

"Where does the ice come from?"

"The members of the band weren't sure, but it seems the mountains stretch back across the Horizon Sea," Scola explained. He wished that he could say more. He hated leaving Calvn Mika's questions unanswered. It was more fun to have the information and be waiting to share it than to have to explain to Calvn Mika why he didn't have the needed information.

"But the seas are not frozen," Calvn Mika said.

Calvn Scola lowered his head. *"I don't claim to explain it. That is why we need to consider what to do concerning them. The sight of them makes the Equus nervous,"* he admitted.

Calvn Mika turned to the group. *"Any suggestions?"*

"We can move further south so they will be out of our sight," Calvn Teon suggested.

"That is only ignoring them. However, if they continue to move south, we will come to the South Sea. Then where will be go? All of our food will be buried beneath the white mountains, and we will stand at the edge of our deaths," Calvn Conllal, a piebald unicorn, explained.

"What would you do?"

"Prepare. Prepare now while we can. Find out what is behind the white mountains. Find other sources of grazing beyond them."

"There is nothing beyond them," Calvn Scola said.

Conllal flicked his tail. *"They must end somewhere. Where is it? Is it a place where we can survive? If we cannot survive in front of the white mountains, then we must survive upon them or beyond them."*

"Equ would not let us perish," Calvn Mika argued.

"Who is to say this is not Equ's plan?"

"The council must be united in their position about the white mountains. Do we hold and ignore them, move south, or move beyond them? These are our options."

As he spoke, Calvn Mika pointed his nose toward a different area of the depression for each option. Once he had finished speaking, the Calvns moved toward the area that matched their choice. Eight Calvns chose to move beyond the white mountains; eleven chose to move south and eighteen chose to remain where they were.

Calvn Mika made the counts and said, *"The choice is made. The Equ will remain in the central plains and trust in the love of Equ."*

In the morning, the Calvns gathered their herds at the Ranglan Depression before the pegasus competition began. The Equus were anxious to hear what the Calvn Council had decided about Calvn Gee and the astounding charges against him.

Calvn Mika said, *"We have reached a decision on Capsta's charge against the unicorns of Calvn Gee's Herd. Calvn Gee and Capsta, come forward and accept the judgment of the Calvn Council."*

The unicorn and stallion walked from their positions in the gathering to stand in front of Calvn Mika.

"The Calvns have found for Capsta in his charge against the unicorns. As such, the council's judgment is that Gee's Herd may not compete for the rest of Champion Days nor will Equus be allowed to leave or enter the herd as new members."

"That is no punishment!" Capsta shouted through the mind-link.

"It is the decision of the Calvn Council, and it is final."

"It punishes all Equus in the herd but the unicorns. They have had their day to compete and make their exchanges."

Calvn Mika bobbed his head in indifference. *"Is it my fault you waited until after the unicorn competition to place your charge before the council? The decision has been rendered. Do you seek to declare yourself and any who would follow you renegades who will not follow the council's judgment?"*

Capsta looked around himself, trying to gauge his support.

"I do not seek to be a renegade. I only seek justice," Capsta said, his head drooping.

"And you have it." Calvn Mika paused. *"Another matter has come to the attention of the Calvn Council. That of the white mountains."*

The angry murmurs from the previous decision died down, and Scola pricked his ears forward to show his interest in how Calvn Mika phrased his decision.

"The Equus will continue as they always have. The mountains are not predators, and we have no reason to fear them. Were we not surrounded by mountains in Etrasco? And were we not safe there? This is only a test from Equ to prepare us to return to Etrasco. This is the decision of the council," Calvn Mika said.

Many of the Equus flicked their tails in displeasure, particularly the horses. Scola could almost see fault lines developing among species and herds, but he ignored them. The Equus had thrived because of their unity of purpose, but how much longer would that last?

Sooner or later, they would have to learn to accept the wisdom of the Calvn Council.

17

Jalon landed in the middle of the ring of pegasuses. These thirty-nine pegasuses were the herd leaders of the Equus herds. For issues dealing with the pegasus, they held even more power than the Calvns. Jalon faced Chinarvo, her own herd leader and bowed her head to the ground to imitate eating grass.

"I have come as I was summoned, pegasus leader," Jalon said.

"Very good, Jalon," Chinarvo told her. *"My fellow pegasuses would like to hear the story of your encounter with the griffins."*

Jalon stared at their faces and saw doubt in many of them. They had believed for all their lives that the pegasuses had destroyed all the griffins during the Griffin War. Could Jalon fault them for their doubt in what she had to say? She had believed the same thing.

Jalon told them her story of her sighting and near escape from the griffins. She didn't tell her story so much with direct thoughts through the mind-link, though. She relaxed her body and opened her memories to them so that the pegasus leaders could see for themselves through her own eyes how she had identified the griffins and then her desperate flight and gallop to escape them. Even knowing she was only recalling memories, she still felt the same fear of the griffins and desperation at trying to survive.

"Griffins haven't been seen in a dozen generations," Xanel of Sarcophi's Herd said.

"But that was what I saw, wasn't it?" Jalon asked.

"No one alive has seen a griffin, but your memories match the description that the ponies have passed down," Xanel said as he nodded.

"Where have they been for twelve generations?" Chinarvo asked

his peers.

"Perhaps they are not the same drift of griffins we knew. Jalon saw these griffins come from the north. Maybe these griffins came from wherever the white mountains begin," Plutonis of Mika's Herd suggested.

Jalon shook her head. *"I don't think so, unless griffins can go longer without food and water than the pegasus. The white mountains are a wasteland offering no sustenance to any creature."*

"But if they didn't come from across the white mountains," Kyli of Friez's Herd said, *"then that means they weren't all killed in the Griffin War."*

"So it would seem," Chinarvo said as he nodded.

"Then where have they been for the past twelve generations that we haven't seen them? That's a long time to stay hidden."

Chinarvo pawed at the dirt as he flicked his ears back and forth. *"They have been rebuilding their drift. They must have been rebuilding their aviaries in the Meshacks or in the western forests. If they had been anywhere else, we would have noticed them before now,"* Chinarvo surmised.

Jalon shivered at the realization. The griffins had always been with them, even when the pegasuses had thought themselves safe. For the griffins to show themselves now would mean that they felt confident in the strength and size of their drift. How many griffins would give them that confidence? One hundred? Five hundred? It would be enough that they wouldn't worry about their existence being known to the pegasuses.

"We need current information about them to know how to react against them," Xanel said. *"We may be entering the second Griffin War, and I want to survive it. It was close before. If the pegasuses had not united, we might not have survived, and then all the Equus would have eventually fallen."*

"We have to find their aviaries and count the eggs as well as the actual griffins. All the eggs would have to be destroyed. If even one male and one female were missed and hatched, we could be facing this same problem in twelve more generations. The griffins must be

totally destroyed this time if we wish to maintain the balance of life on Hemlaza," Kyli added.

"How can we find them this time if we haven't even seen a sign of their presence before now, and only by accident?" Chinarvo asked.

"We haven't been looking for them," Jalon said. *"If we search for them, we can find them. We already know that they are in the mountains or the forests."*

The pegasus leaders turned to stare at her. *"Will you be the one who looks, Jalon?"* Xanel asked her.

The offer was before her. As the only living Equus to have seen a griffin, she was the only one who knew what to expect from them. And how much knowledge was that? She had been too intent on getting away from them to study them. But then, who better than her?

She nodded her head. *"I will go."*

"What will you need?" Chinarvo asked.

"Five strong flyers to accompany me and a lot of luck."

"The flyers we can provide," Xanel said. *"Choose the five pegasuses you wish from any herd. The pegasuses will unite in this effort so that we might again triumph over the griffins. As for the luck, you will have to make that for yourself."*

Jalon sighed and considered who she would want at her side if she found the griffins. They would have to be fast flyers. They would also have to be strong enough to fight, and fight well, if it came to that.

"Your mission, Jalon, is to find the aviaries and count the griffins. Report these things back to us and we will take action before the season's eggs hatch."

Jalon bowed her head. *"I will leave by dusk."*

18

Carn spent the first day of these so-called Champion Days ingratiating himself with Oralum, the unicorn; Bronelin, Conllal's Herd's zebra leader; and Calvn Conllal. He would need all of their support if he were to join their herd. Ingratiating himself was hard to do. In fact, he hadn't done it since the decades he had spent convincing his mother to allow her children the right to create and populate this world with their creatures. So he might be a little out of practice, but the Equus wouldn't be as hard to convince as his mother had been.

Speaking with Conllal only showed Carn more of Oralum's foolishness. Oralum might want to take over Conllal's Herd when the Calvn died, but Conllal was only eight years old. By the time Conllal died, Oralum would be too old to lead a herd, and besides, Carn would not wait years to destroy this herd. He still had the destruction of the thirty-eight other herds to plan. The problem, as Carn saw it, was that Conllal still had many years left to lead unless something drastic happened, and Carn was something drastic.

Oralum sought out Carn in the evening. The gray unicorn considered Entro the zebra his most devoted supporter. As Carn watched the unicorn approach, he saw half a dozen pegasuses fly off into the night. Where were they going? No patrols were flying because a herd this large didn't worry about predators. So why would a small band fly off like that?

"What is that?" Carn asked.

"The pegasuses have launched a scouting patrol to find the griffins," Oralum said as he stared in the direction Carn had nodded.

"I thought the griffins were dead."

The pegasuses had killed them all over a century ago. It had angered Carn'd sister, Sarton, to the point where she nearly took on the Equus all herself. Carn and another sister, Jaccon, convinced Sarton otherwise. "There are better ways to extract your revenge," Jaccon had told her. Carn was beginning his plan now, but perhaps Sarton had come up with her own plan of revenge. He wouldn't begrudge her a few of the herds, but Carn still wanted the majority.

"One of the pegasuses says she ran into some griffins the other day while going to explore the white mountains. I don't believe her, but she convinced the pegasus herd leaders. Now they want her to find them," Oralum explained.

"You can't find something that isn't there," Carn replied.

Oralum nodded vigorously. *"Exactly."* He paused. *"What did you think of your new Calvn?"*

"He is adequate as a leader and wise." Conllal seemed better than adequate, but Oralum didn't want to hear the truth. He wanted to hear someone support his own opinion of the Calvn, which was that Conllal wasn't the leader Oralum considered himself. While that was true, Oralum wasn't the leader he considered himself.

Oralum's tail flicked. *"Wise?"*

"An adequate leader would not be able to hold a herd together, but a wise unicorn would listen to ideas from better leaders, such as yourself, and incorporate their ideas as his own," Carn said.

Oralum nodded. *"Yes, yes. That is what he does. I have spoken many ideas to the Calvn, and I have heard those ideas presented as his own."*

Carn tried not to snort. Calvn Conllal might not be a perfect leader, but he was strong enough to hold a herd on his own without relying on any Equus as petty and jealous as Oralum. Carn wondered if Conllal even spoke to Oralum, except when he had no choice.

"Then I would say that the mantle of leadership will pass to you. For if I can see your strengths after such a brief time as part of the herd, then certainly those who have been in your herd much longer see your strong qualities also," Carn said.

"You would think so, wouldn't you? There are others like you who will follow me when I lead," Oralum boasted.

"Enough to form a herd of your own?"

Oralum shook his head. *"No, not enough for that."* He looked around. *"We need to be circumspect when we talk. Otherwise, Calvn Conllal could exile us from his herd if he were to learn of my ambitions."*

Carn nodded. *"A wise decision."* A coward's choice.

Carn waited all day, hoping to catch Calvn Conllal alone. The black unicorn spent most of his time with the Calvn Council. Carn had considered shape shifting into a swarm of bees and destroying all the Calvns while they were in the Ranglan Depression. He imagined that might restart the Herd Wars between the Equus, but then, it also might unite the herds against a Ravager.

Restarting the Herd Wars was a desirable goal. The Equus had nearly annihilated themselves then. It had been a lovely time. Carn had tried to help it along as much as he could.

It would take planning over a brute force attack to start the Equus on that productive road once again, though. No, Carn had to be cleverer than the Equus, which shouldn't be too hard. He also had to be cleverer than Equ, which would be more difficult.

Carn caught Calvn Conllal by himself when the Council broke up to rejoin their herds for the evening. Carn followed the unicorn at a discreet distance, trying to make sure that no one else was watching the Calvn to meet with him.

As Carn watched his surroundings, he detached some hairs from his mane and tail and let them fall to the ground. He commanded the detached parts of himself to form a brown viper that blended well with the ground and shadows. He sent the viper after Calvn Conllal.

A few moments later, Calvn Conllal reared up, screaming. *"A snake! A snake bit me!"*

Since Carn was closest to the unicorn, he rushed over to him. He tried to look like he was helping Conllal, but he was actually reabsorbing the viper into his own body. It wrapped itself around his ankles. First, it changed from its brown color to white and black to match Carn's coloring. Then it sank into Carn's hoof until it had vanished.

Carn called out, *"A horse! We need a horse over here!"*

While he pretended concern, he knew that the Calvn was already dead. Carn had made the viper's venom potent.

Three horses rushed over to Calvn Conllal and examined him.

"He's dead. Calvn Conllal is dead," one horse pronounced.

"What species of snake bit him? Did you see the snake?" a second horse asked Carn.

The zebra shook his head. *"I was the closest to him, and I saw nothing."*

"Calvn Mika, Calvn Conllal is dead," the first horse called.

"Then we must select a new Calvn for his herd while the moons show the path to the Ranglan Stone," came back the reply from the senior Calvn.

Oralum came galloping over to the dead unicorn. *"My Calvn! I cannot believe that he is dead. The horses can help him."*

The horses shook their heads. *"Not unless you have a way to bring the dead back to life,"* one of them said.

Oralum snorted. *"Well then, find the snake that killed him and destroy it before it kills another Equus."*

The horses sent out orders through the mind-link to watch out for any snakes on the ground and to kill the ones they could.

Carn almost whinnied. The Equus were very amusing sometimes.

"Since my herd is without a Calvn, I will act as the interim Calvn until a new Calvn can return with the Ranglan Stone. I, also, will take part in the search for the stone," Oralum said.

"I accept you as interim Calvn until the Calvn Council chooses a new Calvn," Calvn Mika said.

So did Carn. Conllal's Herd, now Oralum's Herd, was halfway to its destruction.

<h1 style="text-align:center">19</h1>

"Varon, I'm hungry," Pautin called to Varon.

Pautin always seemed to know when Varon least wanted her to interrupt him, and that was the time she chose to call for him.

Varon didn't turn his attention from the aerial acrobatics of the competing pegasuses on the second day of Champion Days. The pegasus herd leaders judged their contests on their complexity and beauty. Jalon was not competing. Although she was good enough to be herd champion, she had left the Ranglan Depression last night with five other pegasuses.

Pegasus competitions had always fascinated Varon. He could watch them for days. He enjoyed seeing them trick gravity into allowing them to twist, turn, and leap without plunging to the ground. At least he would have enjoyed watching if Pautin wasn't hungry.

"We're in the middle of a gathering. I just brought you enough grass to feed two mares a short time ago," he told her. In fact, he had spent the entire morning foraging just for her, hoping she wouldn't interrupt him during the competition. So much for that hope.

"So? I'm feeding both myself and your foal. Your foal! And I'm hungry now."

"Can't you wait until after the pegasus competition?"

"No! I am hungry now. You can see pegasuses fly anytime."

"Why don't you go where the donkeys have stored our herd's pile of grass?"

Varon wanted to watch the pegasus competition. It was his favorite competition of Champion Days, but with Pautin so close, her voice boomed in his head.

"I don't want grass donkeys have already chewed."

"They don't chew it, Pautin." She knew that. She just wanted to be difficult. He would not win this argument. Pautin was in one of her moods. *"What do you want me to do?"*

"Find some fresh grass and bring it to me."

Now Varon turned to stare at her, wondering if she was doing this just to anger him. Pautin stared back at him, silently daring him to challenge her right as his season mate. It was his duty as her season mate to care for her needs while she carried his foal.

"Fresh grass?" The nearest fresh grass might be half a day or more from here. She couldn't be that hungry if she could wait that long. The donkeys were spending most of their time foraging for the rest of the Equus. *"Aren't you worried about eating grass that I have already chewed on?"* he asked.

She looked at him as if she thought he had mind-sickness. *"Of course not. You're a horse."*

Varon blew out a sharp breath through his mouth, letting his lips flap. Pautin was letting her species bias show.

"I will find you some grass," he said, but with no tenderness.

Pautin tossed her head back. *"No, not grass. I've changed my mind. I need something moister. I have heard that there is edible moss in the river. I want some of that."*

Varon remembered the Creator Moss and what it had done to Lacinus' Herd. He did not want to see Pautin staggering around and falling down. He hoped that there was no Creator Moss nearby.

"Who told you this?" Varon asked.

"Some other mares who have tasted it. They said it is delicious and helps to settle the stomach," Pautin told him.

"Is that all it does?"

"I suppose. What else might it do?"

Varon shook his head. *"Never mind. I'll try to find you some moss."*

He walked away from the gathering so she could continue to watch the aerial acrobatics.

As Varon walked to the edge of the gathering, he saw many of the donkeys coming in from their latest foraging outing.

"How goes the hunt for food?" he called to one donkey.

"Not well. The cool temperatures have kept the grasses hidden even where the Equus have not eaten it down to the root."

The chill in the air might keep flies and mosquitoes away, but it also kept fresh grass and grains away.

"Will there be enough to last for all the Champion Days?"

The donkey bobbed her head up and down. *"We will find it somehow. We always do, though it wouldn't surprise me if we will be taking day-long journeys to find grass by the end of Champion Days."*

"Luck to you, sister."

The donkey's ear leaned forward at the use of the word "sister." Donkeys were rarely called brother or sister by any except of their own kind. Varon called all Equus brother or sister because that is how he imagined they had addressed each other in Etrasco. He didn't know where he had come by that idea, but it helped keep Etrasco foremost in his mind.

Varon found the stream that ran near the Ranglan Depression. During the herd wars, it had run red with blood. Now it was clear and freezing. He walked along the bank looking for moss-covered rocks. When he found them, he stopped. He couldn't tell if the blue-green moss he was looking at was Creator Moss or not. There was only one way to tell. He was reluctant to try it because he didn't want to become like the Equus of Lacinus' Herd. The pegasuses would probably find them lying on the ground and rolling around, having forgotten all about Champion Days. However, better that Varon should eat the moss and suffer the effects than Pautin. Who knew how the moss would affect the foal she carried in her?

Varon struck at the rock with his hoof until a piece of the moss pulled away. He bent down and sniffed it. It didn't smell any different from other moss he had eaten.

He took a small bite, chewed it up, and swallowed. It was moist, but he didn't find the taste appealing. It might be just what Pautin's altered tastes desired, though. Nothing bad seemed to be happening to him after eating the moss.

He pulled up more of the moss from the rock until he was holding a long strip in his mouth. Pautin would probably want it moist, which meant he would make multiple trips back here to get moss for her. Hopefully, this phase of her appetite would pass.

As he lowered his head to moisten the moss in the water, movement across the river caught his eye. Varon held his head still and studied the landscape across the river. This time, when he saw movement, he could pinpoint it to one of the few scrub trees on the plains.

He looked through the branches and saw a creature. For a moment, Varon wondered if it was a Ravager. However, Ravagers chose familiar forms so that their prey wouldn't bolt at the sight of them. This creature was unusual.

From its neck to its hooves—no, not hooves, but paws like a monkey—it had skin like a bear, but the black hair of its body was of a different color than that on its head.

Varon watched the creature crawl further up into the tree. It seemed to be able to grip with its forepaws, but its rear paws were covered, or maybe they were hooves. Varon wasn't sure which. Though the creature had no toes, its foot seemed suppler than a hoof.

However, when the creature climbed higher, Varon saw a gap in its fur. Its fur wasn't natural. It was wearing the skin of a bear.

Amazing!

The creature didn't look big enough or strong enough to defeat a bear, and yet a bear would not give up his skin without a fight.

What was this weird, unfamiliar creature of the creators who could climb trees and slay bears?

Was it a predator bold enough to challenge a gathering of all the Equus? It was foolishness for any of the predators Varon knew of, but was it foolish for this new creature? Did it have the strength and ability to match any predator with which the Equus were familiar?

Varon looked around for more of the weird creatures. Surely this one was not the only one of its kind? Now that predators were gathering in greater numbers, even they could overcome this bear slayer.

Being alone was foolish; it was death.

Varon didn't see any other creatures, though.

He wondered if he should call out a warning to the other Equus. For one weird creature? He decided not to. He would tell the other horse leaders about it, and they could watch out for the creature themselves. If it proved to be a harmless new creature, they wouldn't do anything more about it. Only if it showed itself to be a predator of the Equus would they tell the Calvns.

Varon turned away from the stream with the moss in his mouth. As he walked back across the field, his legs shook. Varon stopped moving forward and stiffened his legs. That didn't help. The muscles in his legs twitched and threatened to topple him.

What was wrong?

Had he suddenly taken ill?

He was about to call for a horse to administer to him when his sight changed. He was no longer walking across the field near the Ranglan Depression. He was flying, soaring above Hemlaza.

Flying?

He turned to see how he could move through the air like a pegasus. He could see no wings on his back and his legs were still locked in their straight position. How could he be moving?

Then he stopped worrying about how he was moving and instead concentrated on what was happening beneath him. A mass of creatures moved below him. As he flew closer, he saw predators slaughtering the Equus. The Equus were gathered in a large, defensive circle on the white mountains. The young were in the very center, then the mares, and finally the stallions.

Every type of predator imagined—griffins, wolves, bears, lions, tigers, and more–surrounded them. They were all there and all attacking; only stopping when they could pull a kill away to feast on it. The predators moved among each other, some of them ignoring their own natural enemies. They were intent only on destroying and devouring the Equus. They were hunger maddened.

Varon watched in horror as the sheer number of desperate predators overwhelmed the Equus and ripped them apart. Their blood turned the surface of the white mountains red.

"This shall be," a voice said in Varon's head. He didn't recognize the feminine voice, but he didn't know how he could be shown the future either.

The scene shifted. The predators vanished, and now Varon saw the Equus in new positions. They were still together as a single group that stretched so far it would be a day's travel from end to end. Pegasuses and donkeys came to the main herd to deposit foraged food, which some Equus stopped to eat. They walked along the top of the white mountains, away from Hemlaza. Pegasus scouts flew ahead of the Equus herd. Varon did not understand where they were going. He only realized that they were alive. Predators hadn't decimated them.

"This shall be," the strange voice said.

How could two contradictory futures exist?

"You shall decide."

The scene changed again, and Varon was standing alone in the field near the river again. He'd seen an illusion. Both scenes had been an illusion. He hadn't flown. He hadn't seen the future.

He turned around and looked for the strange bipedal creature that he had seen in the tree. He couldn't find it again. Had it been an illusion, too? It didn't seem to fit with either of the other two illusions.

"Cesi," Varon called to a horse in his herd.

"Varon."

"I need help, Cesi. I think I am sick."

"Where are you?"

"Near the river, to the west of the gathering."

"I am on my way."

Varon realized he still had the moss in his mouth. He spit it out. It had to be Creator Moss. Only Creator Moss could do to him what he had just been through. He wouldn't allow Pautin to eat it, no matter how much she complained. There was no telling what she might do to herself if she saw the right illusion. She could harm herself and the foal.

Varon stood still, waiting for Cesi. He was too nervous to venture forth even a step. He didn't trust the strength of his legs to hold him up.

Cesi came trotting over to him a short time later. He was a tall chestnut horse. He stopped in front of Varon and then walked around the stallion, examining him, then sniffing with his nose.

"I am sick," Varon told the horse.

"What is wrong? What are you feeling?"

"Moss. I ate Creator Moss."

Cesi looked around and saw the strip of moss on the ground.

"Is this the moss you ate?" Cesi asked, smelling the moist moss.

"Yes."

"This is common river moss. It's not the best thing for you to eat, but some Equus have developed a taste for it with so little else to eat."

"No, it is Creator Moss. Lacinus' Herd uses it. I have seen it. The zebras have led them to believe that eating the moss brings them closer to Equ, but it harms them. It leaves them open to attack."

"I have not heard of this."

"It's true. I can tell you the others to talk to, and you'll see the evidence yourself when Calvn Lacinus' Herd finally arrives."

"I believe you." He tasted the moss, chewed it, and swilled it around in his mouth. *"But this is just common moss, Varon. I recognize the taste, smell, and color. Do you have a recent stool nearby? Maybe it is something else you ate that caused your hallucinations."*

Varon shook his head. *"No."*

Varon believed Cesi's pronouncement. However, if what he had eaten was only common river moss, then what had caused his hallucinations?

20

In the first light of the rising sun, the Equus filed by the corpse of Calvn Conllal and covered him with grasses; most of which probably carried a plea to Equ to end the Seeking Season and bring them home to Etrasco. The Calvn Council, now including Calvn Oralum, stood in a row behind the corpse.

Varon hated to see their hard-to-find grass used in such a way, but the council would have it no other way. Calvn Conllal was granted a send off befitting a Calvn, which meant that it had to be twice as elaborate and use twice as much grass as would have been required for any other Equus.

After the memorial send off, the horse races were held. As the Calvns chose their champions for the stallion race, and the stallions and mares raced five times around the Ranglan Depression to see who would be the horse champion of the Equus, Varon slipped away from the gathering with Capsta and the other horse leaders.

He was still nervous about what had happened to him yesterday. He'd had no further hallucinations since then, but his sleep last night had been troubled because he had feared that he might tempt more distressing visions while he was sleeping.

He and Cesi had discussed whether Varon had mind-sickness. The thought worried Varon, coming so soon after Tola's death. They had decided that Varon was fine, but Varon had also been careful to not eat any more moss regardless if it was Creator Moss or not.

"Are you alright?" Co, the horse leader of Vinc's Herd, asked him.

"Why do you ask? Do I look ill?" Varon replied, worried.

Co shook his head, making his black mane flip back and forth.

"Not that. You seem distracted."

Varon snorted. *"I am. The ages are changing, and I am not sure that the Equus are ready to deal with the changes that the white mountains signal."*

"Your worry is not a worry of the Equus, just the horses of Scola's Herd."

"What affects the horses in Scola's Herd in this case also affects all the Equus," Varon snapped.

"How do you know what changes the white mountains signal?" Co asked.

"I know."

"You worry too much over the white mountains, Varon. They do not move that quickly. Even if they will cover all of Hemlaza, we will be long dead when it happens."

"And so you think we should ignore them because it will only harm our colts and fillies when they are grown and are sires and dams?"

"It will be their problem."

Varon stamped a hoof. *"It is our problem. We can't ignore the white mountains. It is the fact that the white mountains move at all that worries me. Until two moons cycles ago, we did not know they existed. They are not natural. They are too large, too powerful, and too fast. They have appeared to us for us to deal with."*

"But what can we do about them?" Capsta asked.

"You sound like Calvn Scola, trying to ignore them," Varon said.

Capsta's nostrils flared, and he tossed his tail. *"Never, never compare me with a unicorn. Unicorns are killers, as bad as predators."*

Varon bowed his head to the older horse. He knew how much Capsta hated the unicorns after what they had done to him by acting like they were agreeing with his charges while doing nothing about them. *"Fine, but you're still trying to ignore the problem. If we don't explore our options, we will never know if there are options."*

"But the council…" Co said.

"Since when is the Calvn Council infallible? Scola is my Calvn, and I know all too well of his many faults. Is he the only one? Is your

Calvn infallible?"

Co flicked his tail. *"No, but there are worse."*

"Then why do you assume doing nothing and ignoring the white mountains will make them go away? They are not storm clouds or nightmares. They are solid and coming for us."

Co and Capsta had no reply. They walked in silence to a spot from the Ranglan Depression where a band of stallions from Conllal's Herd had gathered.

"How many have seen the colt?" Varon asked.

Capsta's ears took opposing positions, one forward and one back. *"Seen him? Many. Most of my herd,"* Capsta replied.

"How many know what he is then?"

"Few. My season mate and myself. The horse leaders in some of the herds."

"What do you intend to do with him?"

"Raise him and let him live as a stallion among horses where he will be appreciated for what he is and not hated for what he isn't."

"Even though he is a unicorn and not a horse," Varon said.

Capsta pivoted to glare at Varon. *"If that becomes known, then his life is in danger. He won't be told of his true parents; otherwise, it might affect his actions,"* Capsta said. *"He is Equus. That is enough."*

Varon nodded.

"Then let me see this marvel of nature." Varon refused to name the colt as an aberration or a freak. He chose instead to think of the possibilities such a creature might present for uniting all the Equus. The colt showed all who would only look just how alike the species were.

The band of horses parted, making a path for Varon and the others. Although the colt appeared as any other horse, they still worked to hide it from view.

At the center of the small band was a young colt, perhaps two weeks old. He was reddish brown with a good shape to his legs. The only mark that Varon found interesting was the white circle on the colt's forehead where a horn would have been. His mane was still short and dark brown. As Varon watched, the young colt finished nursing from his adopted mother and looked around. He seemed confused at the attention he was drawing.

"Could you tell him from a herd of colts?" Capsta asked.

Varon shook his head. *"And he has no horse blood?"*

"None. He is... was a unicorn of Calvn blood. Now he is a horse."

"Then, if you are so sure of his appearance, why do you protect and hide him, marking him as special?" Varon asked.

"Scent. I fear his mother still might recognize him if she were to get close to him during Champion Days," Capsta explained.

"Then hiding him will do no good. Besides, if the mother is as ashamed of what happened as you say, she would not claim him. Besides, his birth scent will have changed by now, since he is drawing milk from your season mate."

Capsta nodded. *"Perhaps, but I choose to be careful. I don't want Gee to know the foal's alive, or Gee might kill him just to get even with me."*

"Why?"

"Because this colt is proof."

"Proof of what?"

"Proof that all Equus evolved from horses," Capsta said in an exasperated tone as if Varon was a fool.

Now Varon's ears shifted forward and back. *"How can you say that? No one knows the order of creation."*

"It stands to reason, Varon. Ponies look like stunted horses. Zebras and donkeys are even more stunted. Pegasus are horses with wings, and unicorns are horses with horns. All species are but variations on the basic form, which is the horse."

"That is one explanation."

Capsta stamped one of his forehooves. *"It is the right one, and this colt proves it."*

Varon did not like such philosophical arguments because they served no purpose other than to create tension among the Equus. Each species had created its own beliefs in the order of creation, placing itself as the first created species and the favored species by Equ. However, they seemed to forget the old meaning of their name. Equus meant "all equal under Equ." No longer was that true. Did that mean that the Equus were no longer Equus but individual species?

Sometimes Varon feared that was true. There were too many herds, too many factions, too much jealousy and hatred for the Equus to be a united, equal species.

Varon walked forward and groomed the young colt.

"Be the omen they say you are," he told only the colt. *"But unite the Equus. Show us we truly are the same. Bring us together."*

Varon lifted his head and moved to leave. The colt looked at him, but he was too young to use his mind-voice and the mind-link.

Varon could hear the Calvns calling for the horse champions to come forward for their race. It was time he returned to watch Scola's Herd champions, Syltene and Chrys, carry the glory of Scola's horses to the race.

Varon found Pautin at the edge of the gathering nearest the race area. She stared at the herd champions, particularly Chrys, with a deep sadness in her eyes. Even without asking, Varon knew she was remembering her year as herd champion and wishing she could have been so again this year. Being season mate to a horse leader was not a position of pride for her, for it was Varon's position she basked in, not her own.

Unasked, Varon groomed her neck and withers, hoping to ease the tension from the stiff muscles along her neck.

"If this foal had come earlier, I might have had a chance to be herd champion," Pautin told him. *"Everyone says I could have done it."*

"I'm sure you could have, but Equ wasn't ready for our foal to be born yet."

"But this was my last chance to be herd champion."

"There will be other Champion Days," Varon counseled her.

Pautin turned to him. *"Will there be? Things are changing. The ages are changing. Isn't that what you tell others?"*

Pautin was more perceptive than he gave her credit for. He

would have to remember that. Just because she might be disagreeable didn't mean that she was an idiot.

"I do say that. Things are changing, but I don't know how quickly," Varon said. *"Besides, very few other Equus believe me, so I may be wrong."*

"You aren't." She paused. *"Things are changing too quickly for me."*

"And me, too, I think."

The horse races had barely ended when herd scouts reported that the pegasus band seeking Lacinus' Herd was returning. The eight pegasuses landed in front of Calvn Mika, who was standing on the raised area near the Ranglan Depression. They swept their wide wings forward and lowered their heads.

"What news do you bring us, winged Equus?" Calvn Mika asked.

"Calvn Lacinus' Herd is destroyed," Ulam said.

The news echoed through the mind-link.

"All of them?" Calvn Mika asked.

"We could find no one living. We counted 342 dead Equus."

The news reverberated through all the Equus herds, and each herd gathered in tighter. That number of dead Equus hadn't been seen since the days of the herd wars. Always before, when predators had attacked a herd, most of the Equus in the herd had escaped with the news.

"Could predators have taken down an entire herd?" Calvn Mika asked.

"One would assume that the pegasuses of Lacinus' Herd could have gotten away from ground predators, but we found them among the dead. Stallions can usually outdistance wolves, but they too were dead. Because there are no survivors to tell us differently, we must assume a great number and variety of predators attacked Lacinus' Herd."

"How? Predators don't cooperate in that way."

"I cannot explain how it happened, Calvn. I am only describing what I saw."

Calvn Mika nodded. *"This is very disturbing news. We have not lost an entire herd since the Herd Wars. This is a dangerous time for the Equus. We must remain within easy travel of each other and communicate regularly. The white mountains have changed the behavior patterns of predators. They have panicked and have now become even a greater danger to us."* He paused. *"Until further notice, I need to receive a messenger from each herd on the full moon. If I don't receive a messenger from one herd, I will mount a gathering of Equus to bring help if it is not too late."*

It amazed Varon. He had known that the white mountains would bring change, but Calvn Mika's call to protect the Equus was the first step to reuniting the Equus under one Calvn and as one herd. It seemed an impossible feat for one Calvn to command the thousands of Equus. It hadn't happened since the original Calvn did it 193 generations ago. Varon could not imagine the individual Calvns giving up their power, and he could not imagine the Hemlaza Plains supporting a single herd that was the size of all the Equus combined. They would have to stay on the move to find fresh grass. Even now, with three days at the Ranglan Depression, grasses were depleted for a day's travel in every direction.

A uniting of the Equus might mark the beginning of something good, a uniting of purpose and a return to Etrasco, but the thought of such a monumental change scared him.

Varon found Calvn Scola after the gathering broke up. The Calvn was walking with his head drooping. He hadn't taken the news of sending messengers to Calvn Mika well.

"My Calvn, I request to speak to you," he said formally because he could tell that Calvn Scola was not happy with the proclamation.

Calvn Scola raised his head. *"Speak, my horse leader."*

"My Calvn, yesterday, I had vision."

"A vision? You?"

Varon nodded. *"I can explain it no other way. I thought at first that I might be hallucinating, but Cesi said no."*

"What was this vision?"

"From what I can tell, it was a vision of the future, two imagina-

ble futures for the Equus." He left out the part about the strange creature in the tree.

Calvn Scola sighed. "*What were these futures?*"

"*One was the destruction of all the Equus in much the same way Lacinus' Herd was destroyed. The predators will unite against us and kill us on the southern cliffs.*"

"*And the other?*"

"*We must leave Hemlaza. We must set off across the white mountains and follow them to their beginnings. There we will find a new place to live.*"

Calvn Scola whinnied. The Calvn rarely showed his mirth, but when he did, it was always derogatory.

"*What do you find humorous, Calvn?*" Varon asked.

"*You, Varon. You believe you had a vision, don't you?*"

"*It is the only explanation.*"

Varon didn't enjoy being ridiculed. He was trying to help the Equus, but Calvn Scola was too worried about his own power and position to care about the Equus as a whole. He'd already had some of his authority usurped by Calvn Mika, and now Varon was telling him that a horse had had a vision.

"*It is the only explanation that you want to consider,*" Calvn Scola said.

"*Then what is the answer?*"

"*Perhaps you ate some fermented berries. I don't know. What do I look like? A horse?*"

"*I am a horse, and I know better than to eat too many fermented berries. Cesi said...*"

Calvn Scola stamped his hoof. "*I don't care what Cesi said. I'm telling you that if Equ would speak to the Equus, it would not be through a horse.*"

"*Why not?*"

"*Because as Calvn, I am not only of the blood of the Equ's most diligent servant, but I am of Equ himself,*" Scola said.

Now Varon thought the Calvn was going too far. "*Of Equ?*"

"*Was not the golden-horned unicorn the form in which he chose above all? Unicorns are beloved among the Equus,"* Scola explained.

"I had a vision, Calvn." Now Varon was doubting himself, his twitching ear betraying him. What if Calvn Scola was right for once? And what would he think if Varon had told him about the odd creature he had seen in the tree? Was that why Varon had left that part of the story out?

"Varon, I know the appearance of the white mountains has upset you, but you must trust in the wisdom of the Calvn. Equ placed the Calvns above the Equus to lead you, which we do according to our wisdom."

Varon was tempted to remind Calvn Scola of the Herd Wars that the Calvns had led the Equus into, nearly destroying them all.

Varon lowered his head and imitated grazing. *"I will leave now and consider this,"* he said.

"Do that, Varon. I won't lead you astray."

Varon walked away. He saw Vinel, the zebra from his exploratory band to the white mountains.

"May I speak with you, Vinel?" Varon asked the zebra.

"Speak, horse leader. I will listen."

Varon told the zebra of his visions and what Calvn Scola had said, adding, *"The Calvn will not even consider that they were true visions."*

"That is because they are not," Vinel replied quickly.

"Then what are they?"

Vinel shook his head. *"Delusions, perhaps. Equ does not speak to the Equus through visions. He set the proper path before the Equus when we left Etrasco. If the Equus would but follow that, we would return to his presence."*

"What path is that?"

"The Return. The zebras teach it daily, and yet, how few understand it. I think Calvn Mika understands, or is at least beginning to."

"How so? Is it because of his declaration today?"

Vinel nodded. *"Yes. He unites the Equus. It is only when we are one in number and purpose that we can hope to return to Etrasco. It is only then that Equ will show the way to the zebras, and we will explain to the Calvn."*

"But that fits with the second vision that the Equus, as one, will set forth across the white mountains to return to Etrasco," Varon insisted.

"No, because Return will be accomplished in how we were brought here, through the power of Equ. The path will not be a journey but a doorway from the plains of Hemlaza to Etrasco."

"Then why call it a path?"

Vinel didn't understand how even Return matched Varon's vision.

"Because that is what it has always been called."

"But what if the path is a path? What if crossing the white mountains would take us to Etrasco?" Varon asked.

"You've seen the white mountains, Varon, and you've heard what Jalon said about her explorations across them. It is not possible. Do you doubt her?"

Now Varon realized Vinel was looking for a way to drive a wedge between the horses and the other species. So much for uniting in number and purpose.

Varon flicked his tail. *"No, Jalon does not lie, but she took only one path. Perhaps it is not* the *path across the white mountains."*

"No, Varon, Equ placed the Equus here, and it is here that he will come for us when it is time to return," Vinel snapped.

With that, Vinel turned, lifted his tail and walked away from Varon.

They were wrong. Varon knew that. Unless the Equus united, they would be destroyed. Unless they left their homeland of Hemlaza, they would be destroyed. Varon had seen a true vision.

21

The thirty-eight Calvns of the Calvn Council gathered at dusk around the edge of the Ranglan Depression. The rest of the Equus species gathered near them, facing them.

Calvn Mika said, *"The time has come to replace the Calvn of Conllal's Herd. Who among the unicorns seeks this position?"*

Four unicorns stepped forward. Two of the unicorns were from Conllal's Herd. One was Oralum, which was expected. He was the interim Calvn and would want to make it a permanent position. The second unicorn from Conllal's Herd was Miskala. The other two were from different herds. A unicorn did not have to be a member of the herd needing a Calvn to claim the position. The only requirement was that the unicorn had to have Calvn blood.

Miskala wasn't sure why he had stepped forward when Calvn Mika had called for seekers of the position. He had no particular desire to be Calvn. It had been a spur-of-the-moment reaction that seemed right. In the day that Oralum had acted as Calvn of the herd, Miskala had felt a slight shift away from the policies of Calvn Conllal. Calvn Conllal had been more open in discussing what he intended to do for the herd with the herd. Oralum kept things to himself or spoke only with his advisors. It shouldn't have surprised Miskala things would change with a new Calvn, but it did, and he didn't like it.

"Are you all sired by Calvn?" Calvn Mika asked.

The unicorns each then recited their lineage back to Calvn to prove their qualifications for the position. When they finished, Calvn Mika bowed his head and said, *"You all have a worthy lineage. That being the case, here is the quest I set you upon to claim your title."*

179

He tilted his head up to look at a bright star in the night sky. *"There hangs Creator's Blessings. Directly below it lies the Valley of the Equus where your sire died. You must journey there tonight under the light of Creator's Blessings. Once in the valley, the first of you to find the Ranglan Stone and return to this gathering with it will become of Calvn of Conllal's Herd. However, you must complete the quest before the sun sets again in the east."*

"How will we know the stone we find is the Ranglan Stone, and where will we find it inside the valley?" one unicorn asked.

"If you are true progeny of Calvn, your blood will burn as you near the stone, for Calvn will guide you to its location."

"And if we cannot return by sunset even if we have the Ranglan Stone?"

"Then your ability as Calvn does not measure up to the standard set by your first sire." Calvn Mika paused again and looked at the star. *"May Creator's Blessings be upon you and may the one whose blood burns the strongest return."*

With that, the unicorns took off galloping south.

Miskala wondered if who was Calvn of a herd even mattered in the grand scheme of Equ's plan. He stared up at Creator's Blessings. Where did the Valley of the Equus lie? No non-Calvn had found it, and many had searched. Even unicorns not set on the path by the elder Calvn could not find the valley. It was a guarded secret among the Calvns and a source of their power.

Miskala galloped hard. He was glad that he had been galloping a lot with the horses lately. Because of that, the hard run wasn't such a shock to his system as it might have been, say, one moon ago. Even so, the other unicorns in the group began to pass him the further they got from the Ranglan Depression. Miskala lowered his head and pressed himself to gallop even faster. He thought he could feel himself speed up, but not enough. He managed to keep the others in view, though.

He looked at the path that the unicorns followed. In a straight line, it would take them to a spot in the Meshack Mountains below Creator's Blessings. However, by the time they reached the mountains, Creator's Blessings would have moved. So which location was correct?

Calvn Mika had told them to follow the path of Creator's Blessings. *Path? What path?*

At this time of year, Creator's Blessings moved between the two moons over Hemlaza. At nightfall, Creator's Blessings appeared next to the larger moon, but by dusk, it would have moved across the sky and appeared to be swallowed by the smaller moon.

Was that the path of Creator's Blessings?

It had to be.

Instead of trying to position himself under Creator's Blessings, he should just gallop to where the star would be when it disappeared, which would be next to the smaller moon.

Miskala shifted his course further to the south. The gap between him and the other unicorns widened until he lost sight of them. Miskala kept the smaller moon in front of him and ran towards it.

When he reached the mountain foothills, he slowed to a trot. He was under the smaller moon, but he could be anywhere within a short distance of his current position and still seem like he was under the moon. How would he find the Valley of the Equus within such a wide area?

Calvn Mika had said something about their blood burning. What did that mean? Miskala didn't feel his blood burning.

He closed his eyes.

In his mind, he saw a faint image of a lush valley. Etrasco. The valley of creation. Was that what he was seeking now? Was the Valley of the Equus the same as Etrasco?

Miskala shook his head. No, that made little sense. If they were the same, then the Calvns would have returned the Equus to Etrasco long ago.

Still, why should he think of Etrasco now?

The vision changed before him as if he were walking through Etrasco. Miskala walked in that direction without opening his eyes. When the direction in the vision changed, so did the direction that Miskala walked. Another unicorn appeared in the distance. Miskala walked toward him, but not directly. He turned and wove, but the unicorn waited patiently. As he drew closer, the vision became brighter and more real.

When Miskala finally stood in front of the great, white unicorn, he noticed the unicorn had a golden horn. Miskala stood in front of Equ. Then the vision faded.

Miskala opened his eyes. He was standing in front of an opening in the mountain. Miskala looked around. He had traveled from the foothills through a ravine to stand where he was now. He had done it with his eyes closed by following his vision. Would the other unicorns receive similar visions if they came to stand in the general area of the valley? Was that the burning of the blood?

The entrance into the valley was narrow and not very tall. Miskala could walk through it without ducking his head, but his sides would brush against the rock walls. How could this small opening be the entrance to the Valley of the Equus? Surely it was only an entrance to a cave.

But the vision had brought him here.

Miskala took a deep breath and started inside. The narrow entryway continued for about twenty yards. Then it ended. Miskala stood at the bottom of a gorge about 100 yards across. The sides were sheer and steep with no paths up the sides. The night sky shone down into the valley, and the light from the small moon seemed to be brighter within the valley as the pale stone walls amplified it.

This was the Valley of the Equus, and he was the first unicorn to arrive here. Was it possible that he might become the Calvn of his own herd?

Now all he had to do was find the Ranglan Stone. He knew what it looked like, having seen it at the announcing of other Calvns. It was a small stone to find in such a large valley.

As he walked along the narrow valley, Miskala noticed the scratchings on the wall. Each of the Calvns had left their marks and stories on the wall. Miskala didn't recognize many of them. That didn't mean all were unknown. He saw the six-point star of Calvn Mika. The mountains of Calvn Erlin. The rainbow of Calvn Conllal.

Miskala recognized dozens of the symbols. The Calvns sometimes scratched their marks into trees and rocks to mark their grazing areas.

Miskala quickened his pace. He couldn't afford to dawdle, knowing that the other unicorns might be here at any moment. Even if none of the other unicorns made it to the valley, Miskala still had to find the Ranglan Stone and return to the Ranglan Depression by morning.

He turned a curve in the valley and stopped. On the ground in front of him was a unicorn's skull. The skull's long, white horn pierced the Ranglan Stone. Miskala didn't know whose skull he was looking at, but it was probably a former Calvn's, or maybe even Calvn's himself. It was said that this was the valley where he had died.

Miskala walked forward, feeling uneasy looking at the skull and knowing it would be his future. He used his own horn to slide the stone up the horn until it tumbled over the tip and fell to the ground. Then Miskala placed his own horn in the center of the stone and lifted it. The Ranglan Stone rattled as it slid down his horn until it rested against his forehead.

Two points of light glowed in the skull's empty eye sockets.

"You seek to lead the Equus, but are you worthy?" a mind-voice asked.

"Who are you?"

"You seek to lead the Equus, but are you worthy?" the mind-voice repeated. Miskala couldn't see anyone around him.

"When I return to the Ranglan Depression, will I not be worthy?"

"The stone is only a symbol that you have passed the challenge. You do not take the stone. It must be given."

The ground trembled, and the skull rose from the ground. Miskala saw it was still attached to the neck bones. The entire skeleton slid up through the ground. When the skeleton stood before him, the trembling in the ground stopped.

Miskala stepped back.

"How do you answer the challenge?" the skeleton asked him.

"I must accept."

The skeleton nodded.

"Then those who have gone before you shall judge you."

A circle of unicorns appeared around him. Miskala raised his head, preparing to face the challenge; whatever it might be.

"He is of my blood, but very little," one black unicorn said. Startled, Miskala realized this was Calvn… the original Calvn.

"His heart is pure," said a chestnut unicorn.

"But his mind is not open."

"He can lead," said a roan unicorn.

"But can he follow!"

One by one, the unicorns lowered their horns toward him.

"You have failed," the skeleton said.

Failed? But he had found the Ranglan Stone. All he had to do now was to return with it to the Ranglan Depression, and the Calvn Council would name him Calvn of his own herd.

"But why have I failed?" Miskala asked.

"You are not the one meant to be the guide," the skeleton said.

"But other unicorns have become Calvns who were worse than I," Miskala insisted. He couldn't believe that he was the only unicorn to have failed this eerie test. He had found the valley and the stone! None of the others had. All he had to do now was return to the Ranglan Depression.

"None has ever passed the test, which is why the Ranglan Stone has never been given."

"But I have seen it outside of the valley."

"Yet it always returns to me. The Ranglan Stone cannot be taken. It will only be given to the guide," the skeleton explained.

The spirit unicorns charged, goring Miskala with their horns. He screamed as he reared up and kicked out at the phantoms. Then he collapsed, unconscious.

When he awoke, Miskala was surprised to find himself alive. The spirit unicorns were gone and the skeletal unicorn was once again only a skull on the ground. Miskala shook his head, surprised to find the Ranglan Stone still on his horn.

How could that be if he had failed the test? Did he even deserve to wear the Ranglan Stone?

But no one had passed the test. The unicorn skeleton had told him so.

No one.

And yet, they had all worn the Ranglan Stone, all of the Calvns.

Who was it who could pass the test? Who was the guide, and what was his purpose?

Miskala stared at the skull and asked, *"What do I do now?"*

The skull offered no answers.

Miskala looked up at the sky. He was surprised to find it had dawned and that the sun had passed overhead while he was unconscious. How long had he been unconscious? What had happened to him? He had never heard of an experience like this. The Calvns hadn't even hinted that this was what might happen.

He backed away from the skull until he rounded the curve and couldn't see the skull any longer. He was afraid to turn his back on the skull as if turning around would cause the apparitions to appear again and attack him.

He turned and hurried through the opening and out of the valley. He found it hard to believe that of the four unicorns, he was the only one to find the valley.

Once he was outside the tight entry tunnel, he galloped down the ravine. He took his bearings once he was in the foothills and was surprised to find he was a lot further south than he had supposed.

He galloped hard, hoping to reach the Ranglan Depression before the sun had even touched the horizon. He hadn't gone far when he heard Oralum say, *"Miskala, did you have any success?"*

"I think so."

"Think? Either you have the Ranglan Stone or you don't."

"I have it."

Miskala saw Oralum come up behind him galloping hard and fast. He thought the older unicorn would gallop with him back to the Ranglan Depression. Two Equus would be better protected from predators than a single one.

Oralum galloped close to him, bumping Miskala with his shoulder.

"Is that the Ranglan Stone on your horn?"

"Yes."

Oralum suddenly lowered his horn. Miskala recognized the threatening gesture, having seen it so recently made by the spirit unicorns. He slid to a halt and Oralum's charge hit only the air where Miskala would have been if he hadn't stopped galloping.

"What are you doing?" Miskala asked.

"I will be Calvn."

"I found the Ranglan Stone, not you."

"But finding the stone doesn't make you Calvn. You must return to the gathering with it."

Miskala was tempted to tell him that finding the stone bore its own challenges, but he felt restrained to do so. Oralum was looking for an easy way to leadership. He would never understand what the spirit unicorns had told Miskala.

Miskala turned away and galloped faster. Oralum adjusted his position and chased after him. Miskala knew he couldn't outrun the other unicorn. If he meant to reach the Ranglan Depression with the stone, he would have to find a way to slow Oralum down.

"It doesn't have to be this way," Oralum said.

"I'm not the one trying to kill."

"I don't mean to kill you, Miskala. Equus does not kill Equus, but I will mark you if I must. I am Calvn. The herd is mine now. I won't have it taken from me by you or any other unicorn."

Oralum gained on Miskala, who purposely slowed. When Oralum charged again, Miskala kicked his rear legs out, catching Oralum on the shoulder. The older unicorn squealed and veered away from Miskala. Urged on by his fear, Miskala surged ahead as soon as rear hooves touched the ground.

He had to get a sizeable lead or he wouldn't be able to reach the Ranglan Depression ahead of Oralum. Oralum galloped after him, but he only managed to limp along at nothing faster than a canter. He stayed within sight of Miskala all the way to the Ranglan Depression.

"You won't have the herd, Miskala. It's mine," Oralum promised.

With the morning, the Calvns began preparing for the pony contests. The ponies would compete in a wrestling competition. It moved smoothly, and Plinth of Tona's Herd won the competition.

As night fell, the Equus gathered around the Ranglan Depression to see who would return from the Valley of the Equus. The sun had just touched the horizon when the pegasus scouting for an advance sighting of the future Calvn called out that one unicorn was returning.

The herd called out to the approaching unicorn.

"Hail, Calvn."

"It is Miskala," the unicorn told them.

"Did you find the Ranglan Stone?"

"I have it."

"Then come forward, Calvn Miskala."

Miskala slowed his gallop to a prance as he approached the herd. He arched his neck and held his tail up. He felt that a Calvn should act more regal. A Calvn was a position of pride and responsibility.

Miskala walked down the path as the Equus parted in front of him. He stopped in front of the gathering of Calvns and lowered the tip of his horn to the ground in front of Calvn Mika. With a gentle shake of his horn, the Ranglan Stone slid down the horn to the ground.

"So you found the Ranglan Stone?" Calvn Mika said, staring at the stone.

"I..."

"No!" Oralum said sharply as he limped among the Equus. *"I found the stone in the Valley of the Equus. Miskala attacked me on my way back to the depression and stole the stone from me."*

"He lies!" Miskala said. *"I was the one who found the stone. Oralum tried to attack me."*

"It matters not who found the stone; only who returned with it," Calvn Mika said. *"Miskala has returned with it, and so Miskala will be named Calvn."*

"But I found it, Calvn Mika. I can prove it. In the valley..." Miskala said.

"No!" Mika said. *"Speak nothing of your experience until the members of the council have spoken to you in private. Then we will*

know if you found the Ranglan Stone as you say."

Calvn Mika bowed his head and picked up the Ranglan Stone between his teeth.

"Bow, Miskala."

Miskala lowered his head until his white horn pointed straight out. Calvn Mika slid the stone onto the ridged horn.

"Rise, Calvn Miskala," Calvn Mika said.

Miskala's head came up. He looked over the herd of Equus. He still wasn't sure how he felt about this. He couldn't believe he was now Calvn of a herd.

"Come with us now and we will talk to you of what is required of a Calvn."

The Calvns walked down into the Ranglan Depression in a tight group. Miskala walked with them, holding his head high.

22

Jalon placed her right front hoof down gently on the ground. She tested her weight on the spot before inching forward. She moved slowly up the side of the Meshack Mountains with the five pegasuses who had accompanied her on the scouting mission. In her opinion, they were moving forward too slowly. She was used to flying quickly on the winds. She was not used to stealth. That was the ponies' and donkeys' area of expertise. Pegasuses were meant to fly, not creep.

Still, she reminded herself, she would rather creep than battle a griffin, which is what would happen if the griffin perimeter guards heard the pegasuses coming. Her pegasus patrol had found feces when they had returned to the area where Jalon had first seen the griffins and suspected it was from griffins. The patrol had made swinging arcs to the east then, assuming the griffins had been returning to the mountains when Jalon had seen them. The patrol had come across more feces until the trail had led them to the foothills of the Meshack Mountains.

They had seen a griffin patrol flying then and had to drop to the ground and hide under a rock overhang. Since then, they had been creeping up the mountainside.

"How much further?" Tyni asked.

"I don't know. We have to be near where that last patrol came from," Jalon told him. One advantage of the mind-link was that they could communicate, causing no noise that the griffins could hear. No other animals shared the Equus' mind-link. They might have their own mind-links; Jalon wasn't sure.

"What are we going to do if we find them?"

"That depends on what we find. I'd like to find the aviary nest unguarded, crush the eggs, then bring all the pegasuses back here and

finish the living griffins. Our patrol isn't large enough to face more than two or three griffins at once; at least not if we hope to face them and live," Jalon explained.

"Jalon, I saw something move in the east," Chas, a spotted pegasus, said.

The pegasuses all froze in place. They studied the trees and rocks uphill to the east.

"It's a griffin," Tyni said. *"He's alone, and he's on the ground. He must be one of their perimeter guards for the aviary."*

Male griffins served as terrifying and effective guards. Although they had no wings, they had a horn similar to a unicorns and spikes covering their bodies. In essence, griffins were a creator's nightmare version of Equus.

That meant that they were getting close.

"We'll wait and see if there are any others close by," Jalon said.

The griffin nearly passed from their sight before he turned back. He was patrolling a set area, but he seemed to be alone.

"We still need to get past him," Jalon said. *"I want to see the nests so that we know how many griffins we are facing."*

They inched forward as fast as they dared, then Tyni flew into the air to draw the griffin's attention. The griffin raised his wings to take flight through the trees after the pegasus, and his attention was focused on the sky. The other five pegasuses charged forward, striking the griffin with their hooves. They snapped the griffin's wings first to keep him from flying away. The creature opened his beak to squawk a warning, but Tyni dropped from the sky, using his hooves to smash the griffin's beak. The pegasus pounded the griffin, slicing through his hide and cracking bones. The griffin was ferocious, but he couldn't focus his ferocity on any one pegasus. He was quickly overwhelmed and killed.

"I would not want to do that too often," Chas said, trying to catch his breath.

"Let's keep going. I'd like to find what we came for and be away before another griffin realizes that this guard is dead," Jalon said.

They crept forward even more carefully than before. Now they knew that they were nearing the object of their search, but the danger of discovery had also increased. To make matters worse, as they crept higher, the trees thinned out.

"We're losing our cover," Havis noted.

"Hopefully, what we are seeking will be in the clearing ahead," Tyni told him.

"Hopefully, it will be close enough to see," Jalon said. *"Once the trees are gone, the mountains will be clear to the top. The nests could be anywhere. I'm hoping the peaks will be too cold, though, and they will be near the tree line."*

They were close enough. Within the clearing beyond the tree line, Jalon counted fifty dirt-mound nests, each with a female griffin sitting atop it. No males were nearby. They would either be searching for food or patrolling the nesting site. The nests were in the open so that the sun could help warm them, which was critical given that altitude and the extra-long Seeking Season.

"With an average of three eggs per nest, we're looking at about 150 griffins waiting to hatch," Jalon said, suppressing a shudder. That was another reason griffins were so dangerous to the Equus; they reproduced quicker than the Equus.

"If this is the only aviary," Tyni added.

Jalon turned to look at him. *"You think there are more?"*

"There could be, but I hope not. I think if the flock were much larger, they wouldn't have been able to hide at all. If we can end the threat here, we can end it for good."

"Even if this is the only aviary, at the rate they are laying eggs, they will rival the Equus again in a couple of years," Havis estimated.

"But how could even this many griffins be alive without an Equus seeing them before I stumbled across them?" Jalon asked.

Tyni said, *"Maybe you weren't the first to see them; only the first to get away. They tried to chase you down."*

"This group isn't so large that they would have needed to go beyond the mountains for food before now. With much of their prey moving south and their drift growing in size, they have outgrown their territory," Chas said.

"Outgrown their territory and into ours," Jalon added.

"We're only six pegasuses. What can we do against fifty females, not to mention the males on the perimeter?" Tyni asked her.

Jalon studied the layout of the aviary again, then said to the others, *"Poole and Chas, you two head back the way we came up the mountain. Don't take to the air until you are beyond the foothills. Once you do, get back to the gathering and bring all the pegasuses back to the aviary. The rest of us will stay here so that the pegasuses can find the aviary without landing and climbing the mountains like we did. They can just track us once we establish a mind-link. Make sure that the pegasus leaders know we need to destroy the griffins now, or they will destroy us later if these eggs hatch."*

The two pegasuses didn't argue with her. Jalon wasn't sure if that meant they were willing to accept her authority or they just wanted to be away from the aviary. Chas and Poole turned and headed down the mountainside. The remaining four pegasuses watched them go, saying nothing.

"What will we do now?" Tyni asked when he felt Poole and Chas break from the mind-link.

"We wait until the pegasuses return and re-establish the mind-link with us. By being able to come in directly and attack without warning, they will gain some advantage," Jalon told him.

"A lot of pegasuses will die."

Jalon nodded. *"A lot more will die if those eggs hatch, the young grow up, and they lay their own eggs. It will mean that many more griffins will have to be killed if the Equus are to survive. The pegasus leaders realize that, I'm sure. That's why they sent us to find the aviary."*

The four pegasuses stood still. The lighter colored ones stood behind the trees or their darker companions. Hidden as they were in the shadows of the trees, they became a part of the landscape. They were within the ring of perimeter guards, but outside the nesting area. They were as safe as they could be within a drift of griffins.

"How long do you think we will have to wait?" Algo asked.

"I don't think the pegasus herd will get back here before midmorning, but a dawn attack would be good. The griffins should nearly all be here then," Jalon guessed.

She heard an angry squawk from down the mountain behind them. It was answered by a second warning squawk far to her right. The females in their nests fluttered their wings. They wanted to be on the move, but they needed to stay with the eggs.

"I think they found the dead guard," Havis said.

"Maybe they will think a pack of wolves did it," Algo suggested.

Jalon shook her head. *"The markings on the ground will be hoof prints, not paw prints. They will know it was Equus."*

"Do we stay here?" Tyni asked.

"If we don't, it will make it harder for the pegasus herd to attack when they arrive."

"If we do, we might not be alive to lead them here, anyway."

Jalon quickly considered her options and made a decision. *"It's night. Be still, and they probably won't see us. Keep your ears moving. If you hear anything, we'll move then."*

Tyni looked doubtful, but he obeyed her, as did the others. They waited in the shadows and listened. Jalon watched griffins arrive and form a tighter defensive circle around the females and nests.

"It looks like they will work their way outward from the nests and reform a new perimeter defense that they know is clear inside," Havis said as he studied the aviary.

Jalon listened and observed. She caught sight of a shadow moving downhill from them. It was a griffin. Then she saw other shadows.

"It's worse than that," she said. *"They will try to catch us between them. There is a line of griffins moving toward the nests as well."*

"What do we do now?"

"Start moving back down the mountain. We can hope that their line is stretched thin enough that we can slip through a gap."

Jalon was doubtful, but she didn't have a better idea. They picked their way carefully down the mountain. The griffins made so much noise, roaring and screeching, that they couldn't hear the Equus. They were trying to flush the Equus into the clearing where they would be easy prey for a drift of griffins. Instead, the Equus were moving away from the clearing.

One of the griffins spotted the band and squawked a warning to his companions. The four pegasuses attacked him and killed him with their hooves, but the warning had been given. The griffins tightened their net, moving in massed force from areas where they knew the Equus weren't to where they were.

Jalon looked up. The tangle of tree limbs was too thick to fly safely through, but on the other hand, the female griffins couldn't attack them from above either. This would be a two-dimensional battle.

"We need to punch a hole through the bottom line. We have to retreat," Jalon said.

"Easier said than done," Tyni shot back.

The four pegasuses looked at the line of griffins coming up the mountain toward them.

"We can't get through their line. They are two deep," Havis said.

Jalon looked at the approaching line and came up with a desperate idea. *"We'll fly over them."*

"Over them?" Tyni said. *"Those branches will tear our wings apart."*

Jalon shook her head. *"We're not going to fly into the sky, just over them. We charge and fly just high enough to get over them. Then we gallop until we are clear of the trees and can fly."*

They galloped down the mountain, looking as if they would bowl over any griffins in their path. The griffins braced themselves for the collision. Then, a mere yard in front of the griffins, the pegasuses launched themselves over the griffins' heads. The action startled the griffins, but some of them reacted. They reared up and caught Algo as she passed low over their heads.

Their beaks bit into her legs, locking onto her and pulling her down. Algo squealed as griffins pulled her from the air, but the scream was abruptly cut off as the griffins swarmed over her.

Havis turned back to help.

"You can't do anything for her, but you're wasting the few seconds her life bought us," Jalon told him.

Havis turned, and the three pegasuses galloped downhill. They accelerated so quickly because of the steep slope, Jalon was worried that she would outrun herself and stumble. She could see the griffins falling behind, since their legs were shorter than the pegasuses.

"How much further?" Jalon asked.

"I don't know. Just run until you see clear sky," Tyni said.

"Then what?" Havis asked. *"Flying will only slow us down and speed them up."*

Havis was right. Jalon remembered that it had only been when she had started galloping that she had been able to outdistance the griffins.

"You're right. We've got to stay on the ground and keep them on the ground, too. That gives us the advantage," Jalon said.

"Not much of one," Havis quipped.

"Gully ahead," Tyni warned.

The gully was too wide to leap, so the pegasuses spread their wings and glided across the twenty-foot breach. The female griffins chasing them followed them across a few seconds later, the wingless males forced to an abrupt halt. However, the glide slowed down the momentum the pegasuses had built up, and the females were gaining on them.

"We need to turn before our galloping gets out of control again," Jalon said.

"Turn? If we do that, they'll be on top of us," Tyni warned.

"If we reach open air, they will be on top of us."

They turned to the south and galloped uphill. The griffins shifted with them, gaining a little ground.

"Don't take us back to the aviary," Havis said. *"You'll trap us between the females and the males."*

"I'll swing wide, but I wouldn't mind drawing the remaining females off the nests," Jalon told him.

Tyni said, *"They won't come off those nests; not while they know we're in the area. They know what we want, and they are protecting those eggs."*

The pegasuses galloped uphill in a much more controlled gallop, but the squawks from the griffins seemed to grow louder. Then the drift veered off to the north.

"What are they doing?" Tyni asked.

"Could they know a way to circle around us?" Jalon said.

"They know these mountains better than we do."

"Jalon, we are coming," Chinarvo said as his mind-voice joined the small band's mind-link. She had never been so glad to hear the voice of another Equus.

"They are south of our position, Chinarvo. Follow the link and we will meet you at the aviary," Jalon told him.

"One of you is missing."

"Algo was killed."

"Then her death shall be avenged."

Jalon listened as Chinarvo ordered the other pegasuses to the north of her position to attack the aviary. There were several hundred pegasuses in the mind-link now.

"Kill them all," Chinarvo ordered.

Then the attack was joined. Jalon heard the screams in the mind-link as pegasuses died, and she could only assume that more griffins were dying. They all had to die. If even one mating pair was left alive, the griffins might again grow their drift in secret until it was large enough to overcome the pegasuses. With the pegasuses dead, the Equus as a whole would be the next to fall.

Jalon and the others turned to the north and headed toward the aviary. As they neared the area, Jalon heard squawks and squeals, whinnies and screeches. Near the edge of the tree line, she saw the first dead body. It was a pegasus; not one she knew. His neck had been ripped open. The next three bodies were those of griffins. The aviary area was no longer brown and gray from dirt, but red with blood.

They fought both on the ground and in the air. A pegasus fell from the air into the midst of a ground fight and was clawed to death. Some griffin females tried to defend their nests and were overcome. They were the main targets of the attack. Them and their eggs.

Jalon raced forward and joined in a fight between two pegasuses and a griffin. The fight was going badly for the pegasus. She came from behind and leaped into the air. She came down with all of her weight on the griffin's back, breaking it.

The battle lasted until just after dawn. When it became obvious that the battle would go against the griffins, both males and females were quick to break off the fighting and try to escape. Bands of pegasuses flew after them, knowing that if the purpose of this obliteration was to work, it had to be complete.

When all resistance from the griffins ended, the remaining pegasus made sure that all the eggs in the nests were crushed. Others checked the dead to make sure they were dead and not just wounded. Jalon realized it was a good thing that they had overwhelming numbers in their favor because there were just as many pegasuses dead as griffins.

Chinarvo walked over to Jalon as she looked through a dirt-mound nest for buried eggs.

"It's over this time," Jalon said.

"You think so?"

A confused Jalon said, *"We killed all the griffins."*

"We also did so last time."

Jalon shook her head. *"We couldn't have. Otherwise, this never would have happened."*

"Jalon, all reports say all the griffins were killed at the end of the Griffin War. The pegasuses at the time were fanatical about it."

"Then how do you explain this?" She pawed at the bloody mud under foot.

"How do you explain it?"

Jalon thought about the question and said, *"Sarton."*

Chinarvo nodded.

Sarton was the creator of the griffins, as well as many other fearsome predator species.

"She recreated them," Jalon said.

"That is what I think. It also means that you have made a deadly enemy in ferreting out the aviary and guiding the pegasuses to the battle."

Jalon looked around at all the dead bodies. If Sarton was just going to recreate the griffins, then it meant that all the dead had died for nothing. This would just have to happen again in another generation, and more and more pegasuses would die until the pegasuses would not have replaced their dead quickly enough to defeat the griffins.

Then the griffins would win, and the Equus would die.

23

Miskala looked around at the various bands of Equus. The celebration of the pegasus' victory over the griffins was still going on. While he thought it was wonderful to honor the pegasuses who had returned from the Meshack Mountains, the 300 pegasuses who hadn't returned couldn't be forgotten either.

He found Tyven standing near one of the few trees in the area around the Ranglan Depression. Tyven looked tired after his ordeal in the mountains. More so, he looked older than his seven years. The slaughter of the griffins seemed to have prematurely aged him. Miskala was only now beginning to understand how leadership could weigh on a soul.

"I want to leave tonight, Tyven. I'd like to give the herd a better chance of finding food along the way. We'll find a lot of bare acres immediately around here. We will go hungry for a while," Miskala said.

"We'll find a lot of bare areas all over Hemlaza."

"Can you be ready with the pegasuses? I wouldn't want to interfere with your victory celebration. It is well deserved and hard won," Miskala asked.

Tyven nodded. *"We can be ready, Calvn."*

"Good." Miskala turned away, but he stopped and asked, *"Tyven, I don't know how many have said this to you, but I thank you and all the pegasuses for what you did for the Equus. You placed yourselves at risk to keep the rest of us safe."*

Tyven stared at Miskala and said, *"I didn't look at it as a pegasus matter, Calvn. It was an Equus matter that the pegasuses could handle better than anyone else. What we did for you, we did for our-*

selves. All equal under Equ."

Miskala nodded. *"True words, but your actions proved that your hearts were truer still."*

As Miskala walked away, he pondered Tyven's words: *"All equal under Equ."*

Was that really true among the Equus? Should it be?

Miskala saw Oralum approaching him and swerved to avoid him. Since Miskala had become Calvn, the older unicorn had been ingratiating. However, Miskala couldn't help but remember how Oralum had seemed willing to kill him the night that Miskala returned with the Ranglan Stone. That was something that Miskala could not forget. He did not trust Oralum and never would.

"Calvn, I told the donkeys that they would have to forage tonight so we would be ready to leave tomorrow, and they refused," Oralum complained to him.

"Why would you tell them that?" Miskala asked. He hadn't told Oralum to do it. Oralum still liked to pretend that he was Calvn with those members of the herd whom he could intimidate, like the donkeys.

"Because we will need to eat on our journey."

Oralum had a condescending tone that Miskala hated. Though Oralum would say that Miskala was his Calvn, he didn't seem to accept it. He just seemed to bide his time.

"We will find food as we move, and we're moving tonight," Miskala said.

"Tonight? Moving at night is foolish, Calvn."

At times like this, a glimmer of Oralum's true personality showed through. He might play the subordinate, but he considered himself the superior.

"I am Calvn, and it is my decision, Oralum."

Oralum stiffened. *"May I ask why we are leaving at night when predators will be on the prowl?"*

"You may ask, but I won't answer. I am the chosen Calvn of this herd, and you will accept my will, or I will make an exchange before we leave."

Oralum lowered his head. *"I was born in this herd. I will die in this herd."*

"Then you will obey me if you wish for that to remain true."

Oralum said nothing. He kept his head bowed, turned and walked away. Miskala shook his head. Leading a herd was hard enough without Equus like Oralum, making his work more difficult. But then, there always seemed to be an Oralum in every herd. If the Calvn was stronger, then the herd got larger. If the Calvn was weak, the herd floundered.

Which type of Calvn was Miskala?

When the small moon passed below the larger one, Miskala called his herd together. He asked the zebras to take a count and make sure that every Equus in his herd was there.

"I count 403 Equus, Calvn Miskala," Bronelin, the zebra leader, said.

Miskala nodded. *"Fellow Equus, Champion Days has come to an end. It is time to move on and get on with the job of surviving this odd weather. We will move south. Pegasuses, if you will fly as our vanguard and find grazing areas for the herd, I would appreciate it."*

Tyven nodded. *"It will be done, my Calvn."*

The eighteen pegasuses took wing and flew toward the south. It saddened Miskala to see such a small number. Twice as many had flown before the battle with the griffins.

"Are we running from the white mountains, my Calvn?" Oralum asked.

"No, we go to where we can live until the land can provide for us. The land is in flux right now. We must survive until it settles, and we can once again learn what we shall do."

"Don't you know?"

"I know we shall survive. It is the will of Equ that we do so. However, we must survive as a herd. We are herd creatures. That is how we function and live. I believe that we are being told that it is time to leave Hemlaza. Unfortunately, a majority of the Calvns do not agree with me. Until they do, we will prepare for the time when we must leave."

"But where will we go?"

"I don't know, but Equ will provide a way."

Oralum snorted, and Entro turned to stare at him.

"Miskala is a fool," Oralum said so that only Entro could hear him.

"You and I both know that, but that is because the rest of the herd is not as wise as you or they would not accept Miskala as the Calvn," Entro said.

"No, they aren't; fools that they are. It just shows that they need me all the more. I could lead this herd and make it grow to rival Friez's."

Entro nodded. *"True, but until you convince the herd of your abilities, you don't have the authority."*

"Even if I convince the herd, I still won't hold the authority," Oralum said.

Unlike other species, a Calvn could only be chosen at Champion Days and by a journey to the Valley of the Equus to retrieve the Ranglan Stone. Despite his best attempts, Oralum hadn't been able to find the valley. Nor had any of the other unicorns.

Except for Miskala.

The fool had blundered his way into the valley and somehow found the Ranglan Stone. Now he held power over the herd, and Oralum had to call him Calvn. Miskala, the fat, waddling, pitiful unicorn, was a poor excuse for a Calvn.

"You might assume authority in other ways," Entro said.

"How so?"

"If Miskala finds leading a herd not to his taste, he won't do it. Make it too hard for him to lead, and the herd will call you Calvn, not him. You will lead."

Oralum nodded. He liked the idea.

24

In the morning, the different Equus species began separating to their individual herds and moving off in different directions to search for fresh places to forage for food and safe areas where the mares could give birth. The area around the Ranglan Depression was once again, a field of dirt. The departing Equus left a large dust cloud hanging over the area that could be seen from far away. Now that the herds were separating, they would have to once again be on the lookout for predators, and herd scouts would be more important.

The Calvns appointed the two fastest pegasuses in each of their herds to act as the regular messengers to Calvn Mika.

Trying not to add to the cloud of dust, Varon walked away from the Ranglan Depression with his head hanging down. He coughed as he inhaled dust, but he did not raise his head. Pautin waddled next to him, grunting with each step.

"You would think you were the pregnant mare," Pautin told him.

"Leave me alone, Pautin. I'm not in the mood to argue with you," he snapped.

"From what I hear, your mood lately has been worrying everyone."

Varon paid attention to her. *"What do you mean?"*

"I have heard rumors that you may be getting mind-sickness. It looks like it now, watching you trudge along."

His head came up. *"Who says I have mind-sickness?"*

"Don't you listen to the general conversations going through the herd? It started with the unicorns, but it has spread throughout the herd now."

Varon grunted. *"What makes them think I have mind-sickness? They aren't healers."*

"They say you rave about visions and the white mountains."
"Rave? Have you heard me rave?"
"No."
"But you still assume that I do."
"That's what the others say."
Herd thought. Varon hated herd thought.
"And do you tell them differently?" Varon asked.
"Well, no," Pautin admitted.

Varon knew where the rumor had started. It wasn't hard to figure out. Calvn Scola was telling Equus that Varon might have mind-sickness. That was like him. He ignored the message and tried to destroy the messenger. What could Varon do about it, though? He *believed* the white mountains posed a threat, and he *had* seen a vision from Equ. That explained what he had seen, despite what Scola and Vinel said.

Yet now he was walking away; one of a small herd. The Equus were disbanding instead of gathering to cross the white mountains. Were they moving toward their own destiny?

Equ had trusted him as a messenger of warning, and Varon had failed him. Nothing had changed for the Equus.

Pautin went into labor two days later. Being Pautin, it had to be in the middle of the night when most of the herd was asleep. She screamed her pain into their minds.

"It's time!" she yelled.

Since Varon was the closest to her, he was the first one to reach her. He also heard her shout the loudest. She lay on her side, pushing. Soon, other horse mares arrived to help with the delivery. The mares, having gone through this themselves, were the resident experts on deliveries, though most of the horse stallions could have done it. They trained and studied to care for the Equus.

Pautin squealed and at the same time yelled through the Equus mind-link. She lay on the ground on her side. Her hips twitched occasionally as contractions hit. Varon danced around, trying to stay out of the way of the mares. However, at times, curiosity overcame him, and he had to stop and push his nose through the crowd to see what was happening.

He saw the forehooves of the foal pushing out into the night air. The sight froze him in place. This was his foal being born! It would be his first foal.

"I see him, Pautin," Varon said.

Pautin only grunted as she scooted around on the ground to aid her efforts to give birth.

The foal's black nose appeared next, covered in the placenta. One mare used her muzzle to readjust the foal's legs to help it slide free easier.

"Push hard now, Pautin. Once the foal's head is clear, the rest should come easily," one mare told her.

"Push, Pautin," Varon said.

Pautin kicked out, trying to strike him. Varon jumped back out of the range of her hooves.

The foal's head continued to appear as Pautin pushed. The closed eyes appeared, followed thereafter by the ears. Then the head was clear.

"Wonderful, Pautin. The hard part is finished," the mares told her.

The foal slid out relatively quickly after that. The neck appeared. The chest and the belly. The haunches. Pautin had to push hard again to clear the foal's hips, and then it slid free. A mare used her teeth to help pull the placenta off the newborn, which was kicking and shaking its head to free itself.

"It's a colt!" one mare announced.

"A colt!" Varon reared up on his hind legs and kicked out his forehooves. *"A colt!"* he called out to the herd.

He settled to the ground and moved through the mares to nuzzle Pautin. Her face was damp from her efforts.

"You did good, Pautin. Can I get you anything?"

"I want to rest."

"I'll watch over you while you do."

Varon walked over to the newborn colt. The mares were licking him clean. He was liver-chestnut. Varon wondered if that would turn lighter when the colt was cleaned off. He was so small and fragile-looking. He would stand somewhat lower than Varon's shoulders when he could stand.

"Welcome to the world, little one, although I don't know what kind of world you've come into," Varon told his colt.

Varon enjoyed watching the three-week-old colt play with some other young colts and fillies. Chareth ran very well and would be quick when he grew up. Perhaps he would even be a herd champion one day. Pautin was quick to take credit for her colt's speed.

She had regained her sleek form after Chareth's birth. She was already seeking to attract a new season mate for the coming year. The birth of Chareth had ended her and Varon's year as mates. Varon didn't hold it against her that she was so eager to leave him. He was considering looking for a new mate himself. If he did, he thought he would be much more careful about his selection this time.

He watched Chareth leap into the air and then sprawl on the ground when he landed. He climbed to his feet and ran off. The colt must have thought he was part pegasus.

Varon looked across the field and saw a dun mare with an eel stripe named Phyen. She was a four-year-old who seemed sensible. At least she didn't shun the ponies and donkeys in the herd. She was a definite possibility for a season mate, but he would have to communicate with her for some time before he decided. He wanted a season mate who could help him think through his problems the Equus faced. He wanted someone who would tell him if he was wrong and support him if he was right. Varon wanted a mate who didn't think he had mind-sickness.

Pautin hadn't been that type of season mate... at least not for him.

The past moon cycle since they had left the Ranglan Depression had been peaceful. Life continued much as it had this time last year. Still, things had changed. It was impossible to forget that. He and every other Equus saw the proof every morning when the sun shone on the white mountains. Moving south diminished the size of the white mountains, but it did not make them vanish.

Many times in the evening, Varon wondered if he had been wrong about what his vision had meant or if he had even seen it, only to be reminded of the truth that morning.

Scola knew that the peace his herd had known since the end of Champion Days ended the morning that Molinnar flew erratically into his herd. The pegasus landed amid the herd, and unicorns surrounded him and pointed their horns at him.

"Identify yourself!" the unicorns ordered.

"I am Molinnar of Dalth's Herd."

Dalth's Herd? What would Dalth want with him, Scola wondered.

"Why did you not identify yourself properly when challenged earlier?" Fles said.

Molinnar looked over his shoulder into the sky. *"I was scared."*

"Scared? Why?"

"Dalth's Herd was slaughtered. It is no more."

Scola stepped forward, trying to remain calm, though all he felt was extreme anxiety. *"Slaughtered? Are you sure?"*

Molinnar nodded. *"I am the only survivor. I was returning from Mika's Herd after making a report about a bear cave we discovered. Dalth wanted to warn other herds to avoid it. I was one of Dalth's messengers to the senior Calvn. Boa and I saw lions, falcons, and bears attacking Dalth's Herd as we approached. We turned to fly away, but the falcons pursued us. They swarmed over Boa, killing her. I've never seen a flock of falcons attacking an Equus, but they did. Boa was my life mate, and she is dead! Her death was the only reason I was able to escape. I kept flying while she was being killed."*

Pegasuses frequently took life mates; unicorns only did it rarely. That was one reason that Scola considered them so foolish. Varon could see and almost feel Molinnar's anguish over the death of his life mate.

"Were the attackers Ravagers?" Scola asked.

Molinnar shook his head. *"No, they were normal predators, or at least none of them showed themselves as Ravagers."*

"Are you sure?"

"All it would have taken would have been one Ravager to kill me. I can't believe that I left Boa. She deserved better than me."

Scola shook his head. *"But how could the predators form such an unnatural union without Ravagers among them?"*

"My herd has been seeing this since we left the Ranglan Depression. The predators have to hunt harder for their normal prey. The prey has moved south away from the white mountains to where the air is warmer, so the predators have remained in the north and hunt other sources of prey. We never expected them to move against us, though."

"How large was Dalth's Herd?" Scola asked.

"There were 253 Equus in the herd, plus several mares who had yet to foal."

Scola looked around. *"Chinarvo, send a pair of pegasuses to Mika with this news. Varon, get one of your healers to take care of Molinnar. He doesn't look wounded, but he doesn't look healthy, either."*

Calvn Scola turned and walked away, his head drooping.

"Now two herds have been destroyed. The world has gone crazy. Perhaps it is better that Boa left it," Molinnar said.

Would predators overwhelm his herd next?

No!

He wouldn't let it happen. He couldn't let it happen!

"Benju!" Scola called.

"Yes, my Calvn," came the reply from the donkey leader.

"From this point on, I want all the donkeys on the edge of the herd, serving as herd scouts," Scola told him.

"All? Even the mares?"

"Yes, the mares, too. You heard Molinnar's report. The predators, even those that we usually don't consider predators, are a great danger to us," Scola stressed.

"It will be done," Benju said.

Scola looked over his herd. He controlled the lives of nearly 300

Equus now with all the new births. How quickly could they be slaughtered? He stared at them and moved into the mass of the herd. The herd parted for him until he stood within the center of the herd.

He felt somewhat safer now with his herd surrounding him. Predators would have to go through his herd before they would reach him. He was the safest Equus in the herd. It only made sense; he was the most-important Equus in the herd. A Calvn should always be protected. His herd should give their lives so that the blood of Calvn would continue.

He turned in a circle. Yes, he felt safer now.

Then he saw the white mountains and shuddered. Where had the ice mountains come from? Were they going to take over the Hemla-za Plains?

He wanted them gone. He wanted things back to normal. He wanted the white mountains gone and the Season of Life to be felt across the land.

Would that ever happen?

25

Carn found himself having to concentrate more on holding his form. Odd, since being among creatures whose form he was imitating usually made it easier to hold the form. Not so when he was among the Equus.

He wasn't sure whether if it was his hatred of the Equus that made him want to reject the form or his impulse to shift form and kill. Either way, he had to be careful. If the Equus knew he was among them, Equ would step in to protect his creation. Carn's younger brother was too attached to the one form that was the basis for the Equus.

Carn walked to the edge of the herd where the donkeys were patrolling, watching for predators while the actual threat to the herd was within its boundaries.

"I thought I heard something by the river," Carn said to the donkey nearest him.

"Do you wish me to check the river?" the donkey asked. Carn didn't even know this Equus' name; not that it made a difference in whether Carn would kill him.

"That would be best. It may be predators trying to flank us."

"Then I think I should have some other donkeys come with me to examine the river."

Carn shook his head. *"That won't be necessary. I'll go with you. That way, we won't pull any of the others away from their positions."*

The donkey nodded.

The two of them walked away from the herd and down into the streambed. The stream was running shallower than usual, so that there was a wide bank on either side. As soon as Carn was sure that he and the donkey were out of sight of the others in the herd, he shifted form.

Carn reared up on his back legs. He let his left front leg snake out, forming a tentacle that wrapped itself around the donkey's muzzle so he couldn't scream. At the same time, his left front leg shot out, forming a point that punctured the donkey's brain through his eye socket, severing him from the mind-link. The donkey was dead without ever having issued a warning. Carn would have liked to have kept him alive for a while longer, but the donkey could have alerted the others through the mind-link.

Once the donkey was dead, Carn savaged him for no other reason than he needed to vent his fury. He felt anger burning hot to where it threatened to consume him. He bit. He kicked. He ripped the donkey's flesh and broke his bones.

He wasn't sure why he felt such hatred toward the Equus, but it did not overwhelm him to where he became sloppy.

When Carn finished, he took a deep breath and reformed his shape as Entro the zebra. He walked out of the streambed. He saw the faint gleam of moonlight off the glaciers to the north. The sight disturbed him because he knew that while the white mountains appeared natural, they were far from it. They moved too fast to be natural glaciers. What they were was a bridge off of Hemlaza.

Why would Equ re-establish a bridge so many years after he had broken Hemlaza off of the mainland? What was he planning?

Then another thought struck him. What if another creator or even his mother had created the bridge? That opened up more possibilities than Carn wanted to consider. He and his siblings didn't maintain the most open communications. Nor did he always tell his mother what he was doing.

Carn galloped into the herd, calling for Oralum. Oralum found him and tried not to appear worried by the tone of Carn's thoughts.

"What is the problem?" Oralum asked.

"A donkey has been killed."

"By predators?"

"I'm not sure. I went to drink at the stream and I saw the don-

key's body."

Oralum pawed at the ground. *"We can't go there alone. A herd of predators might be by the river."*

Carn had just told him he had been there alone. If there had been predators still around, they would have taken a lone zebra. He internally mocked the Equus' stupidity.

"What should we do then?" Carn asked.

Oralum snorted. *"We'll get Miskala. He wants to be Calvn. Well, this is Calvn's work."*

Carn tried to keep from sneering. Oralum was so eager to be a leader, but when given the opportunity to show leadership, he had turned from it. What would he have done if he had been Calvn now? Ignore the body or assign the duty to someone else?

"Calvn Miskala," Oralum called. *"A donkey has been killed."*

Calvn Miskala hurried over to the unicorn. *"How did it happen?"*

"I didn't see it," Oralum said. *"Entro told me about it."*

"Entro?" Miskala said, turning to look at the zebra.

Carn nodded. *"I went for a drink, and I saw the body. No predators seemed to be around him, but I didn't stay long enough to look."*

"Preis," Miskala called to his pony leader, "circle the young and the elderly in the herd. If there are predators about, the young and older Equus will be their primary targets."

"Right away, Calvn," Preis replied. Then Carn heard him issuing commands to the ponies in the herd.

"Cy," Miskala called to the donkey leader, *"have you seen any signs of predators?"*

"No, but Jevisson is missing. He is probably the dead donkey that Entro saw down by the river," Cy reported to him.

"Zebras and horses, join the donkeys and form a circle search. Try to find out if we're in danger of attack, but don't go anywhere alone."

Carn heard replies of *"Yes, Calvn."*

"Tyven, have your pegasuses take to the skies and assist in the search," Miskala ordered.

"Right away, Calvn."

"Unicorns, come with me while we investigate the body. Entro, please lead us to where you saw the body," Miskala said.

Carn was surprised at how quickly Miskala had organized the search. He had expected the pudgy unicorn to react in much the same way that Oralum had, with a lot of fear and indecision. Miskala looked like he would be as weak as most of the other Equus, but the blood of Calvn seemed to run strong in Miskala. That was not good. Calvn was the only Equus to challenge Carn when he had tried to destroy the Equus centuries ago. Calvn had died for his foolishness in their single combat, but he had bought time for the herd until Equ drove Carn away.

Was Miskala another Calvn in more than name?

Carn would have to make sure that Miskala lost control of this herd before he came into his power and understood what he could do with it.

Miskala looked at Jevisson's body and felt his stomach lurch. The donkey was so mutilated that it was hard to tell he had been a donkey. This was not the work of a normal predator. Too much savagery had been involved in the kill.

"Ravagers," Miskala said, shaking his head.

"So it would appear," Grenn, another unicorn, said.

"It's not like a Ravager to take only one victim, though."

"No, it's not. I wonder why the Ravagers showed such restraint this time?"

"Watch for Ravagers," Miskala announced to the herd. *"No one goes anywhere alone or breaks from the mind-link."*

"Calvn, may I speak with you?" Preis asked.

"Go ahead, Preis."

"Not at a distance, Calvn."

That was another way of saying that he wanted to talk privately.

Miskala galloped to where the ponies had gathered the colts, fillies, and older Equus. He walked up next to the brown pony and stood shoulder to shoulder with the pony leader.

"What is the problem, Preis?" Miskala asked him.

"Calvn, the death smell of a creator is all around the herd."

"All around?"

Preis nodded. "I have smelled it for some time, but I thought it would be fading by now. It is growing stronger."

While a creator might take the form of an Equus, if the donkeys could detect the death smell of a creator, that meant it must be a Ravager.

"But a Ravager wouldn't walk through a herd and not do anything to it."

"All I can tell you is that it feels like most of the herd is walking through a maze of invisible boundaries," Preis explained to him.

"Then that means that this Ravager is disguised as an Equus if he was able to walk among us," Miskala surmised.

"It's more than that. Creators can disguise their presence from our sixth sense if they have a solid shape. It's only when they are shifting shape that their presence becomes known to us."

"So you're saying that we have a creator among us who is shifting shape, and no one noticed?"

"Not yet," Preis said.

Miskala felt fear. Was there a Ravager in his herd? Were they going to end up like Lacinus' and Dalth's Herds in the next few days?

Miskala wouldn't let it happen. He had to stop the Ravager in their midst.

26

Crasini, the pegasus who had delivered the news of Dalth's Herd to Calvn Mika, returned to Scola's Herd in the evening with the news that Calvn Mika had ordered all the Equus herds to increase the number of their herd scouts. Varon didn't think that would do anything to increase the safety of the herd. In fact, it would only endanger the donkeys even more than they usually were by placing more of them in front of predators. Not that it mattered to Scola since he was already using all the donkeys in the herd as herd scouts.

As to who would gather food now that the donkeys were constantly occupied as herd scouts, Calvn Scola decided to create foraging bands using ponies and horses. They would operate much like the donkey foraging bands did during Champion Days. Scola hoped that by not having to move his herd around as much, they would not attract the attention of any large, roving groups of predators of the size that destroyed Dalth's and Lacinus' Herds.

He also had the pegasuses patrolling for predators, besides their duty of finding fresh grass for the herd when the foraging bands went out.

Varon didn't like the idea of the foraging bands. He thought it broke the herd down into small groups that created a danger for the Equus within them. His arguments had no effect on Scola.

Varon went out with his foraging band every other day. They bit off the grass and carried large mouthfuls from the field to the main herd. Even in the chilly air, it was hot, thirsty work. It also made for lengthy trips back and forth. It was not a very efficient way to collect food for a herd, since they couldn't carry much more than a mouthful.

Varon's band comprised of twelve horses and ponies who were

collecting food for a herd many times its number. It was not a sustainable way to feed a herd. Today, they were foraging in the foothills of the Meshack Mountains. The grasses were harder to find here because of the massive boulders and rocks that they had to negotiate around. On the plains, he simply had to lower his head and there would be grass; at least, there would be when they found an area with a decent amount of grass to forage.

Only half of the band would collect grass while the other half watched for predators. Then the two halves would switch places. If they saw any predators, they would have no choice but to run. They didn't have the numbers to face a normal-sized pack. Collecting the grass didn't take long. It was the travel time that was most wearisome.

"We shouldn't have to do this," Marsa complained for the hundredth time, and for the hundredth time, Varon wished having grass in her mouth would have silenced Marsa's thoughts as well as her nickers and whinnies.

"The Equus must eat," Varon told her.

"Then let them come here to where the food is," Marsa snapped.

"Calvn Scola has chosen the way."

"This way is wrong!"

Varon sighed as he went from being a watcher to a gatherer. They had this same conversation nearly every trip to collect food. Marsa just didn't understand, or maybe she understood and just couldn't accept what was obviously a poor decision.

"It is not a decision that you or I would have made, but it was not our choice to make," Varon tried to explain to the mare.

"Calvn Scola is endangering the herd by breaking us into smaller bands like this." Marsa stamped her forehoof.

Varon nodded. *"I think so. You think so. Calvn Scola does not think so. His is the decision that matters for the herd."*

"But I value my life. I don't want to be slaughtered like those in Dalth's Herd. Did he split his herd like Calvn Scola is doing?"

"No, Dalth kept his herd together." Varon thought finding that out might stop Marsa's argument. It only added fuel to the fire.

Marsa tossed her head back. *"See? Even a full herd couldn't stop the predators."*

"Then what do you propose, Calvn Marsa?" Varon asked sarcastically.

"Don't insult me, Varon. I'm only saying what you should be saying as herd leader."

"Don't insult me, Marsa. Don't you think I told him how foolish foraging bands are? He told me if they were good enough to feed all the Equus at Champion Days, they are good enough to feed his herd now."

"But we need to do something. The decisions he is making now could mean our lives or deaths. He is stretching the herd too thin. He is not choosing a direction to travel or a herd champion. He is deciding how well we can survive in this changing land. The herds should join like they do at Champion Days. That is the best way to protect us."

"But not to feed us."

Varon was surprised that through all of his anger, Marsa's beliefs were very close to his own. What did that mean? If they left the herd without Calvn Scola's approval, he could declare them renegades, and they would be as good as dead. They had no choice other than to follow Calvn Scola and remain a member of the herd, at least for now.

Varon moved closer to Bros, a pony, and talked to him about the legends of the Meshack Mountains. By staying close to the pony, their thoughts could be dominant between them and Varon wouldn't have to listen to Marsa continue to complain.

Varon collected a large mouthful of rough crabgrass and raised his head. The herd would not enjoy this meal, but it would be something to eat. His mouth was already starting to salivate. His instinct was to eat the grass, but he had to hold it in his mouth for the lengthy trip back to the main herd. The sad fact was that he wasn't even hungry. The first thing his group always did when they reached new grazing was to eat so they wouldn't need any of the grass they brought back to the herd.

"Is everyone ready?" Varon asked.

"Yes," came the answer.

"Then let's get going."

"What's the rush? Scola will just send us out again if we get back to the herd early enough." That was Marsa, of course.

"Not to here he won't. This is our third day here. We won't get more than enough grass for half of us if we come again, and we must root around for that little," Varon told her.

"Then we'll move south next time. I don't want to go further toward the mountains. It will just get harder to find fresh grass the higher we go."

The band moved off at a canter, heading north and west to catch up with Scola's Herd. It would take a quarter day of steady cantering to reach where the herd had been when Varon's band had left them this morning. The question was where would they be when Varon's band returned with additional food. Would they have moved south on to warmer climes, or would they have waited for all the foraging bands to return with the evening meal? He hoped that the band would find the herd moving south because it would save the band some travel time.

They had been cantering for a brief time when Marsa said, *"I saw something."*

"Where?" Varon asked.

"On the horizon."

"Could you tell what it was?"

Marsa shook her head. *"No. I just detected motion on the horizon."*

Varon debated whether to stop and investigate what Marsa had seen or to continue toward the herd. What if Marsa had imagined what she had seen? If Marsa had seen something, it would have to have been large and large meant predators. Was it worth the risk? He had to decide quickly. If it was predators, they needed to stop now and prepare for an attack.

"Let's stop and verify what Marsa saw," Varon said.

The band stopped and began milling around the barren plain. Some of them dropped the grass in their mouths so they could swallow. They all looked around.

A gray line appeared on the horizon. Varon studied the movement until he recognized it.

It was a pack of wolves.

"Wolves! Form a defensive circle!" Varon called.

The horses circled, alternating between facing in and facing out. It took only a few moments for them to assume the defensive formation.

"How many?" Varon asked.

"Too many. Maybe fifty," Bron told him.

"That's not too large."

"It is when our band numbers only twelve." A pack of wolves this size wouldn't have even threatened a normal-size herd, but this band was far from normal size.

The wolves reached the foraging band and surrounded them. They spent only a few moments growling, trying to frighten the horses into running. When the band held together, the wolves attacked. The one advantage of being a small band was that there wasn't enough room for all the wolves to attack at once.

The horses facing outward directed the defense and used their forehooves to strike at the attacking wolves while the inward-facing horses kicked when they were ordered to do so by Varon. The donkeys had powerful kicks. The dirty plain turned into a muddy grave.

Varon heard some wolves howl as the horses' hooves met their flesh. Unfortunately, he also heard the screams of horses in both his head and ears. The wolves were using their greater numbers to overwhelm the horses.

"Zacc is down," Presi called.

"Is he dead?" Varon wanted to know.

"I can't tell."

"Have the defensive circle shift to surround him. We'll protect him as long as we can." Varon would not give the wolves a wounded Equus to feast on if he could help it.

The shape of the defensive circle shifted so that the Equus surrounded Zacc, an appaloosa pony. Seeing the downed pony only excited the predators to be more ferocious in their attacks. Although many of their own had been killed, they had weakened the defensive circle's strength by one-twelfth. They attacked more savagely.

"Zacc is alive. I can see him breathing," Presi said.

"That is good, but it does not help us now. Concentrate on keeping yourself alive."

The horse next to Varon went down. When she lifted her head to throw one wolf, another wolf bit Gresein's throat and ripped a large chunk away. The blood sprayed over Varon as the horse crumpled in a heap. Varon shifted his position only slightly to close the gap left by the fallen horse. He wouldn't try to protect a horse that was dead, but he wouldn't leave an opening for the wolves.

"Gresein is dead," Varon said.

"No!" Prau, her season mate, yelled.

"We must be careful, or we will soon follow."

The wolves weren't letting up in their attack to collect their bounty. They wanted these Equus dead. The wolves were having just as much trouble feeding themselves as the Equus. Here, they saw the small band of Equus as a feast for the taking.

"Can anyone see a more easily defensible position in the rocks?" Varon asked.

"I don't have time to look at rocks. I've got a pack of wolves coming at me from all directions," Corss snapped.

A wolf leaped at Varon. Even as he watched, a stick suddenly appeared in the wolf's neck. The wolf's expression of fury changed to one of pain. The body fell dead at Varon's hooves.

What had happened?

"The trees are defending us," Presi said.

"What?" Varon asked.

"The trees in the foothills. They are defending us. I just saw one throw a branch into the heart of a wolf leaping at me."

"That's impossible!" Varon shouted.

"He's right! I just saw it happen to a wolf in front of me. A tree branch killed a wolf," Marsa said.

"But trees can't do that!" Varon shouted.

"And mountains can't move!" Marsa snapped. *"I saw it happen!"*

Varon looked around, and he saw that more bodies of wolves lay on the ground with sticks sprouting from their bodies.

"Bleu just fell, but she's alive," Kryi said.

"Surround her," Varon said.

"We don't have enough Equus to surround both her and Zacc."

Varon made a quick leadership decision. *"Then surround Bleu. She's more likely to live through this at this point."*

As the band shifted its position once again, this time to cover the pony Bleu, the wolves moved in on Zacc. However, the first wolf that reached the body fell dead with a stick in its neck.

How could that be happening? Only two small trees were within sight, and neither one was close to the wolf pack. How could they be throwing their branches?

The wolf pack was thinning out. The trees had killed as many wolves as the horses had. "We need to make a run into the foothills," Varon said.

"What about Bleu?"

"I will be able to go," Bleu replied.

"The wolves are being distracted by the branches that are killing them. We must go now. If you can escape the wolves in the foothills, then try to get back to the herd and warn Scola of what has happened," Varon said.

"He won't bring the herd," Marsa said.

"No, but at least they will be warned of the danger."

The band broke from their formation and ran for the foothills where they could use the crags and valleys to hide. Varon had only gone a short distance when he heard a scream that was neither Equus nor wolf.

He stopped galloping and turned in the direction he had heard the scream. His band was on its own now. They would either survive or not. He could do no more for them, but he wanted to know where those branches that had killed the wolves had come from. If the trees were moving on their own as the white mountains were, then the Equus needed to know this, for the trees themselves might become potential predators of the Equus.

Most of the wolves had run off once the Equus had separated and run. Varon sniffed the air, looked around and listened to make sure that the only wolves he saw were the four that were intent on a pine tree. They circled the tree, occasionally stopping to try to jump into its branches.

Did they suspect this tree of attacking them?

Even as Varon watched from behind a rock outcropping, a branch appeared in the neck of one wolf. It howled in pain and fell over, kicking for a few moments before it died. This brought on an intensified attack against the tree until a branch appeared in another wolf's side and it too died. The final two wolves decided not to wait around, and they ran off.

Varon stood watching the tree, wondering if he would see the pine tree suddenly uproot itself and move to another location. The branches along one side of the tree shook without the benefit of the wind. Varon thought he was about to witness another miracle like the white mountains.

Then a creature dropped below the lowest branch, hanging on with its arms. It released the branch and dropped to the ground. When the creature stood up, Varon realized it was the same creature he had seen in the tree at the Ranglan Depression. Well, maybe it wasn't the same creature, but the two were of the same species.

Varon shook his head. Was he hallucinating again?

He couldn't be. He had eaten no moss or taken any kicks to the head during the fight. This must be an actual creature he was seeing, which meant the one he had seen at the Ranglan Depression was real, too. That creature hadn't been a part of his vision.

This was an unknown creature in Hemlaza!

Had it come with the white mountains? The white mountains and the creature appearing at the same time was beyond coincidence.

The creature was bipedal like a bird, or somewhat like the apes in the forests to the west. It was taller than most of the apes, though its arms were shorter. It had a lot of long, brown facial hair and wore the skin of a brown bear. Its legs, which had been bare at the Rang-lan Depression, were now covered with the skins of gray wolves.

The creature walked over to one wolf and prodded it with his toes. When the wolf didn't move, the creature pulled the branch from the body and put it in a skin pouch behind its back. It then moved to all the fallen wolves and pulled the branches free and stored them in the pouch.

The creature pulled a sharp, metal tooth from a fold in the bear skin and sliced open one wolf. The wolf's inner organs spilled out onto the ground, and the creature cut them free and tossed them off to the side. The creature then used the tooth to skin the wolf, and he tossed pieces of wolf meat into the skin.

What manner of creature was this?

"He is a human."

Varon shook his head. It was the same disjointed, feminine voice he had heard at the Ranglan Depression just before...

He saw a herd of Equus in a vast valley so beautiful it could only be Etrasco. No other valley of this size existed on Hemlaza. The Equus milled around in small bands, playing and eating. Then amid them appeared another creature, much like one that had killed all the wolves, except this creature wore no skins and it was a female. She walked among the Equus, petting them and speaking to them. This creature did not appear to be a predator, but a friend to the Equus.

"Humans are my one creation, just as you are my son's only creation, but whether they are here now to help you, I know not," the feminine voice said.

The vision faded and Varon saw the human male standing only a few meters from him. The human watched Varon as he tied the edges of the wolf's skin together to hold the meat.

"So you came back to see who helped you out, did you?" the human said.

Varon didn't know what the man's odd sounds meant, but he was making no threatening gestures.

"I've been watching you and your kind for a couple of weeks now. I can't decide whether I should eat you or try to ride you. You're as fast as the wind, but you're also a lot of meat. Of course, I've got all the meat that I need right now."

Varon shook his head, wondering how he could communicate

with this human. If they were supposed to help each other, shouldn't they be able to communicate?

"You're a beauty, though, and you don't seem dangerous, at least not to something that's not attacking you. You're prettier to look at than the ox I was riding. I bet you probably taste better than he did, too, when I ate him after he dropped dead coming across that white wasteland," the human said.

His voice was soft. He moved closer as he spoke, but Varon wasn't alarmed. This human was a creature of Equ's mother, after all.

"You're a fast runner. I've seen that. I bet you could run across that wasteland in a third of the time it took me to come over on that ox. If only this place wasn't so far away from the Twin Kingdoms, I could make a killing with all the game around here. You could make old Balen a very rich man."

The human chuckled as he stroked Varon's neck. He had a gentle touch as his hand moved up and down Varon's thick neck.

The human grabbed a handful of Varon's mane and swung up on his back. Feeling the sudden weight on his back, Varon reacted instinctively. He arched his back and jumped up. Airborne, he kicked his rear legs out as high as he could.

He felt the weight leave his back and saw the human fly over his head. Without waiting, Varon turned and ran to the north. He would not give the human another chance to do whatever he had been attempting.

27

Scola did not like what he was hearing from the scattered pairs and trios of Equus from Varon's foraging band galloping back to the herd.

"Where is your food?" he asked them.

The herd was hungry and depended on what the foraging bands brought back to survive this detestable weather.

"Wolves attacked us," the Equus told Scola.

"You survived, though," he said.

"Yes, the trees saved us."

"Trees? How?"

"The trees threw their branches into the wolves and killed them."

Scola didn't know what to make of this tale, and he wondered if the band might not have contracted mind-sickness while they were down south foraging. Hadn't Varon's sire contracted it? And this was Varon's foraging band.

Scola shook his head. *"What you're telling me isn't possible."*

"It's true, Calvn. We all saw it."

Scola knew it couldn't be true. Trees did not attack predators. They never had. It wouldn't be possible.

And mountains do not move, he reminded himself as a chill ran up his spine. They were living in an age of change, and changes were happening.

Scola shook his head.

No!

Trees do not fight. The foraging band must have found some fermented berries and feasted on them while the herd starved. It was

224

just like Varon to favor his friends over the herd. Now his foolishness and selfishness was exposed for all to see.

Varon was the last of his band to arrive back with Scola's Herd near nightfall. He came trotting in, looking scared and confused. He had no grass in his mouth. He hadn't been foraging, except for fermented berries.

Varon approached Calvn Scola to make his report. Scola arched his neck. Let the herd see the difference between a superior Calvn and a poor herd leader. As the foraging band leader, it was Varon's responsibility to verify or deny the reports Scola had been hearing since Varon's band began returning, and Scola was very curious about the story that Varon would tell. He wondered if the Equus in the band had agreed to the story before they returned to the herd.

Scola stood with Revan. She had given birth to her foal during the day. The dun colt with a small, nub-like horn was nursing at Revan's teat while Scola hovered protectively nearby. He was sure that Calvn's blood would run strong in the colt.

"I would hear your report, Varon," Calvn Scola said. *"I've been hearing a lot of fanciful stories this afternoon. Hopefully, you can clear them up."*

"Yes, my Calvn. My foraging band had collected our grass and was on our way back to rejoin the herd when a pack of wolves attacked us. Bron estimated that there were fifty. We defended ourselves. Zacc and Greisen were killed. Bleu was badly wounded as well. When the opportunity presented itself, I had the band break up to return here, hoping at least one of us would make it back. I did not know how many predators might be nearby to aid the wolves."

"What is this I've been hearing about a tree throwing branches into the wolves and killing them?" Scola's tone suggested his scorn with the idea.

Varon nodded. *"It was not a tree, Calvn, but a human."*

Calvn Scola looked up, surprised at the change in the story. *"Human? What is that?"*

"It is a creature made by Equ's mother. I saw the human collecting the branches from the wolves' bodies to reuse them. He was hid-

ing in the tree and could somehow throw them hard enough to stick in the wolves' hides."

"None of the other horses or ponies in your band reported seeing this human."

Varon nodded. *"None saw it. After we broke to gallop back here, I turned back to see if certain trees had suddenly become predators. Like you, I was doubtful that trees could be predators. That is when I saw the human lower himself from the pine tree."*

"Drusino!" Calvn Scola called.

"Yes, my Calvn," came the reply through the mind-link.

"What is a human?"

"I do not know," the pony leader said.

"Is it a creature of Equ's mother?"

"It's possible, I suppose."

"You suppose. You are the pony leader, and you know of the most important tales of the Equus. You keep the memory of the Equus among your Equus. Have you ever heard of a human?"

Drusino's tone stiffened, as if Scola had offended his ability to recall knowledge of the Equus. *"Humans are not spoken of in our herd's memory, though I cannot speak for other herds. I have never heard Equ's mother mentioned either, although I suppose he had parents."*

Scola nodded. It was as he had expected to hear. Humans or a creator mother were fiction. Varon was making up stories to raise himself above the other Equus in the herd, including Scola. What worried Scola was the sincerity in Varon's words. The horse leader tried to sound loyal to Scola, and to a lesser mind, Varon did. But Scola knew better. Varon spoke well, but falsely. Either that or he was mad. Either option suggested that Varon was a danger to the herd.

Scola had to show… proof to the herd that Varon was wrong and a danger.

"Thank you, Drusinos." Calvn Scola stared at Varon. *"Sartino."*

"Yes, my Calvn. What can I do for you?" Sartino replied.

"Does Equ have a mother?"

"No, Calvn," came the firm reply from the zebra leader.

"Then what is a human?"

"A what?"

"A human; a creation of Equ's mother."

"I do not understand. I have never heard the word before."

"Thank you, Sartino."

"I serve as I can, Calvn."

Yes, he did. As a zebra leader, Sartino knew his proper place in the herd and that of his species. He worked to make sure both were filled.

"So," Scola said, turning to Varon. *"You saw a creature that doesn't exist that you say was made by a creator who doesn't exist. For your claim to be true, you would be saying that the stories preserved by the ponies are wrong, and the rituals maintained by the zebras are also wrong."*

Scola thought Varon would become unnerved when confronted by the falsity of his claims, but the chestnut horse remained firm. He even had the effrontery to arch his neck.

"Just because Chinarvo and Sartino haven't seen a human yet, doesn't mean they don't exist. They do exist. As does Equ's mother. I saw her in a vision."

Scola rolled his eyes. Now they were back to visions. Scola had thought he had crushed that nonsense back at the Ranglan Depression. With the rumors Scola had spread among the herd, Varon should have been embarrassed to even suggest he'd had another vision.

Why couldn't Varon just accept his place in the herd like Sartino? Why did he feel the need to feel more powerful than the Calvn?

Scola shook his head side to side. *"A vision! I thought we had passed beyond that, Varon. Now you come to me with more stories of visions. I have been patient with you because of your youth, but you overstep your authority, Varon. You seek to place your voice not only above that of the other species leaders of the herd but also above my wisdom. I cannot allow this to stand."*

Varon lowered his head, but he did not retract his statements.

Had he no shame? No sense? Was he so determined to push Scola to the limit?

"Attention, my children!" Scola called out to the herd. *"As Calvn of this herd, it is my duty to dispense wisdom according to the laws of the Equus. I must do that now."*

The herd had gathered in around Scola, waiting to see who would be punished and why.

"Varon, you have overstepped your authority and are seeking to lead the Equus away from the wisdom of the Calvns through your 'visions'. Do the zebras agree?"

"We will confer," Sartino said. The zebras were the judges of the herd. It was their responsibility to decide Varon's guilt or innocence of this charge. After a time, Sartino said, *"The zebras have agreed. We support the charge."*

"Varon, with the zebras' consensus, I sentence you to a three-day exile from the Equus. Should Equ see fit to preserve you for that length of time, you may rejoin the herd. Should you not survive, then your guilt will have been shown to all. Until then, be gone."

Then Calvn Scola flicked his tail and turned his back to Varon.

28

Varon turned from Calvn Scola and looked over the herd. Few of the Equus would look away from him. Most of them stared at him to drive him away. All the unicorns and most of the zebras held anger in their glares, a sign that they not only accepted Calvn Scola's decision, they embraced it. They feared Varon.

"I have done no wrong to this herd," Varon proclaimed.

None of the Equus replied, particularly Scola. An exile had no voice among the herd, and so Varon could not be heard by any of the Equus, or at least none of the Equus could respond to him. For any of the Equus to give refuge to an exile would invite them to be exiled with Varon. Though an exile was temporary–in Varon's case three days–very few Equus ever returned from an exile. Solitary Equus made tempting targets for predators.

"Marsa, tell the Calvn what we saw on the foraging trip," Varon asked.

Marsa glared at the Calvn, but she turned her back to Varon. For all her talk, she did not want to be named an exile with Varon. She did not want to be separated from the herd. She did not want to die.

"Drusinos, surely you don't think I would try to take your authority from you?" Varon asked the pony leader.

Drusinos glanced at Scola and then said, *"It is not for me to say."*

Varon turned to his pegasus friend. *"Jalon, speak for me. You know this is not right. I am not trying to usurp any other Equus' power."*

Jalon blew air through her lips so they flapped. *"My advice would be to find some place to rest for three days. The mind-sickness may pass. Then rejoin the herd."*

Varon's eyes widened. He swung his head back and forth to look at the Equus in the herd. *"Mind-sickness? Is that what is behind all of this? You all think I have mind-sickness because I speak the words of Equ and speak what is in your own hearts?"*

Varon faced their stares, but none of them would lower their heads in submission to his argument. Tola's bout with mind-sickness was still fresh with them. They would rather condemn an innocent Equus than risk getting mind-sickness. They were that afraid of contracting mind-sickness.

Was it possible that he could have the disease, though?

No, he couldn't let Scola's short-sightedness make him doubt himself. Varon had not imagined the human, just as he had not imagined the white mountains or the branch-throwing trees. Others could verify parts of his story, and that would lend support to the rest.

"I do not have the mind-sickness. Calvn Scola is trying to isolate me because he's afraid of the future and the truth just as he fears the white mountains," Varon announced as loudly as he could.

"Unicorns," Calvn Scola said, *"if this exile does not leave the herd now, treat him as a predator."*

The unicorns lowered their heads and pointed their long, white horns toward Varon. Varon snorted and pawed at the ground. He was prepared to fight if need be. Let the blood of fellow Equus be upon these unicorns for violating the First Law. Scola was behaving no better than Calvn Gee had acted with his foal.

Varon directed his comments to Scola and not the unicorns he faced. *"You can silence me, Calvn Scola, but another Equus, horse or other species, will fill my place, speaking the same ideas, and then what will you do? Will you claim that he or she has mind-sickness and order your unicorns to violate the First Law because you fear the truth? Then what of the next Equus who you see as a challenge to your authority and the next Equus and the next one?"*

Reminding the unicorns they were about to violate the First Law disturbed them, but they held their places. They were loyal to the Calvn.

"Varon, please go," Pautin said, stepping forward to be near him. *"Don't force the horses to choose between you and their Calvn. You know what their choice will be. Don't let our colt see his sire killed for being stubborn."*

Varon looked at Pautin, then down at the colt that stood beside her. Chareth stared back at him, not understanding what was going on. His eyes did not show his fear, but even at his young stage, he could sense the tension in the herd. No Equus should have to watch another Equus violate the law basic to their culture.

Was this a fight that Equ wanted him to fight?

No, Equ had other plans for him that did not include him dying here or now. He needed to live to convince the Equus of his visions and of how they might survive the changes that the white mountains announced. He could not do that if he died as a martyr to Scola's fear and Varon's own pride.

He lowered his head and began walking away. The herd parted before him as if they were afraid that by touching him, his supposed mind-sickness would somehow contaminate them. If he had mind-sickness, they were already contaminated. When he reached the edge of the herd, he raised his head and saw no other Equus before him, only the empty plain. Behind him, he watched the Equus, his herd, turn their backs to him.

"I will return in three days," Varon announced.

No one responded to him. He hadn't expected them to. They probably didn't believe he would survive the exile.

He forced himself to walk away from the herd. He wanted them to see him for as long as possible. Varon wanted them to realize that they might send him to his death.

Jalon watched her best friend leave the herd, perhaps forever. Varon might have been walking to his death, and Jalon could not bring herself to be more encouraging when he had asked her for support.

Find some place to rest for three days!

How stupid she must have sounded to Varon, because she knew she sounded stupid to herself.

She looked around at the other Equus, whose backs were turned to Varon. How could they all abandon him? All the horses had turned their backs to him, and Varon had been their herd leader! At least Jalon had not turned her back on Varon.

What good had that done, though? When Varon had asked for her support, all Jalon could do was to tell him to do what he needed to return. That was support?

It was cowardice.

Jalon didn't support Calvn Scola, so why couldn't she support the horse she called her friend? Jalon had faced and fought griffins, who had wanted to kill her, but she wouldn't stand up against a petty Calvn when he was trying to get another Equus killed?

She lowered her head in shame.

"Equ, forgive this fool and lend your strength to Varon. He has earned the right to have your help," Jalon said, offering her plea to their creator.

Varon's stories were odd, but that did not mean that they weren't true. It had been odd to see the white mountains appear and more odd to find out they were made of ice and were moving. They existed, though. She had felt them and walked upon them.

Varon wasn't threatening the herd. He was telling a truth the Calvn, and perhaps the herd, didn't want to face.

Humans? Why couldn't there be a new species on Hemlaza? The griffins had returned after being gone for generations.

The point was: did Jalon believe Varon?

The answer was yes. Varon had never lied to her and had always tried to follow the teachings of Equ in his life. Scola had done nothing to inspire her confidence and loyalty. Yes, Jalon believed what Varon had said.

That being the case, it also meant that by not supporting him, Jalon had betrayed Varon.

Varon walked until he couldn't see the herd behind him. He knew when he had left the mind-link by the silence that filled his head. Only then, when he was too far away from the herd to hear their thoughts, did he allow anguish to overcome him. He let out a pained nicker.

He was alone, utterly alone.

He could hear no thoughts of any Equus. He searched the horizon and skies, hoping to see an Equus coming to check up on him and tell him that his exile had been a mistake. None came.

What of the predators in the area, like the wolves? Where were they? They were gathering in larger groups and forming unusual alliances, which only placed smaller bands or single Equus like Varon at greater risk of attack and death.

How long would Scola's Herd remain where they were? They would have to move soon or the foraging groups would have to travel too far away to find enough food to feed the herd. If they left the area without Varon, would he be able to find them again?

Realizing that he was hungry, Varon walked in circles, looking for grass. He should be able to find small patches of grass and grain left behind by the foraging groups. He didn't need as much as a herd, so he could live on the small patches that foraging groups had left behind.

About half a mile to the north, he found a small patch that more than filled his hunger. When he was finished, he turned to study the terrain. He would have to sleep sometime. How could he watch for predators then? Even a brief nap would leave him open to danger. He was at the mercy of any predator that might stumble upon him.

Varon tried to find a depression in the land that might hide him while he slept. He walked around the area, but the plains were flat. He gave up and laid down, hoping that his coloring would let him blend into the ground. Lying down would at least minimize his form against the horizon, but it would delay his ability to bolt if there was danger nearby. Weighing his alternatives, he would rather keep the predators from seeing him in the first place, rather than having to depend on outrunning them. It was a trade off that he thought was worth it.

At least he hoped so.

"Equ, if you want me to help you take the Equus wherever it is

you want them, then I need you to help me now and keep me alive," Varon said to the night sky.

Then he closed his eyes and went to sleep.

"Awake, Varon."

Varon opened his eyes. He wondered how long he had been asleep. It was still night.

"Predators are coming from the east," a vaguely familiar mind-voice said. *"Run now before they catch your scent."*

Varon stood up, establishing his direction from the stars, and galloped to the west. He wasn't sure if Equ had given him the warning or not, but he would not risk that he had only imagined the warning.

He had only been moving for a few moments when he saw shadows behind him. These shadows were moving familiarly.

The predators!

He tried to gallop faster, but the shadows only grew larger and closer.

"You can't outrun us, Equus."

Varon's gait faltered, and he almost stopped. These were Equus behind him. He was running from Equus! But why had Equ warned him of predators?

Then he remembered that Equus weren't above violating the First Law. Calvn Gee had tried it, and so had Calvn Scola. Were these Equus willing to kill him?

"I've been exiled from my herd. Leave me be!" Varon told them.

"We know. We have come to end your exile," one the Equus in the shadow herd said.

"Only my Calvn can do that."

"So can we."

"And who are you? What herd are you?"

"We are the Ravager's Foals."

Ravager's Foals? Who would want to name themselves after a Ravager? Varon knew one thing. He wanted nothing to do with this herd.

"Leave me be," Varon said.

"We will end your exile, Equus. It is your time to die."

They closed the gap between themselves and Varon even further. Varon tried, but he just couldn't gallop any faster than he already was.

A bright light appeared in front of him. Varon thought it was a lightning strike and veered away from it. His luck was getting worse. First, he ran into predator Equus, and now he would have to outrun a wildfire.

"Run into the light, Varon," the same vaguely familiar voice said in his head.

Varon was surprised that anyone in the shadow herd knew his name, but then he realized that the voice was different. It was a voice that he had heard before; the one he associated with Equ.

He turned back toward the lightning and saw that it wasn't lightning. It was an oval-shaped light that just seemed to sit on the plain. What was it? He didn't want to run into it, not knowing what it was.

The Ravager's Foals galloped only a few dozen yards behind him. He either had to face them or the light.

Varon chose the light.

He ran into it and was surprised to find it growing brighter around him. Then he was in a lush, green valley. He was so surprised at the change of scenery that he slid to a halt. He shook his head, unsure of what he was seeing.

The scenery didn't change. He was still in the most beautiful valley he had ever seen. The valley floor was thick with grass and grain. The air was warm, and the ground beneath his hooves was soft. This was unbelievable. He turned around to see where he had come from, but he couldn't see the patch of oval light. He also couldn't see the Ravager's Foals.

This valley was so beautiful. Why would he want to even think about returning to Hemlaza? Even at the height of the Season of Life, Hemlaza could not match this beauty. Who cared about being an exile? Varon would make his home here.

An oval of darkness appeared in front of him. Varon backed away from it.

"You must pass through the portal, Varon," Equ said.

"Will it take me away from here?"

"You are not ready to return here."

"Return here? I've never been here."

"You were born here. All the Equus were. You are standing where other Equus have only dreamed of standing," Equ told him.

"Etrasco."

"Yes."

"But I don't want to leave here. I have been working all of my life to return here," Varon said. *"You can't bring me here and then tell me to leave."*

"You must. You have work yet undone."

"I don't care about the work undone. This is where I want to be!"

Etrasco. He had returned to the birth land. He was here, standing in the valley of creation. He was home. He had made it!

Then he remembered how he had gotten here. Equ had brought him here to save him because he thought Varon would help him save all the Equus. Now Varon only wanted to save himself. Such was the power of Etrasco over him.

He looked around, trying to drink in all the details, sights, and sensations of this valley. He wanted to recall this place as vividly when he closed his eyes as when they were now open. He blew air through his lips, letting them flap. Then he walked into the darkness.

He found himself back on the dark Hemlaza Plains. He looked up at the sky and realized by the positions of the stars he was not where he had last been. Instead, he was far to the east. The Ravager's Foals were nowhere to be found, either. Varon was alone and safe.

Varon shook his head. He closed his eyes and tried to recall the image of Etrasco and tell himself that it hadn't all been a dream.

"What happened?" he asked Equ.

"You asked for help, and I gave it to you."

"But why couldn't I stay in Etrasco?"

"Because the Equus aren't ready to return there yet. That is what they are being prepared for," Equ explained to Varon.

"Do you know why those Equus wanted to kill me? You knew they were predators," Varon asked.

"Were they Equus?"

"Didn't you see them? They were a herd of Equus."

"Varon, I know all of my children by name, and I did not know any of them."

They had been Equus. Varon knew that much. If Equ knew all his children, though, why hadn't he known who the Ravager's Foals were? It had something to do with their name, Varon was sure. Those Equus didn't identify themselves with Equ, but with Ravagers. Just the thought of that made Varon shudder.

He galloped until he felt that he was safe, and then he slowed to a walk to cool down. Varon decided that without Equ's help, he would not survive this exile. He had never heard of an Equus returning from exile, so why should he be the first? These Ravager's Foals were just the first predators he would face. How many times would Equ rescue him? How valuable was he to Equ's plans?

As he walked, his legs felt shaky. Varon stopped and locked his knees. He was coming to recognize the feeling and what it meant.

"No, I don't want a vision now. I have to watch and protect myself," Varon said.

His vision brightened, and Varon realized that he was seeing his vision as if it was daylight, although he knew it was still night. He saw the Equus and the humans together in great numbers. The humans rode on the Equus' backs, and the Equus pulled carts and wagons filled with grasses, grains, fruits, and vegetables between strange, hollow structures. He saw the Equus protected from predators within stone walls and fences. He saw humans feeding the Equus more than enough food to fill their stomachs. It was a vision of cooperation between the two species.

What he wasn't sure of was if the cooperation was as beneficial for the Equus as it was for the humans. The Equus worked hard in exchange for protection and food, but the humans seemed to receive so much more from the Equus than the Equus got from the humans. The humans got free labor that allowed them to create their large structures and a more efficient way to transport the materials since the Equus were faster and stronger than the humans. What disturbed Varon the most was that the humans seemed in control of the Equus. That shouldn't be. The Equus were free creatures.

The scene shifted.

Now Varon saw the Equus once again gathered as a single herd. Thousands of Equus were being led across the white mountains by a single white unicorn. At the opposite end of the massive herd, predators—bears, wolves, lions, and others—raced to catch up with the herd, and they gained on the Equus.

Varon watched as the unicorns, ponies, and horses at the rear of the herd turned to defend the herd and delay the predators. As they formed a defensive line between the predators and Equus, Varon heard a deep rumbling. The ice plain atop the white mountains shook so violently both the Equus and the predators were thrown to the ground.

A crack appeared in the ice between the Equus and the predators. It grew wider and longer as the white mountains shook. The predators realized what was happening. They dug their claws into the ice to regain their footing and charged the Equus defensive line. A tiger tried to jump the widening gap, but it was already too wide. He fell into the chasm, roaring and growling. Others quickly followed him, especially those who had been near the edge.

The trembling stopped. The Equus regained their footing and some braver ones moved to the edge of the gap and looked over the edge. It was deep, so deep that Varon could see the ocean thousands of yards below the edge. He couldn't see any of the predators that had fallen into the water, though. Some predators had gathered on the opposite edge of the gap, making threatening sounds at the Equus but with no way to carry them out.

The length of the gulf did not stretch entirely from east to west across the white mountains, but it was long enough that it would delay the predators from following the Equus for at least two weeks, maybe even a moon cycle. They would have to circle around the end of the crack and then move back to this position. The Equus were safe for now.

Or they would be.

If the vision from Equ was to be obeyed.

Varon's vision cleared, and he found himself alone on the dark Hemlaza Plains again. He found that he missed the vision now that it was gone. Although he had known that he was experiencing a vision, he had found comfort in seeing the Equus, even if they were only images in his mind.

He looked around to see if he could see anything in the darkness. Convinced he was still alone, Varon lay down and napped. When he awoke, he was quickly on his hooves and searching for food.

He found a prairie dog burrow with young prairie dogs playing outside of it. He approached the three prairie dogs and stood off a distance so that he wouldn't scare them, then he just watched them tumble over each other as they played. They wrestled and nipped at each other and jumped over one another. Varon wished that he could speak with them through the mind-link.

Varon's tail swished back and forth in enjoyment. He wondered how his colt was doing back with the herd. Was Chareth strong and adventurous? Or had he been shunned because of Varon's supposed transgressions against the herd?

Varon stamped his hoof. It caused the prairie dogs to stop their play and look at him. He would survive this exile. It would be temporary. He would return to Scola's Herd and prove his innocence of both Scola's charges and the rumor that he had mind-sickness.

29

Scola held council with his three unicorn advisors. Other Calvns held their herd councils with their herd leaders. It was a sign of their weak leadership that they had to gain the favor of those that they were trying to lead. It gave the herd leaders a near-equal standing to the Calvn when they should have been reminded of who was in control. Scola patterned his herd council after the Calvn Council. Since unicorns were the true leaders among the Equus, why should he council with any Equus but unicorns?

"How is the herd this morning?" Calvn Scola asked.

Greegh, a roan unicorn, said, *"There is still grumbling about Varon's exile. It was not seen favorably."*

"That is to be expected from the horses, since it was their herd leader who was exiled," Scola replied.

"That's the curious thing, Calvn. The horses seem embarrassed by Varon's actions, and they are trying to forget he was their herd leader. They've already selected Stoni as their new horse leader. Most of the grumbling is coming from the donkeys, ponies, and pegasus."

Scola pawed at the ground. *"Really?"*

Greegh nodded.

"Then perhaps Varon was trying to extend his influence beyond leading his own species."

"You mean that's not why he was exiled?" Dola, a bay unicorn, asked.

Scola shook his head. *"No, he was exiled because he was trying to join the Equus under one Calvn, and he speaks obvious lies."*

"How do you know they are lies, Calvn? They weren't obvious to me. I was curious about what he had to say."

"Because there are no such things as visions," Scola snapped.

Dola pranced around a bit. The announcement had upset him. *"Really?"*

Scola had to be careful now; otherwise, he might endanger the legacy of the Calvns. It was widely believed Calvns received visions from Equ, as it was said the original Calvn had. If Scola claimed now that no Calvns, other than the original Calvn, had ever received a vision, he could threaten the unicorns' authority within the Equus herds. The belief in a direct connection to Equ was the source of their power and what gave them the unicorns their authority as the leaders of the Equus.

"Visions don't come to unicorns outside of the bloodline, and they certainly don't come to horses," Scola said to calm Dola.

"Then Varon is claiming to be a Calvn by saying he is receiving visions from Equ," Dola said.

"No," corrected Greegh, *"he is claiming to be something greater than a Calvn by receiving visions from both Equ and Equ's mother."*

The thought gave Scola pause. Dola and Greegh were right. By claiming to receive visions, perhaps Varon sought to act as a Calvn or something greater. Acting as a Calvn without being of the bloodline was an exilable offense. Scola had missed the opportunity to get rid of Varon for good, but now he had claimed if Varon returned after three days, he would be innocent of Scola's charges. It couldn't be allowed to happen.

"Varon must not be allowed to return to the herd," Scola told his advisors.

"But if he survives his three-day exile, he must be allowed to return. It is the law," Plith said.

"What are the chances he will survive, though? Not very good," Dola said.

"He must not survive this short exile. He must not have even his slight chance," Scola said.

"How can we ensure that, Calvn? We can't lead the predators to him. They would devour us before we could ever direct them to Varon," Plith pointed out.

Scola considered that. *"Perhaps... or perhaps it won't be a predator that kills Varon."*

"Then what?" Dola asked.

"Aren't there buffalo nearby?"

"What buffalo?"

"The small herd you saw this morning when you were doing some close-range foraging for your season mate, Dola."

Dola shook his head. *"But I wasn't foraging. I leave that to the foraging bands."*

Scola stared at the bay Equus. *"You were, and poor Varon will startle one of those buffalo, and they will gore him to death when they stampede this evening."*

Dola, Plith, and Greegh looked at one another, wondering if they had missed something their Calvn had explained. They might serve as advisors, but they weren't leaders, even if Plith was of Calvn blood.

"Have you received a vision of Varon's fate, Calvn?" Dola asked.

Scola's tail swished. What a marvelous idea! *"Yes. Yes, I have. Equ has shown me what must be done to protect the herd. He has chosen you three to act as his agents on this mission."*

"Us?" Plith said.

"Yes, you have proven your worth to me. Now you must prove your worth to Equ. How willing are you to do his will?"

"What would he have us do?"

"Make sure that Varon does not return to the herd. His presence among us endangers our very survival," Scola told his advisors.

"But how can we do that?" Greegh asked.

"Slay him."

Now Greegh pranced in front of Scola. *"Slay? But that would violate the First Law of Equus! How could we do that?"*

"The zebras made the First Law, but Equ made the zebras. He says... he has shown me in a vision what he wishes you do. He wishes for Varon to die. I know it is a great deed he asks of you, but you must follow his will," Scola said.

"But we can't make the buffalo kill Varon. They are too gentle," Greegh said.

Scola stepped closer to Greegh. *"Then you report now that buffalo are nearby to allow the idea to become part of the thoughts on the mind-link. You slay Varon tonight, and when he does not return after the third day, it will be assumed that predators killed him. If his body is ever found gored, we can remind the herd of the buffalo that were in the area."*

"Equ wishes that?" Dola sounded skeptical.

Scola nodded. *"He does."*

The three unicorns looked at one another and then turned to Calvn Scola. *"It will be done, my Calvn. Varon will not return to the herd."*

By his second night in exile, Varon thought he might go crazy. He was so mad for companionship he would have welcomed predators just to have something to do. He would have greeted them with neighs and nickers rather than kicks and slashes.

Finding water and grass were no problem for a single Equus. Varon was full, but he wanted someone to link with, even if it was only to hear Pautin's nagging voice now. He would welcome the annoying sound. He hadn't even heard Equ's voice in his head since last night. He needed the companionship of other horses.

In the brief time of his exile, Varon realized one important fact: the Equus were not meant to be alone. They were herd creatures. They needed the security of the mind-link and other Equus as part of their daily lives. Exile was more than a punishment; it was torture. It reminded the offender of the need for Equus companionship, which they had denied themselves through their actions. The punishment was not only being exposed to a greater danger from predators; it was being alone.

"Beware, Varon."

At the sound of Equ's voice, Varon was alert. He lurched to his hooves and looked around. He could see nothing nearby.

"Beware? Beware of what?"

No other reply came, but Varon felt the brush of another Equus mind against his. Had the herd moved toward him during his day? He was still north of the herd, so that would have been the last direction in which Scola would have taken them. He would have moved south if not to be away from Varon, then to move where it was warmer and there were fewer predators.

Were the Equus what Equ was warning him against?

He couldn't see why they would be. Once they recognized Varon as having touched their mind-link, if they were members of Scola's Herd, they would avoid Varon for fear of reprisals from Calvn Scola.

Then Varon felt the brush of another Equus mind again. No thoughts were sent through the link. It was a brush, a tickling of his mind, as if to make sure that Varon was still where he had been.

Something was wrong. Varon could understand the first touch as accidental, but not the second. After the first, the Equus should have moved away from him. They hadn't. They had moved closer during the interval between contacts.

Varon faced in the direction the light touch had come from. He saw a dark shadow against the lighter sky. The shape blocked out stars as it crept closer to him.

"Varon?"

Varon didn't answer. He didn't recognize the mind-voice, and he wondered if Scola was baiting him to see if Varon would violate his exile and establish a mind-link with the herd.

"Varon, my name is Greegh."

Greegh? Greegh was one of Scola's advisors.

The shadow moved closer. Varon backed away.

"Turn," Equ's voice said in his mind.

Varon did as he had been instructed. He turned in time to see another shadow charging him from where his blind spot had been.

Varon jumped to the side, and the unicorn ran past him. If Varon had remained standing where he had been, he would have been gored in the chest. As it was, the white horn scratched his neck. Then the unicorn adjusted his path, and the horn sunk into Varon's haunches.

Varon neighed in terror. He kicked out with his forehooves, drawing blood from the unicorn's own haunches as he ran past him. Varon looked up to see a second unicorn charging from the other side. Varon rose on his rear legs and kicked the horn aside with his forehooves. The unicorn snorted, but his head dropped, which turned his body away from Varon.

What was going on? These Equus were trying to kill him! They would not wait to see if the predators would do it. They were taking it upon themselves.

They were violating the First Law.

Why?

Then Varon recognized Plith, and he realized why. Plith was another one of the Equus the Calvn consulted in place of the herd leaders. Plith wouldn't do anything like this unless he had been instructed to do so by Calvn Scola. His position as an advisor gave him much influence among the herd. He wouldn't risk it by taking on a renegade action the Calvn hadn't sanctioned.

Calvn Scola didn't want Varon to return to the herd. He wanted him dead.

Varon kicked out at a third unicorn to clear a path. Then he galloped as he hadn't run for years. Instead of trying to stay near the herd, he now needed to get as far from Scola's Herd as he could if he wanted to survive.

And Varon wanted to live.

Equ wanted him alive to aid in his plans. Equ had warned him of the danger twice, and even rescued him from certain death twice. Varon had to do his part and stay alive.

His exile had just become permanent.

<h1 style="text-align:center">30</h1>

Miskala trotted along with his herd as they moved south; hopefully toward better forage. *His* herd. He liked the sound of it, though he hadn't ever imagined he would become his herd's Calvn.

He also hadn't imagined all the problems he would have to deal with as Calvn of his own herd. It only made him appreciate what Calvn Conllal had done as leader the herd all the more. Finding adequate grazing was an ever-constant problem this year. Not only did the Equus have to compete with other herds for the diminished food sources, but they had to compete with other creatures. The Equus were better adapted than most animals to eat the nutrient-poor grasses. The Equus could at least find forage where other animals might starve. Small animals didn't need as much food as the Equus. It probably all worked out.

Miskala cantered alongside Preis, the pony leader of his herd. *"Preis, I have a question that I would like to ask you."*

"I will answer it if I can, Calvn."

"I know I possess Calvn blood, but have any of my sires been Calvn of this herd?"

Preis was quiet as he researched the answer in the memory of the Equus. *"Your Calvn blood is from your dam and her dam. Before that, your bloodline was not a part of this herd,"* Preis told him after a few moments. The ponies were amazing for their ability to remember details of a herd's history. It came from the way they had developed a tight and specific mind-link that contained memories and not just thoughts. They were the only species of Equus who had mastered the technique, and with it became their responsibility to serve as the memory of the Equus.

Miskala had hoped if one of his sires had been Calvn, he could find out information about how his sires had governed this herd. He hadn't realized he was only a third-generation unicorn in this herd.

"Thank you," Miskala said.

"Why did you ask, Calvn?"

"I wanted to see if there was one of my blood whom I could emulate. I wanted a Calvn whom I could try to model myself after as I try to lead this herd."

"Then I would suggest that you use the first of your blood, Calvn. You now carry his name and he, too, is your ultimate sire," Preis said.

Miskala blew air through his lips and let them flap. *"No Equus could hope to match his abilities. He is more legend than fact now."*

"Not to the ponies."

"I can't come to you for every decision I need to make, though."

Preis whinnied. *"No, I suppose not, but if you seek to emulate him and fail, you might be better off than if you seek to emulate a lesser Calvn and succeed."*

Miskala saw the wisdom in that. *"You are right, Preis, and I thank you for your advice."* Miskala paused. *"Have you or any others detected any more creator paths?"*

"No, Calvn."

That worried Miskala. He still believed the Ravager was among them, so why hadn't he attacked yet? What was the Ravager's plan?

"Is it possible the paths you detected were old?"

Preis shook his head. *"If they had been, we should have been able to cross them. No, this Ravager just hasn't shifted form again. He is remaining, for all intents and purposes, an Equus."*

Miskala nodded. *"Remain vigilant then. If he shifts at all, I want you to do what you can to narrow down who it might be."*

"That will be hard, Calvn."

"The alternative is to wait until the Ravager is ready to destroy us."

"I understand, Calvn. We will watch."

Miskala shifted his position more toward the edge of the herd.

He spoke quietly with some donkeys, asking if they had seen any predators and complimenting them on their vigilance in protecting the herd. Besides watching for predators, the Equus now had to watch for growing packs of predators that could threaten the safety of the herd. So far they had either been able to avoid such large packs or his herd had been so much larger than the predators that they hadn't dared challenge Miskala's Herd.

When he'd gotten the donkey reports, Miskala had asked for their opinions on other topics, such as where good grazing might be found or even what they thought the significance of the white mountains were. He wanted the donkeys to feel they were a part of the herd, but Miskala was also trying to get a feel for where various Equus felt themselves positioned in the herd.

Having grown up among them, Miskala knew all the Equus in the herd. He had realized that upon becoming Calvn, they all treated him differently, especially his friends who were not unicorns, like Qarel and Capsta. Though the herd hadn't changed, it seemed as if it had. Not because the Equus were any different, but because Miskala was seeing them differently. He was no longer one of them; he was their leader.

Most of the Equus in the herd had accepted the change in leadership in stride. *Most.* There were other Equus – a band within the herd – who seemed hostile toward him. When Miskala spoke to them, they responded with as little actions and thoughts as they could. They glared at him. He had heard from his friends that the hostile Equus taunted him behind his back, mocking his leadership ability and weight and even how his mane lay against his neck. None of this band was openly disobedient; they were just hostile and their doubts made Miskala question himself and his ability.

The herd slowed as they reached adequate grazing for the next few days. To find such grazing was moving his herd further and further south, away from their familiar territory. If other herds were doing this, they would soon push at the edges of each other's grazing territory. Miskala didn't enjoy feeling as if he was running from the white mountains.

"Let the mares and the young eat first," Miskala said as they stopped.

This had been one of his governing decisions. Some Equus argued that the stallions should eat first to maintain their strength, and therefore, the defense of the herd. Miskala would rather keep the unborn foals healthy in the womb and the young strong enough to keep up with the herd since they were moving more than usual.

As the herd grazed, Miskala watched for Lyos. She was a white unicorn. Her hair was so white that it was hard to look at her on sunny days because of the glare coming off her hide. Miskala found her coloring exotic, and during the few times that he had spoken with her, he had also found her very intelligent. She wasn't a part of the hostile band.

He spotted her across the herd. She seemed to stand out from the rest of the herd. He tried to watch her without her knowing it.

Lyos turned her hindquarters to Miskala and lifted her tail. He realized that she had been urinating frequently the past few days. He hadn't thought too much about it because he hadn't been thinking of her as a mate. Now he realized that she was in heat and offering herself to him. He curled his upper lip back and took a deep sniff of the air. The intensity of the smell made him shudder.

She was *definitely* in heat.

Now that he had the invitation, Miskala doubted himself. Was he ready for this? Of course he was. Lyos wasn't a life mate, just a potential season mate.

He tucked his nose down to emphasize the tight arch in his neck. Then he emitted a long, forceful nicker. Hearing the sound come from himself made him slightly self-conscious. It shouldn't have. He had been hearing the sound for the past few weeks as other couples mated. Why shouldn't he mate if felt the desire?

The herd would expect him to continue his Calvn bloodline. Not that being Calvn of the herd was a hereditary role, but many times strong Calvns passed on the strength of their ultimate sire to their offspring. Having a strong source of Calvn blood within a herd was always a good omen. It meant that future Calvns would have grown up in the herd, and therefore, know all the strengths and weaknesses of the various herd members.

Miskala raised his own tail and pranced with high steps around Lyos. He observed her, wondering if she would accept him or if she was taunting him. If she was taunting him, she could do some serious injury to him with a well-placed kick if he got too close.

He made three laps around her and she still stood and watched him. He moved in closer and nuzzled her white neck. When she accepted this close contact with him, he worked his way back to her flanks, grooming her along the way. Satisfied that she was accepting of him as a mate, he nibbled at her tail and back legs.

It was the beginning of a mating ritual, and he gave in to his physical needs. When it was over, his brain took over his passion. He stood next to her, staring at her as she watched him. If she became pregnant, they would become season mates until the foal was born. His doubts resurfaced, and he wondered what sort of world he was trying to bring a foal into. Would it be a barren, ice-covered plain? Would the Equus be a hunted species? Was it wise to want to bring a new life into this erratic time?

The thought so upset him he felt sick to his stomach again. He had been feeling that more and more. He tried not to let his pain show, but it had curbed his attack. Between the sickness and the scarcity of food, Miskala was no longer the overweight stallion he had been three moon cycles ago. He attributed the sickness to the stress of his position. He was unused to leading. He would grow into the position and become the Calvn his herd deserved.

"Is something wrong, Miskala?" Lyos asked. *"Have I displeased you?"*

Miskala began grooming her at the withers. *"No, Lyos, you've made everything wonderful."*

Carn watched Miskala stop grooming his season mate and graze on the nearby grass. How easy it would be to shift form and kill the unicorn; to kill the entire herd. It wouldn't work, though. Many of the herd would bolt before he was through, and his mother would punish him for overstepping his bounds.

No, he would have to wait and follow his plan.

Miskala should have been dead by now. The poison was slow acting, but this was taking too long.

As Miskala grazed, Carn let a few of the hairs in his tail change to vapor and carry the poison from the greyleaf plant to Miskala. The vapor was so light that it was undetectable. It coated the grass, and Miskala ate it unknowingly.

At first, he had tried to alter the structure of the grass to make it poisonous, but it was impossible to alter the structure of something that already existed. So he had settled for this method, which until a couple of weeks ago he had thought would work fine. Now he wondered if he had somehow gotten the structure of the poison wrong or if having it carried in a vapor form diluted its effectiveness.

The first few times Miskala had ingested the poison he had gagged and thrown up. Miskala had blamed it on tension, and everyone had accepted that. Carn had known the true cause, though. Miskala hadn't either gagged or thrown up recently, which is what caused Carn to wonder about the poison's effectiveness.

The delay had given him time to cultivate Oralum into a leader who would divide this herd and turn it upon itself. Just the thought of watching that happen made Carn giddy.

As for Miskala, he would die soon. Even if the poison's potency had been diluted somewhat, the constant build up of it in Miskala's system would have to kill him. He was a walking corpse and didn't even realize it. Carn was doing Miskala a favor. His death would be much swifter and less painful than the death Carn had planned for his herd.

31

Even before Varon stopped galloping away from his attackers, he realized he could not survive for long as an exile. It wasn't just the predators he had to worry about. If he had to continue living as he had for the past two days, he would develop mind-sickness and prove Scola right. Varon needed to find another herd and see if they would adopt him, despite his exile from Scola's Herd.

He galloped to the north to put distance between himself and Scola's advisors, and then he veered to the west. He lost track of how long he galloped because he was too busy making sure that he didn't run headlong into predators. Packs that would avoid a herd would fall on him with relish. He let his thoughts go out, searching for another herd that would acknowledge him.

He found Calvn Alii's Herd near morning. His thoughts brushed the minds of the herd scouts and they called out to him.

"Who are you?" one donkey challenged him.

"I am Varon of Scola's Herd."

"Approach slowly until we allow you to enter our herd," the donkey warned. Alii was keeping his herd at a heightened state of readiness.

Varon slowed his pace to a walk and approached the group of three donkeys who were closest to him. They were tense, as if they expected Varon to attack them. Their eyes, after taking in Varon, continued to roam the horizon for other Equus or predators.

"Have you had trouble with predators, brother?" Varon asked.

"Two days ago, tigers attacked us. We lost two donkeys, a zebra, and a pony before the unicorns could drive them off."

"Then your dead have returned to Etrasco."

"The hard way," the donkey nodded.

"Will Calvn Alii see me?"

"He is holding council with his herd leaders now. You are to wait here until the council is done. He will let me know when to send you to join him."

Varon nodded. He walked back and forth, wondering how he would convince Calvn Alii to adopt him into his herd if it was known that he was an exile from Scola's Herd. If Calvn Alii adopted him before Calvn Scola sent out word about Varon's exile, Alii would find it hard to renounce him. Better yet, if there were ill will between Calvn Alii and Calvn Scola, Alii might adopt Varon despite Scola.

"Calvn Alii will see you now," the donkey told him.

Varon approached him. *"What is your name?"*

"Dissinalit."

"I hope that we will be brothers this day, Dissinalit," Varon said.

Dissinalit looked skeptical. *"I am only a donkey. You are a horse."*

Varon nodded. *"But we are both Equus."*

Varon walked by the donkey and was soon among Alii's Herd. He noticed that the Equus looked somewhat lean in this herd. They must have been having as much trouble finding food as Scola's Herd was.

Varon approached Calvn Alii, bowed his head low to the ground and imitated eating the nonexistent grass. Calvn Alii was a chestnut like Varon's colt, Chareth, and the Calvn was taller than Varon. However, even this fine unicorn was showing signs of having too little to eat. The edges of his ribs were showing beneath his chestnut coat.

"Why are you here, Varon of Scola's Herd?" Calvn Alii asked.

"I seek adoption into this herd."

"This herd? Why? We have not spoken of this before, and my herd scarcely needs another belly to fill with food," the unicorn said.

"I can forage for more than myself, Calvn. I am also an excellent healer."

"You are Scola's horse leader, aren't you?" Varon nodded, though he no longer knew if it was true or not. *"I have no need for a horse leader. Gane does well."*

"I would be happy to be only a horse among your herd. My joy comes in serving as a healer, not as a horse leader."

"Does Calvn Scola know you are here?"

"He knows that I have left his herd."

Alii snorted. *"Do you think I am a fool, Varon?"*

Varon shook his head, *"No, Calvn."*

"Scola sent pegasus out declaring you a renegade."

"But I am not a renegade. That I stand before you should prove that. I was given a three-day exile from my herd that has now ended, and I choose not to return to Scola's Herd. I mean the Equus no harm," Varon protested.

"All renegades say that." Calvn Alii paused and dug the edge of his hoof into the dirt. *"Whether I believe you or not, it is not for me to declare your guilt or innocence. Your Calvn and the zebras did that. A renegade you have been declared, and a renegade you shall remain. Now leave this herd."*

"Calvn Scola is afraid of me."

Calvn Alii's eyes flared with anger, and he pointed his horn at Varon. *"How dare you say that of a Calvn! No wonder Calvn Scola declared you a renegade. Your attitude threatens the structure of our society."*

"But what I say is true. I told Calvn Scola what Equ would have the Equus do. I told him of how the Equus could save themselves, and he feared what I said because he did not want to relinquish his power," Varon declared as he began to leave.

Calvn Alii turned across Varon's line of travel, blocking him. *"And how would you know Equ's wishes? You are not of the bloodline."*

"Equ spoke to me and showed me visions of the future of the Equus."

Alii backed away from Varon. *"So it's true."*

"What's true?"

"You have the mind-sickness. No wonder Scola exiled you. Leave my herd. Now! I will not have mind-sickness infect my herd."

"I do not have mind-sickness."

"Then you are taking upon yourself something that only the

Calvn can receive. As herd leader, only a Calvn can receive visions from Equ. In claiming you are a visionary, you also show that you deserved to be declared a renegade," Calvn Alii said.

Varon flicked his tail in irritation. Calvn Alii was being just as thickheaded as Calvn Scola. It must have something to do with the horn.

"My herd does not and will not accept you as a member. We do not want your mind to be a part of our mind-link," the Calvn told him.

Varon glared at Calvn Alii. *"You're being foolish."*

Calvn Alii arched his neck. *"It is my duty to protect my herd. I am Calvn."*

"Being a fool and Calvn seems to be the same thing nowadays."

Calvn Alii snorted and pawed the ground. *"Leave now before I order the unicorns to drive you away. Your presence among us endangers my herd."*

"It also seems the Calvns have abandoned the First Law. Is it because Calvn Gee got away with it that you think you can, too?" Varon said, referring to the accusation made against Calvn Gee that he left his hornless unicorn colt to die.

Varon turned and trotted away from the Calvn. As he passed the herd scouts on his way out of Calvn Alii's grazing territory, he said, *"Farewell, Dissinalit."*

"Are we not to be brothers, Varon?"

"Not herd brothers, but we will always be brothers. However, your Calvn is as foolish as mine," Varon told him.

Varon broke into a trot. He was reluctant to leave the comfort of the herd, but he didn't want Calvn Alii to change his mind and order the unicorns to attack him. He was not up for another battle. Varon had pushed his luck with the comment about Calvn Gee, but it had shamed Calvn Alii enough to give Varon time to leave the area.

As he passed beyond Alii's Herd's mind-link, he felt the despair of solitude return to him.

What would he do now?

After Return, Scola called his herd together. He looked around at the nearly 250 Equus he controlled. Then he turned to stare for a few moments at the white mountains. His herd's future did not lie beyond them. Scola controlled the future of his herd, and he would not take them to the white mountains and beyond. In fact, they would go further south to escape even the sight of the white mountains.

"My children, last night, I sent my advisors to check on Varon to make sure he had not violated his exile. I am sad to report the mind-sickness had overtaken our former horse leader. Without provocation, he attacked my advisors last night, nearly killing one of them," Scola announced to the herd.

Dola, Greegh, and Plith limped up next to Calvn Scola. They displayed their wounds – a collection of cuts and scrapes – for the herd to see. Scola had ordered them to wound each other even further than Varon had to make his point. Dola's haunches and Greegh's neck had gashes held closed with thorns. Plith had a poultice applied around his horn to strengthen it at the base, although it had not been damaged.

"After consulting with the zebras, I sent the pegasuses out this morning to warn the other Calvns of the danger Varon poses to their herds. I am declaring Varon a renegade, and if the other Calvns are wise, they will avoid him or risk contaminating their own herds with mind-sickness."

"Varon did not seem mind-sick when he left, Calvn," one pony said.

Calvn Scola swung his head toward Dola, Greegh, and Plith. *"Look at my advisors. Would a healthy Equus have tried to violate the First Law? I say no."* He paused. *"May Equ take him swiftly. The foraging groups will go south today, and the herd will follow. The herd will move south until we reach the Shadow Ocean. Once we reach there, I will decide what to do, depending on how good the grazing is there."*

Calvn Scola heard the faint whispers on the mind-link as different Equus spoke to each other while trying not to be heard by other Equus. Even private conversations among life mates created stirring on the mind-link. The thoughts could not be heard or even who they were between; only that they were happening.

"Can you tell what they are saying?" Scola asked Plith.

"No, they are holding their conversations too close to one another. They are afraid to touch the mind-link fully."

"Because they think Varon contaminated it?"

Plith's ears flicked back and forth. *"Or because they are afraid of who will hear their thoughts."*

Scola lowered his head. *"Varon has scarred this herd."*

"But now that he is gone, the wounds will heal. Soon the Equus will obey you without question again," Dola told him.

"The fact that Varon could create such dissension disturbs me the most. It must not happen again," Scola said.

"It won't, Calvn. We will make sure it does not happen again."

How could they make such a promise? His advisors hadn't killed Varon. They had failed in that. *"Watch and listen even harder. I may have to declare a group of these Equus renegades before this is all put to rest,"* Scola said.

"Would that be wise, Calvn? It would just make Varon's supporters seem that much more powerful if you have to drive them away from the herd," Greegh advised.

Calvn Scola snorted. *"You should have killed him. Then I would not have this concern. You have failed both Equ and me."*

"We tried, Calvn. We approached Varon in stealth. He should not have been able to hear us, but somehow he did. As we drew closer, he was on the alert."

Scola shook his head. *"He must have thought you were predators."*

Greegh nodded. *"Yes, so I distracted him while Dola and Plith tried to approach him within his blind spots. He turned and saw us, though."*

Calvn Scola snorted. *"You were three unicorns against one horse. How could he have escaped you?"*

"He still has the speed of youth, and he fought well, striking at anything around him and knowing it would be an enemy," Plith explained.

"But did you wound him?"

"Yes, most definitely. I gored his right haunch on my first pass. It was a deep wound, too."

Calvn Scola nodded. *"Good. If Equ will grant us our desires, it will become infected and we may rid ourselves of Varon after all."*

Varon's breath caught as he waded into the middle of the river. The water was biting cold. He whinnied in pain as it reached the wound in his haunch.

Even the chilly water did not lessen the heat coming from the wound. When he looked at it, it almost seemed to glow red. It didn't take a genius to realize the wound was infected. He should have rinsed it last night, but he had been far from a stream that was deep enough to suit his purposes. He had hoped that Calvn Alii would have accepted him, and Varon could have gotten a horse in Alii's Herd to treat the wound. Varon would have to make a poultice and apply it to his haunch. No Equus would have anything to do with him now that Scola had declared him a renegade.

Varon closed his eyes and sighed. What would he do now?

By now, all the herds would know Calvn Scola had declared him a renegade. Varon wondered what Scola had told the zebras to get them to go along with his decision. Other Calvns didn't have to obey Scola's renegade order, but they would know Varon was considered a trouble-maker and a danger to the Equus. Scola was telling anyone who would listen that Varon had mind-sickness. No herd would want to chance linking with him longer than it took to find out who he was.

Varon walked out of the water. His muscles were stiff with cold. The water drained off of him in small rivers. He shook himself to help get the water off. He hoped that the water was washing away some infection, but if he couldn't clean and close the wound, it would become infected again.

He looked to the north and saw the ever-present white mountains, a reminder of the mission he needed to accomplish for Equ.

But how? What did Equ expect him to do, especially as a renegade?

Now that he was a renegade, he had no influence among the Equus. How could he gather them to take them across the white mountains?

Should he head north and gather the Equus along the way?

"To the east," Equ's voice said in his mind.

East? All that was to the east were the Meshack Mountains. The mountains weren't even range for the Equus. What would he find there? Certainly not Equus.

"Answers," Equ told him.

Varon was now a renegade because of Equ. He had committed his life to following Equ. Why should he balk at following Equ now, when so little of his life was left?

He started walking east.

It took five days to reach the foothills of the Meshack Mountains. Varon stopped to rinse his wound in a river daily. It was the only thing that he could do. He had to hope that the wound would heal on its own.

"I am here, Equ. What would you have me do now?" Varon asked from the middle of the river.

"Go to the other side," came the reply.

"Other side? Of the mountains? No Equus has ever crossed the Meshacks. They are too high and too steep at the top. Even the pegasus cannot fly over them."

"I will show you the way."

"How?"

"Follow the river."

Varon looked down at the water flowing around his body. Then he looked up and followed the flow with his eyes. It came from a point high up the side of the mountains.

He walked out of the water and walked along the bank as it flowed from the foothills. At some points, the banks disappeared, and he was forced to wade through the water against the current. It wasn't bad if the water was shallow, but the deeper areas numbed him if he stayed in them for any amount of time because the water was so cold. Varon followed the river for two days, more inside of it than out.

On the third day, he found himself at the base of a great waterfall hundreds of yards high. The water pounded down so heavily that the spray stung him and the noise deafened him. As he stood neck deep in the water, he looked for a path through the rocks to the top of the waterfall. He saw none. The waterfall was part of a cliff, so the face of the waterfall was a sheer drop. He could go no further up into the mountains, even if he followed the river.

"Is this where you wanted me to be, Equ?" Varon asked.

"No, your destination lies on the other side of the mountains."

"But how do I get there? I can't climb sheer rock faces like a monkey."

"Go behind the waterfall."

Behind!

As Varon approached the waterfall, the roar of the pounding water was so loud that he wondered if he could even hear Equ if the creator spoke to him. The spray from the waterfall blinded him as he worked his way around the side of the waterfall. His hooves lost their footing, and he was forced to swim until he was in shallower water.

Then he saw an opening between the waterfall and the side of the cliff. He kicked his legs harder to move himself toward it.

Behind the waterfall, the roar of the water bounced off the stone, which made it even louder. The gap between the mountain and waterfall was just wide enough to allow him to pass between them. He swam behind it and saw that the cliff face wasn't flat. It bowed inward. There was a cove behind the waterfall that couldn't be seen from the front of the waterfall.

As Varon swam into the cove, he found his footing again as the water became shallow once more. He walked out of the water and onto dry land inside of a cave.

This had to be what Equ wanted him to find.

Varon walked deeper into the cave. The air that flowed through it was cold, and because he was wet, Varon felt even colder. Within a short distance, it was so dark that he could no longer see, and still he kept walking. He moved forward, feeling his way along to make sure he didn't hit his head or step off into some great chasm. The cave remained high enough above his head that he didn't have to duck, nor did the floor of the cave fall away from under his hooves.

Varon wasn't sure how long or how far he walked, but it was long enough that he stopped to sleep at least a half a dozen times.

Sometimes it was hard to tell whether he was sleeping or just staring off into the darkness. There were a difference in what he saw when he closed his eyes. When he grew hungry, he managed to find a bit of moss on the rocks that allowed him to keep going.

He kept walking.

He saw stars above his head. He was out of the cave and standing on a high ledge on the other side of the Meshack Mountains. He could see moonlight reflecting off the sea to the west of Hemlaza and the beach below him.

Varon found a patch of rye grass on the ledge and ate. It stilled the rumbling in his stomach.

"What now, Equ?"

He heard no reply. Varon wondered if he should try to find his way down the mountainside, but he chose not to attempt it in the dark. Tomorrow would be soon enough. Now he was tired. Besides, he was safer from predators up on the ledge than down on the beach.

Varon closed his eyes and went to sleep.

When he awoke as dawn was breaking, he thought he was in a dream. He was standing high above the ocean. The mountain surrounded what he thought had been the beach last night. Now he could see that it was another ledge hundreds of acres in size. Instead of reflecting off of the sand, the moonlight had been reflecting off of millions of bones.

Varon saw a path leading from the ledge he was standing on down to the lower ledge. He followed it. As he drew closer to the bones, he realized that they were from Equus.

But no Equus had ever been beyond the Meshacks, so how had so many bones come to be gathered at this place?

"What happened here?" Varon asked.

His legs felt shaky, and Varon locked his knees. His vision changed, and Varon saw a land that looked familiar, but he knew that he had never seen it before. In the center of the land, he saw a vast herd of Equus being slaughtered by predators. The predators feasted on the dead Equus, ripping the flesh from their bones. They left even more meat lying on the ground rotting. These Equus hadn't been killed for food. Ravagers had killed them!

Were these bones all that remained of those Equus? No, that couldn't be. The Equus in the vision had been on a plain. These Equus were on an isolated ledge between the Meshacks and the sea.

"These were Equus," Varon said. More than Equus, these were dead Equus.

"Here, I gathered my chosen to follow the land back to Etrasco before the time of the Ranglan Stone. Without the Ranglan Stone, they became lost because the barrier I placed over their minds would not allow them to find Etrasco without help. I tried to lead them to Etrasco, but before I could, the Ravagers slaughtered them."

Equ continued, *"In my anger, I destroyed the land bridge between here and another continent that would have led to Etrasco, and I raised these mountains to separate the predators from the Equus. My mother thought I was building a new Etrasco and forbid me to do more than create these mountains. They were not enough. My brothers and sisters created new predators on this island continent. What was worse was during the season of peace that followed the isolation of Hemlaza, the Equus created their own predators."*

That surprised Varon. *"How could we do that? The Equus are not creators."*

"It was during the time of peace that the Equus began the herd wars. The Equus did more harm to themselves than the predators could. By the time I ended the herd wars by delivering the Ranglan Stone, the predators had regained a foothold in the land.

"Walk among the bones, Varon. They are your sires. They are what you and the Equus will become if you fail in this," Equ told him.

Varon had finished walking down the path to the large ledge where the bones were. He stood at the edge of the vast field of bleached bones and stared at them. How could so many Equus have been slaughtered? He lowered his head and stared into the empty eye sockets of the skull of a young Equus.

"Why did you not save these Equus?" Varon asked, jerking his head up. *"If they were doing what you desired, why didn't you protect them from the Ravagers?"*

"It was forbidden."

"By your mother?"

"No, by laws older than my mother. Once created, a creature must be allowed to follow its own nature. It is why I sent the Equus from Etrasco in the first place so they could define the nature of being an Equus," Equ explained.

"Not because we failed you?"

"No, the Equus could not fail me while they were in Etrasco. They had to prove themselves worthy to live in the outside world. Creators are allowed to guide their creations but not take be an active participant in their lives."

Varon stared at the sea of bones around him. *"What is this then? Don't the Ravagers take an active role in our lives? Aren't you taking an active part?"*

"My brothers and sisters can only kill when they take on the form of a predator, and hence, take on their killing nature. Once they are in the form, they amplify the creature's killing desire. For my part, delivering the Ranglan Stone to the Equus was pushing the limit of interfering without changing my form. Otherwise, I am providing guidance that you can use according to your nature."

Varon walked back up the path so he would not have to stand among the bones and disturb the dead. He felt insignificant when he stood among them.

"Who were these Equus? What herd?"

"The leader was named Busilim. He was my Voice, as you are now. He gathered those who would listen to my Voice and led them to Etrasco."

"Wait!" Varon said. *"The ponies teach that Busilim was the first renegade. He divided the Equus until he was driven away from Torg's Herd."*

"In their memories that is what happened. When the Calvns would not humble themselves to become my Voice, I chose another Equus to lead. Varon, you are not the first to become a renegade to follow me."

"But Busilim was a zebra." All the Equus knew that only uni-

corns could lead.

"Yes, he was a zebra. I do not favor one species of Equus over another. Busilim listened and obeyed my will. That is what was important," Equ said.

"I doubt that a zebra would listen today."

"You would be surprised."

Varon took a deep breath and thought, *"So if I am to lead the Equus across the white mountains…"*

"You will not lead them."

"But you said that I am your voice."

"You are, but one thing I learned with Busilim is that when he lost his sense of direction on the open plains, he had no one to consult. This time I have chosen another to lead. You will be my Voice and the guide, but she will be my Eyes and the leader."

Varon flicked his tail. *"She? The Equus will not follow a mare. Stallions who are strong enough to defend their position lead their species in a herd."*

"Then the Equus will perish, for my Eyes are those of a mare."

Varon was silent. Equ had said it so matter-of-factly. If he loved the Equus, how could he allow the Equus to perish like he had these Equus? Equ didn't want the Equus to perish. He was trying to lead them away before something terrible happened to them.

"You won't let that happen again, will you?" Varon asked as he looked back at the bones.

"Even now, I am collecting the Equus who will heed my words."

Varon noticed that Equ hadn't answered the question. He decided that he didn't want to know the answer.

"Then I will be your voice to them," Varon said.

"Before you leave across the white mountains, you must have the Ranglan Stone to show you the path," Equ told him.

"How do I get it? I don't even know where the Valley of the Equus is located. Would you have me ask Calvn Mika to give me, a horse, the symbol of the power of the Equus?"

"It was meant for you to possess. You are my Voice."

Varon just shook his head.

32

Jalon flew toward the north, not paying attention to what was on the ground below her. She was supposed to be looking for grass, grains, or berries for the herd, but she stared toward the white mountains to the north.

Was Varon even now heading toward the mountains to follow his visions? Was he following the will of Equ while she obeyed a Calvn who despised her?

Jalon was still in contact with some pegasuses in her foraging group. She was still part of the mind-link with them. She would fly back to the herd this evening and be a part of the herd mind-link. Varon, though, was alone and feeling abandoned by all those he had known and trusted. He deserved better than that.

It shamed Jalon to know that she had betrayed Varon when he had needed her support the most. How could she abandon someone she called a friend to stand with a leader who despised her and her species? It made no sense, and yet, she had done it. Was the herd instinct so strong within her that she could betray her friend just to be a part of a herd? Scola's Herd was no place for a pegasus. Many other herds treated pegasuses as if they were second in the Equus social structure to the unicorns, but, at least, the herds didn't scorn them.

"Jalon, you're flying too far away from us," Chinarvo warned her.

Jalon didn't answer. She just flapped her wings harder.

"Jalon, what are…"

Then her contact with the mind-link broke, and Jalon was alone with only her own thoughts to keep her company. The others would try to pursue her for a while, but Jalon wasn't worried. She was a fast flyer; one of the fastest in the herd. Even if the others in her scouting band tried to catch up with her, she would ground herself and gallop.

She wasn't sure how her desertion from the herd would be reported to Calvn Scola, but she found herself not caring what Calvn Scola thought of her. The only thing that she was worried about was finding Varon alive. She wanted to help him.

The other pegasuses pursued her. She had caught glimpses of them in the distance, but she stayed well ahead of them until they gave up and turned south. Then Jalon knew that she was alone.

She let her thoughts range out as far ahead of her as she could. She was hoping somehow to sense Varon and establish a mind-link with him. Her plan was to find Varon and then to find a herd that would accept them; a herd that tried to live by Equ's will as well as Varon did.

All equal under Equ.

It was so simple. The Equus needed to live up to their name if they expected to return to Etrasco, and yet, so few of them did.

Varon did.

He saw all Equus as brothers and sisters, not as unicorns, pegasuses, horses, ponies, zebras, and donkeys. That was why Jalon had treasured her friendship with Varon. She had wanted to be like him. She wanted to be worthy of the name Equus.

She wanted to prove herself worthy to be called Varon's friend, and so she flew north and searched.

33

Miskala waited until both moons were high in the night sky to begin his journey. His herd was resting after having found good grazing for the day. He looked around and saw many Equus sleeping, trying to rest before tomorrow, when they would search for grazing again. The herd scouts patrolled around the edges of the herd, and some young played in the darkness. However, the herd was stiller and less alert.

Lyos stood beside him with her chin nestled on his back as she napped. Miskala bent his legs and tried to slip out from under her without waking her. It didn't work.

"Miskala," she murmured.

"What, my season mate?"

"Where are you going?"

"I have Calvn business to attend to. Rest now. I'll be back before morning."

She nodded and closed her eyes. Miskala had been enjoying his time with her; especially since they had found out she was pregnant. Lyos was as wonderful a season mate as he had hoped for.

Miskala walked to the edge of the herd. He waited until the donkeys had passed on their patrols and then slipped between them toward the east. He cleared his mind of all thoughts to not draw attention to himself on the mind-link. Then he walked casually as if he doing nothing more than walking to the stream to drink. He worried about being alone in the night and leaving his herd alone.

His stomach churned, threatening him with vomit. He paused and closed his eyes. He didn't understand why he seemed to be feeling sick every day. He felt healthy otherwise.

Once he no longer felt the herd's mind-link, Miskala galloped toward the Meshack Mountains. It surprised him how easily he found the Valley of the Equus the second time. He was amazed other Equus who weren't Calvns hadn't also discovered it.

He passed through the tunnel and into the valley. He had expected to be afraid of returning here because of the confrontation he had had with the unicorn spirits the first time he had been here. However, he was not a seeker of leadership this time; he was a Calvn. The spirits that inhabited this valley were his sires.

He walked through the valley, looking at the scratchings on the wall. He stopped to look at some of them, wondering what they said. What had the Calvns recorded that was unknown to the Equus in general?

Miskala walked around the curve in the valley and saw the unicorn's skull. He tilted his head forward and let the Ranglan Stone slide from his horn onto the dead unicorn's horn.

"That which was given to you for safekeeping, I now return to you," Miskala said.

The Calvn Council hadn't known why none of the Calvns had passed the test the spirit unicorns had conducted on each of them. They had known they hadn't been forbidden to take the stone from the valley, but they were sure to return it.

The skull's eyes glowed red, and Miskala wondered if he would have another confrontation with the skeleton.

"Then add your name to the memory of the Calvns," a voice said in Miskala's head.

Miskala saw an image in his mind of an upward-pointed triangle with a curved line crossing the apex. He realized that this would be his mark.

He looked around until he found a space on the rock wall. He lowered his horn and scratched the symbol into the stone. When he had finished, he stepped back and stared at it. He was surprised to find another matching symbol a few feet from his mark. He stared at the mark and wondered what it said.

"They have recorded what I said to them," a voice said in his

head, different from the voice he associated with the skull.

Miskala looked around, wondering if another Equus was in the valley. As far as he could see, he was alone.

"What did I write?"

"You wrote what I will say to you now. Follow my Voice, and be true to him."

"Who are you?"

"You know."

Equ? Had Equ spoken to him? He still couldn't make sense of the scratchings, even after being told what it meant. *Follow my Voice and be true to him.* Was that what it said? What did it mean? As a Calvn, Miskala was a Voice of Equ, so should he follow himself or another Calvn? He couldn't make sense of it.

He had now become a part of the memory of the Calvns. Miskala only hoped that he could lead his herd well.

Carn looked up from his grazing and watched Miskala slip away from the herd. The Calvn moved quietly into the night without announcing he was leaving. Carn would have expected the new Calvn to worry about predators, but he didn't seem to. He was either very brave or very foolish.

Now where would the Calvn be going alone in the night? Carn was tempted to follow him, and he would have, if Oralum hadn't been standing so near to him.

"Where do you think our fearless Calvn has to go by himself?" Carn asked Oralum.

Oralum looked up from his grazing. He looked where Carn was staring and saw Miskala leaving. *"We're near the mountains. I suppose he is returning the Ranglan Stone to the Valley of the Equus. That is where it is kept between the times that the unicorns use it to select new Calvns."*

"With that stone, you could be Calvn, Oralum. Why don't you follow him and take the stone from him?" Carn suggested.

Oralum shook his head. *"It isn't just possessing the stone that makes a unicorn a Calvn. The senior Calvn of the Calvn Council would have to recognize me as the Calvn."*

Oralum's lack of initiative to become Calvn of this herd surprised Carn. He was a poor leader. Carn would shape him into the tool he needed him to be.

"We should follow him and find out where the Valley of the Equus is. That way, you could go right to it the next time there is an opportunity for you to be Calvn."

Carn wanted to know so he could return when he was alone. He had never found it over the years and had searched for it since he had known of its existence. Somehow his brother had shielded it from him, but if an Equus led him to it, Carn could claim the Ranglan Stone as his own.

"Only a unicorn can enter the valley," Oralum said.

Where was this valley? How did Equ shield it from the other creators? It must hold all the secrets of the Equus, like the Ranglan Stone, if Equ saw fit to protect it from detection. Carn could sense the power in the piece of meteorite, but he did not understand how to harness it to his advantage.

He supposed that he could take it and it would imbue him with the power to control the Equus. With such power, Carn could command the Equus to destroy themselves.

A new plan took shape within Carn's mind.

<h1 style="text-align:center">34</h1>

Varon retraced his path out of the Meshack Mountains. It seemed to take an even longer time for him to find his way out of the cave than it had for him to find his way through it. That surprised him because he was anxious to be away from the graveyard of Equus. His wounded haunch ached, which caused him to limp and slowed him down.

Why hadn't Equ allowed the winds to sweep the bones into the sea or caused the mountains that made up the sides of the hidden cove to tumble in on the bones and bury them? What purpose did leaving the bones hidden in the cove serve? It was morbid.

Then Varon realized the answer.

The bones weren't hidden from Equ. Even buried, the creator would have known they were there. Could it be that Equ left them there to serve as a constant reminder to himself the price of failure? That was how he had used it when he had revealed the bones to Varon. The sight still shook Varon. He had never considered that Equ might fail in something he attempted. Varon did not think he would ever forget the sight, and he shouldn't.

If Varon failed, the Equus would face mass death. Their future lay across the white mountains to wherever it led. He had to convince the Calvns of that. If even one Calvn could be convinced, that Calvn could lead his herd across the ice, and Varon could join that herd.

It wouldn't be easy. If it had been, Equ could have spoken directly to the Calvns instead of to Varon. How did Equ expect Varon to succeed where he could not?

Varon came out of the Meshack Mountains and projected his

thoughts outward. He didn't sense a mind-link within range of his mind-voice. He decided for no apparent reason he would head west. Hopefully, he could encounter a mind-link within a short distance and begin his search for Calvn Mika's Herd. Calvn Mika was the senior Calvn. If he could be convinced to follow Equ, Mika could lead the other Calvns and Equus across the white mountains. He would also be the Calvn who would allow Varon to have the Ranglan Stone.

Imagine Varon, the horse with the Ranglan Stone! Equ was right when he said that the Equus' way of life was changing. Scola would develop mind-sickness himself when he found out Varon possessed the Ranglan Stone. ...If Varon could find the Ranglan Stone and find the mare who was supposed to be the Eyes of Equ on their journey to Etrasco.

So much to do.

Varon stopped to eat at a small patch of rye he came across while trotting. With his head lowered, he didn't see the donkey approaching.

"Horse, beware!"

Varon's head came up, and he saw the donkey in the distance. He also saw the human sitting atop the donkey's back.

"What happened, brother?"

"I was part of a foraging group jaguars scattered. As I was trying to make my way back to my herd, I saw this creature who is now on my back."

"How did he get there?" Varon asked, remembering how the human had tried to climb onto his back. He had thrown the human off of him.

"He offered me oats. As I ate them, he put something over my head and neck. Before I knew it, he was on my back and what he put on my head allowed him to control my head movements."

Varon stared at the donkey as he approached him. *"Is it painful?"*

"Only if I refuse to move. Then he kicks me in my side with his heels."

"I can help you," Varon said.

"No!" the donkey said quickly. *"If you get too close, he will*

capture you as he did me. He already has another donkey and a pony kept confined."

The sight of the human on the donkey's back angered Varon. He remembered how close he had come to being like this donkey, a slave to the human. Was this Equ's mother's idea of cooperation? The Equus weren't meant to be controlled. They were free.

"I will help you, brother. Be ready," Varon said.

"Be careful."

Varon watched the human and donkey approach him. When they were close enough, Varon charged the two of them. The human kicked the donkey in the sides to move out of Varon's path.

"Hold," Varon ordered him.

The donkey remained still, despite the pain he must have been feeling from the human's kicks. Varon used his head to butt the human from the donkey's back.

The human yelled as he tumbled to the ground, landing hard on his back. He rolled over and staggered to his feet.

"Oh, but you're a feisty one. We must do something about that," the human said in his language that Varon couldn't understand.

The man stood up and uncoiled what looked to Varon like a supple vine. He tied a knot in it and swung it back and forth in gentle, looping arcs.

"That is what he will use to capture you," the donkey warned Varon.

Varon snorted and watched the human. The human twirled a loop of the vine in the air above his head and threw it at Varon. While the vine was in the air, Varon charged the human again, knocking him aside with his shoulder. The human yelled and fell backward onto the ground. The donkey brayed in delight.

Varon turned and ran back to the donkey. He examined the length of vine on the donkey's head. He would have to chew through it to get it off of the donkey.

"Be still, and I will get this off of you as quickly as I can. Then the human can no longer control you," Varon told the donkey.

Varon reached out and took the vine in his teeth. Then he ground his teeth together until the fibers in the vine broke. He took hold of one of the loose ends and pulled the knotted vines binding the donkey's head.

The human stood up, shaking his head.

"Go and free the others now," Varon told the donkey.

"What about you? You could help me," the donkey asked.

Varon wanted to go with the donkey, and he was tempted to do so. Galloping with this donkey would ease his loneliness that he felt because of isolation. However, the donkey had to return to his herd. Varon had a mission to perform for Equ.

"I would like to go with you," Varon said *"but I must find Calvn Mika's Herd."*

"I am from Calvn Mika's Herd."

"Do you know where the herd is now?"

The donkey nodded. *"I know where it was when I was captured. I could help you find the herd. The Calvn will want to know more about this creature. I didn't even know what species it is."*

"It is called a human," Varon recalled.

"The other herds will need to be warned of these humans," the donkey rep ied.

Varon was surprised. Fate or Equ had stepped in to help Varon in his mission. This donkey could not only take Varon to Calvn Mika; he could verify humans existed.

"I will go with you then," Varon said. *"What is your name?"*

"I am Efris."

"Efris, I am Varon."

They galloped to the north and away from the human. The human ran after them for a brief time, but he gave up because his speed on two legs was no match for theirs on four. Efris could gallop faster than Varon since Varon's haunch ached and throbbed with pain, but they still quickly outdistanced the human. The human yelled and shook his fist at Varon and the donkey while he tried to catch his breath.

"If this is what humans are like, why do you think they will work with the Equus and not to dominate us?" Varon called to Equ.

"I don't think it," came the reply from Equ.

"But you showed me a vision of the humans and..."

"A vision? I showed you no vision. I cannot cast visions into your mind, Varon. I can only speak to you through the mind-link."

Varon panicked. He thought for a moment that Scola might be right and Varon had mind-sickness. *"But I saw a vision. I have seen other visions at the times you have spoken to me."*

"What visions?"

"I saw a vision of the Equus and humans working together, another of the possible futures of the Equus, and one of the Equus crossing the white mountains while being pursued by predators," Varon recited.

"Your visions are not from me."

"Then do I truly have mind-sickness?" Varon asked.

"No, your visions are true, but they do not come from me," Equ replied.

"Then who sent them?"

"My mother. She is sending the visions to you. She realizes the Equus need to leave Hemlaza," Equ explained.

"Could she send a vision to the Calvns and make them understand what needs to be done?" Varon asked.

"She could, but if the Calvns don't listen to their creator, what makes you believe they would listen to their creator's mother who they don't even believe exists?"

Varon sighed. Equ was right. He couldn't imagine Sartino admitting he had been wrong about Equ's mother, and Scola wouldn't know what to do if he had a real vision.

"So it still falls on my shoulders," Varon said.

"You can do this, Varon."

"I hope so, but I don't understand how I will do it."

"It will become clearer as you accomplish the various goals."

Varon and the donkey galloped. The donkey led Varon to a large cave in the foothills of the Meshack Mountains. A pile of logs blocked the front of the cave.

"Can we lift the logs off?" Varon asked.

"No. We tried that when we were inside the cave. They are too large and heavy," Efris told him.

Varon examined the structure to find a way inside. Two saplings had been driven into the ground in front of the cave mouth to hold the logs against the side of the cave.

"Knock the saplings down," Varon said.

Varon kicked one sapling away and the donkey kicked the second sapling out of the way. The logs remained in place.

"It didn't work," Efris said, disappointment heavy in his voice.

Varon used his nose to push the top log aside. It tumbled to the ground. Varon jerked back as the rest of the logs shook loose and fell in a clattering pile in front of the cave.

"Praun. Ravison. Are you still within the cave?" Efris called.

A black pony and a lean, gray donkey walked from the darkness of the cave into the sunlight. They looked from Efris to Varon.

"Efris, where is the creature who wears the animal skin?" Praun asked.

"He is far from here. This horse chewed the vines off my head and knocked the creature over," Efris explained.

"Well done," Praun praised Varon.

"Are you both from Mika's Herd?" Varon asked.

"No, I am from Calvn Drai's Herd," Praun said.

"I am from Calvn Quilon's Herd," Ravison said.

"Can you find your ways back to your herds?" Varon asked them. He didn't want to abandon them if they didn't know where they were going.

"Where are you going?" Praun asked.

"I will accompany Efris back to Mika's Herd," Varon answered.

"Then we will go with you. It is safer that way. Too many strange occurrences and creatures are afoot," Praun said.

"What about your own herds?" Varon asked.

"Mika receives reports from each herd. Ravison and I can find out where our herds are located from the pegasuses who report from them," Praun suggested.

Varon couldn't say that he would regret the extra company. He had been alone for a week now. He was eager to speak with other Equus, especially ones who seemed not to have heard the rumors of his mind-sickness and his renegade status. The small band began galloping to the west, following Efris. Varon wondered what other Equus would think if they saw a horse, a pony, and a donkey following another donkey, but Efris was the one who knew where Mika's Herd had been before he had been captured, so he was the one they would follow.

"What is wrong with your haunch? Did the human wound you?" Ravison asked. He had noticed that Varon was favoring his right rear leg.

"I was wounded in an earlier fight," Varon replied.

"With a predator?"

"No."

Varon didn't want to elaborate on that. He wasn't sure how these Equus would react to hearing that unicorns were willing to violate the First Law. They might not believe him; just as they hadn't believed Capsta at Champion Days.

His haunch still hurt, though. He needed to see another horse in Mika's Herd to have him treat his wound before it became even worse. He hadn't been able to wash it since he had left the Meshack Mountains, and if the infection spread, Varon would die or least be crippled enough that predators could take him, which was the same thing.

They galloped through mid-day before they brushed the mind-link of Calvn Mika's Herd. The sudden surge in size of the mind-link brought Varon joy.

"Identify yourself," came the challenge from the herd scouts.

"It's Efris, Har."

"Efris? Where have you been for the past moon cycle?"

"A new type of creature captured me," Efris explained.

"A new creature?"

"Yes, and it also captured my current companions. They seek to stay with our herd until they find out where their herds are now. We will also tell Calvn Mika of this unfamiliar creature."

"Then come in. I will tell Calvn Mika that you are coming. He will want to hear if a new creature is on Hemlaza."

The quartet walked past the herd scouts, pausing while Efris and Har groomed each other. Many other Equus greeted Efris and peppered him with questions. He answered some and ignored others. Varon watched Efris arch his neck as he became the center of attention.

The four approached Calvn Mika and lowered their heads to the ground to imitate grazing. The black unicorn walked in front of the four and stopped.

"Efris, welcome back to the herd. You have been missed," Calvn Mika said.

Efris raised his head. *"Thank you, my Calvn."*

"We thought a predator had taken you."

One of Efris' ears leaned forward and the other backward. *"I don't know if I would consider this creature a predator, but he can kill. I have seen him eating burned rabbit and wolf."*

"How many of these creatures are there?"

"Just one that I have seen, but he is clever, and he can manipulate things with his hands like a monkey."

When Scola's Herd had been in the western forest, monkeys had jumped on Varon's back, but they had not tried to control him. They had just been playful.

"What kind of creature was this? What is it called?" Calvn Mika asked.

"I don't know, but my companion knows."

Varon raised his head. *"It is called a human, Calvn, and I have seen two different ones.."*

"Who are you?" Calvn Mika asked, focusing his attention on Varon.

"I am Varon."

"You are the one Calvn Scola exiled."

"He exiled me because he said I had mind-sickness. I don't. I tried to tell him about this creature. He did not believe in humans."

"Calvn Scola said you tried to attack his advisors when they came to see if you were honoring your exile," Calvn Mika said.

Varon snorted. *"I did not attack them. The three of them attacked me. I have the wound from one of the unicorn's horns to prove it."*

"They also have wounds," Calvn Mika said.

"Calvn Mika," Efris said, *"Varon freed not only me but these other two Equus. He has been an aid, not a hindrance, in our efforts to escape the human."*

Calvn Mika turned to stare at Varon and said, *"Since you have a name for this new creature, do you know where this human comes from?"*

"I am not sure, but I think he comes from across the white mountains."

"What makes you say that?" Calvn Mika asked.

"If the human lived on Hemlaza, we would have seen him or others before now. Since we haven't, he must have come from somewhere else. Where? Hemlaza is an island. The only thing that connects Hemlaza to anywhere is the white mountains," Varon explained.

Calvn Mika nodded. *"Calvn Scola said you had a particular fixation with the white mountains."*

Varon snorted and tried to keep his anger from showing. *"Fixation or not, two donkeys, a horse, and a pony have all seen the human. Can you explain how the human came to be here in any other way, Calvn Mika?"*

"No," Calvn Mika admitted. *"This does not bode well for the Equus. The last thing we need at this time of predator massings is another predator hunting us."*

"There is a way for the Equus to survive," Varon said.

"You speak of your prophecies again."

"What I have spoken to this point have not been my prophecies. They are Equ's, and they are proving accurate. That should give me some credibility," Varon suggested.

"It does. It's the reason I haven't run you off so far, but do not press this point. Scola has declared you a mind-sick renegade, and as such, I should drive you from my herd."

Varon lowered his head to the ground in an act of submission. He did not want to be alone again. He had Calvn Mika's attention now. He had to succeed.

"So how can the Equus survive?" Calvn Mika asked.

"The Ranglan Stone will lead us to safety."

"It will? How?"

"I am not sure, but when it is used by the Voice of Equ, it will serve as a guide."

Calvn Mika nodded. *"If what you say is true, I can retrieve the stone from the Valley of the Equus, and since I am the Voice of all the Equus, I can lead the herds to safety."*

"Not you, Calvn," Varon corrected him.

"If not me, then whom? I am the Voice of Equ."

"You are the Voice of the Equus, chosen by the Equus. I am the Voice of Equ, chosen by Equ."

"You?" Varon nodded. *"You must be mind-sick if you think I would turn the Ranglan Stone over to a horse. It is a sign of the Calvns' power, and I am the leader of the Calvns. If the Equus are to be led anywhere, I will lead them."* His thoughts gradually increased in intensity until he attracted the attention of the rest of the herd. *"You must be mind-sick, Varon. Scola was right. You cannot lead the Equus with the Ranglan Stone, and you will not possess it."*

Varon stomped his left hoof, raising a small cloud of dust. *"I seek to save the Equus."*

"You seek to become Calvn. Scola was right about you after all."

Varon shook his head. *"What I have said will happen. I seek to preserve the Equus, but you seek to preserve your power."*

Calvn Mika snorted and flicked his tail. *"You are exiled from this herd. If I ever look upon your face again, I will treat you as a predator. Now leave my herd and my sight. You disgust me."* Then he turned away from Varon.

Varon didn't even bother to argue. He knew it would do no good. Calvn Mika had been trying to gather power to himself since Champion Days. He would not give it away now, especially to a horse.

"You will not have the Ranglan Stone, Calvn Mika. Equ will not let you keep it," Varon warned Mika.

"Then let Equ come to me and ask for it. Only then will I surrender it."

"We will see."

35

Jalon's thoughts brushed against a mind-link. As soon as she realized it was a herd, she changed her flying direction until she was alone again. She was searching for the single mind of a particular horse, not for a herd. Trying to find information about Varon from herds hadn't been successful so far. The herds only knew Calvn Scola had declared Varon a renegade, and they didn't want to have anything to do with an Equus who was looking for Varon, especially the pegasus who she learned from encountering other Equus that Scola had also declared an exile. As if Scola's decision mattered when she was already in a self-imposed exile!

So Varon was alone now. Having been declared a renegade, he couldn't go back to Scola's Herd. She also couldn't return to Scola's Herd. Somehow having her choice made for her of whether or not to return was a relief. Now she didn't have to decide. She could concentrate on finding Varon. Her future was forward, not back.

The wind shifted, so it was blowing against Jalon. She flapped her great wings harder and leaned into the wind, stretching her neck forward to cut down resistance. With the shifting winds, the black clouds to her south moved northward.

She sighed. Rain would cut down on her visibility, but she still should be able to reach Varon through the mind-link if she flew near enough to him.

Equ was not making this easy on her. If Varon's visions were true, and she believed they were, then she had hoped that Equ would guide her to Varon. She only wanted to help him. Now she wondered if she would ever find him alive. If predators had killed him, she would never forgive herself for abandoning him when he had needed her most.

A short time later, the rain was on her, cutting her visibility even more than the clouds did. It stung, and she realized it wasn't rain, but sleet. She would have to be careful. If ice built on her wings, it would be harder to fly and the extra weight would tire her out more quickly.

If she were smart, she would set down and wait out the storm. However, the ground in this area was little more than an open plain. She didn't even have the other Equus in a herd to huddle against for warmth. She might as well continue on. There was a lot of land to cover to find Varon.

Lightning crackled near her.

The flash blinded her. Though the lightning didn't hit her, its nearness singed her feathers. She reacted by jerking herself away from the pain. The extra weight on her wings from the ice overbalanced her, and she spun sideways, flipping over and over.

Jalon lost her sense of direction even as she tried to right herself. She locked her wings in position, hoping to glide to the ground.

As she stopped spinning, she realized she was upside down. She forced herself into a roll to the left to right herself, and she slammed into the ground.

Stunned, she lay on her side on the ground. She knew that she needed to move. Lying there, she was a meal for any nearby predator. She was too numb to move, though. She knew that the lightning hadn't hit her, but she wondered if she had broken bones in the fall.

She tried to move her legs, but her body was numb. She could feel it, but everything seemed to tingle. Her eyes were still blind from the lightning, so she couldn't see if there were any wounds on her body.

There must be something she could do to help herself, but her thoughts were too muddled to think what it was. She had to concentrate.

Then she felt the touch of the mind-link.

"See, I told you I sensed an Equus."

"You were right, but I never questioned you, Redo," a second voice interjected.

"Frim did."

"I just said that I didn't sense an Equus. I meant no offense,"

Frim defended.

There was a long pause. *"The lightning makes me nervous,"* the second mind-voice said.

"It does all of us, Zeph," Frim said.

"At least it didn't hit any of us," Redo added.

"Do you think she is dead?" Zeph asked.

"Her chest still moves and I can sense her mind-voice, though muddled."

"She's not responding to my prodding, though, and her eyes are open."

Prodding? One Equus was close enough to touch her and she couldn't feel him or see him? Jalon tried to form her thoughts and join the mind-link and communicate with the Equus, but she couldn't concentrate and she still couldn't move.

"So what should we do?" Frim asked.

"We should help her," Zeph said.

"Help her? She could endanger our existence. We should run as far from her as we can."

"How can she harm us? She is alone. There is no herd that is a part of her mind-link. I do not think she is with the Ravager's Foals. She is an exile like us," Zeph said.

"But the storm could have separated her from her herd, and since she's unconscious, we can't ask her," Frim argued.

"No, I don't think so."

"If we leave her, then we would be no better than the others," Redo said.

"That's not true," Frim replied.

"It is. If we leave her, she will die," Redo said.

"If we help her and she returns to her herd, then the Equus will know of us and of our existence. They will hunt us down," Frim countered.

"It's a risk we should take. Our entire lives are risks. This one won't betray us. Equ has brought her to us to aid us in our quest," Zeph said.

Jalon heard nothing after that because she lost consciousness.

36

The lightning pounded the ground for a third time, sending tremors through it. All around him, Miskala heard Equus whinnying or squealing. It was getting harder to keep them from stampeding in all directions. Many of the Equus worried that the lightning would hit them.

"Keep the herd together and move them south," Miskala told the donkeys. He had sent all of them to the outskirts of the herd to keep the Equus within together.

The storm had come up from the south. Miskala wouldn't have worried too much about the sleet, but the lightning was another matter. They seemed to be right in the center of the worst of the strikes.

"Calvn Miskala," a zebra named Talo called out.

"What?"

"A donkey nipped at me when I tried to pass him. I demand that you punish him for overstepping his authority."

"Why did you try to get past him? Didn't I tell the herd to stay together?" Talo was one of the hostile band within the herd. Miskala was beginning to discover who stood against him and who was for him. Oralum led the band against him. Something would have to be done about him soon.

Talo hesitated. *"Well, I... I wanted to be away from where the lightning was striking. I have no desire to die."*

"None of us do, Talo. The lightning isn't striking the herd, and we are moving away from the strike zone. I told the herd to stay together and the donkeys to keep them together. If you tried to get past them, you were disobeying my orders. Perhaps it is you who I should punish and not the donkey," Miskala told him. The weather had put

him on edge, and he was in no mood for diplomacy.

"A donkey has no right to attack me," Talo argued.

"I gave him the right! If you wish to no longer be a part of this herd so you might disobey my orders, then I can have the donkeys declare you an exile and you can go where you wish."

"Calvn!" Talo said, shocked.

"You are the one who tried to leave the herd against my wishes, Talo. Do you expect me to reward your disobedience?"

Talo lowered his head. *"I am sorry, Calvn. I did not know there was a reason behind our confinement."*

Miskala glared at Talo until the zebra turned away from him. *"I have a reason, Talo. I am trying to take my herd to safety."*

"Of course, Calvn."

The lightning strikes were frightening, but they were only at one spot for a few moments. It was the wildfires caused by the lightning strikes that worried Miskala more.

Still, Miskala would have felt more comfortable if he could watch the lightning hit from a great distance away and not just a few hundred yards.

Lightning hit again. The ground heaved itself up. This was the closest time yet.

Too close.

Miskala knew even before the ringing in his ears had stopped that one of the Equus had been hit this time.

"Close the gap! Hold them in!" Miskala heard Cy, the donkey leader, shouting.

"What happened?" Miskala asked.

"The lightning hit and injured one of my donkeys," Cy told him.

"Just one?"

"Yes, Calvn. Don't worry. We've still got the herd together and are moving them south."

"Get a horse to help the donkey that was hit. They will have to catch up later."

Miskala had had plenty of doubts, but he would not tell them to Cy. At the moment, he was too proud of the donkeys to let them know he had doubted them. They had kept the herd together even when it had cost one of their own lives. Miskala had thought if lightning had struck within the herd that the panic would have been too great for the donkeys to hold back, but they had managed the job and held the line. They were stronger than most other Equus gave them credit for.

Their pace increased as they moved south, partly from fear and partly from the donkeys' urgings. They hurried from a trot to a canter and moved out of the lightning strike zone; soon they were only experiencing sleet and rain.

Once all the lightning strikes were at least a mile away, Miskala had the herd slow to a stop so they could huddle together for warmth.

"Well done," Miskala told Cy.

"Thank you, Calvn."

Miskala looked around for Lyos. She had been near him earlier, but the ebb and flow of bodies within the herd had taken her away from him. Now he wanted nothing more than to stand next to her and groom her.

He spotted her familiar white coat and walked toward her. He felt his knees go weak and the familiar pains in his stomach returned. He staggered and almost fell.

Be strong. He couldn't let the herd see his weakness. At a time like this, his herd needed to see he was strong, not weak. The hostile band would take advantage of that in a moment if they saw him fall.

Why was he still having stomach pains, anyway?

Miskala stopped and took a deep breath.

"Are you all right?" Lyos asked him.

"Was it that obvious?" Miskala replied.

"I don't think so, but I was looking directly at you."

"Can you join me here? I don't trust myself to walk right now."

"Is it the stomach pains again?"

Miskala nodded. *"Yes, and they're getting worse, not better."*

"You should talk to a horse."

Miskala shook his head. *"No, not until I feel more comfortable as Calvn. I don't want the horses gossiping to the herd about my condition."*

"So what if they do? You are a Calvn, not a creator. You have led them well while you were sick. They shouldn't feel that that would change if you were better."

"Perhaps."

Miskala closed his eyes and relaxed his mind. He didn't concentrate on being part of the mind-link. He just let it happen as if it were as natural to him as breathing. He let his mind touch all the thoughts of the herd except those that were kept private. He did not contact each Equus. He brushed against the link whenever his thoughts touched another Equus. When he did that, the mind-link pushed back.

Miskala let the energy from that push come back to him. Hundreds of pushes and hundreds of quick jolts of energy returned, strengthening him.

It was a trick he had developed weeks ago in trying to combat the stomach pain. He was thrilled with the results. It brought him a rejuvenating burst of strength, and it made him feel closer to the other Equus in the herd.

Miskala opened his eyes and touched the side of his muzzle to Lyos. She nickered.

"Don't worry," Miskala told her. *"Everything will be fine."*

"I hope so."

Carn had seen Miskala stagger. It was with joy that he thought the time had come and Miskala would succumb to the poison. Then the unicorn had stood still and seemed to drift away in a daze. Whatever he had done had seemed to rejuvenate him.

Carn couldn't understand what Miskala was doing.

That only made Carn angry. He was losing patience with Miskala. He had expected the Calvn to fall over days ago from the poison that Carn had been adding to Miskala's food. At the least, Miskala should be in such obvious pain and unable to lead that Oralum could take over the herd.

Oralum had rallied the other dissidents against Miskala. They were a cowardly bunch, though, and they were waiting for a sign that would bring them to power. Carn hoped that Miskala's untimely and unknown death would be such a sign. With Oralum leading, Carn could turn Equus against Equus, but not before he sent Oralum to get the Ranglan Stone. With the power of the stone, Carn could control and destroy all the Equus.

The problem was that Miskala wasn't cooperating. He was stronger than he seemed. Either that, or the poisons that Carn had been adding to the forage weren't as powerful as he had thought.

It wasn't the poisons. Carn had used them before and knew they were potent.

Something was protecting Miskala. Something, or someone.

Could Equ be protecting him? No, Equ would have confronted Carn if he knew that Carn was sabotaging this herd. It was something else.

Miskala had found a way on his own to protect himself from the poison, whether or not he realized it. Now Carn would have to find out what it was and circumvent that protection. There were ways to get at the Calvn other than a direct attack, and Carn was a master of them all.

Miskala's days as Calvn were numbered.

37

Varon slowed his canter to a walk, but even that hurt his hips. Just the increase of any weight on his haunches sent pain shooting through his body. The wound he'd received the night Scola's advisors had attacked him was infected, and no river nearby that he could drink from let alone rinse his wound clean. Not that he thought that would be much help to him now.

He was also running a fever. He could feel the flush through his head beyond the normal feeling he got from running. Blood pounded within him.

Varon needed help. He needed a horse to treat his wound, but no herd would accept him. They feared him, or at least feared what he had to say.

His right rear leg gave out and Varon stumbled. He regained his balance, but he didn't allow himself to put any weight on it, which hobbled him even more. At this rate, he wouldn't be able to walk anytime soon, but he probably would crawl by nightfall.

He needed to rest. It had been awhile since he had eaten, but he found no grasses on which he could graze. This area had been picked clean of anything edible unless dirt and rock could be eaten. Varon hobbled northward, pushed on by the memory of the Equus graveyard on the other side of the Meshacks. Busilim had at least gathered enough Equus to attempt a return to Etrasco. Would Varon not even get that far?

He wasn't sure how long he walked, but he stopped when the sun set.

Collapsed better described it.

His fever still raged, and he hadn't eaten all day. His strength was gone.

"Father Equ, hear my plea. Father Equ, come for us. Return us to the birth land. Father Equ, help us. We want to be with you," Varon said.

In his pain and delirium, it was all that Varon could think to say. If Equ wanted Varon's help, he had chosen his Voice unwisely. Varon was not even helping himself, let alone the creator. The smallest predator could kill Varon now. He was helpless.

"Father Equ, hear my plea. Father Equ, come for us. Return us to the birth land. Father Equ, help us. We want to be with you."

Varon heard something in front of him; the click of a hoof on rock. Varon stopped stumbling forward and looked up. It hurt to raise his head.

A large, white unicorn stood in front of him. Startled, Varon backed up. He stumbled and almost fell. The unicorn hadn't been in view when Varon had looked up earlier.

The unicorn must have stood at least two heads taller than Varon, and his horn was golden. It was the unicorn he had seen fight the Ravager. How had the unicorn survived that fight? Varon had to be imagining this, or he was seeing Equ.

Then Varon saw a small brown monkey peer around the side of the unicorn's thick neck. The monkey was sitting on the unicorn's back. The monkey frowned when she saw Varon.

As Varon watched, the monkey shifted shape, turning itself into a long, green snake. The snake twisted itself around the unicorn's neck, sliding through the white mane until her diamond-shaped head rested against the unicorn's ear.

"He has failed," the snake said.

"He has not," the unicorn replied.

"He is dying."

"But he is not dead."

The snake hissed. It twisted itself higher on the unicorn until it was coiled around the golden horn. Then the snake shifted shape until it was a red falcon perched on the unicorn's horn.

"Is he worth it?" the falcon asked.

The unicorn nodded. *"Yes, Perl. He struggles to obey my voice when no one else will even listen. He is the one."*

Obey his voice? But Varon obeyed Equ's voice. Was this unicorn Equ?

The falcon tilted its beak upward and squawked. Soon after, birds of all sizes and colors flew in and land in front of Varon. They dropped grasses and grains in front of Varon. Varon felt the breeze from hundreds of wings fluttering from the birds. The breeze they created cooled him down somewhat.

"Is that enough, little brother?" the falcon asked.

"Yes, thank you."

"I hope he is worth it."

"He is."

Then the falcon faded from view, and Varon was left staring at the unicorn's golden horn. The unicorn turned to look at him.

"Are you Equ?" Varon asked.

The unicorn nodded. *"Yes, Varon. Now eat. Fill your belly."*

Varon lowered his head and began munching on the grass and grain at his hooves. It tasted delicious, but he would need more than a full belly to accomplish his mission for Equ. This feast had only solved one problem to present him with the greater problem.

The unicorn walked over to look at Varon's wounded haunch. Varon tried to turn his body away from the massive unicorn.

"Be still," Equ said.

Varon obeyed the command because he recognized the mind-voice as Equ's.

"You should have responded quicker when I warned you about Scola's advisors," Equ said.

"I wasn't sure what you meant at first, and then I couldn't believe they would so easily violate the First Law," Varon said.

"Now you see the problem Busilim had. When I am disembodied, the mind-link is not always as clear or as loud as it should be."

"Is that why Busilim's Equus were lost?"

"In part."

Equ leaned his head forward so that the tip of his golden horn touched Varon's wound. Varon felt his haunch tingle, and then the pain and burning of the wound was gone. Equ moved away and Varon could no longer see the hole in his flank. He tested his weight on his leg and felt no pain. The touch of a unicorn's horn had healed him.

"What did you do?"

"I healed your wound with your body's own energies. You will need to rest here until you recover."

"How long will that be?"

"Not too long. You're strong. Eat until you're content, and maybe you'll be ready to move on tomorrow," the golden-horned unicorn said.

Varon lowered his head and said, *"Father Equ, hear my plea. Father Equ, come for us. Return us to the birth land. Father Equ, help us. We want to be with you."* Varon thought the best way to honor and thank Equ was to utter the call for Return.

"Don't give me rote pleas, Equ. My ears have turned deaf to hearing the same thing over and over again," Equ told him.

"But you answered my plea."

Equ shook his head. *"No, I answered your need. There is a difference."*

"Then how am I to communicate with you if you don't respond to pleas?" Varon asked.

Equ lowered his head so he could stare into Varon's eyes. Varon wasn't used to such direct eye contact, but he couldn't look away. Equ's gaze held his attention.

"Tell me the desires of your heart," Equ said.

"I don't understand."

"What is it you wish for most at this moment?"

Varon hesitated before he said, *"To live."*

Equ nodded. *"Good, that is a beginning. That is why you and the Equus have been placed on Hemlaza, so you might live."*

"I don't understand."

"No, I did not think you would. I couldn't understand why at one point in my life, but now I think I do. If living is your greatest desire,

what would then be your next-greatest desire?" Equ asked.

This question caused Varon to think. Besides living, what did he want from the life he had been given? What would he do anything for, short of dying?

"To know your will. To know what you would have me do to explain the mystery that you have placed in my mind. Tola and Poins raised me to want to honor you, but how can I do that when I don't know what you want?" Varon replied.

Equ nodded. *"Good. Again, good. But why? Why would you have me tell you my will?"*

"To serve you," Varon said.

"Really? To serve me? What if I told you to do something so horrible that you could not accept it? Would you still do it?"

"You would not tell me to do something horrible."

"But if I did?" Equ countered.

Varon's ears flicked forward and back. *"I don't know what I would do."*

Equ nodded. *"An honest answer, and that is why the Equus are still away from Etrasco. They do not know why they do what they do. My children should be followers of me, not because they feel they must be, but because they want to be. It must be the greatest desire of your hearts to want to return to me. And when it is... when service is the truest desire of your heart, knowing all the choices available, then I shall bring you all home, but not until then."*

"I want to serve you, Equ," Varon said.

"For glory?"

Varon flicked his tail. *"How could you think that? Doing what I have done for you so far has not brought me glory. It's brought me exile from my herd and near death."*

"And do you still serve me, knowing how few accept you as my Voice, knowing that you will only be able to save a seed of the Equus? Would you serve me even if I gave you a chance to be a part of a herd again, but not the Voice of Equ?"

Varon nodded. *"I would."*

"Then you will have that chance."

Equ turned and walked away. As he did, he seemed to shimmer, as if Varon was staring at him through heat waves. Then he was gone.

Now what was Varon going to do? He might be healed, but he was still no closer to finding the seed of the Equus that Equ wanted him to gather.

Varon felt the touch of a mind-link and looked around, wondering if Equ had returned. A tan pegasus landed a few yards from him.

"Who are you?" the pegasus asked.

"My name is Varon, brother." He left out his herd identification since he no longer had a herd to which he belonged.

"I am Tyni of Miskala's Herd. I thought I saw another Equus with you as I approached," the pegasus said, looking around. *"Are you part of a foraging band?"* He nodded at the piles of grain and grass.

Varon debated whether he wanted to explain about Equ's appearance to this pegasus at this point. He decided he might as well save his story for the Calvn of this herd and see if he could find refuge with them. He still had his mission to perform.

"No, I'm alone out here," Varon said. *"Are you hungry? Please, eat."*

Tyni walked over and started eating some of the grain. *"You're taking a chance with the profusion of predators around."*

"Equ will protect me."

"I don't know how much Equ has to do with everything that's been going on."

Varon heard the despair in the pegasus' mind-voice that saddened him. This pegasus was young, and yet, he seemed older than his years.

"The battle with the griffins changed you, didn't it?" Varon guessed.

The pegasus hesitated and then nodded. *"I can't imagine a pegasus who wasn't changed. It's a hard thing to have to kill. We destroyed eggs. The eggs weren't trying to kill us, but we had to smash them then or they would have hatched and grown to griffins that would have tried to kill us. Still, they were just eggs!"*

"I can only imagine, but my guess is that with all the changes happening there will come a time when the Equus will face something more horrible than griffins and you will be all the better prepared for having survived the horror of the battle with the griffins." Varon was surprised to hear himself sounding so much like Equ, but he was Equ's Voice, so he should not have been surprised.

The pegasus shook his head. *"I can't imagine anything worse."*

"I can't either, but then again, I couldn't imagine mountains that can move." Varon nodded toward the white mountains.

The pegasus nodded. *"Yes, I know another pegasus that has been there. Her name is Jalon of Scola's Herd."*

Varon's ears perked up. *"Jalon! I know her. She is a wonderful friend."*

"She is also a talented leader. She kept a small band of pegasus alive at the griffin aviary until help arrived," Tyni said.

Varon nodded his agreement.

"So why are you here and not with a herd?" Tyni asked.

"Truth?"

Tyni's head bobbed up and down. *"That is always best."*

"Scola exiled me. He thought I was overreaching my position by trying to have the Equus live up to their name," Varon explained.

"All equal under Equ."

"Ah, you remember. That is good. Too many have forgotten."

"Calvn Miskala has been trying to remind us of that."

Varon remembered that Miskala was the new Calvn chosen at Champion Days.

"Miskala is a new Calvn with excellent ideas then."

"And Scola is a pegasus-hating unicorn," Tyni snapped. *"I don't see why the pegasuses stay with that herd. I would have left long ago."*

"Horses prefer to remain with their birth herd. It holds a powerful attraction to us. It is familiar. Is it not so with pegasuses?" Varon asked him.

"At some point, the attraction and species bias cancel each

other out."

"You would think, but the pegasuses of Scola's Herd haven't reached that point yet." Varon paused. *"Tyni, I think I would like to speak with Calvn Miskala. I think he and I would be in agreement on issues that tore Scola and I apart."*

Tyni nodded. *"I think so, too. Why don't you follow me back to the herd?"*

"I'd be happy to."

Varon was hoping he had found a herd where he would be accepted for what he was. He hoped Miskala's Herd was the beginning of the seed of Equus.

38

Capsta stood and watched the colt romp with the other colts and fillies in the herd.

His colt, he reminded himself.

Gerrish was his colt, his blood. Unless Capsta came to believe it and lived it as if it were true, how could he expect others to do so? What would happen if the Calvn Council ever found out that Gerrish was Calvn Gee's hornless foal?

Gerrish stared at the chocolate-colored colt wrestling with the other young. Then he lowered his head and charged another colt. Gerrish's head smashed into the other colt's chest, sending it sprawling. However, the impact also knocked Gerrish back, though he didn't lose his footing. Gerrish shook his head to clear it and whinnied in triumph.

"Why did you butt him with your head, Gerrish?" Capsta asked. The colt used that attack often, even though he saw the other horse colts using their hooves.

"It feels right."

"Even when your head is ringing?" Capsta said.

"I'm still standing."

"The point is to still be standing with a clear head to defend yourself against a follow-up attack," Capsta pointed out.

Gerrish might look like a horse, but he still had the natural instincts of a unicorn; he attacked head first. Why hadn't any of the other Equus noticed that Gerrish acted like a unicorn? How much longer could the deception continue?

The only part of his appearance that suggested he was a unicorn was the white, round spot on his forehead that marked where his

297

horn would have been. The Equus couldn't imagine a unicorn without a horn, and so they saw none where there was one. Even Capsta had never heard of a hornless unicorn before Gerrish.

"Come along, Gerrish. You can play later. The herd is preparing to move to new grazing," Capsta told him.

"Yes, Father." To the other colt, Gerrish said, *"Come on, Pan. Get up and canter with me. Keep up, if you can."*

The two colts galloped off, each trying to outpace the other. The canter was forgotten amid their competition, and they galloped hard with the energy of youth.

Capsta turned and started moving east with the herd. Gerrish was out of sight, but he would be safe if he stayed within the herd, and he knew that he should.

Shortly past midday, the herd halted. At least part of the herd stopped.

"What's going on?" Calvn Miskala asked.

"There's a creator path here," Preis, the pony leader, said.

Bronelin, the zebra leader, said, *"I don't want to hear about your sixth sense again."*

"It's true. Look."

Capsta looked along with everyone else. All the horses, ponies, and donkeys were stopped in a straight line, while a few yards away were the unicorns, the pegasuses, and the zebras.

Capsta's heart chilled when he saw that Gerrish was standing on the wrong side of the line. He had no sixth sense! Of course not. He was a unicorn, not a horse. Capsta wasn't the only one who noticed the colt's mistake.

"If it's true, why is Gerrish on our side of the creator path?" Bronelin asked.

"See, I've been saying that they fake their sixth sense. The teaching just didn't take with Gerrish," Oralum added.

Gerrish looked around. His split ears showed the confusion that he was feeling. He did not enjoy being the center of attention. Capsta didn't want him to be the center of attention, either.

"Father?" Gerrish called.

"Come here, Gerrish," Capsta said.

Gerrish walked to his supposed sire, again effortlessly passing across the creator path. Capsta groomed the colt to ease Gerrish's tension. As he lowered his head to Gerrish's neck, he could feel the colt's pulse pounding hard.

"Our sense is not faked. Gerrish just found a weak point in the line," Preis said.

"Then you follow him through the weak point," Oralum challenged.

The pony leader tried to cross the line where Gerrish had, but he couldn't force himself through it. He gave up trying and stared at Gerrish in amazement.

"I can't do it," he said.

The zebras, unicorns, and pegasuses whinnied.

"Maybe the horses, ponies, and donkeys are evolving," Oralum said.

"Preis," Calvn Miskala said, *"is it the one we are seeking?"*

Preis nodded. *"I have ponies tracing the path, but it keeps breaking and restarting. Because of that, it's hard to tell what is the newest end of the path."*

"Find it, Preis."

"We're trying, Calvn."

The herd had no choice now but to wait for the creator path to fade enough for the horses, ponies, and donkeys to pass through the path. No amount of cajoling could bring the horses, ponies, and donkeys across the line before its power had faded.

"Did I do something wrong, Father?" Gerrish asked.

"No, Gerrish. I did. I've been lax in your training. It is my responsibility to turn you into a fine horse, and I haven't been doing a good job of that yet."

"But you have."

Capsta shook his head. *"I haven't, but I will."*

39

Pautin inhaled deeply and thought perhaps the air was a few degrees warmer. They had been moving south for days now. It should be. The white mountains were just a low white line on the horizon.

She was tired of the Seeking Season and wanted to see fresh grass, flowers, and berries. She wanted to shed her heavy coat instead of remaining in this in-between state that made her appear sloppy and unkempt.

She felt a tugging at her teat and kicked out, although she knew it was Chareth. He neighed and dodged away from her hoof.

"Get away," Pautin told him.

"I'm hungry."

"You're old enough to forage for yourself."

"But there's nothing to eat," he whined. Pautin hated when he did that. He must have gotten that trait from his sire. He certainly didn't get it from her.

"Don't look to me for an easy meal," she warned him.

"But you're my mother."

In answer to that, Pautin urinated. She was in heat anyway; not that she was attracting any stallions. Many of the horses resented the way she had treated Varon, thinking she should have supported him more. Like they had defended him when Calvn Scola had exiled him? She had only been Varon's season mate, not his life mate. They had joined their bodies, not their souls. If Varon was wrong, why should she support him?

Those who didn't resent her seemed to think of her only as Varon's mate. They wanted nothing to do with her, as if associating with her would associate them with Varon. She couldn't win either way.

Dalis still wanted to mate with her. He was such a disappointment in his efforts to become horse leader that so far, she had rebuffed all of his approaches. If a better mate didn't come along soon though, she might allow him to mate with her just so she would be associated with Dalis instead of Varon. The prospect didn't thrill her.

What a mistake it had been to mate with Varon! Not only had being pregnant with her colt kept her from competing in Champion Days, it had isolated her from the herd. Why did he have to go crazy about the white mountains? It might not have been mind-sickness, but it was a dangerous obsession. The white mountains might bring change, but Varon couldn't. The Equus didn't handle change well. Varon should have known that. He was too foolish, and his foolishness had cost him the safety of the herd and probably his life.

Chareth would have to show that he was better than his sire.

"Chareth, are you that hungry?" Pautin asked her colt.

"Yes, Mother." He pranced around her, waiting for the opportunity to eat at his dam's teat.

"Then it's time for your lessons."

Chareth stood still.

"Now? Can I eat first?" Pautin gritted her teeth at the whining tone.

"No, only if you perform well."

Chareth blew air through his lips and let his lips flap.

"The Calvn has superior wisdom. Repeat," Pautin said.

"The Calvn has superior wisdom," Chareth said.

"Never doubt the Calvn. It is folly. Repeat."

Varon might not have learned these lessons, but Pautin would be sure that Chareth did.

"Never doubt the Calvn. It is folly," Chareth said.

Then she had Chareth continue repeating both lines over and over. It was her way of making sure that Chareth wouldn't follow his sire. She had him do his lessons at least three times a day each day. Chareth would be loyal to his herd. She would see to it.

"May I eat now?" Chareth asked.

"Yes."

Pautin nodded and felt her colt's lips lock on her teat and tug.

It wasn't only Pautin who had experienced change because of Varon, though. Since Varon had left, the entire herd's demeanor had shifted subtly. She heard fewer conversations in the mind-link, and many of those who conversed through the mind-link used more intimate links that couldn't be heard on the general mind-link. The donkeys seemed more downtrodden than ever. Many of the horses seemed scared since one horse leader had contracted mind-sickness and a second horse leader had been declared a renegade. The pegasuses had lost a third of their number in the battle with the griffins. They patrolled regularly now, as if they wanted to stay as far away from the herd for as long as they could. The unicorns dominated the herd more, particularly abusing the donkeys. The zebras sided with the unicorns because the zebras sensed where the power in this herd lay. Only the ponies seemed unchanged as they took in everything and stored it in the herd's memory.

"You're teaching your colt very well, Pautin."

Pautin raised her head and looked around. She saw Calvn Scola staring at her from a few yards away.

"I try, my Calvn," she said.

He nodded. *"I can see that. You know your place in the herd and fill it well."*

"Thank you."

"For the herd to survive, every Equus must know his or her place within the herd."

"Yes," Pautin agreed.

"That was Varon's problem. He wouldn't submit. In contrast, you are an excellent example of what a horse should be." He paused. *"The donkeys collected some blueberries this morning, but I couldn't finish all of them. Do you like blueberries?"*

"Yes, Calvn." She loved them.

"Then why don't you go tell Benju that I told you it is all right for you to eat your fill of the remaining berries," Calvn Scola told her.

"Thank you, Calvn. I will."

When Chareth had drunk his fill and moved away to play, Pautin walked through the herd to find Benju. The donkey leader glared at her as she approached him. His nostrils flared with suppressed anger.

"Don't look at me like that," she said. *"Calvn Scola said that I could eat what is left of the blueberries."*

"I know," Benju replied as he stepped aside. She saw a small pile of berries and brush on the ground. It took all of Pautin's control not to charge at the pile.

"Why are you glaring at me?" she asked.

"No reason," he said without altering his glare.

Then she remembered that Varon had befriended the donkeys and tried to raise them above their station. All Equus needed to know their place in the herd.

She walked by him and picked the berries from the brush with her lips. They weren't as sweet as they could have been, but they were much better than grass.

As she savored the berries, she realized that Calvn Scola was using the same technique to ensure her loyalty as she was using to train Chareth to be loyal to the herd. She didn't mind, though. She was a loyal Equus. Even the Calvn had admitted she was what a horse should be.

40

Tyni locked his wings in position as he glided down, landing on the ground near Miskala. He bowed his head and spread his wings forward. Carn moved himself closer to the pair so he might hear the conversation without disrupting closer conversations on the mind-link.

"I can't believe the pegasus was foolish enough to invite a renegade to be a part of our herd," Oralum said near Carn.

Carn nodded his agreement. This was what he had wanted to avoid. Oralum's mind-voice would overpower the conversation between Miskala and Tyni. However, for once, Oralum was right. It seemed a foolish thing to do, even for an Equus.

"But he did do it. Now we can see what our Calvn will do about it. He may give us more evidence to use against him." Carn just wanted Oralum to be quiet. The unicorn seemed to think that unless he was putting his thoughts on the mind-link almost constantly, he would be forgotten.

Miskala snorted and said to Tyni, *"You've placed me in a bad position, pegasus leader."* His tone was stiff and formal to show his displeasure.

"I don't think so, Calvn. Just speak with this horse, and I think you'll see in him what I saw," Tyni replied as he lowered his head.

"I will, Tyni," Miskala said, softening somewhat. *"I won't let another Equus' judgment be mine without good reason. I wouldn't want to turn an Equus out onto the plains and leave him for the predators, but I won't endanger my entire herd for the sake of one Equus. I know you wouldn't either."*

"I am glad to hear you care so much for your herd, Calvn Miskala. I don't intend to endanger your herd. Hopefully, I will be able to save

them," the chestnut stallion said as he walked into the herd.

"You are Varon," Calvn Miskala said.

The stallion lowered his head to the ground and imitated eating grass to show his submission to Miskala's authority. *"I am."*

"I have heard about you."

"I am sure Calvn Scola is happy to spread his lies about me."

Calvn Miskala cocked his head to the side. *"Lying is a very serious charge to make against a Calvn because you are trying to shake the belief that Equ leads him."*

Varon raised his head. *"Are you?"*

"Am I what?"

"Are you led by Equ? I know Calvn Scola is not. If he was, I would not be here."

Carn didn't like Varon. Just the sight of the stallion prickled the hair along his spine. What was worse was that when he examined his feelings, he found that he feared Varon. That confused Carn because he feared no single Equus.

"I would like to think Equ guides me," Miskala said, answering Varon's question.

"But has he ever spoken directly to you?"

Miskala nodded without hesitation. *"Yes, when I wore the Ranglan Stone."*

Carn was surprised. He had thought his youngest brother had taken to leaving his creations to develop on their own because he had "hated to see them in pain." The last time Carn had seen Equ, his brother had been weeping about the self-destruction his creations were doing during their herd wars. Now it seemed that Equ was communicating with his leaders through the Ranglan Stone. Carn would have to pay careful attention to the Ranglan Stone the next time that he saw it. It might be useful in his plan.

"And when Equ spoke to you, did you listen?" Varon asked.

"He told me to follow the Voice of Equ, which I do. I follow Calvn Mika, who is the senior Calvn and the Voice of Equ," Miskala explained.

Carn cut in. *"Don't let this happen, Calvn."*

"What is happening that shouldn't?" Miskala asked.

"This horse is trying to lead you into something foolish by twisting the truth. A horse who will so easily speak against his former Calvn will do the same thing to you," Carn warned.

Oralum nodded. *"I agree. Calvn Miskala, this horse has been declared a renegade by Calvn Scola. If you follow the Voice of Equ, then why would you dispute another Calvn's decision? He, too, is a Voice of Equ."*

"Because Calvns are not infallible, Oralum, and they are not without their faults and pettiness," Miskala told him without away looking from Varon.

"But it is said that Varon might have mind-sickness. He tried to kill three unicorns!"

Varon flicked his tail. *"I did not! Calvn Scola's advisors attacked me. Besides, I was exiled five days ago and the rumors of my mind-sickness began even before then. If I had the mind-sickness, it would be very apparent by now."*

Tyni interrupted the argument. *"Calvn, Varon is also a follower of Equ."*

"We all follow Equ!" Oralum snapped.

Tyni shook his head. *"No, we all say we follow Equ, but our actions speak otherwise. Varon follows Equ in trying to live up to our name, and in doing so, he has set himself apart from most other Equus."*

"How do you know this?"

"Because Jalon, the leader of the attack against the griffins and also a member of Scola's Herd, speaks highly of him."

Varon said, *"Calvn Miskala, I seek a herd to be a part of."*

"Is that all?"

Varon hesitated. *"No, I seek to teach others the truth about what Equ would have the Equus do to survive."*

"And you are the decider of truth?" Oralum mocked him.

Varon shook his head. *"No, but I am an Equus who knows the truth."*

"How?"

"Equ has spoken to me."

That caused a murmur through the herd. Even Miskala looked uneasy for a moment. Now Carn knew why he hated Varon. Varon was his brother's chosen champion, just as Busilim had been before the herd wars and the original Calvn before him.

"You see, Calvn!" Carn exclaimed. *"This horse seeks your power. Is it so hard to see why Calvn Scola said that he had mind-sickness? Only a fool would think a horse could be Calvn."*

"I don't seek to be Calvn," Varon said.

"But you claim to be the Voice of Equ."

"The two aren't the same. In fact, Equ told me I won't lead the Equus where they need to go. I am only Equus Equ uses to speak to his leader."

Carn had to concentrate on holding his form. He wanted to shift shape from the zebra he appeared to be and kill Varon; kill him before he could say anymore. Did Equ know what Carn was planning? Was he seeking to thwart Carn's plan of destruction? It couldn't happen that way.

Carn wouldn't let it.

"What is this seed that you speak of?" Miskala asked.

No! Miskala was listening to Varon. He might believe Varon.

"As Tyni said, not all the Equus follow Equ or will follow him. Not all will heed my warning either, but it must be given, and the Equus must be given a chance to hear the truth. The decision will be theirs. A monumental change is coming to Hemlaza, as we have seen with the white mountains appearing and the griffins reappearing, among other things. Those who will not follow Equ will perish," Varon told him.

"And those who follow him won't perish?"

Varon shook his head. *"No. Those who follow our creator will at least have a chance to survive."*

Calvn Miskala shook his head. *"You are a fool or a tool, Varon."*

"A fool," Oralum chimed in.

Miskala ignored him and said, *"I must think on this for a time. Until I reach my decision, Varon, you have the safety of this herd since it is obvious you don't have the mind-sickness."*

"Thank you, Calvn," Varon said, lowering his head.

"But Calvn..." Oralum interjected.

"I said that I need to think about this," Miskala snapped.

Then Calvn Miskala turned and walked away.

Carn thought Varon had scared many of the Equus in the herd with his talk of the Equus perishing, but he had given many others cause to reexamine how they lived their lives. One of those had been Miskala. He was considering letting Varon stay with the herd. If that happened, Carn's plans for this herd might unravel. Varon might hold them together while Carn was trying to turn them against each other. Varon was the Voice of Equ, and therefore, an enemy to be destroyed.

Miskala walked with Lyos around the edge of the herd. All his conflicted feelings confused him. The conversations in the mind-link showed a similar confusion.

"What if Varon is right and not foolish at all?" Miskala asked.

"You must think he is if you gave him the safety of the herd," Lyos said.

Miskala nodded. *"But I fear what he said. What if what he says about the Equus perishing is right?"*

"Then we should follow him. Didn't you say Equ told you to follow the Voice of Equ?"

"Yes, but Varon paints such a bleak picture for the Equus. I want to see a better future for the Equus. How can I follow the Voice of Equ if he leads me to destruction?"

"Varon paints a picture of survival, and that is all you can hope for."

They walked in silence as Miskala considered the problem of Varon. If he accepted Varon into the herd, he was accepting what Varon proclaimed. Judging by Oralum's reactions to Varon, that would only lend strength to the hostile band within the herd. They would grouse that Miskala had reversed the wisdom of another Calvn and allowed a renegade to join the herd. To ignore the truth, though, would be foolish. He would condemn the herd to death just to gain the approval of a small group who had already shown Miskala that they couldn't be pleased.

His stomach clenched into a knot so tight that Miskala staggered. Pain burned through his entire body. He sent out his pushes against the mind-link, waiting for strength to return to him. It did, but it wasn't enough to ease his pain. He gagged, but nothing came up.

"What's wrong, Miskala?" Lyos asked.

"My stomach."

"Again?"

"Worse this time. Worse than ever."

Miskala felt a nose prodding his side, and he squealed in pain. He pulled away and almost stumbled and fell.

"Open your lips, Calvn," Varon ordered.

"Varon?"

What was Varon doing near him?

"Open your lips. I need to see your teeth," Varon repeated.

"My teeth? Why?" Miskala asked.

"What are you doing?" Lyos asked.

"I'm trying to help him," Varon replied. *"I'm a healer. Open your mouth, Calvn."*

Miskala did so. Varon leaned in close to stare into his mouth.

"Stick out your tongue," Varon told him.

Miskala obeyed. His stomach clenched up in pain, and he snorted.

"Groom him, Lyos. Help calm him down," Varon said.

Lyos began working her lips into her season mate's withers.

Varon asked, *"Has there been any blood in your feces lately?"*

"Some," Miskala admitted.

"How long ago did you eat?"

"Just before you came in with Tyni," Miskala told him.

"Did another Equus bring your food to you?"

Miskala shook his head. The pain was getting worse. He was seeing spots in front of his eyes. *"No."*

Varon walked around to Miskala's side and kicked him in the stomach with his rear hooves. Miskala squealed in pain, drawing the herd's attention. His knees buckled, and he fell to the ground. Then he began vomiting.

"What are you doing?" Lyos screamed through the mind-link.

She began kicking at Varon. Varon remained calm and stayed out of range of her hooves.

"Miskala has been poisoned!" he told Lyos. *"He should have been dead already. I don't know why he is still alive, but he will not be alive for long. I need to get the poison out of his system if he wants a chance to live."*

"Why did you kick him?"

"To force him to vomit. I had to empty his stomach, and I didn't have time to search for a purging herb."

Poisoned? The word stuck in Miskala's mind. He had been poisoned?

"Lyos, leave him alone," Miskala said. To Varon he said, *"How did you know that I had been poisoned?"*

"You looked healthy when I first saw you, but then you were staggering as you walked with Lyos. That was a warning sign, and it brought me over to you. Your gums and tongue are discolored, and there's blood in your feces. Those are the signs of poison."

"But how was I poisoned?"

Varon shook his head. *"That's what I don't understand. I also don't know why your own horses wouldn't have picked up on the signs of the poisoning before now."*

"I've been hiding it from them. I mean, I didn't know I was poisoned, but I wasn't telling them I've been in pain for a while."

"Why not?"

"Because I thought the pain was tension caused by being the new Calvn of the herd," Miskala said.

"As you said earlier, Calvns are not infallible." Varon paused. *"How long have you been having stomach pains?"*

"Since just after Champion Days."

"But that was many moon cycles ago. This poison should have killed you within a couple of weeks. You must have amazing stamina."

Miskala shook his head. *"I've just developed ways to handle the pain."*

"I would love to hear about them sometime. They might help other Equus survive their bouts with illness," Varon predicted.

"Will I live?" Miskala asked.

"That depends on how you were poisoned and if we can stop it

from happening again."

"But I don't know how it happened."

"You must have eaten the poison at some point and have been doing so continually. I assume you know what plants are poisonous."

"Of course I do, and I've been eating what the rest of our herd has been eating. Why aren't they dropping over dead?"

"Have the donkeys been bringing any forage to you?"

Miskala shook his head. *"That's a waste of time. We've just been moving as a herd to where we needed to feed. It's more efficient that way."*

Varon walked over to the pile of vomit and sniffed at it. *"This is laced with greyleaf."*

Miskala shook his head. *"I would never eat greyleaf. I know what it looks like."*

"You had to eat it. It was in your stomach."

"I didn't eat it," Miskala insisted.

"Then somehow one of the Equus in your herd can get you to eat it without you knowing any better," Varon told him.

The hostile band. Miskala felt guilty about the thought, but they were the obvious choice for the poisoners. It could have been one or all of them working together.

"How do I protect myself?" Miskala asked.

"All that I can tell you is to drink a lot more water than usual to keep your system flushed, and if you feel stomach pains again, find some cowsbreath or sunspot to purge yourself."

"That will be better than getting one of the Equus to kick me."

"If you can't find a purging herb, getting kicked may be your only choice if you want to live."

"Thank you, Varon."

"I'm sorry, Calvn."

Miskala cocked his head to the side. *"Sorry? Sorry for what? You saved my life."*

"I thought your herd might be the seed that I sought, but one of your own herd is trying to kill you. That is not an Equus who should be saved."

"And so you would condemn my entire herd for the actions of one?"

"Do you know that it was only one?"

"I don't, but I would hope that no more than one Equus wants to kill me," Miskala admitted.

Miskala staggered to his feet. He still felt shaky and unsure of if he could walk. Lyos hurried to his side to give him support should he need it.

"Walk with me, Varon," Miskala said.

"I'll leave you two to talk," Lyos said. Miskala liked that he didn't have to tell her this was a private conversation with Varon. She was very sensitive to his emotions and feelings.

As she walked away, Varon said, *"She is a sound choice for a mate. She was quick to come to your defense when I kicked you."*

Miskala nodded. *"Yes, she is wonderful."*

"I wish I had chosen my season mate as well."

"Then the Voice of Equ can be as infallible as Calvns," Miskala noted.

"I never denied it. If I was infallible, I wouldn't have been declared a renegade. I would have known of a way to convince all the Equus of the truth of what I say, even Calvn Scola."

Miskala snorted. *"That brings up another problem, Varon."*

"What would that be?"

"You are a renegade. Whatever his reasons, Scola is a Calvn, and he has the power to declare you a renegade. I can't change that."

"So, will you turn me away?"

"How can I? You have placed me in your debt by kicking me."

Varon nickered. *"Then you will accept me?"*

"You may not want to be a part of this herd, Varon, especially if you follow Equ. I am not the only Equus in danger here."

"More have been poisoned?"

Miskala shook his head. *"From time to time, we detect a creator path in our midst."*

"How can that be? Your horses should have sensed it before your herd was among it."

"They should have, but they didn't. What does that tell you, Varon?"

Varon thought for a moment. *"One of the Equus in your herd is a Ravager who has not made him- or herself known yet by killing."*

Miskala nodded. *"Yes."*

"Or perhaps it is only a creator who wants to observe your herd. I've never heard of a Ravager who didn't attack."

"It's not a creator observing us. A few of the times, the horses have detected a death scent, and it is throughout the herd. Some members of our herd have died."

"What will you do?"

Miskala's ears flicked back and forth. *"What can I do? I won't abandon my herd. I can only hope to identify the Ravager and get the rest of the herd away from him before it is too late."*

"Your herd is calm."

Miskala didn't understand what Varon meant at first. *"Calm? Oh, they don't know about it. At least the unicorns, pegasus, and zebras don't. The rest of the herd may suspect, but they have said nothing that is not general knowledge."*

"I would still like to be a part of your herd, Calvn Miskala," Varon told him.

"You don't value your life then."

"On the contrary, I do, but I have also been given work to do. It cannot begin until I am part of a herd," Varon explained to him.

Miskala nodded.

"My children," Miskala said on the mind-link. *"I find no wrong with this Equus and no sickness about him. In finding neither cause for his original exile, I also find that I have no reason to deny him inclusion in my herd. I look forward to hearing his truths and judging them on their own merits. Varon is now Varon of Miskala's Herd."*

<h1 style="text-align:center">41</h1>

Jalon startled herself awake with a jerk of her head. She'd been dreaming about griffins attacking her. She opened her eyes and lifted her head from the ground to look around.

How long had she been unconscious?

The rain had ended, and it was late in the day. She must have been unconscious for a long time. Too long.

"Ah, she awakes from the long slumber."

Jalon jumped at the sound of the unfamiliar mind-voice in her head. She looked behind her and saw an unknown zebra standing there.

"Who are you?" she asked.

"I am Redond. Some Equus call me Redo, though." He walked around to face her so she did not have to twist her neck uncomfortably.

"I recognize your voice. I heard you talking with others before. Where are they?"

"They have removed themselves because we did not know your intentions."

"My intentions? It sounded like one of those others wanted me to die earlier."

Redo nodded. *"That was Frim. She is young and afraid. At times like that, she forgets that the Equus are interdependent. Please don't hold it against her. She is a fine pony. We do not know if you mean to expose us to earn your way back into your herd."*

"What do you mean? I'm not out to cause harm to you or any other Equus. I am searching for a horse named Varon."

Redond cocked his head to the side. *"Then you are not an exile?"*

Jalon hesitated. *"From what I have heard, I have been named an exile, but that was after I left my herd by my own choice."*

Redond made the odd, hiccupping neigh of a zebra. *"Interesting. I have known very few Equus who have done that. Those who did heard the call and answered it."*

"Call?"

"The call of Equ to gather."

Jalon shook her head. *"I don't understand."*

Redond neighed. *"Leave it to old Redo to forget the important information. No wonder the others didn't argue when I volunteered to stay behind."*

"What important information?"

"Why, that my herd is a herd of renegades who have banded together to survive our exiles and to live as Equ intended."

Jalon's eyes widened. *"Exiles? I thought all exiles died."*

"All that lives dies, youngster. I am sure we will eventually, but then so will the senior Calvn."

Jalon shook her head. *"No, I mean, I thought predators killed all the exiles."*

Redond lifted his head and stared at her. *"You don't believe that or you wouldn't be searching for Varon. Predators kill many exiles and their foals, but others join our herd. Still others live in total isolation."*

"What of me?" Jalon asked.

"As an exile, you will have to make such a decision, too. You can stay among us if you wish, or you can forge your own path."

"And if I want to leave?"

Jalon rolled over onto her knees. She wasn't sure if she trusted the strength in her legs enough to stand yet.

"That is why I am here with you, and we are alone. My herd seeks protection now. Later, they will find us to find out your choice. We won't fully expose ourselves to you because we would not want you to be able to lead the Calvns back to our herd," Redond said.

Jalon shook her head. *"I've done my share of leading others to battle, to not want to do it again. Besides, why would the Calvns care about your herd?"*

Redond leaned close to her as if he wanted to speak privately.

"Do I look dead to you? I am an exile from Alii's Herd. You have been taught that to be exiled is to die, and the power to exile becomes a powerful way to control those who might oppose you. Who wants to face exile if they believe they will die? But if they believed they could find the truth, that is another story," Redond explained.

"What truth?"

"We call ourselves Equ's Herd and there are no castes in our herd. We have a leader, whom we call Leader. In the past, all species have had at least one of their own serve as leader. Currently, the leader is Druin, a unicorn mare."

Startled, Jalon repeated, *"Mare?"*

Redond nodded. It was hard for Jalon to imagine a herd being led by a mare. She couldn't imagine a donkey leading a herd. Calvns were always unicorn stallions. They had the blood of Calvn in their veins.

"Is she a good leader?" Jalon asked.

"Not the best, perhaps, but she is very good."

Jalon felt a brush from a mind-link. Redond straightened up and looked around.

"Jalon, if you wish to live, we need to leave now," he told her.

"Why?" Jalon asked as she pushed herself up on all four hooves. She was glad that she could stand without swaying.

"The Ravager's Foals have found us."

"You mentioned Ravager's Foals before. What are they? I've never heard of them," Jalon said.

"The Ravager's Foals are killers. They are exiles like us, but they have allowed their hatred of being exiled to consume them."

Jalon shook her head. *"I don't believe it. To kill another Equus because you were exiled makes little sense."*

"These are the exiles who deserved to be exiled."

"You didn't deserve your exile."

Redond nodded. *"No, I was exiled because I spoke out to support the donkeys too often and Calvn Alii thought I was trying to usurp his authority."*

"You and Varon will have a lot to speak about, then."

Jalon saw a herd of Equus appear on the horizon, galloping toward them.

"We need to reach the forests," Redond said. *"We will be safe there."*

"Why?"

"Because the forests are protected."

They galloped with the Ravager's Foals closing the gap. Jalon watched the edge of the forest grow large in front of them. The Ravager's Foals grew even larger behind them.

Jalon knew that she was the reason for their slowness. She hadn't regained the full strength of her legs, and she felt dizzy from running after being stationary for so long. Redond was holding back to stay with her.

"Go on ahead," she said. *"You can gallop faster than me."*

"Now, how good of a protector would I be if I left you to the Ravager's Foals?" Redond said.

"A live one."

Redond snorted. *"A live one who knew that he was alive only because he was willing to abandon another Equus to death or worse."*

"I'm not afraid to die."

"That's because dying is easy, Jalon. It's living and fulfilling your potential that is hard. Keep galloping."

Jalon tried to gallop faster. She even flapped her numb wings, hoping that it might lighten the weight on her legs. She stayed with Redond and tried to pass him so he knew he could gallop faster. He didn't slow until they were well inside the shadows of the trees.

They slowed to a walk, and Jalon turned to see if the Ravager's Foals were pursuing them. She saw them approach the edge of the forest. As they crossed the perimeter, swarms of birds of every kind swept out of the trees and attacked the Equus.

"What is happening?" Jalon asked.

"They are the protectors of this forest."

"Why didn't they attack us?"

"Because we do not come to harm others. We only seek to live in peace and follow Equ."

Jalon felt uneasy in the forest. The deciduous trees were barren and looked like skeletons. The patches of evergreens blocked her view of anything else. She was at home on the open plains where she could see all around her. She needed the open space of the plains, and more importantly, the open space of the skies. Too many things could jump out at her in the forest; too many places for a predator to hide. It also reminded her too much of the forests on the side of the Meshack Mountains where the griffins had hidden.

"How can you live here?" she asked, feeling very claustrophobic.

"It is my territory."

"But how can you live without other Equus?"

"We do live with other Equus. We are a herd."

"But you don't have contact with the other herds."

"What do we miss by being a single herd and not part of a group? Do we miss the animosities and pettiness between herds? Do we miss Champion Days where the Calvn Council seeks to promote themselves even higher?" Jalon had no answer for that. *"We thrive, as you will see if you are lucky. We live full lives without the contact of other herds."*

"How will I get to see this herd?"

"You have to commit to follow Equ, truly follow him. If you can do that, then you will be committed to our herd."

"So does that mean you will stay with me until I decide what I will do?" Jalon asked.

Redond nodded. *"If needed."*

"I can admire your herd, Redond, but I must find Varon. He's been declared a renegade, and he is just the type of Equus your herd wants. He was exiled because he spoke of his visions from Equ to the Calvn of our herd."

Redond stopped walking. *"Visions?"*

"Yes, Equ speaks to him."

"Truly? He doesn't have the mind-sickness?"

Jalon shook her head. *"No, and also, I think he has seen Equ. A Ravager tried to attack him once, and a great white unicorn with a golden horn saved him."*

Redond's ears flicked back and forth. *"Amazing. I would like to meet this Varon."*

"You take the fact that he speaks with Equ a lot easier than the other Equus did."

"My herd tries to follow Equ. We know that many have been called together, so it is not surprising he would speak to others."

"Then you can see why I need to find him."

Redond nodded. *"Do you have any idea where he might be?"*

"I was heading toward the white mountains. Varon seemed to think the Equus would eventually have to cross them. I thought he might have headed toward them, hoping that other Equus might get the same message from Equ."

"I don't see how the Equus could cross those mountains."

"Nor do I."

"I think you are right. We must find Varon because he will know the way across. As you said, I believe he will want to help our herd," Redond told her.

Jalon nodded. *"Yes."*

"That still leaves open the question of your loyalties."

Jalon arched her neck. *"I am loyal to Varon. I decided that when I left my herd."*

Redond stared at her. *"And Varon is a horse?"*

"What does that have to do with anything?"

Redond nickered in the zebra way, making it sound like a squeal. *"I just think it's too bad. With such loyalty as you possess, you two would make suitable mates."*

Jalon whinnied. *"I think not."*

"Would you serve my herd, though?"

"I will if Varon serves it."

Redond shook his head. *"That is not good enough. If Varon should fail to follow Equ, what would you do?"*

"He wouldn't."

"You don't know that. Good Equus, very good Equus, have failed. Calvn himself failed. If Varon should fail, where would your loyalties lie?"

Jalon couldn't answer him because she didn't know the answer. She had struggled so hard to come to terms with her first denial of Varon that she didn't think she could do it again. However, she had denied him once, so she knew that she could deny him. It was within her.

She shook her head. *"I don't know. You ask me to decide my loyalties between a herd I have never seen and a horse who has been a loyal friend to me. I can't."*

"I'm not asking you to make that decision. I'm asking you to follow Equ as much as you say that Varon follows him," Redond said.

"Yes!" she exclaimed. *"What Varon is doing is right. I believe in that."*

Redond nodded. *"Good."* He paused. *"Druin, did you hear that? Are you satisfied?"*

"I am," came the reply in a feminine mind-voice. *"Bring her in."*

"Who was that?" Jalon asked, not sensing where the other voice in the mind-link had come from. It was as if it was a voice without a body.

"Our Leader."

"Why didn't I sense where she was in the mind-link?"

"The ponies have been monitoring us in the way that they record memories, and they opened their memories to the Leader so she could also hear us without her presence being sensed," Redond explained.

"I didn't know that could be done."

"Come, I'll take you to meet the herd, and we can decide how to best find Varon."

They trotted until they came to an open clearing. As they slowed to a stop, Equus began stepping out from between the trees to look at Redond and Jalon. Many of the Equus were very old or very young.

"Do you have trouble supporting these Equus within the forest, especially with the long Seeking Season?" Jalon asked.

"We're having more trouble than usual, but we will survive. We always do. The young and old stay here because we have hot springs here that keep the growing season going year round near them. It is

enough food to supplement that which the foraging bands bring in. Otherwise, the able-bodied Equus in our herd work," Redond told her.

"Work how?"

"They search out those who have been exiled. We may find only one Equus a year who has been exiled, but we try to find him or her before the predators do."

"We take care of our own here," Druin said.

Jalon turned and saw the white unicorn walking into the clearing. She was about ten years old. Her neck had a proud arch in it, but she did not have the arrogance in her stride that Scola did.

"I see that you can take care of them," Jalon said.

"I am Druin."

"Then I am Jalon of Druin's Herd," Jalon asserted.

Redond nickered with amusement.

"We call ourselves Equ's Herd," Druin said.

"The Ravager's Foals tried to follow us," Redond said. *"We lost them at the edge of the forest, but I'm sure they are still nearby."*

Druin nodded and said to Jalon, *"We must talk about Varon. You believe he is the Voice of Equ?"*

"Yes."

"Why?"

"He says he is." Jalon thought this herd was very suspicious, but maybe they had to be, knowing they were alone on Hemlaza. Alone was relative. If the number of young and old in this herd was the same proportion as it was in most herds, then Equ's Herd numbered close to 800 Equus, making it about three times larger than most Equus herds led by a Calvn.

"And why do you believe Varon?" Druin asked.

"Because Varon doesn't lie, and he lives the way I imagine Equ would want us to live," Jalon told her.

"You will see that same lifestyle here. We welcome you to our herd, Jalon." She paused. *"I guess that we should concentrate on finding the Voice of Equ. Lantz, are you nearby?"*

"Yes, Leader. I'm watching the Ravager's Foals at the edge of

the forest. They're beginning to move away," a male mind-voice said.

"Good. I need you to get a message out to all the bands that we are searching for an exile named Varon, formerly of Scola's Herd. It is important that we find him and bring him back here. He may be near the white mountains."

"I'll get right on it, Leader. The messengers should arrive soon. I'll send them out with our wishes," Lantz told her.

"Very good, Lantz."

Jalon asked, *"May I go out also to search for Varon? He is my friend."*

"You don't have to go. We have enough bands out who will search for him," Druin replied.

"I want to, though. If I'm to be a part of this herd, then I need to do my part."

Druin nodded. *"Well spoken, Jalon. You will be an asset to the herd. Go with our creator's blessings."*

42

Miskala looked over his herd and was saddened by what he saw. The fracture lines were becoming apparent to many in the herd. The Equus were separating into two groups; those who believed Varon was the Voice of Equ and those who didn't, and by association, those who believed in Miskala's leadership and those who didn't.

Miskala believed Varon was telling the truth, but he was in the smaller group. Accepting Varon into the herd had swelled the size of the hostile band until they were no longer even attempting to hide their hostility toward Miskala and Varon.

What would this herd be like in a moon cycle? Would the invisible fracture lines become actual divisions in the herd?

"What is wrong, my mate?" Lyos asked. She began grooming Miskala, and he relaxed somewhat.

"I am failing my herd."

"Perhaps it is the herd that fails you, Miskala. The ages are changing, and the Equus resist change. If things had remained as they were, you would have become a fine Calvn."

Miskala looked at her. *"Meaning that since the ages are changing, I won't be a fine Calvn?"*

"You are leading and making the wisest choices, but when most of the herd resists following those choices, they sentence themselves to the consequences."

"But if the majority resist, does that mean I am making poor choices?"

"What do you believe? Is Varon the Voice of Equ?"

Miskala didn't even have to consider his answer. He had decided. *"Yes."*

"Then if you are to follow Equ, does that mean you are going against the voice of the herd?" Lyos asked him.

"It may."

"So which should you follow: Equ or the herd?"

"Equ, of course." He paused. *"But I'm the Calvn. Shouldn't I be able to convince the herd to do what is right?"*

"Miskala, you are not the only Calvn who has had his authority challenged. You've heard the rumblings at Champion Days against the decisions of the Calvn Council. You've rumbled yourself. No Calvn has total support within his herd, but the differences between you and some others are that your conflicts come because you want to follow Equ. Many other Calvns find conflict when they try to take what is not theirs."

Miskala blew air out of his mouth and let his lips flap.

"If this herd represents the entire Equus, then it does not bode well for our future survival," he said.

"Perhaps you should worry about your future."

"Why?"

"These Equus don't want to follow Equ. Will you follow them to their destruction, or will you lead the ones who want to do what is right?"

"My responsibility is to the entire herd."

Lyos nodded. *"For now, it is one herd, but the time is coming when it will split. With whom does your responsibility lie, then?"*

"You see the split also? Is it that obvious?"

Again, she nodded. *"In some ways. Some who support you will not converse or associate with those who doubt you. You've noticed that there are more fights among the herd, too. Varon's truth is disturbing, but it does not mean it is any less true."*

He had noticed the fights and was thankful that no one had been injured.

Miskala stamped his front hoof. *"I shouldn't have brought Varon into the herd. He will split it for sure, and then what will happen to us?"*

"I'm not sure you did the wrong thing, Miskala. The herd al-

ready had divisions before Varon came. He only brought them to the surface."

Miskala nodded. *"I know, but he makes it harder for me to hold the herd together."*

"But would you have forsaken learning Equ had chosen his own Voice?"

Miskala was quiet as he considered it. *"No, it restores my faith in Equ, knowing he has not spoken through the likes of Calvn Mika,"* he said.

"Then you have no choice."

"You mean I should help Varon? If he is given the Ranglan Stone, he will be killed. The Calvn Council will not allow a horse to possess the symbol of their power."

"It is only a symbol to them. Varon says he needs it. It is a tool to him."

Miskala nodded his head. *"I know. That is why we are here."*

"Here? Where?"

"Near the Valley of the Equus."

Lyos stopped her grooming. *"You intend to bring Varon to the stone."*

Miskala nodded. *"If that is what Equ requires."*

Varon was speaking to a group of donkeys when Miskala approached him. Miskala stopped to listen to him speak.

"I cannot say whether the social structure of the Equus will change after the exodus. I do know that the exodus brings us one step closer to Etrasco, and if we return to Etrasco, all will be equal. For isn't that the meaning of our name? All equal under Equ. So if our social structure changes on our way there, it will be for the best," Varon explained.

"Can you ask Equ?" one donkey asked.

Varon nodded. *"I can, but it doesn't mean he will choose this time to reply. All I can say is that he has shown me that all the species of Equus must leave Hemlaza. The donkey to the unicorn; none of us are safe here."*

"Varon," Miskala interrupted.

"Yes, my Calvn," Varon replied.

"Can we walk?"

Walking was not only a way of movement among the Equus, but it also allowed those walking to stay close enough to speak privately.

"Of course." Varon paused. *"I must go now, brothers, but consider what I have said. Then look to the north toward the white mountains and consider more."*

Varon turned away from the donkeys and walked alongside the Calvn.

"Do you make much progress?" Miskala asked.

"Some. Not as much as I would hope, but the more I speak as the Voice of Equ, the more I come to believe he will not save all the Equus."

"Why not?"

"Not all of them will heed him. If he intended to save us all, he could move us in a thought, but he has chosen this way and me, know-ing what would happen. I don't have to like it, though. If it was up to me, I wouldn't lose any Equus," Varon told him.

Miskala shook his head and looked over Varon's head, wondering if he had to choose a portion of his herd to save who it would be. *"It sounds heartless to save only a seed."*

"Is that not what you do as Calvn if a predator attacks? You save a seed," Varon asked.

"I attempt to save all of them," Miskala said, knowing it was not completely true. He would sacrifice herd scouts and older Equus to predators if he had to.

"But do you not choose who will most likely survive, such as the mares and foals?"

Miskala thought it interesting that Varon thought in terms of who would live instead of who would die.

Miskala nodded. *"Yes, I see your point."*

"So it is with Equ. He asks for all Equus to return to Etrasco, but will take those who heed his call. Those are the Equus who still believe all are equal under Equ enough to listen when he speaks to them."

"How many seeds can you save, then?"

Varon's head dropped and his tail swished back and forth. *"Few.*

Too few, I fear. Time grows short. We are being driven from Hemlaza by the white mountains, and we will either face the future or die."

"Short? You mean that you know when you will leave for Etrasco?"

Varon shook his head. *"No, but I know as long as Hemlaza has food, the Equus will try to pretend that nothing has changed. But as food grows scarcer, predators will become bolder and could very well kill the Equus who listen to Equ. I have seen the early signs of this, as I'm sure you have. I do not know when Equ will say we must leave, so I have to work hard to gather those I can before that time and leave before all is lost."*

"And you also need the Ranglan Stone."

Varon nodded. *"I need the Ranglan Stone."*

Miskala looked around to make sure that no one was near him. *"I will take you."*

Varon neighed. *"I suspect that was hard for you to offer."*

"Yes, I endanger my life and yours."

"I understand."

Miskala wondered if he did. Did Varon realize the treachery he was asking Miskala to commit? *"We will need to be careful. Tensions are high among the herd. Those who wish me or you to be exiled or worse would use this as an excuse to press their cause."*

"I will follow your advice then, my Calvn."

Miskala nickered. He thought it amusing that Varon was calling him his Calvn when Miskala was following him.

"Good. We are near the Valley of the Equus. No one other than perhaps Oralum realizes it, but if he did, it would be the worst thing to happen to us. We need to do this in a way that we aren't missed."

Varon nodded.

"Tonight then."

Slipping away from a herd was difficult. Equus, because of their need to be alert, slept only in brief stretches of less than half the night, and very little of that sleep was deep. Therefore, it was not a matter of waiting until Oralum, Entro, and the other Equus hostile to Varon and Miskala slept. Varon and Miskala had to leave with none of the hostile band realizing they had left.

As night fell, Varon approached Miskala and said, *"Calvn, I need to leave the herd for a time."*

"Why? It's night and dangerous, Varon, especially with the predators massing with unusual alliances. Do you value your life so little?"

"I value my life a great deal, but Equ has need of me to do something."

"What does Equ require of you?" Oralum asked, interrupting the conversation as if he had been a part of it.

"He has not told me yet. He has only told me to leave the herd for a time. I will return by morning," Varon answered.

"Do you go east to the mountains again?"

"No, not this time. He has told me to go to the north."

"Toward the white mountains?" Oralum asked, surprised.

"As much as the white mountains are to the north."

"Maybe he will tell you to leave Hemlaza," Oralum said with some amusement.

"Not yet, Oralum, but I'm sad that when I do finally leave this herd, you won't be accompanying me," Varon told the unicorn.

Oralum snorted. *"I would not make a fool's journey."*

Varon shook his head. *"No, you would rather suffer a fool's end."*

"Enough!" Miskala said. *"You are each entitled to your opinions."* He said to Varon, *"Do you require or desire an escort?"*

"No, my Calvn. This is something I need to do alone."

Miskala nodded. *"Fine, some of us will look forward to your return."*

Varon turned and galloped away.

"Maybe the predators will find him," Oralum mused.

Miskala turned to face Oralum and glare at him. *"Oralum, you may not like him, but don't wish him ill."*

"What does it matter what I wish? Equ will protect him," the other unicorn said as his tail flipped up and down with irritation.

Miskala grew tired of Oralum trying to frustrate his leadership and struck back. *"I think I understand why you were never chosen as a Calvn."*

"Why is that, Calvn? I would seek to know how I might change that." His tail was moving at a furious pace now.

"A Calvn is the leader of his herd. He must place the concerns of his herd above his own. I have yet to see you do that."

Oralum chose not to make a reply in his anger, or he might have given Miskala the grounds to exile him. It was one of the few times he had shown wisdom or self-restraint.

"Get out of my sight, Oralum. I don't want to deal with you to-night," Miskala said.

"As you wish, my Calvn."

Oralum turned and walked away. Entro and some other members of the hostile band followed him to the edge of the herd.

Miskala sighed. He had wondered how he could put distance between himself and Oralum. The argument had worked out well for him.

"You shouldn't antagonize him," Capsta, the horse leader of the herd, said.

"Well, the rest of the herd seems to be taking sides in support or against Varon. Maybe it's time I started making my feelings known about the issue."

"Yes, but if your animosity comes out in the open, Oralum might act. He hasn't until now because it would put him in a poor light."

"Act how?"

"He wants power. He will try to take it when the herd opinion is strong enough to support him," Capsta said.

Miskala shook his head. *"He won't do it yet. If he does, he will become a renegade."*

"Let us hope that he never acts."

Miskala nodded and walked away. He sought out Lyos. He needed the comfort of her presence and the wisdom of her reasoning.

"I have to leave for a while, Lyos. You must keep anyone from searching for me. Mislead them if need be. It's important," Miskala told her while they were grooming each other.

"Why?"

"Because I'm about to do something rash."

"And you won't tell me what."

"You'll know soon enough. It's better you don't know more in case things go wrong," Miskala explained to her.

"Then go help Varon," Lyos said.

Somehow, it didn't surprise Miskala that his mate knew his heart and his thoughts. She would make a suitable life mate. He wondered if she would want to make that kind of commitment to him.

Miskala waited until full dark. He still saw a lot of movement among the herd so his own movements wouldn't attract attention, and he couldn't be seen in the darkness. He galloped south at first and swung to the east. He let his thoughts roam and couldn't detect another Equus mind.

Satisfied, he continued on eastward until he touched another mind with his mind-voice, that of a single Equus.

"Varon."

"Yes," came the reply.

Miskala closed the gap until he stood beside Varon.

"Were you followed?" Miskala asked.

"No."

"We need to be back with the herd before morning. We can't delay."

Miskala broke into a gallop and Varon followed. Miskala slowed to a walk and stopped in front of an opening in the mountains.

"This is the Valley of the Equus."

"It's smaller than I imagined," Varon said.

Miskala looked at Varon to see if he was being sarcastic. He wasn't. He had pictured the Valley of the Equus to look a certain way.

"This is the only entrance to the valley. It opens up wider within a short distance. The Ranglan Stone is kept upon a unicorn's horn inside the valley."

"A unicorn's horn?"

Miskala nodded. *"It is still attached to his skull."*

"Gruesome."

"I would call it frightening."

Miskala ducked his head and started through the opening. As with his previous visit, he felt a chill down his back when he entered the valley. He was afraid of the symbol of his power, especially after the spirits he had seen when he was here.

Varon moved to follow Miskala, but stopped at the entrance.

Miskala saw him stopped and asked, *"What's wrong?"*

"I can't pass through."

"Why not? The entrance is wide enough."

"It's not that. The valley is haunted."

"Haunted?"

"Spirits are within the valley," Varon said.

How had he known that? Miskala had never heard of the sixth sense detecting spirits. *"They don't mean you any harm. You are the Voice of Equ. You are the one they have been waiting for,"* Miskala said.

"It doesn't matter. My body is acting as if a herd of Equus stands in front of me, blocking my way," Varon told him.

"But Equ is leading you."

"He leads you, too, brother."

Miskala shook his head. *"Not in this instance. I have chosen my path, and it is to follow the will of Equ and you. You must enter with me. I can show you the Ranglan Stone, but I don't know how to use it. Also, you might need other information in the valley you will find."*

"What information?"

"A history of the Equus and the Ranglan Stone. The Ranglan Stone has acted oddly at times."

"Oddly?"

"The Ranglan Stone is not just a stone. Equ sent it to us to end the herd wars. That is the reason the Calvns have used this stone as a symbol of their power. It has power."

"Power the Calvns have never learned to harness," Varon guessed.

"Power we haven't even been able to understand. When one is chosen Calvn, the stone is placed on their horn and the Calvn may hear... a voice," Miskala explained.

"It is Equ," Varon said. *"What does the voice say?"*

"Sometimes it is soft, sometimes loud. It always seems to say something different to whoever wears the stone."

"What did he say to you?"

"Why are those who are all equal to me different to you? Follow my Voice and be true to him."

Varon nodded. *"Meaning me."*

"That's what I believe. So you see why you need to see the record. All the Calvns have recorded what they have heard and how the Ranglan Stone has acted over the years. It is not a part of the ponies' memory," Miskala said.

"It may show me how to use the Ranglan Stone. Can you read it?"

Miskala shook his head. *"I haven't learned the language of the Calvns yet. I only know what Calvn Mika told me when I returned to the Ranglan Depression with the stone."*

"So this is how you honor the Equus." Oralum, followed by three zebras, galloped up to face Miskala and Varon. *"You've violated the trust of the Calvns,"* Oralum said.

"As you have," Miskala told him, though he did not understand how Oralum had realized what was happening or how he had followed him without being detected.

"I had to bring the zebras to show them what you have done. It requires the full consent of all the zebras to replace the Calvn of a herd with an interim Calvn."

"So you seek to steal what you can never earn," Miskala said.

Oralum arched his neck. *"Your actions allow it."*

"I refuse you and call upon the herd to support me."

Oralum tossed his head back. *"Fine. Those Equus who support the minority position will become renegades."*

Oralum had agreed too easily. Miskala remembered what Capsta had told him about when Oralum would act. Did Oralum have the support of the herd? Miskala would have to trust them. He couldn't believe the herd would want Oralum to lead them, and he couldn't back down now.

"Agreed," Miskala said.

"Agreed."

All Miskala could recall was his dream of the herd splitting and how few his supporters had been. It was not a good omen.

43

The zebras of Miskala's Herd called the herd together. Miskala stood at the end of the row of zebras, and Oralum stood at the opposite end.

"Equus of this herd, hear me," Bronelin, the zebra leader, said. *"Oralum has charged Miskala with violating his duties as Calvn of this herd, and Calvn Miskala has called for the support of the herd. The choice will be yours. Oralum, as the accuser, will speak his accusations against the Calvn first. Then Calvn Miskala will respond to the accusations."*

Bronelin stepped back to stand with the zebras who would litigate this confrontation.

Oralum reared up to attract the entire herd's attention. *"Fellow Equus, we have survived on our own through many disasters; lightning strikes on the plains, hurricanes, heavy snows. Through all this, it has been our traditions, our rules of conduct, which have kept us together as a herd. Those traditions and rules tell us the Calvn is the leader of the herd because he is the Voice of Equ.*

"And yet, our Calvn has allowed a horse from another herd— no, a horse exiled from two other herds—to come among us and claim the honor of being the Voice of Equ. Two Calvns have seen fit to ban him from their mind-links. However, our Calvn has allowed this exile to join our herd and to preach his sedition among us.

"Finally, Miskala further violated his duties to this herd by leading one not of the blood of Calvn to the Valley of the Equus to take the Ranglan Stone." He paused as the herd murmured amongst themselves. *"I deduced what was happening and stopped the two of them before it was too late. The Ranglan Stone still rests in the val-*

333

ley. All along, Equus, it has been I who have sought to maintain our rich traditions that have served us so well in the past.

"Now, I call upon the herd to support me, lest Miskala and Varon lead us away to our deaths. Has not the Calvn Council declared the white mountains no threat, and are they not the Voice of Equ? Support me and live as the Equus always have. Support me and continue the rich traditions of our heritage for our young."

Miskala pawed at the ground. He looked at Varon and said, *"He's playing to their fears. He is scaring them into believing he is their savior."*

"All you can give them is the truth," Varon told him.

Miskala looked up. Oralum had finished, and now it was his turn to speak. *"Where have those rules and rich traditions of the Equus brought us, my children? We have changed from 'all equal under Equ' to a species of castes that places unicorns above all and donkeys at the bottom. Is that equality? Is that the will of Equ?*

"I say no. We hold to the laws of the Equus, but do we obey their spirit, the meaning behind those laws? The First Law of the Equus is that Equus shall not kill Equus. Yet, the Calvn Council admits in private that Calvn Gee exiled his own colt because it did not look like a unicorn. They won't take action against Gee because he is not only a unicorn but a Calvn. If the laws are so important, why can the Calvn Council violate them at will? I tell you, my children, the Equus have always changed and adapted whether or not you realize it. Herds grow, die, and are reformed. I tell you now the Calvns are not the Voice of Equ. They speak in their own interest, and their own interests are to maintain their power. Varon brought us the truth; truth he shared with you all. Truth, all of you, if you were to look within your hearts, would realize.

"Support me and show the other herds the Equus can truly be 'all equal under Equ,' for it is only through our adherence to the teachings of Equ we will live. What is his will? He told all of us when he named us Equus. All equal under Equ. All. That means donkeys as well as unicorns, zebras, and pegasuses. The ages are changing, my children. If the Equus do not change, they will die."

Bronelin once again moved forward. *"So it has been spoken and given to the herd to decide. Choose you now where you will stand."*

The Equus separated, moving to stand behind either Miskala or Oralum. Varon remained standing in the middle and found himself alone as the Equus decided with whom they would stand. Most of the unicorns, pegasuses, and horses went with Oralum. Varon stepped toward Miskala and felt his knees go weak.

No, this was not the time for a vision! He had to show his support for Miskala.

But he was no longer with Miskala's Herd. He stood alone within the Valley of the Equus. No, not alone, for Oralum was also in the valley. The gray unicorn wore the Ranglan Stone on his horn as he prepared to have the zebras who had supported him during the split declare him interim Calvn of Miskala's Herd. Varon didn't know where Miskala and his band were, but he was sure they waited for him somewhere. He was a part of them now.

Varon approached Oralum, and the unicorn turned to look at him.

"Will you not accept defeat?" Oralum said.

Varon shook his head. *"No, because Equ will not."*

"Equ does not speak through you. I am the Voice of Equ. I am Calvn of Oralum's Herd," Oralum declared.

"Then what does he tell you?" Varon asked.

"I told him to return the stone to you," Equ said in Varon's head.

"He said that the white mountains are no threat," Oralum said.

"Liar, your words have proven you to be the threat to the Equus and Miskala's Herd. Not me. Not Miskala," Varon said.

"I am no liar. I am Calvn of Oralum's Herd. If I speak it, it is Equ's will."

Oralum turned and walked away.

"Equ told you to give the stone to me."

Oralum stopped. When he turned to face Varon, he said, *"You guess or hope, I know not which, but I told you what he spoke to me."*

Varon reared up, flailing his legs. One hoof struck Oralum on the nose, the other struck him on the side of the head. Oralum collapsed and lay still.

Varon had killed an Equus.

Varon's vision cleared, and he stood alone between the two bands of Equus. It dismayed him to see how much smaller Miskala's band was than Oralum's. Was Miskala's band the seed he was to save, a band even smaller than a herd?

It couldn't be. Varon had seen many Equus crossing the white mountains. At least half of all the Equus had been in the great herd.

"You stand alone, Varon. Which band do you choose?" Bronelin asked.

"Was there any doubt?"

Varon walked over to stand behind Miskala.

"I have failed you, Varon," Miskala said. It was obvious which band would be exiled.

"Nonsense. You've given me my first success. Together, we will find others. If we have to take fifty Equus from every herd, we will. Equ won't let us fail him."

"How can you say that?"

"Because he is afraid to fail us. He had already pressed the limits of what he should do to help us. We will succeed," Varon said with confidence he wasn't sure he felt.

"Will we?"

"I have seen it."

Varon would rather think about that than what else he had seen. How could Equ's mother ever think Varon would violate the First Law of the Equus? It had to be only a possible future, like when he had seen all the Equus being destroyed in his first vision.

"Now the zebras will choose who they will follow," Bronelin said.

Nine zebras came to stand with Miskala. Thirty-three stood with Oralum.

Oralum reared up, kicking his front legs. *"The herd has decided, Miskala. They stand with me. As the new Calvn, I declare Miskala and his band of renegades to be forsaken by all Equus. Leave our presence now, renegades."*

Miskala was the first to turn and walk away from his former herd.

"What do we do now, Calvn?" one donkey asked.

"I am no longer Calvn."

"But you are still our leader."

Miskala spun around. *"I am not. This band was formed because we followed the Voice of Equ, and so follow him we shall. Varon is our leader."*

Varon stopped as all the Equus in the band turned to look at him.

He shook his head. *"I will lead for now until the one chosen by Equ to lead is identified. It will not be me, though."*

"Then who?" Miskala asked.

"I don't know who it will be, but she will be a unicorn."

Miskala was startled. *"She? But a mare has never been a Calvn."*

"And this unicorn will not be, either. She will be the Eyes of Equ as I am his Voice. Ultimately, Equ will lead us."

The band walked again.

"What shall we do?" Miskala asked Varon.

"I set out to claim the Ranglan Stone, and I have not yet found it. We must have it before we leave," Varon said.

"But how?"

"We're close to the Valley of the Equus now. We'll circle around Oralum and his band and take the Ranglan Stone before Oralum can take it to proclaim himself Calvn to Calvn Mika."

The band galloped toward the north, well beyond Oralum's Herd's mind-link. Then they turned to the east as Miskala led them to the Valley of the Equus. Miskala was dismayed to see Oralum's Herd arrayed in front of the entrance to the valley. They must have galloped at top speed to get there ahead of Miskala and the others, and they must have realized what Varon would do before he had known it.

"I see you don't mind violating the traditions of the Calvn when it suits you," Miskala said to Oralum.

"We seek only to protect the Valley of the Equus from renegades. None but me will enter," Oralum said as he arched his neck and tail and pranced in front of his herd.

"We need the Ranglan Stone," Miskala said.

"You will not have it. Now leave. As renegades, you are no long-

er considered Equus, and we are free to kill you." Oralum saw Varon and said, "What does Equ tell you now?"

"He has said that I will save a seed of the Equus while the plant will perish. If the Equus are the plant, then you, Oralum, must be a thorn."

Oralum snorted. "At least I remain a part of the plant. Your band is like the leaves that drop from the tree in the fall to wither and die. Now go!"

Varon turned and led his band away. They would not force their way into the valley with the other Equus there.

"What now?" Miskala asked Varon.

"If we do the will of Equ, why doesn't he help us accomplish our goals?" a pony asked and others agreed.

"Have we been declared renegades only to die?" one of the nine zebras in the band asked.

"You must find the Ranglan Stone alone," Equ said in Varon's head.

"No," Varon replied.

"You refuse?"

"I have seen what might happen if I enter the valley alone, Equ. Do not put me into that position," Varon told their creator.

"Are you afraid to die?" Equ asked.

"No, I won't die. That is not what my vision showed me."

"Then what did my mother show you?"

"Can she show possible futures?" Varon asked.

"It depends."

"On what?"

"She shows what should be for her plan to come to be, but what should be and what will be can be different. This choice is always yours. I do not control you, nor does she. I have learned that her decision is the wisest one."

"But is her plan your plan?" Varon countered.

Equ didn't answer for the longest time. "In general, yes. In specific, not necessarily. What did she show you, Varon? I can feel your turmoil over it."

"That's because I think I know what I must do." Varon expanded his thoughts and said to the band. *"I will go into the valley alone and retrieve the Ranglan Stone."*

"Alone? What of the hauntings? You couldn't enter the valley before," Miskala said.

Varon sighed. *"I will find a way. I must. Our future begins with me going into the valley."*

"I will go with you."

Varon shook his head. *"No, I must go alone. If you go, it only increases the chances I will be seen and stopped."*

Varon left his band in Miskala's care and headed back toward the valley.

"Is there another way into the valley?" Varon asked Miskala as he walked away.

"None I saw."

"Can you and the band distract Oralum's Herd while I sneak inside?"

"Yes, but you will have to be quick about it. You can't freeze at the entrance because your sixth sense detects something," Miskala warned him.

"I know."

Varon slipped around Oralum's Herd and crept as close to the valley as he dared. Miskala and his band came galloping out of the night, screaming to disrupt the mind-link. They charged the herd and dashed among them and then back out toward the plains.

"Follow them and chase them from anywhere near the valley!" Entro ordered the herd.

Most of the herd galloped off after Miskala and his band. A few zebras remained behind him with their attention directed forward to guard the way into the valley. Varon crept behind them, hoping they wouldn't notice the movement behind them.

As he approached the entrance to the valley, he broke into a gallop and charged through the opening with his eyes closed. His senses were assaulted and screamed for him to stop, but he plowed forward. His head scraped the ceiling, and he ducked. His legs locked in fear of the unseen terror before him. Varon was moving so fast, though, that he sprawled forward and he was through the protective barrier around the valley. The silent alarm in his head stopped sounding.

Varon stood up. He had thought it would be large, but it was larger than even he imagined. The mountains rose on both sides of the valley so that Varon could see why there was no other way inside.

He walked closer to the walls of the valley. He saw the scratchings on the walls that Miskala had told him about. Some figures repeated themselves. Varon looked around. The scratchings covered all the walls from the ground to above his head.

This was the history of the Calvns. Did he need to know what these scratchings said? Varon did not know the language of the Calvns.

"I can tell you all that you need to know about the Ranglan Stone," Equ told him.

"Why couldn't you just bring it to me then?" Varon asked.

"It would go beyond my ability to interfere. You had to want it enough to find a way inside. This is a test of your will to do my will," Equ explained.

Varon stopped walking. *"Then you know what I am supposed to do?"*

"I suspect."

Varon rounded a turn in the valley's path, and he saw Oralum ahead of him. The unicorn lifted the Ranglan Stone off a unicorn's horn that held it in one place on the valley floor. This was just as Varon had seen in his vision. His time for a decision was near.

Varon took a step toward the gray unicorn. Oralum watched him approach.

"Will you not accept defeat?" Oralum said.

Varon wondered if he should say something different and change his vision to avoid the outcome. *"I am not yet defeated."*

How much would that difference change his vision?

"But you have been. I hold the Ranglan Stone, and I will carry it to Calvn Mika and claim my place as Calvn."

If the stone reached Calvn Mika, Varon would never get it back.

"I must have the stone," Varon said.

"Then perhaps Equ will give it to you."

"I wish it were that easy."

"Be gone from here, renegade, and I may let you live."

"I will leave with the stone."

Oralum tilted his head back and slid the Ranglan Stone further onto his horn. It rattled its way down the length of the two-foot-long horn. His attention was directed at the air in front of him. He neighed in terror at something Varon couldn't see.

"What's happening?" Varon asked Equ.

"He's finding out he does not live up to an ideal," Equ told him after a moment.

Oralum lowered his head, as if he was subjecting himself to a better Equus. Varon noticed that the unicorn was careful not to allow the Ranglan Stone to slide to the ground.

Oralum suddenly jumped to the side, screaming on the mind-link. Varon was tempted to take the Ranglan Stone and run, but Oralum was moving too erratically. Varon didn't want to get in the way of Oralum's horn.

After one final scream, Oralum stood still and regained his composure. When he saw Varon watching him, he said, *"You're still here. I had hoped that you were an unpleasant dream, too."*

"I'm not finished what I came to do," Varon told him.

"Then you will die in this valley," Oralum said.

Oralum lowered his head and charged Varon.

Varon hopped to the side and Oralum's horn missed him. Oralum was older and wasn't as fast as Varon. As Oralum slowed to turn, Varon kicked out his rear legs and hit Oralum in the haunch. The unicorn faltered but turned.

"Don't force this," Varon warned him.

"I force nothing. You brought this on yourself."

"I don't want to kill you."

Oralum neighed. *"You can't. I am Calvn."*

"Calvns die."

"Not now. Not here."

Oralum charged with his horn lowered. Varon raised up his rear legs and kicked out at Oralum's horn. It forced Oralum's head down even further, throwing Oralum off balance. His front legs buckled, and his horn plowed into the ground between Varon's legs. When Varon came down, he hit the unicorn on the neck, snapping it with a loud crack.

Oralum whinnied, stumbled, and then fell to his side. He lay still, except for a few heaving breaths, and then even those ended.

Varon backed away from the dead unicorn. He had violated the First Law of the Equus. He had tried to change the future, and it had still turned out the same way.

Varon turned back toward the end of the valley. How could he face the others in the band, knowing what he had done?

"Take the Ranglan Stone," Equ said.

"I can't," Varon told him.

"You must take the Ranglan Stone."

"But he's dead. I violated the First Law. I am not worthy."

"It was unavoidable. If you do not take the stone, then all you have done here will have been wasted," Equ said.

Varon walked forward and leaned his nose down toward Oralum's face. The body was still warm. Despite the thick muscles in Oralum's neck, Varon could see it was broken. His eyes stared up at Varon.

"I'm sorry, Oralum. I didn't want it to end this way. You were too stubborn."

Varon used his lips to pull the Ranglan Stone off of Oralum's horn. He closed his eyes and suppressed the wave of revulsion going through him. When the stone was free, he held it in his mouth and galloped for the exit from the valley. His terror at what he had done was already so great that the spirits that surrounded the valley barely registered in his mind.

He burst from the valley, startling Oralum's Herd, and he kept on running. He heard shouts in his mind as Entro tried to rally the herd to pursue Varon. Varon was out of range of the mind-link before anyone moved to follow him.

44

When Carn saw Varon gallop full tilt from the Valley of the Equus with the Ranglan Stone in his mouth, he panicked. Carn had taken advantage of the opportunity presented when Oralum took control of Miskala's Herd to send the unicorn after the Ranglan Stone. Carn meant to take it away from him when he left the valley. His reasoning was if he could control the source of the Equus power, he could control the Equus.

Instead, it was Varon who left the valley with the stone.

If Varon kept the stone, it would ruin Carn's plans. He yelled into the mind-link for the herd to capture Varon, but the horse already had a running start and was moving away fast. Carn had to catch him before he got away with the Ranglan Stone.

Carn shifted shape, expanding and morphing into a large green dragon with iridescent wings even wider than those of a pegasus. The Equus around him screamed in fright as they watched him change and fly into the air. He flew straight for Varon.

Though Carn tried to come in behind Varon so he wouldn't be seen, the screams on the mind-link alerted the horse. Varon dodged to the side. Carn's talons only raked him along the side instead of impaling him. Varon stumbled and fell into the dirt. The Ranglan Stone flew from his mouth.

Carn swooped down and snatched the Ranglan Stone from off the ground. As he flew away, he felt his concentration falter. His body changed without him willing it, and he fell to the ground. He was in his natural state now; a combination of living molecules held together by a powerful will, but his will wouldn't let him reform his body.

Carn had never been so terrified. He couldn't control his own body. It swirled around as if it was nothing more than a cloud of dust. Without solidity, he lost his grip on the Ranglan Stone, and it tumbled to the ground.

Varon staggered to his hooves. The Ravager had finally made himself known. Varon watched the dragon snatch the Ranglan Stone from off the ground and fly off.

Then an amazing thing happened. The dragon froze in mid-flight and dissolved into a cloud of dust. The Ranglan Stone tumbled to the ground.

"Take the stone," Equ commanded Varon.

"But the dragon."

"The dragon was Carn, but he can't do anything at the moment until he is no longer near the Ranglan Stone," Equ explained.

"What does Carn want with the Ranglan Stone?" Varon had no desire to face down a Ravager. Once in his life was enough, and he had been lucky to escape that time.

"He thinks it is powerful."

"It is powerful."

"Not the power he thinks it has. That comes from the mind-link," Equ said.

Varon galloped over and grabbed the stone off the ground with his mouth. Carn's cloud of dust stung as it hit him, but only that. He galloped away as fast as he could.

Behind him, Varon could see Carn reforming into what appeared to be a large lizard that walked on two legs.

When Miskala saw the dragon appear, he stopped amidst a fight with a zebra who had supported Oralum.

Entro! Entro had been the Ravager!

The herd panicked, fleeing in all directions at the sight of a Ravager among them. Then the dragon dissolved, but the herd didn't seem to notice the disappearance. Screams and cries filled the mind-link; neighs of terror filled the air.

"Stop, my children! Don't separate! Come to me!" Miskala

commanded through the mind-link.

Many of the Equus stopped, but only a few made the move to return to him. They wanted to be as far away from the Ravager as they could.

Then the Ravager reformed into a great lizard and came back to them. It bit Jobi the pony across the back, severing him in two. Then it swung its huge head back and forth, looking for something else to attack.

Miskala took that moment to charge the creature. He lowered his horn and aimed for the lizard's underbelly. He had to do his best to destroy the lizard before it destroyed the herd.

The lizard saw him coming and turned to face him. When it darted its head toward Miskala, he dodged and sunk his horn into the creature's softer underbelly. The lizard reared back its head and roared, but as he did, his tail swung around and knocked Miskala into the air.

Miskala landed on his side and felt a couple of his ribs break. The creature advanced on him, even as the hole in its stomach healed. Miskala knew then that he wouldn't be able to kill this lizard. It was a Ravager, a creator. It could create life, and it could take it away.

Suddenly, Lyos stood over him, prancing around in anger.

"Lyos, get away," Miskala told her.

"No, we'll go together. Get up."

Then the lizard was on them. Its jaws opened wide and Miskala saw his season mate bitten in half as the Ravager bit through her neck. Her lifeless head fell near his. He screamed through the mind-link and squealed in terror.

Miskala was on his hooves in moments. He attacked and jabbed at the lizard with his horn, even kicking it when the opportunity presented itself. The two of them danced around each other as Miskala kept away from the lizard's tail and jaws. Miskala was tiring, though. He couldn't keep up his aggressive posture forever, especially with a Ravager. He could only hope that he was buying enough time with his life for his herd to get away from here.

Varon stopped galloping when he heard Miskala's scream. Was he dead? No, the scream continued, but it sounded insane.

"*Miskala,*" he called.

His only answer was Miskala's scream.

The power Carn thinks it has is the mind-link, Varon remembered Equ saying.

Why should Varon think of that in all of this chaos? The mind-link controlled herd thought, which Varon hated. It had driven him from his herd and killed his dam. Where was the power in that? Not the power of one, the power of many. Predators stayed away from large herds because many Equus were an awesome force. Ravagers were predators. Could the power of many repel them?

He spun around and galloped back in the direction that he had run from.

"*Where are you going?*" Equ asked.

"*The mind-link gives Equus the power to oppose the Ravagers.*"

"*It took you long enough to realize that.*"

"*Why didn't you tell me directly if you wanted me to know it?*" Varon asked.

"*Because you can only harness the mind-link's power if you truly realize what you are doing,*" Equ explained to him.

"*Then I can just command the Equus to attack Carn?*"

"*'All equal under Equ' can also be translated as 'All are one under Equ.' United, you have power, but you will have to allow the ponies to use their power. You can't think about what you're doing; let it happen as if by instinct.*"

That made no sense to Varon. "*I don't understand.*"

"*If you've gotten this far, you will understand at the proper time.*"

As Varon approached the valley, he saw Miskala sparring with the giant lizard. It dismayed him to see the former Calvn fighting alone when Equ had just said that the Equus needed to stand together. How could Varon control the Equus to help Miskala? He was only a horse.

"*Ponies, take my thoughts into your herd memory,*" Varon said.

"What? The herd is no more," one pony said.

"Just do it now!"

Varon tried to relax, but it was hard to do with a Ravager so close by. He felt the minds of the ponies entering his mind as they searched out his memories. Varon was seeing things not only from his life but also from generations past.

He reached out with his mind to the ponies. They tried to withdraw and re-establish a normal mind-link, but they were too slow. Varon had caught them off guard and had already established a conduit to them. It was shaky, but it held. He could feel the power of the ponies in him.

"How am I doing this?"

"The Ranglan Stone hones the natural ability of the unicorns and gives it to those species without it. You have the Ranglan Stone, so you now have the true power of a unicorn. It is creating the true mind-link," Equ said.

Varon pushed his thoughts out from the ponies, using their unique form of storing memories to build his controlling mind-link. Varon felt the number of minds joining his growing. Each mind added its own power to the link until he had touched all the Equus minds within his range.

He looked at Miskala growing weaker in his battle against the lizard, and Varon knew the Calvn's mind was better suited to lead this battle than his. Varon passed the control of the mind-link to Miskala.

Miskala's sagging head perked up as his body surged with the power of the mind-link, and 300 Equus galloped in from all directions to attack the lizard. They charged and retreated in a coordinated attack. They attacked at the lizard's blind side. The lizard would turn to meet the attack, only to have another group charge and retreat at its new blind side.

The Equus circled the lizard. They were without fear because Miskala felt no fear as he coordinated the attacks. His thoughts became reality, and the Equus obeyed without hesitation. Some Equus still died, but the herd did not falter because of Miskala's control.

Still, Varon could see something he didn't think Miskala realized in the heat of the battle. For all the damage the herd was inflicting on Carn, he healed just as quickly. Miskala's Herd might carry on this attack for days, but as long as the lizard kept healing, it could kill the Equus one by one until it had won the battle.

"They can't win, can they?" Varon asked Equ.

"Not if they seek to kill Carn. I could not and would not give you the power to kill a creator. Death is not the object of your existence, Varon."

"Life is."

"Yes, you understand. I gave the Equus the power to survive what they might face in this world, including Ravagers, and live on."

Even as Varon watched, another Equus in the circle died from the savage attack of the lizard's tail, which had sprouted half a dozen spikes. Carn was adapting to their attacks and become less confused by their coordinated movements.

What if he shifted shape to something even more dangerous than the giant lizard?

Carn had to be kept in a state of confusion, but what more could the Equus do? What if Varon gave him what he wanted? Would Carn be so distracted trying to get the Ranglan Stone that the Equus could keep him confused?

Varon rushed forward through the line of Equus and flung the Ranglan Stone at the lizard. As the stone hit Carn, it passed through him as if he were a hallucination. The lizard roared and dissolved, just as the dragon had when it had touched the Ranglan Stone.

The swirling dust moved away from the Ranglan Stone. Carn tried to reform himself, but Miskala directed the Equus to rush in and attack anything that looked solid. Varon picked up the Ranglan Stone again and tossed it into the cloud. If it had dissolved the lizard just by touching him, then it should be able to keep him dissolved.

The dust cloud swirled into a tight column and disappeared.

"It's dead, and may he burn forever," Miskala said. It was the first thing Varon had heard him say since the battle had begun. Miskala had controlled the herd with his unvoiced thoughts;

thoughts not on the mind-link.

"No, I've seen this happen before with Equ. He's only gone to whatever realm he is from," Varon explained.

"Will he be back?" Miskala asked.

"Not soon, I think. You can release your control."

Miskala did, and the Equus who had been standing ready to attack Carn should he reappear, pranced around. The mind-link was filled with questions and confusion. Miskala neighed and ran over to Lyos' body.

"What happened, Varon?" Miskala asked him.

"You filled your role as Calvn, as Equ wanted the role to be filled. You led the Equus in a way that kept them alive."

Miskala's gaze never left Lyos' dead eyes. He kneeled down beside her and groomed her bloody withers. Varon wasn't sure what to do.

"How did I do it? I've never heard of a Calvn having that kind of control... that kind of power over his herd," Miskala said.

"I think you were on the verge of discovering it on your own, Miskala. It is like the way you treated your stomach pains." Miskala had allowed the power of the herd strengthen him. It had been a reflexive, almost desperate effort. He had opened his mind to the herd in a way he had never heard of being done. Varon continued, *"I still don't understand fully either, but what can be done once, can be done again if need be. You saved your herd."*

Miskala nodded. He whined in a way that sounded similar to a donkey's bray. *"But at what cost? I lost Lyos."*

"Equ doesn't promise us that individuals will live, Miskala, only the species."

"That's easy to say when it's not your mate."

Varon walked over to stand next to his friend. *"But it was my sire and dam. I loved and respected them, and I lost both of them,"* Varon told him.

"Were we successful, really?" Miskala asked as the rest of his herd gathered around him. Horses tended the wounded, but Miskala remained next to Lyos.

Varon lowered his head and dropped the Ranglan Stone in front of the unicorn.

"We live and we survive knowing that will help us continue to live," Varon said.

"You made it into the valley."

"In some ways, I wish I hadn't. Destiny guided me through, though I attempted to change it," Varon explained.

Miskala stared at the Ranglan Stone. Both he and Varon noticed the blood on it.

"I did what I had to do," Varon said as he looked away.

Miskala sighed. Finally, he said, *"We all did. I know you will follow the way of Equ in whatever direction it will take you."*

"You sound so sure."

"I had better be. Lyos died to follow me and you."

Varon nodded, but he didn't look at Miskala.

"What do we do with the Ranglan Stone now?" Miskala asked.

"You should wear it until we find the unicorn leader to whom Equ will lead us. I don't want to carry it. I don't deserve to wear it. You, however, have proven your ability as a Calvn."

Miskala lowered his head so that the tip of his horn slid through the hole in the Ranglan Stone. Miskala lifted his head, and the stone slid down his horn.

Varon nodded and walked away.

"Where do we go now?" Miskala asked.

"Let Equ tell you. I need to forget some things."

As Varon left him, rain fell. It was a warm rain, given the icy chill in the air.

Varon considered exiling himself from this herd. How could he urge the Equus to follow Equ when he had broken the First Law of the Equus? He didn't deserve to be the Voice of Equ.

"You are my Voice," Equ said.

"But I have killed another Equus."

"You did what needed to be done, Varon. The responsibility for the outcome is not yours, but mine. You are innocent in this."

"Innocent?" Varon said. *"I killed. I am no better than Scola,*

Gee, or Oralum. Actually, I am worse because I succeeded. They failed in their attempts. I am not innocent."

"Oralum disobeyed me. His wrong decisions led him to his death."

"Carn led him astray," Varon corrected him.

"I do not dismiss my brother's role in all this, but I told Oralum when he placed the Ranglan Stone on his horn to give it to you. He would not heed my words. You did. You acted on my behalf and I accept your pains and responsibility as my own. You submitted your will to mine, and so you are innocent."

"Was that the test, then?"

"Yes," Equ said.

"Why did it have to be so harsh?"

"You don't know harsh yet, Varon. This is preparing you for the future, and when that future comes, you will wish for this day and think it is easy."

"Then I fear for my future," Varon said.

"And I fear for the future of the Equus."

45

Varon walked around the small band as they rested and grazed on a sizeable area of uneaten alfalfa. He avoided the herd scouts and didn't converse with anyone, including Miskala.

He was unworthy to be with these Equus. These Equus had given up their herd, and some their families, to follow the will of Equ. Miskala had seen his own season mate sacrifice her life so he might live. They looked to Varon to lead them, but what right did he have to lead them? He had violated the First Law of the Equus. Every time that Varon closed his eyes, he saw his hooves breaking Oralum's neck. He heard the snap of bone and relived the realization of what he had done.

"Varon?"

"What?" Varon snapped.

"This is not a good sign for one who is my Voice, Varon. I had to call your name four times before you answered me," Equ told him.

"I was thinking of Oralum."

"You were feeling self-pity. That is dangerous. It could leave you vulnerable to predators."

"Does it matter? The Ranglan Stone is retrieved, and a unicorn will lead the seed of the Equus to safety," Varon snapped.

"It matters to me. You are my Voice. You are my foal."

"I am not worthy of that honor."

"You are, or I would not be speaking with you." Equ paused. *"Look to the north, Varon."*

Varon looked up. At first, he saw nothing but the night, but then he saw the white unicorn with the golden horn step out of the darkness. He seemed to glow with his own inner light.

"Equ?"

"Let's walk," Equ commanded him.

Varon approached his creator with his head lowered, his mouth chewing imaginary grass. He did not want Equ to see the guilt on his face. He was a murderer of Equ's foals.

"Why are you here, Equ?" Varon asked the tall unicorn. Beside him, Varon looked like a newborn colt.

"Your need has called me. It is easier to communicate with you in your form, so I am in your form. The mind-link is even clearer than if you were to use the Ranglan Stone."

They walked across the rolling foothills that marked the beginning of the Meshack Mountains.

"One reason I placed the Equus on Hemlaza was so they could live," Equ explained to Varon.

"Did we not live in Etrasco?"

Equ's ears flicked back and forth to show his indecision. *"You existed, but you did not live. I can see that now. I did not then."*

"I don't understand."

"Neither did I at first, but I have changed, matured, much as the Equus have. Neither of us can remain static and live. To live, you must experience the range of possibilities your world offers. That includes the bad as well as the good. As a group, the Equus have experienced a lot of the good and now will come the bad. I have experienced the bad myself in having to send the Equus from me. This separation from my children has made me harder. Perhaps it is a good thing to come from the bad. I am not sure. Once I could have told you, with certainty, not to kill another Equus. It would have hurt me as much as it hurts you. Now, I know I must tell you that to kill one Equus to save many more is not a terrible thing."

Varon shook his head. *"Why me? Why not Miskala? He is a Calvn and the Calvns already believe they are the Voice of Equ."*

"I speak to them, but they cannot hear me over their own talking. Even Miskala, who listens better than most, cannot hear me as well as you do. One must take the time to listen if he or she wants me to speak to them. Because you are the one who listened and acted, you

are the one with whom I speak. Others have heard my voice and shied from the weight of the responsibility. Miskala was one of those. You gave him the strength to act. He could not have held his own against Carn had you not convinced him he was doing my will. Others have heard my voice and ignored it as a hallucination. Only you have both listened and acted."

"And now what will you have me do?" Varon asked.

"Find the seed I have prepared and gather them."

"Isn't this band... the seed?"

"They are a part, a part that comes only because you convinced them of the truth. Others await to hear you and be convinced by you, and now I must do what I came to do." Equ turned to face Varon. *"Varon, raise your head high."*

Varon did as he was told. Equ lowered his golden horn and touched it to the top of Varon's head between his ears. Then he ran it down Varon's face. Varon felt a warmth fill him. His guilt over Oralum washed away, and Varon found himself more determined to carry out Equ's will.

"Thank you," Varon said.

"I help as I can," Equ told him.

As the first signs of dawn appeared in the sky, Varon found Miskala. The unicorn was grazing alone and staring at Lyos' body covered with grass. She had been sent away with the Equus' pleas earlier in the day.

Miskala raised his head to look at Varon. *"I could have made her my life mate. I was thinking about it. I wanted to ask her, but I didn't feel worthy,"* he said.

"She would have been a wonderful choice," Varon agreed.

"She was better than me. She made me want to be better."

Varon nodded. *"Those are the best kind of mates; those that make us better."*

Miskala sighed and asked, *"Are you ready to leave, Voice of Equ? The grass here won't last more than another day or two."*

"Nearly. I now know how to use the Ranglan Stone. Equ gave me some instruction when I spoke with him about how to use it. Besides

helping a unicorn command a herd, it is also a guide, which is why I needed it."

"How?"

Varon lowered his head. *"If you would lay the stone on the ground, please?"*

Miskala tipped his horn forward and the purple-black stone slid off and dropped into the dirt. Varon used his lips to turn the stone on its side.

"I am the Voice of Equ. Show me where I must go. I command it," Varon said to the stone.

The stone wobbled, and then rolled a few inches in a northwest direction. Miskala backed away from the stone as if it was a predator.

"I have never heard of it doing that! I don't think the Calvns know," Miskala said in amazement.

"They have no reason to know it. They were never taught the proper way to command it because it wasn't needed in that way. It has shown us the direction we must travel."

Miskala looked up. *"Northwest? What is there? Etrasco?"*

"My guess is it's the seeds we must gather before we leave. This stone helps us understand the will of Equ and follow it," Varon said.

"Will this seed we are gathering follow you?"

"Not me. They follow Equ. I only know we must gather all those who will listen and leave Hemlaza. It is a dying land," Varon told him.

Miskala blew air through his lips and glanced at Lyos. *"I only hope this is worth the price we are paying."*

Varon nodded. *"It is. We will return to Etrasco."*

Epilogue

Equ opened his eyes and steadied his form. After so many years of existing as a unicorn, it was second nature to him to be a golden-horned unicorn. He sighed and looked around at the empty valley of Etrasco. How he missed the sights and sounds of his children at play!

Was this chosen path the best thing for the Equus? It was so… so harsh.

A great blue heron landed in front of him. It cocked its head to the side and stared at him.

"They are confused and hurting, Mother," Equ said.

His mother's form shifted, and she became a spotted fawn who walked up next to Equ and rubbed herself against his chest.

"It's not the first time, Equ," she reminded him.

"But this time, Carn and the others will kill them if they don't change. Look at how close Carn came to killing Varon and the others. They stopped him, but Carn won't give up."

"It is a challenging time for us all. As for Carn, I will discipline him. He pushed the limits too far this time."

Equ looked down at his mother. "How can you be so calm? We are depending on one horse to change the learning of generations of Equus. One horse, no matter how pure of heart, is not strong enough to accomplish such a great task."

"But he can rely on the strength of others to lend him theirs."

Equ shook his head. "Will that give him strength, or will it weaken him because he knows he cannot complete his life's work alone?"

"How can you doubt the Equus so easily? You chose Varon to serve as your Voice and guide the Equus from Hemlaza," his mother said.

"I know their weaknesses. I created them."

The fawn nuzzled against him as if seeking safety. "But I know what the Equus are capable of because I created you. You wish them to return to you, but for that to happen, they must once again move forward like they did after their Herd Wars ended."

"Will they, though?"

The fawn nodded. "I think so. You created them, didn't you?"

About the Author

J. R. Rada is the Amazon.com bestselling author of *Kachina, The Man Who Killed Edgar Allan Poe,* and *Welcome to Peaceful Journey.*

He works as a freelance writer in Gettysburg, Pennsylvania, where he also lives with his wife and sons. James has received many awards from the Maryland-Delaware-DC Press Association, Associated Press, Maryland State Teachers Association and Community Newspapers Holdings, Inc. for his newspaper writing.

To see J. R. Rada's other books, visit his website (jamesrada.com/jrrada).

If you would like to be kept up to date on when J. R. Rada's new books are published or ask him questions, you can e-mail him at *jimrada@yahoo.com.*

PLEASE LEAVE A REVIEW

If you enjoyed this book, please help other readers find it. Reviews help the author get more exposure for his books. Please take a few minutes to review this book at Amazon.com or Goodreads.com.

If you enjoyed *Dawn in Etrasco* keep up to date on new releases, news, and specials from J. R. Rada by joining his mail list. When you sign-up at http://bit.ly/3MVuSA2, you'll get *Polderbeest* as a FREE gift.